When a playful knock sounded at the door, she jumped in her chair. Her hands gripped the armrests. He was here!

God, did she need to check the mirror again? Was her lip gloss smeared from the glass of ginger ale?

"I'm losing my mind," she mumbled, forcing herself up. "Be calm, composed, and collected. Just like old times."

But this wasn't her figure skating days, because when a melodic pattern of knocks sounded, reminding her of a jingle she couldn't place, a smile started to tug at her mouth. *Elevated dopamine levels*, her academic side told her while another new side of her practically sang, *Isn't he cute, knocking like that?*

When she opened the door, she felt as if she were floating off the floor in pure joy. Brock held a bouquet of white calla lilies, and he was wearing a sexy blue suit with a white dress shirt—no tie—clean-shaven. His usual scent of pine and cloves was stronger tonight, combined with notes of musk and lime.

All sexy male, and for tonight, all hers.

Maybe courtship wasn't so bad.

PRAISE FOR AVA MILES' NOVELS
SEE WHAT ALL THE BUZZ IS ABOUT...

"Ava's story is witty and charming."

> BARBARA FREETHY #1 *NYT* BESTSELLING AUTHOR

"If you like Nora Roberts type books, this is a must-read."

> READERS' FAVORITE

"If ever there was a contemporary romance that rated a 10 on a scale of 1 to 5 for me, this one is it!"

> THE ROMANCE REVIEWS

"I could not stop flipping the pages. I can't wait to read the next book in this series."

> FRESH FICTION

"I've read Susan Mallery and Debbie Macomber... but never have I been so moved as by the books Ava Miles writes."

> BOOKTALK WITH EILEEN

"Ava Miles is fast becoming one of my favorite light contemporary romance writers."

TOME TENDER

"One word for Ava Miles is WOW."

MY BOOK CRAVINGS

"Her engaging story and characters kept me turning the pages."

BOOKFAN

"On par with Nicholas Sparks' love stories."

JENNIFER'S CORNER BLOG

"The constant love, and the tasteful sexual interludes, bring a sensual, dynamic tension to this appealing story."

PUBLISHER'S WEEKLY

"Miles' story savvy, sense of humor, respect for her readers and empathy for her characters shine through…"

USA TODAY

OTHER AVA TITLES TO BINGE

The Paris Roommates

Your dreams are around the corner...

The Paris Roommates: Thea

The Paris Roommates: Dean

The Paris Roommates: Brooke

The Paris Roommates: Sawyer

The Unexpected Prince Charming Series

Love with a kiss of the Irish...

Beside Golden Irish Fields

Beneath Pearly Irish Skies

Through Crimson Irish Light

After Indigo Irish Nights

Beyond Rosy Irish Twilight

Over Verdant Irish Hills

Against Ebony Irish Seas

The Merriams Series

Chock full of family and happily ever afters...

Wild Irish Rose

Love Among Lavender

Valley of Stars
Sunflower Alley
A Forever of Orange Blossoms
A Breath of Jasmine

The Love Letter Series
The Merriams grandparents' epic love affair...
Letters Across An Open Sea
Along Waters of Sunshine and Shadow

The Friends & Neighbors Novels
A feast for all the senses...
The House of Hope & Chocolate
The Dreamer's Flower Shoppe

The Dare River Series
Filled with down-home charm...
Country Heaven
The Chocolate Garden
Fireflies and Magnolias
The Promise of Rainbows
The Fountain Of Infinite Wishes
The Patchwork Quilt Of Happiness

Country Heaven Cookbook

The Chocolate Garden: A Magical Tale (Children's Book)

The Dare Valley Series

Awash in small town fabulousness...

Nora Roberts Land

French Roast

The Grand Opening

The Holiday Serenade

The Town Square

The Park of Sunset Dreams

The Perfect Ingredient

The Bridge to a Better Life

The Calendar of New Beginnings

Home Sweet Love

The Moonlight Serenade

The Sky of Endless Blue

Daring Brides

Daring Declarations

Dare Valley Meets Paris Billionaire Mini-Series

Small town charm meets big city romance...

The Billionaire's Gamble

The Billionaire's Secret

The Billionaire's Courtship

The Billionaire's Return

Dare Valley Meets Paris Compilation

The Once Upon a Dare Series

Falling in love is a contact sport...

The Gate to Everything

The Standalones

A Very UN-Shakespeare Romance

The Hockey Experiment

Love and Other Trials

Non-Fiction

The Happiness Corner: Reflections So Far

The Post-Covid Wellness Playbook

Cookbooks

Home Baked Happiness Cookbook

Country Heaven Cookbook

The Lost Guides to Living Your Best Life Series

Reclaim Your Superpowers

Courage Is Your Superpower

Expression Is Your Superpower

Peace Is Your Superpower

Confidence Is Your Superpower

Happiness Is Your Superpower

———

Children's Books

The Chocolate Garden: A Magical Tale

———

To see all of Ava's titles, check out her handy printable booklist.

THE HOCKEY EXPERIMENT

AVA MILES

Copyright June 2025, Ava Miles.
ISBN: 978-1-949092-72-1

All rights reserved. No part of this book may be reproduced or transmitted in any form by any means—graphic, electronic or mechanical—without permission in writing from the author, except by a reviewer who may quote brief passages in a review.
This is a work of fiction. All of the characters, organizations, and events portrayed in this novel are either the products of the author's imagination or are used fictionally.

www.avamiles.com
Ava Miles

To teachers—like my cultural anthropology professor, Dr. Carolyn Nordstrom.

Thank you for the passion and magic you bring to the classroom and into our lives.

ONE

What is it about men?
What. Is. It. About. Men?
WHAT IS IT ABOUT MEN????

"Darla... why are you shouting in your field diary?" Dr. Valentina Hargrove pointed to her friend's carefully printed diatribe, sensing latent dating anger.

Dr. Darla James screwed up her oval face. "One word: asshole Peter."

Since her longtime research colleague was also her best friend, she didn't point out the use of two words, not one. "Right. He ghosted you. But shouldn't you be writing something more germane? Like the question we're here to study? Look, I've already written it at the top of my page."

Are hockey players modern cavemen?

After a quick glance at Val's field journal, Darla discreetly flicked her hand toward the hockey rink. "Well,

Val... My question seemed more pertinent than, *What is it about cavemen?* Since I've never met one."

Val gave in to the unacademic urge to snort. The errant swearing and grunts from the Alexandria Eagles muffled any minor sounds in the massive outdoor arena where they were sitting on cold, *freeze-her-bottom* bleachers, fitting for late February in Minneapolis. Difficult to adjust to after returning from the hot and humid Congo.

Although she was also having another unacademic compulsion: to deeply inhale the smell of fresh, cold ice after being away from it for so long. Four years, as a matter of fact.

The happy little two-year-old she'd been when she'd first started ice skating would never have believed she'd be able to keep away from "the magic glass" so long. The young woman who'd won three junior Olympic golds and retired from skating with a peptic ulcer at fifteen easily could.

"I beg to disagree, Darla." Academic discourse had been her salvation after leaving ice skating, and she welcomed the feeling as she leveled her friend a knowing look. "Your last three dates were total cavemen in the slang sense of the word, asshole Peter leading the pack."

"Har-de-har-har." Darla nudged her playfully before leaning forward, her gaze glued to the male specimens slapping furiously to take the puck away from each other during afternoon practice. "You know, Val, some would say we're the two luckiest women in the world to be spending part of a hockey season with a full access pass to these men."

"I don't see how luck factors into it." To her, the hockey players held the same academic interest as the Pygmies in the Congo she and Darla had studied this past year for their newest article in *Cultural Anthropology Today*.

While these professional athletes might not be sitting

around an evening fire in the jungle, preparing to eat the dinner they'd hunted themselves, their monosyllabic discourse and guttural intonations held exciting academic similarities. Her insides were completely titillated.

Granted, hockey players didn't wear loincloths with their bodies painted white like Pygmies, but still...

"You just don't get it, Val," Darla said with a sigh as she smoothed her severely straight black ponytail, courtesy of extensions, over her shoulder. She gave Val one of her frustrated looks, the kind that portended personal trouble.

"You're right, I don't, if we're talking about what I think we're talking about," she replied and folded her hands. Even so, her friend's discourse on men and mating rituals never failed to both educate and amuse her. Today, the distraction was also welcome since it was difficult to tune out the beautiful crisp noise of skates on ice. She would have to become accustomed to blocking it out while she was on this study.

Darla tapped her mouth with her fingertip like she was trying to work out a problem. "Val, hockey players make me question my understanding of modern male and female relations."

Yes, please give me something else to focus on. "Outline it for me."

"I like to think I'm an independent woman."

"You are." Maybe it was their over-the-top nerdy assistant disguises that had Darla doubting herself. "With a PhD in cultural anthropology from Oxford. Like me."

Darla's fake tortoiseshell-framed glasses remained on the large males weaving and attacking each other on the ice in white, blue, and red practice jerseys. "All that male...ness has my girl juices swimming. They're all so big. And rough. And *umm*."

"*Umm?*" Darla was already muttering worrisome

guttural intonations herself, as if the hockey-caveman similarities were catching. "And that signifies—"

Her best friend since boarding school looked as if she were imploring the heavens, the way they'd witnessed people doing in the last fertility dance they'd attended during the full moon. "You know how I am, Val. Those men make me just want to—"

"Let's take a pause and refocus, shall we? I can tell you're flooding your system with stress hormones."

"Cortisol hates me." She cupped the gentle curve of her belly, hidden under her baggy black T-shirt, identical to the one Val was wearing. "This pudge never goes away, and while I've come to accept my curves—"

"Again, we're refocusing."

Darla went through this same inner turmoil with every study involving the male sex, something they were becoming academically known for in the small, exciting world of cultural anthropology. Some days she had to pinch herself. Hargrove and James were making a name for themselves, almost like Masters and Johnson, and Marie and Pierre Curie—only she and Darla weren't romantically involved, of course.

"Then refocus me hard!" Darla gripped her arm, her golden eyes pleading. "Give it to me, Dr. Hargrove. I admire your ever-present stoicism as always. Especially with men. You're an academic goddess. Perched in Oxford's black robes, presiding at the front of the class, completely in command of herself."

"I wouldn't go that far. A goddess, I am not, while you have had *scores* of marriage offers. Don't you remember how that one chief told me my hips were too small for childbearing? While he thought you were the perfect goddess of a woman come to life. Clearly fertile because of your curves, and powerful because you could also throw a spear."

"Yeah, but the last guy I dated in Johannesburg told me my hips and the rest of me were too big. You can't please men."

There should be a special place in Dante's hell for men like Asshole Pete and the others who'd hurt Darla. "Why try? I think you're perfect as you are."

"That's because you're a girl and you get me." Her friend looked ready to hug her. "We return to my question: *what is it about men?*"

"I have no idea, and honestly, I don't want to." Val choked on a laugh. "These hockey players don't present such quandaries for me. I admire their hard work and commitment, but I can't imagine ever seeing one of them as a male like you're suggesting."

"God, I envy you in times like this." Darla uttered a heartfelt sigh and let go of the death grip on her arm. "Even though I worry about your lack of interest in the male species in your personal life. You study them but you don't want to get down with them much. Outside of carefully orchestrated interactions."

Val was not going to let Darla jump onto *that* topic. Nor was she going to point out she preferred a scientific approach when engaging with life, including interactions with the opposite sex. She preferred it that way after the chaos of her youth. "We knew going into this study that you were going to be affected."

Darla bit her unpainted bottom lip, her black ponytail swaying as she shook her head in distress. "It's horrible! I hate this primal reaction I have to them. It's like I take a giant whiff of their *leave your reason behind and throw off your panties* pheromones, and I turn into someone else. I can't seem to stop falling for really big, gorgeous, tough guys."

"With terribly dangerous jobs, most of the time." Val folded her hands over her field journal, sensing Darla's need to express her frustration before they could move forward. "Diamond smuggling. Mercenary work. Darla, I know you're somehow wired for the kind of man who—"

"Has gorgeous muscles and oozes aggression and charm?" She put her hand to her forehead and tapped it like she was trying to reprogram her neurons. "I swear, Val, it's all my mother's fault..."

Val gave voice to the words she knew would come next. "If you weren't the love child of an R&B singer and her then-married record producer..."

"I'd have better judgment in men," Darla finished mournfully.

Val patted her on the back and consoled her like she had since their first discussion about Darla's taste in men in Swiss boarding school. She certainly wouldn't bring up how she'd figured out a way to turn off her own prurient interest in men, given her own mother being on her fifth marriage and her father having three. To Val, eight marriages by two people was statistically significant. But Darla needed encouragement, and as her best friend, that was her job.

"You'll manage like always." She removed Darla's hand from her forehead and looked her straight in the eye. "Focus on the bright side. At least hockey players won't land you in jail or get you killed."

Darla spurted out a laugh. "You *would* say that."

"Consider this then... Even if you are attracted to one of them, you can't date him. It's completely against our academic guidelines for any study, and you are a serious professional, Dr. James. Despite your intense biological reaction to the male sex."

Val thanked the fertility gods—if they existed—that she had not received such hormonal wiring.

"You're damn right I am." Darla sat up straighter, like she might in a lecture hall on early human migration. "What else have you written down, Val? You're always light years ahead of me in the first couple of weeks of a study, no matter how much research and prep work we do before we hit the ground."

That's why their academic collaborations worked so well. Val had a quick, clinical mind able to define concepts, identify patterns, and draw immediate hypotheses while Darla had a more holistic approach to amassing information and making nuanced conclusions later on. Val observed. Darla empathized. Even better, as best friends they enjoyed each other's company on long field trips around the world, often to places where there were no phones or internet, running water notwithstanding. Another reason they'd taken this job.

Val turned the page of her field diary so Darla could see her initial thoughts, a smile tugging at her lips. She was pretty proud of the conclusions she'd already drawn. Simple and straightforward was always best.

> *Cavemen: early humans with physically dense, highly muscular bodies; known for aggression and territorialism; capable of using tools like a club; with simple linguistic capability*
>
> *Hockey players: modern humans with physically dense, highly muscular bodies; known for aggres-*

sion and territorialism; capable of using tools like a hockey stick; with simple linguistic capability

"The similarities are striking, don't you think?" The kick of scientific excitement was coursing through her already, as the punch in her usually one-note lecture voice proved. "This is going to be fun."

Her inner war about skating notwithstanding.

Darla looked back to the rink and let out a little breathy sigh. "Physically dense, highly muscular bodies is an understatement. Not to be sexist, but Val, those men are grade A in every way."

Val looked back at the men on the ice. With their protective gear on, they looked even larger than they did off the ice. She knew the player stats for every single Alexandria Eagles player as well as their physical stats. Most of them topped out at around six feet, with the defense and goalie positions running a little taller. The ideal weight requirements were around two hundred pounds. All solid muscle.

Women around the world—Darla included—thought they were gods of masculinity. Val understood why clinically. Their physical stature embodied the ultimate potential of the male body. Their testosterone levels alone would attract female interest, pheromones notwithstanding. These men professionally trained their bodies to be dominant and powerful, and that translated both on and off the ice. Constant competition gave them an edge many other humans didn't possess but could certainly admire.

As a former competitor in figure skating, Val knew all about refining her body to meet an ultimate standard. Small. Sleek. Toned. Beautiful in a doll-like way except for the beauty mark by her lip. Her skill as much as her form had attracted people's attention and admiration. As a young girl, she'd been uncomfortable with such adulation.

Then again, women experienced attention from the opposite sex differently. She'd felt vulnerable.

Most men, however, puffed out like roosters for being told they were the gold standard of masculinity. As Val had seen in their off-the-ice behavior, most hockey players loved such attention, craved it even. Unfortunately, that behavior was bleeding into the Eagles' performance on the ice.

She and Darla were here to help change that. Hockey alone couldn't have tempted her, but this was her father's team, and he'd asked for help. Coupled with their travel fatigue—and her and Darla's desire for modern plumbing and other luxuries they'd been without in the field—it had seemed like a win-win, the perfect study.

Then Darla had experienced one of her light bulb marketing moments a few days ago, which had excited them enough to order another round of margaritas to celebrate. Helping this team win the Stanley Cup would position them to provide other sports teams, and perhaps even corporations, with their brand of analysis to help management achieve their goals. Human nature was at the root of many conflicts, and they were experts in analyzing such issues and offering solutions.

"Physically, these hockey players might meet the ultimate male standard, but they are championship deficient," she added, tapping her field diary for emphasis. "Which is why we're here to help my father with his team."

Part of her still couldn't believe he'd asked her and Darla to conduct this assignment after finishing their most recent grant. Then again, while he'd never say so, her father would prefer for her to be in Minnesota than a country like

Congo. Less parental worry for him. Because Ebola was nothing to laugh at, and that wasn't even mentioning the armed guerrillas and hairy gorillas, as Darla liked to joke. And don't get her started on the large venomous snakes slithering into her tent or the way baboons' enormous teeth shone in the moonlight when they made a surprise appearance.

"This topic of study," Darla said gamely, wagging her finger at the ice, "might be a bit crazy to some, but your father doesn't do anything that doesn't make sense. Or money. I admire him for that."

She glanced at the Eagles' coach, who was barking at someone on the ice about a missed assignment. "This is his out-of-the-box effort to make his new team win the Stanley Cup with Chuck. To date, this team can't win 'the big one.'"

"And your father's identity does not include being a loser." Darla gave Val's chin a playful tap. "He's an overachiever like his daughter."

She wished she were the type of person who could roll her eyes, but it wasn't in her nature. Facts were indisputable, after all, and she *did* meet the classical definition of an overachiever: a person who does more than they are expected to do or who is more successful than others.

Her father was one certainly, and her mother had been the same way, but after winning her last Olympic Gold in her late twenties, she'd retired and pretty much stopped achieving anything. Well, except for husbands. Now she collected husbands like Olympic medals. To Val, her father was the only one who'd been gold.

"Dad and Chuck think our study might light a fire under these players to focus them to win, especially as we get closer to the playoffs."

"While we get to turn in our suitcases and bask in

running water and electricity." Darla put her arm around her companionably, and Val didn't have the heart to remind her to be professional. "Val, I do a little dance every time I go into my bathroom. A toilet! Hot water in a shower! A heated floor! It's a miracle every time."

She felt an indulgent smile play across her lips. "I cannot disagree, Dr. James. For me, it's sleeping in my Egyptian cotton sheets with a light comforter. Every time I got tangled up in mosquito netting, I'd wake up thinking I was covered in a giant spiderweb."

"It's almost like a vacation, isn't it?" Darla started a sultry happy dance, a little reminiscent of her mother's last music video for her song "I Need You Like the Air I Breathe," which had gone platinum. "Even though it's Minneapolis."

"I'm pleased with what I've seen so far. No, it's not Bora Bora, but we knew that going in."

Darla gave one of her crowd-attracting husky laughs, courtesy of her voice having the kind of musical quality that screamed Grammys were in her bloodlines. "I tell myself, if it was good enough for Prince... But back to our study. Val, this baby is going to make headlines. Just you watch. And not all the good kind, I think. Because cavemen are one misunderstood bunch."

"That's not our concern," Val reminded her as Chuck blew his whistle in three consecutive bursts, his anger evident. "We observe. We study. We find patterns. We make conclusions. We meet the conditions of our contract. That's our job."

Even though it was her father who was paying them, she'd insisted they follow their normal protocols to the letter. He had wisely suggested that they work in disguise, wearing team badges devoid of their names to keep their identities secret. No hockey player was going to recognize the famous cultural anthropologists, Hargrove and James, of course, but they might not like it if they knew Ted Bass had signed his daughter up to study his new team.

They certainly wouldn't recognize her as his daughter in this outfit, however, notwithstanding the fact that she favored her mother. And since she was in the field so much, few people had captured recent photos of her and her father together. Even so, she had purposefully chosen the most revolting pair of glasses in history to hide her features and make her repellant to the male sex.

"In your world, it's that simple, yes." Darla closed her field diary and nibbled on the end of her pen. "I don't need or want some very angry six-foot, two-hundred-pound hockey player mad at me for comparing him to a caveman without the proper understanding should they hear we're involved."

Val found that highly unlikely. "I still don't understand why they would be mad." She closed her diary as well, studying the rink as one of the hockey players flipped another teammate off—using silent communication to convey dislike or humor, something she would note in her diary later. "While the modern slang for caveman implies an ignoramus, we both know they were quite brilliant. They took down woolly mammoths. They survived the Ice Age."

"Your geekiness is showing, Dr. Hargrove, which I love, but I'm not sure that's how those guys would see it." She threw her field diary and pen in her leather satchel. "Male egos are a tricky business."

"I don't deal with those." Val paused as Darla chortled. "Laugh all you like, but I stopped catering to anyone's ego a long time ago." Her attempts to please her mother had been a PhD study in all the reasons she should stop; it only led to ulcers, literally. "I understand human posturing, but I respect only those whose excellence and talent are real. I don't respect people who lord their talents, real or imagined, over others."

"Which is why I adore you." Darla patted her hand sweetly. "God, these glasses are going to drive me nuts. Not only do they look dreadful, but they keep sliding off my nose." She straightened them before shooting out of her chair with her usual enthusiasm. "Come on, Val. Practice should be over soon. Let's go see your dad."

As Val followed her and walked down the concrete stairs to leave the rink, two men crashed into the plexiglass wall. Val turned toward the commotion. She caught a flash of two large male bodies fighting for supremacy in a flurry of strength, muscles straining, jaws locking, sweat trickling down the sides of their faces. An arresting visual, to be sure. Val appreciated the primal outlet.

But then the man pinned against the wall trained his eyes her way...

His entire focus seemed to latch on to her. It was rather unnerving, the intensity of his gaze.

But she held it, sensing something important.

Some moments happened that way. Everything slowed down, and a connection was forged.

She was aware of her heart rate increasing. Her skin didn't feel as cold as it had previously. Interesting, she noted, and unexpected.

The icy blue eyes holding hers belonged to Brock "The Rock," the Eagles' captain. She'd read articles on him as part of her early research, and his eyes seemed to command as much media copy as his skating, passing, shooting, and stick-handling skills. He was considered one of the most dangerous offensive players in the NHL while also being a guy's guy and a nice one at that. The Alpha in a pack of strong men. Quite the feat, she knew.

He was still staring at her, all his muscles rippling in response to his opponent pinning him to the glass...

Only he seemed in no hurry to end the fight. In fact, despite his position relative to the aggressor, he seemed in charge of the situation.

One more second passed.

And another.

Val reasoned she was a new arrival to his territory, so with his blood up from the sport, it made sense that he'd home in on her to see if she was a threat. Even pinned as he was.

Then his nostrils flared, like she'd seen animals do in the Serengeti when they caught a whiff of their mate.

No, that couldn't be the reason.

But her heart immediately began to pound to a primal drumbeat in her ears.

Totally unnerving.

She watched a trail of sweat trickle out of the curly black hair escaping his helmet. Noted his rock-hard jaw and broad forehead. From this distance, she couldn't make out the scar along his jawline, but she'd seen photos of him and knew it was there. It only added to his hardened masculinity. He *was* handsome. There was no denying it.

Yet it wasn't something she should notice. She fell back on her training. Remained still. Continued to observe. Took shallow breaths to offset her emotional and physical response to him. But her brain started tugging at a question.

Was he responding on some primal level to her as a woman?

She hadn't imagined that possibility. Her outfit was intended to disguise her female attributes and repel interest.

Did pheromones travel easier across cold surfaces like the ice? She would have to look that up. The reptilian brain was a masterpiece of scientific interest.

His regard of her continued as the other player struggled to keep him pinned, grunting as he pushed to hold him in place. Only Brock wasn't fighting him anymore. She thought she heard a growl emerge from him. Her mouth immediately went dry, and she had the urge to wet her lips. A shocking reaction.

She was here to observe, not to engage.

A sharp hit from his opponent to his kidneys knocked him into the wall hard and ended his focus on her, returning it to the fight for male supremacy. She watched as he shoved back against his opponent with all his strength.

Val noted the excitement within her—as if she were rooting for him—as he broke free with the puck, slicing quickly across the ice toward the central line.

She made herself turn away from the rink. Darla was waiting for her closer to the bench—and the action—studying players.

Val swallowed thickly, wishing she had a glass of water.

Her reaction was not appreciated, she decided. Her feet felt heavy, and her respiration was choppy, as if she'd been doing sprints. She forced herself to take a few deep breaths, welcoming the frigid air rushing through her airways, the smell of rubber mats and cold ice filling her senses. A sense of longing came over her. For the ice. It had to be for the ice.

Clearing her throat, she forced herself to walk forward. She would be fine. The moment had been strange was all. But it made sense that her own reptilian brain was acclimatizing itself to the new environment and the dominant players. Like Brock Thomson.

Yes, that explanation made sense.

TWO

"What is it about women?"

He asked the question of his good friend and old teammate as they were packing up to leave. His sister's text had prompted the question, but he couldn't deny a similar question had clanged around in his mind as the water hit his still-electric skin in the showers: *What is it about that woman?*

He still couldn't believe she'd captured his attention: the nerdy one in the mannish, baggy clothes wearing the ugliest glasses he'd ever seen. While Mason had him up against the glass, no less.

He'd seen her enter the arena with the woman she'd sat beside. She was clearly a new employee since he didn't recognize her. She certainly fit Chuck's no fuss, no muss attitude. Another analyst or trainer likely. They had millions of those around.

But that didn't explain why he'd been aware of her throughout practice when usually his complete focus was on the ice.

Then Mason had pulled his usual shit with the body

check as Brock had noted her coming down the steps. But he hadn't given the kid's harsh breathing or taunts any attention, because everything other than her had faded to the background. He'd been so incapable of looking away from her that he'd practically memorized her appearance, from her auburn ponytail to the beauty mark just outside the corner of her mouth.

What a weird moment that had been.

Maybe he'd taken too many hits to the head and it was finally adding up, but he hadn't been able to look away. There was just something about her. Maybe it was the way she held herself so still, or how she hadn't flinched away from what was happening. Usually, women balked in horror or got into the blood sport of things. Not her...

The moment had been charged with something he couldn't name. The way she'd stopped and stared at him... Like she was cataloging him completely. He'd felt as pinned by her gaze as he had by Mason's body.

Jesus, he probably needed his head examined. Brock tossed his phone in his leather duffel bag and growled darkly after rereading the last text that had come through, ready to set aside his strange reaction to Mystery Girl.

"Since you aren't dating anyone, I'll assume your sister texted you something about the kids. You said she's out of town for work." Finn clapped a meaty hand on his shoulder in solidarity. "So what is it this time?"

Brock reached deep for patience. He really did. His sister was getting divorced from her deadbeat husband. Her whole world was falling apart. She had two kids to take care of as well as a career as a medical sales rep, which she deeply loved. It would be tricky for her to find a new balance, and in the meantime, he'd agreed to step in and help.

Forget that hockey season was in full swing. Susan was his sister. Kinsley and Zeke were his niece and nephew. Family. She'd called him in tears, saying the only thing that had made Zeke feel better about the divorce was the possibility that they could stay with Brock.

Jesus. Of course he'd said yes! He'd told her they could stay forever.

But he was discovering on a whole new level that he *really* didn't understand women, something he'd already learned after getting divorced in his mid-twenties. "Susan is having the babysitter drop the kids here and not at my house, because she thinks it'll be easier for them if *I* go home with them. Do you know what that even means?"

Finn made a comic face before tugging on his lucky fisherman's sweater from his favorite store in Halifax. Brock was glad he hadn't worn one of the many sweaters Finn had given him over the years since they'd first started playing together in college, or they would have matched like Mystery Girl and her colleague.

"I'm not dating anyone either right now, so I've got no answer for you, man." Finn grimaced, highlighting the cut to his lip he'd gotten in practice. "I love women, but they completely mystify me."

"If that's not enough, Chuck told me to head upstairs to see him and Ted."

"Mason's going to love that when it gets around," Finn said in practically a stage whisper, seeing as how they were still in the locker room. Sure, there weren't too many players left. He'd lingered in a cold shower to reduce the swelling from the bruises Mason had given him on the ice with that last hit.

When he'd stopped and watched that nerdy-looking new assistant. Whom Coach had hired...

The thought of Chuck refocused him. "We just need to do what we're here to do, Finn."

"I'm locked," he said, his eyes going flat.

"That's something I can always count on."

Brock nodded to a few of the other guys who were heading out.

They'd been playing together almost six months since preseason had started. Brock was still getting to know the team, even though he'd reached out to many of them in the off-season. Working out together and socializing had helped them get off to a running start as a team. But it was nearly March now, and they needed to gel. It still hadn't happened. They had a competitive record, but they were barely scraping by when they won because of stupid penalties and lack of team cohesion.

Mason "The Marvel" was the proverbial stick in their spokes. That punk had taken it personally that Brock had been recruited to play for his old coach and be the Eagles' savior, and he'd been extra aggressive in practice and games since the beginning, trying to prove who was better. They traded who was the highest scorer in every game, and the kid was driven to outdo him.

Brock was having none of it. He'd gone up against talented players with giant egos his whole career and won. He planned on doing the same here. The kid needed to get with the program. Now. They had eight weeks to make the conference championship and make the playoffs.

He clipped on his Swiss watch and checked the time. "Kinsley and Zeke are going to be here in five minutes, and I'm going to have to park them in the executive offices to wait for God knows how long."

"I can wait with them." Finn zipped his worn duffel shut—the same one they'd both gotten when they'd played for Harvard. "No idea what I'm going to say to your niece. Kinsley's a little terrifying right now. When I swung by your house last week, she'd written UNWANTED on a plain white T-shirt with a black Sharpie."

He hated how tight his chest felt. It made him feel guilty that he was so out of sorts because his family was staying with him. Before a season started, he put everything in a particular order, from the suits he was going to wear for road trips—bought by his personal shopper—to the latest magazines lambasting him and his team and their chances at victory. Nothing fed his motivation like doubters and people who outright insulted him and his abilities.

But the magazines were out of order now, covered by Zeke's PlayStation controller and Kinsley's schoolwork. Susan tried to keep the house tidy, but Zeke's numerous pairs of shoes littered the floor. So did the occasional candy wrapper.

Brock was living in an emotionally fraught circus, and it was going to require all of his mental focus to keep his mind on winning and the job he'd come to do, back in his hometown, for his old coach and the Eagles' new owner, Ted Bass.

He could feel tension begin to worm its way into his body. "It's the tent Kinsley's pitched in my family room that kills me."

Finn rubbed the back of his massive neck with a grimace. "She still hasn't agreed to sleep in one of your guest rooms?"

"Kinsley hasn't left her tent." He felt his jaw pop as the image of the teetering green canvas atrocity flashed through his mind. "Despite me promising to decorate her room any way she wants. But what kills me is the big posterboard sign she's taped to the tent. *I am not an inconvenience.*"

Finn cursed as he finger-combed his blond hair. "That's not good."

"*Right?* I don't even know what to do about that. I remember being really pissed off at my dad when I was a kid. He was the principal at my elementary school, so sometimes the whole student and son thing got crossed."

"Understandable," Finn concurred, leaning back against his locker. "Your dad likes his rules."

Something Brock appreciated better as an adult. "But this kind of teenage agony? It's worse than having a tooth knocked out. I wish Kinsley was five years old again, and I could get her a teddy bear and an ice cream cone. I was her hero of an uncle back then. Now I'm just another adult who doesn't understand her. Like Susan and her dad. I don't know what to do for her."

"You're stepping up and giving them all a place to land." Finn crossed and zipped up Brock's bag for him with a knowing look. "Taking care of shit. Man, you're doing more than most would."

Still, it didn't feel like enough. Certainly, it wasn't fixing anything. "I wish I could cut off one of Darren's balls and use it for puck practice while he watches, bleeding and crying from the stands."

Finn's laugh boomed out in the locker room, making a few other players stop dressing and send over inquiring looks. The old guys were still trying to figure them out.

"He deserves that and more." Finn made a slashing motion across his neck. "What kind of man tells his wife that she and their kids are an inconvenience?"

"An asshole." Brock picked up his duffel. "Thanks for watching out for them. I'll be as fast as I can with Chuck and Ted."

"Good luck with that," Finn called as Brock hurried out of the locker room.

Mason was loitering outside of the dressing room with some of the team's younger hockey players. Of course he was wearing his famous black fur coat, the one modeled after Tyler Durden in *Fight Club*. Apparently, Mason's dad used to watch the movie with him before hockey games to get him into fight mode, and the tradition had stuck. Brock had his own so-called rituals and superstitions—a peanut butter, honey, and banana sandwich had been his pregame go-to for years, started by his mother—but he thought Mason had taken the movie a little too far.

Sure, the kid abided with the NHL dress code before games, wearing the usual suit, tie, and pants, but the fur coat skirted the line. And then there was his off-the-ice wardrobe...

The kid had drawn big press for his crazy graphic shirts, silk pants, leather jackets, and aviator sunglasses—many items he'd endorsed, bringing in serious bank. He'd been quoted in *Sports Illustrated* saying he loved the color red because of the movie, since it symbolized blood and violence. Just how he liked his hockey.

Not Brock's style. He usually respected other players and how they chose to carry themselves, but Mason put his particular brand of hockey in everyone's face.

The kid had incredible stats, the reason he'd been named Rookie of the Year and earned the nickname "The Marvel." But even though the Eagles had made the playoffs over the past couple of years, partly thanks to him, he'd racked up more penalties than anyone else on the team, sometimes costing them games.

The Eagles had been brushed with the worst refrain any good team could incur: they couldn't finish. They couldn't bring in the big win. They were their own worst enemy, Mason being Enemy Number One.

Which was why the Eagles had been given a hard spring cleaning this year. The old owner had sold the team to Ted Bass, who had brought in his old friend, Chuck Collins, who in turn had traded two underperforming players to bring in him and Finn. Chuck had coached them at Harvard, and together they'd won three hockey national championships.

Instead of welcoming Brock as a resource who'd help them finally win the Stanley Cup, Mason had brought an enemy and payback mentality to their relationship from the first day they'd met. The kid clung to old grievances, like the fact that Brock had been on a team that had beaten Mason twice in the playoffs. Shortsighted to Brock's mind.

The only thing they both agreed on was what Brock considered their common ground: neither of them had won a Stanley Cup and both wanted one. He tried to remember that whenever Mason put him to the wall or gave him a hard time. Which was about to happen right now. Because Brock knew the kid was waiting for him after that stunt on the ice. He gritted his teeth and increased his stride.

"Brock, my man." Mason held out his arms, his large black fur coat making him seem like a giant grizzly waiting for prey. "Are you feeling a little bruised from where I put you up against the wall? Do you need Mommy to kiss it?"

He leveled him a flat stare. "First, my mother has passed, and second, you're going to have to work harder to get me to cry uncle. Focus on winning instead. I'm not your enemy, Mason. I'm your teammate. You boys have a good evening. I'm off to see Chuck and Ted."

Mason's mouth flattened. According to locker room gossip, he still hadn't met with Ted Bass privately. Mostly because Ted was smart and knew the lack of distinction ate at Mason's ego. When he heard a crash behind him, Brock smiled all the way to the front office.

If only they could channel that kid's energy toward championship success...

But that's why Ted had hired Chuck, who was known for some pretty off-the-wall motivational strategies when their butts were in a sling, as he liked to say. Brock was part of that strategy, but he'd only agreed to stay for a year so they could make their run at the Cup. A one-year contract for ten million, and after the year was through, Cup or no Cup, his professional career would be over. One of the best high school hockey coaches was retiring and wanted him to take over. The job happened to be fifty minutes from Minneapolis, and he would be able to coach his nephew—a dream for both of them.

But first, they had to win so he could meet his final hockey goals. Every day Brock visualized lifting the beautiful Stanley Cup trophy over his head.

He would accept no other outcome.

THREE

"What is it about men and jealousy?"

Val glanced over at her friend, who was tapping her foot in time to an inaudible beat while they waited to see Val's father. "Jealousy as a rule is generally ascribed to women, although both sexes fall prey to it. What are you referring to?"

Darla waggled her brows. "I'm still trying to get over that last hit against the glass as we left. That was Mason 'The Marvel,' the Eagles' very talented rookie, asserting his dominance over the Eagles' oldest player and new captain, Brock 'The Rock.' According to what I researched, fighting like that usually doesn't happen in practice."

Val didn't mention she was trying to put that very moment from her mind. "I would suspect primal instincts here. Probably because the older, more experienced man has a better shot at survival than the younger one, and the younger one knows this."

Darla snickered. "I think the young Alpha is looking to make a statement about whose club is bigger, don't you?"

She shot her friend a look. "Are you going to make club and stick jokes during our entire study?"

"You bet I am." She gave an adorable smile, the kind she sported when they were drinking alcohol, whether from a gourd, a goat skin, or a giant margarita glass. "And I'm so taking you to the locker room."

Val fought a groan. "I wish it weren't necessary, but—"

"Bathing rituals—especially male-only rituals—are critical to our study."

"Sell it." She let herself chuckle softly. "Maybe I'll 'forget' my glasses and let you describe the scene to me."

"I can already tell you how it's going to be." Darla opened her arms full length. "Big and bigger."

Val tried to hold on to her professional reserve, but her mouth was twitching. "Describing male anatomy really isn't within our scope of study, Dr. James." Unless it was part of fertility rituals or artistic symbols, of course.

"Yet it feeds a woman's soul and gives her something to dream about on lonely nights." She tugged on Val's satchel cozily resting against her stomach. "You could use a little dreaming. The last time you had a real date was before we went to Congo. That was over a year ago."

While Darla had found a way to go out during that time. With a peacekeeper. With a humanitarian worker. With a volunteer doctor. All manly and sexy specimens. "You know me. I'm not as interested in the opposite sex as you. I prefer carefully scheduled encounters with suitable candidates."

"Like it's lab day or something." Darla lifted her hands in surrender in response to the look Val gave her. "All right, I'll stop getting on your case. I know you're choosy, Val, and you should be. I should be more like you."

"No, you should be *you*." She gave in to the urge to put

her hand on her friend's arm. "Because who you are is wonderful."

"Ah... Don't make me give you a big ol' hug right here in Dad's reception. Good thing I didn't feel that urge in the arena. We'd stop practice. Men love girl-on-girl action."

Her mouth twisted in distaste. "Another aspect of the reptilian brain that puzzles me."

Darla lowered her glasses and gave a playful wink. "I'll explain it to you sometime over giant margaritas."

Val schooled her features since Chuck was bearing down on them. He didn't even crack a smile as he reached them, even though she'd known him for over ten years as one of her father's friends.

Not that he'd changed much. He was grayer, sure, with thinning hair, but he still wore long-sleeved polo shirts that always looked wrinkled and somehow a bit disreputable, along with black athletic pants. "Hello, Chuck."

He inclined his round chin at her and then Darla. "Ted busy?" he asked quietly.

"On a call. We're waiting for Lavinia's all-clear."

Her father's executive assistant had worked for him since before Val was born. She'd seen him through three marriages. Found Val the perfect schooling, everything from tutors to boarding schools.

"Have them call me," Chuck bit off, starting for the exit.

The sound of the office door snicking open had him stopping and heading back. She and Darla rose as Lavinia appeared. "Sorry about the delay. You can go in now. Chuck, are you planning on joining our new employees?" Her teasing remark was for their benefit, Val knew.

"Why else would I be up here?" he barked, heading for the door without waiting.

Darla was fighting a smile as Val bit the inside of her cheek. "He's a character."

"Always has been. Like you two, it seems. I didn't have a chance to say so earlier, but I'm mad about the outfits," Lavinia commented as she marched them swiftly toward the double doors with the name plaque reading Ted Bass.

"We thought they were rather brilliant," Darla commented as Lavinia stopped them in the doorway.

"You also received your skates, yes?" Lavinia asked a little too innocently. "Your father insisted you have them while you're here. He wanted me to mention that you should use the ice whenever the Eagles aren't."

Because he knew about her inner war and would never want to pressure her directly. He'd sent her the skates and asked Lavinia to make the suggestion, leaving the rest up to her. Except the pressure in her diaphragm had surged anyway. She'd won the gold with those skates.

"You didn't tell me that!" Darla exclaimed. "You're going to take advantage of the rink and skate some, aren't you? I know you miss it."

She fought the urge to rub the area of her former agony. "We'll see. We're here to work."

"Hmm..." was all Darla said in her smooth-as-honey voice, and to Val's ears, Darla's murmur sounded like trouble.

Lavinia only patted her arm as they walked into the office before closing the door behind them.

"My God!" Val's father slowly rose from his chair in front of a fleet of windows reflecting downtown Minneapolis and scratched his perfectly styled white shock of hair before hugging first her and then Darla.

"What's the matter?" her friend asked innocently.

He gestured to them, his cuff links flashing. "I knew you

two were going incognito, but what have you done with my daughter and her best friend?"

"Other than using our first names, we've erased Dr. Hargrove and Dr. James completely." Val smiled easily. "As agreed. No one would suspect we're cultural anthropologists."

"Or Ted Bass' daughter," Lavinia commented, taking her usual seat where she monitored most of Val's father's meetings. "Not to mention your folks, Darla."

Darla gave her a wink. "I wish my parents could see me like this. Mama would probably faint, and Daddy would call for a shot of Hennessey."

"Part of me can't blame J-Mac." Her father leaned forward from his lofty height of six-five and studied them. "Is that your real prescription, Val? My God, those glasses are an inch thick and preposterously hideous! Henry Kissinger's were more attractive."

"We went for complete authenticity," Val stated practically.

"So I see." Her father walked around them both, ruefully shaking his head. "When you accepted our crazy plan, I knew you were going to figure out a disguise to protect your identity. This is so simple, but it beats anything I could imagine."

"Personally, I love the nerdy outfits." Chuck grabbed a bottle of water from her father's fridge. "They look like number crunchers, Ted. I don't want any of the players giving them a hard time."

"As women?" Her father's voice was sharp. "I know our players have reputations with the ladies but tell me they aren't harassing female staff. Because I won't tolerate that, Chuck. I'll kick them off this team so fast their heads will spin."

"Hang on." Chuck dropped down onto the cream sofa against the side wall and guzzled his water, some dribbling down his chin. "I haven't seen or heard of anything to suggest harassment."

"Neither have I, Ted," Lavinia added in her no-nonsense tone. "And you can be sure I've looked into it."

Her father's frown vanished, and he motioned for Val and Darla to sit. "Good. That makes me feel better."

"Us too." Val gestured vaguely with her hands as she took a seat. "Darla and I can handle ourselves, but such regard would hurt the study."

Her father kicked his feet out as he sat on one of the matching sofa chairs. "Why am I not surprised you'd say that? But I want you two to feel completely safe and comfortable while you're here."

Chuck thrust out his half-downed water bottle. "They will, Ted. I plan on telling the players and the staff that Val and Darla have worked with me before as analysts and will have full access. I expect some of the younger ones to give them a little prodding. The guys like to know who's in the organization and what they're doing. It's inevitable, Ted. Which is why I asked Brock to come upstairs to meet them. I knew they'd be swinging by your office after practice."

Val was aware of her mouth going dry again, and she didn't like it. She rose to grab a bottle of water for herself and one for Darla. After opening hers, she did her best to take normal sips and steel herself to see the Eagles' captain again.

"Good." Val's father steepled his fingers. "So, you saw your first practice. Any impressions?"

Val caught Darla's nod, indicating that she should answer. "Well, there are obvious correlations up front. Aggression. Territoriality. Use of tools."

"Dental problems," Darla joked.

"What about the Paleo diet?" Her father laughed. "Val, did you know the 'Paleo' in the Paleo diet referred to the Paleolithic period? Lavinia told me the other morning, and I was stunned I hadn't made the connection before."

Darla was biting her lip to keep from smiling, and Val couldn't blame her. Ted Bass was known for his brilliance in business, but he knew very little outside of those interests. Even his knowledge of hockey had come after he'd bought the team as an investment last year, thinking his good friend, Chuck, could turn it around, should he want to jump from his old team to Ted's. He had. "Yes, Daddy. We knew that."

"I'm not sure how 'Paleo' my players actually are on their off hours." Chuck swigged the last of his water. "They have nutritional coaches and guidelines, but—"

"Sometimes you've got to munch." Darla patted her hip, making the curves visible under the baggy shirt. "Gets me into trouble, but I do love some junk food and sweets. Of course Val doesn't."

"Val has the kind of mental focus and physical discipline I wish most of our players had." Her father shot her the winning smile he was known for, the one that had graced every major business magazine around the world. "Too bad you're only here to observe. You could give those guys a lecture or two in gritting out a win under pressure. Hell, when I think of how you won that last gold in the Junior Olympics with a stomach ulcer. I'm not sure we have players that tough, Chuck."

"Neither am I, Ted. Yet." He crushed the water bottle with his bare hands, the noise as much as the act making her wonder if Chuck needed to be in the caveman study. "Everything's good with that now, though, right?"

Val laid her hands in her lap to keep her nerves calm. When she thought of how stressed she'd been as a young girl, sometimes old anger resurfaced. Back then, she'd been expected to smile through anything. Pain. Failure. Disappointment. A rude question from a reporter. A harsh word from her coach. Or her own mother. And she usually had to do it with cameras trained on her. That girl hadn't known how to handle all the pressure or the emotions attached to it other than to put them into a box.

The ulcer had been her body's answer to the unrelenting pressure, and ultimately, it had given Val a ticket to a better life. Of course, her mother had objected to her quitting. She'd wanted her to continue to grit through and compete as an adult. Her father had nearly blown a gasket. It had ended their marriage.

Her father had always had her back. His loyalty to her had been one of the most treasured gifts of her life besides Darla. Now she would have his back. He wanted her to do this study, hoping it would help motivate his team to win. She wouldn't let him down.

"I'm healthy as a horse, to use an idiomatic phrase." Val tapped her knee and playfully mimed a doctor checking out her reflexes. "But competition can eat away at you if you let it."

"That's a good point." Chuck rose and grabbed another water. "Let's get down to brass tacks. I came in this year with high hopes of turning around this team. I brought Brock in, along with his old friend from college hockey days, Finn Landry, hoping their maturity and leadership would help focus the rest of the team and get us rolling. Despite their talent, the team continues to underperform and make headlines off the ice. We're talented enough to win the Stanley Cup, but we don't have the discipline yet.

We're lucky to be eking out wins. That's where you come in."

Val and Darla both nodded before Val said, "We're glad to help."

"Chuck is known for using some pretty unconventional motivational strategies when warranted," Ted broke in.

"Infamous is more like it." Chuck laughed and cracked his knuckles. "But these are hockey players. Thick skulls. And this team has the thickest I've come across. Rather like cavemen. Your area."

Their area was actually much more expansive than his supposition, but Val was not going to point that out. Neither was Darla.

Her friend leaned forward in her chair and lowered her glasses. "Despite the common references to cavemen being stupid, you should know that cavemen were quite smart, with large brains. They were dominant and territorial and worked together for the collective good. Much like your hockey players, I imagine."

"We could use a whole hell of a lot more working together, let me tell you," Coach shot back.

Val thought of her early findings. "Yes, I can imagine. There's a lot they can take away from the cavemen. Their tools and orchestrated teamwork are recognized as the reason they survived the Ice Age. I think that would motivate the players when the ongoing rigors of competition and travel test their will to win."

"Well said," her father commented, sending her a smile. "I knew you'd understand."

She did. Only too well.

"This kind of motivational strategy is only something I reach for if my team starts losing enough games to put us out of the playoffs." Chuck rubbed the back of his neck.

"We've got fifteen losses right now, and every season I know in my gut when we've reached what I call 'The Skids.' It's the moment in a season when you can't take any more losses and are in serious jeopardy of not making the playoffs."

"Chuck has a bad feeling he's going to need to pull out the big guns," her father added. "So do I. But even if he doesn't, you'll still have all the access you need to finish your academic article. I want to assure you of that."

"Thank you," she and Darla both echoed at the same time.

"Now, what exactly do you need for your study?" Chuck's eyes narrowed. "I'd prefer you not interview the players about whether they think they're modern cavemen."

Darla laughed before she could smother it. "Darn. I was also hoping to ask 'The Marvel' if he felt his excessive penalties were due to territorialism or not being respected by his elders on the team."

Chuck hooted. "That's a good one."

Val fought a smile before glancing over at Darla. "We are able to fully conduct this study through research and direct observation, don't worry. We appreciate the full access to the team, and we're here to support you in any way we can."

Besides, in addition to helping her father, they would be getting an incredible academic article out of the bargain and positioning themselves for more stateside work.

"Perfect." Chuck chugged more water. "Then we all understand each other."

Her father leaned forward and took her hand. "Thanks, honey. Because I'm not owning a losing team."

"Let's focus on winning, Ted." Chuck crunched yet another water bottle, making Darla's mouth twitch with amusement. "And letting Val and Darla do their jobs."

She and Darla traded another look. From the Congo to the horn of Africa, she and Darla had worked in some pretty tight spots.

This assignment would be a piece of cake.

"Great, I'm glad we've got all that settled. Lavinia, will you bring Brock back here?"

All the blood left Val's forebrain. She'd forgotten about the Eagles' captain joining them.

Maybe this assignment wasn't going to be as easy as she'd thought.

FOUR

HOW COULD A WOMAN WHO LOOKED SO DETERMINEDLY unfeminine do this to him?

Brock had been in the league for a long time, so meeting with management didn't give him the butterflies it had as a young player. But he had to cover his surprise at seeing the woman from earlier—the one who'd stopped him from fighting Mason against the wall. She was with the other woman he'd seen her with in the bleachers during practice.

Suddenly, his heart was drumming in his chest.

They were both sitting comfortably in Ted's seating area along with Chuck and Ted's executive assistant, so they had to be pretty important people...

They looked like prototypical female athletic trainers in those baggy black T-shirts, khaki pants, white tennis shoes, and ponytails, with no makeup. He couldn't understand why anyone would willingly choose glasses like that, but what did he know? He peeled his gaze away from Mystery Woman, but he couldn't shake the feeling that the whole outfit was off. Somehow, it didn't seem to fit her.

So who were they? More importantly, who was the very

contained one with the incredible posture who held him in her thrall?

He gave the group a polite smile. "Ted. Coach. Ladies."

Ted crossed and shook his hand. "Good to see you, Brock. Thanks for coming up. Chuck and I wanted you to meet two new members of the Eagles' staff who are going to be with us for a while—and hopefully help us get to the playoffs and a Stanley Cup win."

He made sure to nod emphatically. If he were dressed in his uniform, he would have cracked his knuckles to show Ted how much he wanted that trophy.

"Brock, this is Val and Darla." Chuck paused to chug water like a camel, something Brock was used to seeing since Coach never drank while they were on the ice. "I've known them for a long time, and they're top-grade analysts."

So not trainers. He inclined his chin at the two women since a handshake didn't feel right. "Nice to meet you two."

The woman named Darla smiled warmly. The other one—Val—didn't. She remained cool as a cucumber as she watched him intently, her posture elegant even in her baggy clothing. As a pair, they couldn't be more of a contrast. Darla had light brown skin while Val's was almost as light as his mother's porcelain china.

Even seated, she sat a few inches taller than her companion. Brock had judged her to be five-eight when he'd first seen her, with Darla being about five-four. Where Val was slender, Darla was curvy. If he were going out on a limb, he'd say Darla was the friendly and outgoing one while Val was more guarded.

Except her reserve was compelling, almost charismatic. Up close, he could see beyond her unflattering style and home in on other details. The beauty mark added a note of sensuality to what could have been cool beauty. She was elegant, regal even. He must be losing his mind.

Coach took another swig from the water bottle before saying, "Val and Darla will be working with me behind the scenes on the best way to motivate the team."

He almost smiled then. Chuck was known for his off-the-wall thinking. One time he'd inflated the opposing team's stats to make them seem tougher as opponents. He'd done it to keep them from treating the game like a cakewalk.

His strategy had worked with most players, but Brock had a mind for numbers. He'd thought Coach had made a computing mistake and had pointed it out privately, earning him a slap on the back and a "Let's keep my little motivating strategy a secret."

Brock hadn't said a word. The guy was his coach. Plus, the strategy had worked.

And who could forget the geriatric ballerina Chuck had hired once to teach the team a lesson?

But hiring *two people* to help Chuck full-time?

Holy—

Ted clearly wanted the Stanley Cup as much as Chuck did. Of course, forking out the money for two employees to help turn this team around would be nothing to him. Everyone knew Ted Bass didn't fail, something Brock mirrored in his own career and side businesses.

Chuck crushed the now-empty water bottle and laid it on the table beside the other three he'd prepared for the recycling bin. "As the captain, I wanted you to know so you could spread the word and look out for them. You get me?"

He nodded his head crisply. Chuck was probably concerned about Mason harassing them. The kid wanted to be everyone's center of attention, and when it didn't happen, which wasn't often, he laid on the charm. Even though it was as shallow as black ice.

"You got it, Coach. Anything they need."

"Okay, that's it." Chuck stood up and went to Ted's fridge for another water.

Ted inclined his head toward Chuck with a wry smile. "I wonder sometimes why he doesn't line up all the bottles and simply down them all."

Brock knew Ted's humor meant he hadn't yet been dismissed.

Were the two analysts going to do anything but watch him? Neither had so much as smiled except for that brief greeting by Darla. Val sat with the kind of stoicism he'd seen from some of the Nordic players he'd faced off against over his career.

She wasn't watching him like he was a piece of meat, though. She was watching him like she was trying to figure him out. His early coaches in hockey had sported similar expressions when he'd joined their teams.

"Coach used to say it was good exercise to get up and grab his own water," he responded with a rueful shrug. "Crunching the bottles helps your heart, right, Coach?"

"Better than a stress ball," Chuck responded, flopping back onto the sofa and twisting off another bottle cap.

"Everything going okay with your family?" Ted asked out of the blue. "I heard you're helping your sister out during her divorce. Susan has two kids, right?"

He nodded, unsure where this was going. "Yeah, Zeke's twelve and Kinsley's fourteen. It's a tough time for them, but you don't need to be concerned. I'm handling it. I'm locked, Ted."

"Of course you are." The older man stood up and walked over, gripping his shoulder as he walked him to the door. "I wasn't suggesting anything else, Brock. I only wanted you to know that Lavinia can help out in a pinch. Finding a last-minute babysitter. Or a tutor. She's the true 'Marvel' of the Eagles if you ask me. My daughter was around that age when I got divorced. Without Lavinia, I wouldn't have made it. I just wanted you to know you have support here."

He looked Ted Bass straight in the eye. Not too many people did, but Brock knew this was the moment to do it. "I appreciate that, Ted. Thanks. Speaking of, the babysitter is dropping the kids off here for me to take home. I need to run."

"Go." Ted opened the door, proving why people liked him—he didn't have an ego and treated everyone with respect. "We'll talk soon."

Letting himself out, he watched the door close behind him. God, what a strange meeting. But if those two women could help Chuck figure out a way to motivate this team to ultimate victory, Mason especially, Brock was all for it.

"Uncle Brock!"

Turning, he smiled as Zeke sprinted toward him, his backpack jumping on his back as he ran. Brock caught him up in a bear hug, even though the kid was getting bigger by the day and starting to shoot up in height. He wasn't too cool yet for these displays of affection.

Brock inclined his chin to Finn over Zeke's shoulder. His friend stood beside a very pissed-off Kinsley, who was wearing another one of her T-shirts. INVISIBLE was handwritten in bold black letters. She was holding her coat in her arms like she'd taken it off so people could see the bold message. God help them.

"Hey, buddy!" He ruffled Zeke's curly black hair with

one hand as he set him down. "How was school? Did you rock your math test?"

"I think so." Zeke looked up at him with his big brown eyes filled with hero worship. "I asked Mom if I could practice with you on the ice. Can you? Can you?"

"We have homework, you moron." Kinsley gave one of her annoyed huffs and threw her straight black hair over her shoulder. "Besides, this whole place smells. Even here."

"It smells like guys are supposed to smell." Zeke turned to him for confirmation. "Like men."

Brock fought a smile as he traded a look with Finn. "I'm kind of used to it. Finn?"

"It stinks." He wrinkled his broad nose. "That's why men wear deodorant and cologne."

"Not enough, clearly," Kinsley responded in that same unhappy tone.

The sound of a door clicking open reached him, and he turned to see Chuck and the two women leaving the executive suite. Brock nodded to his coach as the man muttered greetings, high-fived Zeke, and continued past them, not breaking stride. Coach didn't do small talk.

But the women were frowning—even the one with the ironclad reserve. He looked away uneasily, trying not to wonder why, and laid a hand on Zeke's shoulder. "How about we practice before school tomorrow? That way you'll be fresh in the morning, and you'll have your homework done. It's important for athletes to keep their grades up."

"Okay," Zeke muttered before glaring at his sister. "But Kinsley will have to come to practice with us since Mom is out of town and Aggie doesn't like to drive in morning traffic downtown."

"Whatever." She made her choppy bangs move with another annoyed huff. "I wish Aggie would just stop pretending to care about us. All she wants to do is text her boyfriend."

"Well, on that note..." Finn started to back slowly away, murmuring his goodbyes.

Brock couldn't blame him, although he filed away the info about Aggie.

He spotted Darla walking briskly toward them with Val hot on her heels, and he stepped aside with Zeke to clear the path so they could go by.

Only Darla stopped in front of Kinsley and gestured to her front. "Honey, take it from someone who's been there. *You are not invisible.* No matter what's happened, you don't let anyone make you feel that way. Okay?"

If Brock hadn't been a master at schooling his expression, his mouth would have gaped like Kinsley's. As much from the woman's comments as her gorgeous voice. He wasn't one to wax poetic, but it sounded like liquid gold.

Kinsley finally closed her mouth and nodded quickly to the woman, gripping the ends of her T-shirt. "Yeah...I mean, sure."

"Good." Darla gave some kind of affirming female nod Brock didn't understand. "I like your style, though. Way to make the people around you feel guilty."

Brock lifted a brow. That sounded like a skull shrinker's comment if he'd ever heard one. But it wasn't far off, and he was glad the truth was out in the open.

"She's mad because our dad left us." Zeke stuck out his chin, almost mulishly. "Not like we need him. He was never around much anyway. His music was always *so* important. It's not like he's even that good."

"God, a musician!" Darla gestured to the ceiling like she was imploring the heavens. "They make the worst parents."

Val was clenching her hands now. "Will you wait a moment, please? I'd like to do something."

He realized the question was directed at him. Again, he studied the woman before him. He'd been right about her height, given where the top of her head came up to on his body. He sensed she was thin under the ill-fitting clothes. Her high cheekbones under those atrociously thick black glasses suggested as much, along with the elegant neck sticking out above the baggy T-shirt.

What in the world was Chuck up to with these two?

"Sure thing. We can wait."

He watched as Val walked back into the executive office after a brief knock, making Brock nearly rock back on his heels. She clearly had no fear of interrupting Ted Bass. She emerged a moment later with Lavinia, and together they disappeared through another door behind the executive suite. She reappeared with what looked like two white Eagles T-shirts. Lavinia handed her two Sharpies, and then she was writing something on the plain backs.

After finishing, she gracefully glided back toward them. She moved like a gazelle. Even in her ugly white tennis shoes.

"If I could be so bold..." She extended the first T-shirt to Zeke. "This one is for you."

Brock almost blew out a heavy breath as he read SURVIVOR written on the back in black ink. The kid's face screwed up before his manners kicked in and he said, "Thanks, lady."

"My name is Val, and this is my friend and colleague, Darla. We're here to help the team, and because you are part of the team's family, we're here for you too. Now, you, Kinsley. Your uncle mentioned your name inside. This shirt is for you."

When the T-shirt unfolded in her hands, Brock's mouth did gape. The message was simple but powerful.

SEE ME.

Kinsley's face was turning pink, but her entire demeanor had changed. The washed-out, pissed-off, slightly bored expression was gone. Her hazel eyes were sparkling. God, were those tears?

"Thank you," she whispered, a moment before she was hugging Val and then Darla.

Zeke looked up at him in shock, and he put his arm around the boy before turning to the two women. "Thank you, Val. Thank you, Darla. That was very...kind." God, he'd almost stuttered he was so stunned.

Darla fussed with Kinsley's bangs, and they traded a smile only women managed with each other. God, he hoped these two *were* skull shrinkers because he could use more of their help keeping Kinsley like this. Like she used to be. Before her dick father broke her heart.

"It's a pleasure," Darla said again, hugging Kinsley and kissing the top of her head as the young girl practically clung to her. "When you come back to see your uncle, make sure to find us. We'll have some special girl time. Right, Val?"

"Yes, that would be good." She didn't hug Kinsley, but she reached out and touched her shoulder, her awkwardness telling him she didn't make physical gestures often. *"I see you, Kinsley."*

"So do I." Darla bumped Kinsley slightly, making his niece cough out a laugh.

"I'll find you. When I come, ah...next time." She was blushing fiercely now. "Thanks. I'm glad...I met you two."

Her speech was awkward, and she was beet red, but

there was a sweet smile on her face. Brock had never seen such a transformation. His heart had a funny reaction.

"We are too, honey," Darla said in her smooth voice with a soft smile. "We invisible girls need to stick together."

Brock noted the inclusive language. Darla was implying she had felt the same way. Did Val? Is that why she'd offered the kids those T-shirts?

God, what was he thinking? It was none of his business.

"Again, thank you." He lifted his chin in their direction. "I'll see you around the facility."

"You'd better believe it," Darla answered with a quirk of a smile.

Val shot her a look before turning to him. "Enjoy your afternoon."

Kinsley didn't talk much in the car, but there was something different about her silence—less sulky and more contemplative. Zeke, who sat in the front, babbled on about school and hockey. When the boy mentioned those "weird women" and held up his new T-shirt with an eye roll, Kinsley leaned forward in the car and punched her brother lightly.

"*I* thought they were cool," she said with heat in her voice.

Brock realized she was clutching her new T-shirt to her chest. "So did I," he agreed, and when she met his eyes in the rearview mirror, they shared a smile.

His heart lifted, and for the first time since Susan had called him about the divorce, he felt hopeful. Like the kids were going to be all right, Kinsley especially. He'd known Zeke's anger was going to propel him forward. But this? Man, he couldn't wait for Susan to see the change in Kinsley when she got back from her trip tomorrow.

When they arrived home, he covertly watched as

Kinsley approached her tent. Would she finally take it down? Hope beat in his chest, and Zeke sidled up to him and put an arm around his waist, as if they were two sentinels keeping watch over someone they both loved.

Kinsley paused outside the tent rather than throwing herself inside it with a huff like usual. Her stillness had him holding his breath.

Take the sign down, please, baby girl.

But instead, she dropped to the floor and took a spiral notebook and a Sharpie out of her backpack. He couldn't see what she was writing. Apparently, she was carrying scotch tape with her now because seconds later she was affixing it to the side of the tent with a practiced ease that made him nervous. He read the sign as she stepped back.

I WANT YOU TO SEE ME.

He tried to keep his sigh quiet, but Zeke elbowed him, rolling his eyes before heading into the kitchen for a snack.

As Kinsley was unzipping her tent to head inside her sanctuary, Val's earlier words came back to him. Maybe it was time to try and speak his niece's language.

"Hey, Kinsley," he called, making her turn slightly. "I see you too."

Something bright flashed in her hazel eyes, and she gave him a crooked smile. He felt an answering one touch his lips before she disappeared into the tent.

Those women were miracle workers, he decided, and he was going to help them in any way he could.

He couldn't wait to see what they were going to do to motivate the team.

FIVE

Why are men as a species so protective of their turf?

VAL GLANCED UP FROM WRITING IN HER FIELD DIARY. Her heading was Territorialism, and her question applied both to cavemen and hockey players.

It was Day Two of their study, and the players had filed into the movie theater-style team room for the morning meeting after arriving at the rink by eight thirty a.m. At Chuck's decree, they'd skipped breakfast and the taping of their sticks to rush to the meeting. A meeting she and Darla were attending after having been briefly introduced by name. Chuck had purposefully provided no other details about them.

Now, they were sitting in the last row against the wall, the best place to observe. Darla had on her polite smile, the one she used during the first days around a new culture they were studying. Open, but not too chummy.

Val had on her usual expression. Stoic. It had always

suited her. She was aware of the stares they were getting, mostly from the chiseled-jawed guys sitting in the back with them, but they were behind her invisible glass wall, a people-coping technique one of her early figure skating coaches had taught her. She postulated these unfocused players were not the Eagles' best given their distance from the front, where Chuck stood, and their wandering attention.

Darla tapped her field diary as she began to scribble in black ink. Val knew even before she looked that the note was for her. Darla had been writing notes to her since their first class in boarding school.

> Chuck kind of made us more interesting by saying nothing about us, didn't he?

Val leaned over and wrote the required response.

> *What could he say? Did you expect ceremonial feathers and a blessing from the hockey gods? The less the better, I think.*

Darla's mouth worked before she wrote her response.

> Probably. But the stares are INTENSE. Maybe it's because they're coming from really hot guys with volcanic focus.

Val almost snorted.

Volcanic focus? Did you watch "Joe Versus the Volcano" again?

You know you love it. Wink.

I really don't. Now, let's get back to observing, Dr. James.

Right. I'll tell my girl parts to settle down, Dr. Hargrove.

You do that. PLEASE...

Val jumped a little when Darla poked her playfully in the side. It wasn't unexpected. Sitting still too long made Darla restless, and so far, the meeting had been a dry overview of the team's approach to their next slate of games, one Val would summarize easily into: *we will work hard and prepare hard and we will win.* Very Chuck.

She casually scanned the room. Brock, who had sent a welcoming smile their way upon arrival, was in much the same wardrobe he'd been wearing when he'd met her father in his office: green cashmere sweater with black wool pants and black leather shoes.

He was sitting in the center front row next to Finn Landry, his Harvard teammate, who wore a more casual navy fisherman's sweater and slacks. Both of their postures were strong and commanding.

The pecking order was clear. Brock was the captain, and his sidekicks were like the elders of this group, imbued with authority from their chief, Chuck, who held the ultimate elevated spot at the podium, the center of everyone's attention.

Territorialism personified.

Mason "The Marvel" was seated with a posse of young players to Brock's right, one row behind, wearing a Gucci-inspired turquoise graphic print hoodie with what looked like bullfighting pants. The other players in his crew were all attempting to dress like him, connoting them as a mini unit. They were the next generation. Still proving their worth to the group. Eager to take over but not to be weighed down by responsibility. Their dislike for their elders was obvious in their cocky body language and whispered comments, ones that earned them a sharp glance from their chief.

Chuck was gesturing to the movie-like screen with a metal presentation pointer in his hand—an obvious modern male extension of a phallus. The first team the Eagles would play was the object. They were to identify this team's weaknesses and then work together to take them down.

Val reasoned it wasn't too different from the Pygmies' approach to hunting dangerous wild pigs or laser-fast antelope.

Chuck mentioned something called a muffin, but since he was pointing at the screen, she suspected he wasn't talking about a snack. Darla nudged her, angled her notebook over, and started writing.

> Hockey appears to use food-inspired words to describe play.
> Not unlike tribal cultures.

> So far I've got: apple, biscuit, egg, lettuce, cheese.
> Now I'm hungry.

Val fought a smile. Darla was always hungry. She wrote back:

> *We'll look up these terms, but it IS fascinating.*
>
> *Also, considering how large these men are and all the calories they must burn, the fact that no one's stomach is gurgling with hunger suggests it must be common to use these terms in a non-food fashion.*

Darla coughed to cover up a laugh.

> You would think that. I'm dreaming of a steak sandwich.

Val pushed Darla's field diary away and wrote down the terms in her own record. She was aware of pressure at the base of her brain from all the names and concepts, but they would understand the lingo better as time passed. When Chuck finally called out, "Okay, that's it," she found herself relieved for the break.

She knew from the schedule Chuck had provided what to expect most days when the team was home and didn't have a game, which she'd logged in her field diary with some postulated cavemen comparisons.

Arrival at rink by 8:30 am
Breakfast (bonding ritual)
Tape sticks (superstition and war ritual)
Team meeting (warrior forum)
Warm-ups, including off-ice exercises (warrior practice)
Dressing for on-ice practice (ritual)
10 am practice on ice until 11:30 am (warrior practice)
Media engagement (community relations)
Post practice workout like strength training (warrior practice)
Shower (male bathing ritual)
Lunch 12:30 – 2 pm (bonding ritual)
More practice until 4 pm (warrior practice)

Sometime soon, she would ask Chuck to arrange for them to watch the players tape their hockey sticks; from what she'd researched, it was loaded with ritual and superstition. She leaned over to Darla as players started to file out of the room.

The curious looks were expected, but Mason "The Marvel" whispered something to his pack of young wolves as they all stood to leave, making them all laugh and chortle. She knew she and Darla must have been the butt of his joke. As he strutted by in that wild turquoise outfit, looking much like a cockatoo to her mind, his lips were twitching as if she had been dropped on earth to be the brunt of his amusement. That she would not tolerate.

She met his gaze dead-on. Like she used to when facing a very nasty figure skater whom she believed had secretly dreamed of doing to her what Tonya Harding had done to Nancy Kerrigan at the U.S. Figure Skating Championships in Detroit in 1994.

From the flicker of shock that briefly crossed his face, she knew she'd caught him off guard with her stare-down. Val imagined he wasn't as confident as he tried to project. Classic male inferiority complex masked by exterior projecting.

"Ooh, I love it when you get that face on," Darla whispered, crossing her ankles as he left the room. "Mason doesn't seem to like us."

"He doesn't need to like us, but outward disrespect is bad for us and what we've been hired to do. While he's not the captain or the coach, he does lead a good portion of the younger players. We want cooperation. Not ridicule."

"It's not like we haven't been the butt of male humor or hostility before. Oh, how I'd like to knock them down a peg or two. They're like the artists in the music industry that I can't stand. Overinflated egos and total self-absorption. Drives me nuts!"

"Let's refocus." She watched as Chuck stopped Brock and Finn from leaving, gesturing heatedly toward the back of the room—in the direction Mason had left. She couldn't hear what he was saying, but his frustration was obvious in his curt tone.

"Yes, lay it on me." Darla danced a little in her seat to shake off her mood. "Make it good."

Val knew exactly what would improve her friend's spirits. "I was reading about why hockey players tape their sticks last night, and did you know they call a part of the stick their shaft—"

"Usually I love a good shaft discussion." Darla closed

her field diary and gave her *that* look. "This is what you did instead of being my wingwoman last night?"

She would not feel guilty. "It was technically a school night. Tuesday! I know we're back to civilization, so to speak, but—"

"This place has restaurants and bars," Darla whisper-hissed. "I want to check out the music venues on First Avenue. All of them. I want to go to a movie."

"We'll get there." She pressed her lips together as friendship fought with duty. "You know I don't like to go out as much as you do, especially with work."

"But we're back where there are things to do besides listening to jungle sounds, fighting off baboons, and getting drunk on homemade hooch from a gourd!" Darla took her by the shoulders. "I need to go out, Val."

Her voice carried, because her mother's siren voice had been passed down to her. Chuck stopped speaking and looked over. So did Brock and Finn. Then Chuck muttered something and stormed out, nodding in their direction as he passed.

Had they broken up his sidebar? She turned in her chair, giving Darla her whole focus. "Let's have this discussion when everyone's gone," she whispered.

Darla bit her lip. "Sorry," she said in a quiet voice. "You know my voice carries."

Everyone from reporters at *Rolling Stone* magazine to her fans said Regina Eastman could whisper to someone in the worst seats in a concert venue. Darla's voice perhaps didn't have that much oomph, but it certainly had a power a normal human voice did not. Val still couldn't explain it scientifically. One African chief had said her voice box was blessed by the gods, and if you ever heard Darla sing, you wouldn't dispute that.

Val became aware of a solid male presence coming down the empty row where they were sitting. Her heart rate began to pick up.

"Hey, Darla." The deep baritone voice confirmed it was Brock Thomson. "Hey, Val."

She turned in her chair to look at him. He took up the entire row, towering over them, a powerful figure in his soft cashmere and wool slacks. There was an endearing, hesitant smile on his face. The icy blue eyes he was known for on the ice—the ones she'd seen in all his hockey photos—were a warm blue today.

Her gaze took in the stubble on his chiseled jaw, lined with a small scar, and the curly hair protecting his powerful skull. A scent of pine and cloves reached her nose. His aftershave, she reasoned.

She was aware of yet more uncomfortable physical reactions to him. Tension in her rib cage. Accelerated heart rate. Dryness in her mouth. She was becoming a walking lab specimen under the file of Brock Thomson.

"Don't mean to interrupt, but I wanted to thank you for being so kind to my niece and nephew, Kinsley especially." Brock sat two seats away, but Val still thought he felt too close, too overwhelming to her acute senses. "You helped her spirits a lot, and I wanted to tell you I'm grateful. It's been really rough, not knowing how to help her. Zeke is easier for me. He loves hockey. And food. We both love pizza."

He looked almost embarrassed revealing that, which only made Val like him more.

"We get each other, I mean." He lifted his shoulder. "But Kinsley is—"

"A misunderstood girl whom you can't fix with a hockey

practice or a pizza," Darla broke in, practically leaning into Val's lap.

Part of her wished her friend hadn't engaged. They weren't supposed to get this personal with their subjects. She'd wondered a half dozen times last night if she'd overstepped, giving his niece and nephew those T-shirts. But Darla was right. They'd both been that girl. How different might it have been for them if an older woman had taken notice and tried to help? Even one moment of kindness could change a life. She'd seen it again and again. It was one of the best characteristics of the human species, in her mind.

"Yeah, pizza and stuff won't work," Brock replied with a long exhale, laying his large hands on his powerful thighs, making her uncomfortably aware of his physicality. "Glad you get what I'm trying to say here. By the way, did I hear you mention wanting to go out? You guys are new to town, right? I was born and raised here. I'd be happy to show you around. Plus, it would be the least I can do for your kindness."

"That would be—" Darla stopped herself and looked at Val, her gold eyes big behind her tortoiseshell glasses. "Would that work for you, Val?"

Val appreciated her dialing it back and asking her. Darla's professionalism always kicked in...eventually. Her mind quickly ran through the metrics she'd drafted for their study. Sightseeing with an elder of the so-called tribe was something they'd done before. In fact, it came under their ethnographic category of building rapport with their new community. "That is a gracious offer. Thank you. Brock. We accept."

Her voice sounded stilted, and she felt like she'd tripped over his name. Embarrassing, given it being one syllable.

The *Globus pharynges* phenomenon: something obstructing her throat.

Brock's smile broadened. His gaze stayed on her long enough to make her have difficulty swallowing. Then he tilted his head to the side. Had Darla said he possessed volcanic focus? She felt like he was studying her like he would hockey film.

"You're most welcome." His richly deep voice possessed a chord that affected her in the pelvic region. "Val."

The gruff way he said her name made her mouth go even drier. Her physical response was not good...

So not even in the realm of professional.

God, what was next? Nervous laughter? Twirling her hair? Drawing hearts in her field diary?

She *had* to bring her reactivity to him under control somehow.

Darla was waiting for her to respond, and she could only hope her friend hadn't noted her awkward responses to this man.

"Maybe you can bring Zeke and Kinsley along," she suggested after searching for a polite response. The children would be a good distraction from Brock. She could focus on Kinsley especially. Better that than for Brock to be her sole focus in close proximity.

God, if Darla ever found out what was going on, she would love it. It was a rare thing for Val to be the one responding to the man "stick," so to speak.

Haha, Darla would say. *About time, Val*.

Catastrophic.

Then Brock's smile transformed to a grin, and the end of Val's world didn't seem imminent: it felt like it was beginning. Like in some silly love song crooned by Darla's mother.

"Kinsley and Zeke would love that. How about this Friday? We could pick you up around six. Sightsee a bit. My sister will be back in town by then."

"Have her come along too," Val said in a rush.

"Yes, please, we'd love to meet her," Darla practically beamed, pressing her hand to her chest. "Let me give you my number. We don't know anyone here. I was just telling Val how much I want to explore Minneapolis, especially the music scene."

She didn't glare at her friend, who was clearly fishing, as Brock entered Darla's information into his phone.

Finished, he leaned back in the seat and crossed his arms. "I wondered if you sang. With that voice of yours. If that's all right to say."

Darla lifted her shoulder. "Nothing wrong with saying what's true. People comment on my speaking voice as much as they do on Val's eyes."

Val had the urge to bury her head in her lap.

"Your eyes?" Brock leaned toward her, studying her face with an avid intensity that made her skin tingle. "I hadn't noticed."

Now his face seemed puzzled.

She lowered her gaze. He didn't need to know she had green eyes reporters had called everything from luminous to vibrant, depending on her mood. It had no relevance toward her time with the team. "Darla is being funny. Who could see my eyes behind these glasses?"

He didn't laugh. Probably because she wasn't funny. His eyes narrowed, making her think of powerful Antarctic glaciers and blue ice, as if he were trying to see what was behind her thick lenses.

"You probably need to move along to warm-ups so you can get dressed and on the ice soon," she found herself saying, her insides now jumping at his regard. "Chuck is a stickler for rules."

"I know." He inhaled some kind of giant breath and exhaled slowly, the sound all rough and masculine. "But I'm a pretty good taskmaster myself."

That was all it took for her to see him on top of her, both of them naked, as he held her hands over her head, pressing her down in the most delicious of ways. Her thighs gave a clench. She blinked at him in shock. Her mind had just drawn up sexcapades, as Darla liked to joke.

What on earth was going on with her?

"I'll bet you are," Darla teased, making Val want to sink into her chair. "Thanks again for the invite. You tell that beautiful niece of yours to hang in there. We'll work on propping her up more on Friday."

That was three days away. Surely Val could get herself under control by then.

"You're the best." Brock uncurled from the seat slowly, and the researcher in her knew it meant he was reluctant to leave. "I'll tell her." Then he smiled again, warm and kind and slightly sexy, and she fought the urge to grip her knees to hold on to her focus.

"If you have any trouble with anyone..."

They all knew who he was referring to.

"If you need anything—anything...." he continued in that same steadfast tone.

Her thighs clenched at the repetition of the word.

"You let me know," he finished. Another crooked, sexy smile. "I'll see you around."

When he walked down the row, Val had a good view of his backside. Had she ever noticed the strong muscles of a man's *gluteus maximus*? Now the Latin word made sense—

largest of the buttocks. Yes, that was what Brock had. Large, thick, defined muscles. Utterly captivating.

She was beginning to feel the stirrings of hyperventilation. "Excuse me, Darla, I need to find the restroom."

She stood up, scattering her pen and field diary and practically tripping over her satchel. Gathering them up quickly, she stuffed them into her bag. Darla thankfully said nothing. Pressing her shoulders back, she glided out of the meeting room only to realize she'd forgotten her satchel.

Only Brock was still in sight, walking in front of her, the defined muscles of his backside visible.

Her reptilian brain uttered a sultry *yum*.

Pausing in the hall seemed a smart move. To stop a reaction, one had to remove the stimulus. She took deep breaths, praying she wouldn't need a paper bag to offset imminent hyperventilation.

Darla appeared, carrying both of their satchels. "What happened? You were totally out of sorts back there. Did you get a whiff of the ice or something? Feel the urge to get out there and skate?"

She couldn't tell Darla her early scientific conclusion: *she was attracted to Brock Thomson*.

Not only was it unprofessional, but she wasn't sure how Darla would react. Her friend might abandon professionalism and encourage her. It wouldn't be unlike Darla to say something like: *Brock is your unicorn, Val. You have to ride it.*

She also could not use her longing to be on the ice as an excuse, because while Darla wasn't pressuring her—and wouldn't—she knew her friend was hoping she'd strap on her skates. That meant she had to use her standard excuse.

"I think I need to eat something." One thing she'd

learned about Darla over the years...any crisis could be blamed on a drop in blood sugar.

Her friend immediately dug into her satchel and pulled out a granola bar, unwrapping it for her. "I knew this was going to happen with us living apart. You eat like a bird when I'm not with you night and day. What did you eat last night?"

"A Caesar salad." She took the granola bar and sunk her teeth into it for show.

"I had a steak and a baked potato with a side of creamed corn." Darla clucked her tongue. "Don't make me start having you keep a food journal, Val."

Anxiety spiked within her. "That was low."

Darla knew how much she'd hated having one when she'd been a figure skater, something her mother had insisted on.

"When I need to, I play dirty." Darla shoved her ponytail out of the way as she rummaged through her bag and took out a water bottle. "Here. Let's get you fed and watered, and then we need to head to the ice for practice."

After Val ate the entire granola bar and downed half the water, she insisted, "I'm fine now, Darla. Really."

She hoped so. The distance between her and her physical stimuli had helped. With Brock gone, her heart rate was normal now. The dryness in her mouth was gone. She catalogued her current state. All that remained was the tension in her chest and a slight—what should she call it?—electricity dancing across her skin. Almost like how her skin felt before a massive thunderstorm in Kenya, when static energy filled the air. A phenomenon researchers—and poets—called desire.

She wanted to cradle her head in her hands. This had never happened to her before. Never on a study. And never with this intensity. Brock *was* her unicorn, and she wished he would head back into his magical forest and free her from his spell.

"Wasn't it great of Brock to offer to show us around?" Darla asked as they started walking toward the rink. She was assessing her with that mother hen regard, so Val made sure to nod with one of her neutral smiles as they reached the arena while she did her best not to inhale the smell of ice.

"I'm so glad you mentioned bringing Kinsley and the rest of the family along," her friend continued.

So was she, because she should not be alone with her unicorn!

God, was she starting to hyperventilate? This needed to stop.

Darla put a protective hand to Val's elbow as they ascended the concrete steps to find a seat in the stands. For a moment, Val nearly froze, the smell of pine and cloves reaching her. Brock's scent.

All the way from where he was standing at center line...

"We both enjoyed helping Kinsley," Val managed to say as she took her seat, listening to the melodic sound of skates on the ice, hoping it would distract her for once. "It was nice hearing it had made a difference."

"Yeah, it was." Darla plopped down beside her, her satchel making a thunk as she dropped it on the ground. "She's a sweetheart, and she's lucky she has a nice man like Brock who cares about her. He seems like a good guy, doesn't he? Did you know the media calls him one of the nicest guys in hockey?"

Val had read that as part of her research about the team. Now it held more meaning. Because he was being nice to *her*, which made her physical response to him even more dangerous. She liked the man *and* found him attractive.

Damn unicorn.

Darla scooted in place next to her, giving a little cry as she sat, taking Val's mind off mythical fairy creatures and her unusual need to swear.

"Something wrong?" she asked her friend, going on the offensive to keep Darla from catching on. "You can't say you have ants in your pants here. We aren't sitting on a log in the jungle."

"A thought I'll be adding to my gratitude list tonight before bed." She wiggled in place. "No, I might need to buy myself a heated cushion. My sweet little bottom needs some love, and this cold seat ain't giving it to her."

Val's off-the-rails mind brought up an image of Brock's bottom in his black slacks, the hard muscles moving back and forth under the wool. Heat rose up her neck as she thought about what it would be like to touch that butt.

Her eyes tracked to locate him on the ice. She didn't even need the number seven on his jersey to find him. He was making figure eights, his ease and power tangible. God, he could skate. He had a smoothness to the way he flowed on the ice, punctuated with explosive breaks of speed.

He made her miss skating like no other person out there. She could tell he understood the dance of it all...the flow. God, he was beautiful to watch. He slashed across the ice, a picture of male power. Her heart rate began to accelerate again, her mouth turning to dry toast.

The unicorn was stealing her peace.

When she got home, she would research unwelcome physical reactions to the opposite sex. The academic in her would find a way forward.

Because otherwise their entire study would be in jeopardy.

SIX

"Why do girls take so long to get dressed?"

Brock looked up from his watch toward Zeke. The kid was slouching on the couch in his winter coat, his triangular face scrunched up in annoyance.

He'd been wondering the same thing as they waited for Kinsley to emerge from the bathroom—for thirty minutes. Susan must have known this wait was possible since she'd mentioned catching up on paperwork. He hadn't had the heart or courage to move her along, but if he'd known it would take this long, he would have played more hockey tape for him and Zeke. "I still have no clue, Zeke."

"Ugh! But you're a grown-up!" His nephew pulled at his spiky hair. "How could you not know?"

Because he was a guy, but that answer wouldn't satisfy Zeke. "Have you asked your mom?"

His nephew kicked at Brock's hardwood floor with his tennis shoes. "She said girls like to look nice. I thought it was only for boys, but she said it's for anything. Even girls."

Brock didn't quite get that. He understood competition and jealousy between women. God knew he'd seen plenty himself as they'd vied for him. But Kinsley taking thirty minutes to look nice for two women? That seemed excessive.

"Kinsley!" Zeke yelled as he shoved off the couch. "We're going to leave you if you don't come out."

"We are not." Brock strode through the living room—past the tent in the corner beside his ficus tree—and down the hallway to the guest bathroom. "Kinsley, sweetheart. I know you want to be on time for our new friends, so we need to leave here in two minutes. Because Friday traffic—"

The door opened, and Brock's mouth gaped before slamming shut. His niece's long black hair fell in fresh waves down her back. She had pink lip gloss on her mouth, something Susan had told him in their rules meeting that she allowed. But it was his niece's clothes that heralded the biggest change. She was wearing a soft pink sweater and jeans with red hearts stenciled on the front pockets along with glittery pink flats.

For a moment, he bit his lip. What was he supposed to say here? He went with the truth. "You look great, Kinsley."

She lifted her shoulder and peered at him through her choppy black bangs. "You think so?"

Insecurity was in her voice, making his heart clutch. Susan used to be like this, he remembered. Before a school dance. Before a date. And later, before her wedding. Brock had always thought life was harder for Susan because she was a woman. Now he had Kinsley to show him that truth. "Yeah. I really like the hearts on your jeans. And the glitter. It makes you sparkle."

Her whole face brightened. "Good. That's good. I really want Darla and Val to like me."

Another knock to his heart. "They already like you,

sweetheart. Trust me. When adults pay attention to someone, that's a sign."

"Yeah, I know that." Her entire posture was slouching now. "My dad never paid attention to me."

He ground his teeth. He and Susan had talked about the best things to say to the kids when the topic of their dad and the divorce came up. But he thought his sister was being a little too nice. She'd tried to explain the whole "inconvenience" comment they'd overhead as stress and the result of frustrated dreams. Brock wasn't a parent, but he'd have admitted it was a hurtful comment. "He never paid much attention to me either, Kinsley."

That had her clutching the hem of her sweater and staring up at him. "He didn't? But everybody pays attention to you, Uncle Brock."

He puffed out a self-deprecating laugh. "Only hockey fans." Which wasn't completely true, because women paid him attention, hockey fans or not, but he wasn't about to tell his niece that. "You ready? I don't like to be late when I'm picking people up, especially the first time."

"Yeah, it might make them worry you're not really excited about seeing them." She sailed down the hall in a blur. "Mom, we're going."

He followed, musing over her words. Had he ever had that kind of thought? If someone was late, he figured they'd gotten caught up. Was this another female perspective? He'd have to ask Susan. You'd think he'd know something after his two-year marriage, which had ended years ago, but like he'd told Finn, if he'd known anything about women, he'd still be married.

The chatter clued him in that the kids were in the entryway with their mother. For a change, Susan had a huge smile on her tired face as she looked at Kinsley. His sister might not be wearing INVISIBLE T-shirts like Kinsley, but her business clothes weren't as crisp as usual, and her shoulder-length black hair wasn't shiny or styled. He imagined she wasn't sleeping well. Only Zeke seemed to be managing so far, and Brock thought it was because he had hockey as an outlet for his emotions.

The game had always given him the same thing, especially during his divorce, when he'd felt like such a failure. His demanding schedule hadn't allowed him to give enough, and when Erin had finally decided she wanted more, he'd let her go. Not seeing a way to give her what she wanted. Figuring she'd be happier if she left.

After that, he'd promised himself that if he found someone else to love, he would leave hockey and pursue the business interests he'd carefully been establishing since early in his career. His Harvard business degree and alumni connections, especially when he'd played in Boston, had been golden tickets to profitable investments and opportunities.

So far, he hadn't met that perfect person, and with retirement looming, he felt more open to whatever possibilities showed up. Life was funny that way. His sister and her kids were living with him. Who could have imagined that?

"You sure you don't want to come?" he asked Susan when she inclined her head at Kinsley with a smile as if to say *Do you see my daughter? She's back.*

"Come on, Mom!" Zeke crooned. Susan tugged him to her side, and he wrapped his arm around her willingly. "You were gone this week, and there's always paperwork."

The guilt punch. Brock cocked his brow at his nephew, who only hugged his mother harder.

"Well, I'd wanted to catch up on some work, so I'll be ready for someone's big hockey game tomorrow."

Zeke let out a yelp. "We're going to kick butt."

"I wish I weren't traveling tomorrow for our game," Brock told him. "But I'll watch your game with you when I get back since your mom plans to video it for me."

"That's awesome!" Zeke let go of his mom and jumped up in the air in excitement. "I need to be as good as you, Uncle Brock, if I'm going to go to St. Lawrence so you can coach me."

Brock smiled at the mention of his alma mater, but the deal wasn't done yet. The coach didn't want him to announce he was retiring until the season was over. Plus, he wanted to keep the focus on winning the Cup. "You keep working hard, Zeke. The rest will fall into place."

When Zeke had first shared his dream of going to the famed prep school fifty minutes outside Minneapolis, Susan had asked Brock point-blank if he thought there was a chance. He'd told her yes—if Zeke continued to position himself to join like Brock had at fourteen.

The only downside was that Zeke would be living at school. Like their mother, Susan wasn't thrilled about that, but she knew getting in opened the door to another world.

Brock had promised to do everything he could to help the boy prepare. Now that he was back in Minneapolis, he was training with Zeke two mornings a week before school, an extra practice he had to be careful to balance. Coach had ordered him to make sure he wasn't putting in too much extra ice time.

He held up his key fob and jingled it in the air. "All right, kiddos. We ready to go?"

Kinsley beamed. "Come on, Mom! Please come. You'll love Darla and Val."

"Well... Maybe I can tag along. I am curious about them."

Brock knew that was an understatement given the turnaround in Kinsley.

His sister tugged at her clothing. "I'll just change quickly. Maybe you can help me, Kinsley."

Zeke rolled his eyes as the two of them rushed upstairs. "We're never going to leave now."

Brock frowned when he checked the time. "Maybe they'll be down soon."

"Right. You saw how long it took Kinsley." He walked to the front door, fiddling with the knob.

"Why don't you show me some of your practice shots?"

"Now?" He gestured to his jacket. "But I'm not dressed."

"Champions don't care what they wear. Come on."

Zeke didn't hesitate. Ever since Brock had moved back to Minneapolis last June, his nephew had wanted to spend every waking minute with him. And now that his dad had up and left them, he was a little more...needy wasn't the right word. Present. Every time Brock came into a room, Zeke practically zoomed to his side. The kid even talked to him with his mouth full or strolled in while he was shaving.

They ran some drills until Susan and Kinsley came down. His sister had transformed a little, wearing jeans and boots and her favorite winter white jacket. He gave her a thumbs-up. Then he herded everyone outside to where he'd left his black Range Rover in the driveway and got the show on the road, thinking they had a decent shot of being on time if traffic wasn't egregious.

He was actually looking forward to seeing them outside the arena. Finn had thought he was crazy, taking the women around, given how close they were to Chuck and Ted, but Brock wanted to thank them for their help with Kinsley. Besides, they'd asked him to bring the kids, and he thought

Kinsley would benefit from more of their focused attention. Win-win. He was all about wins—in whatever form they came.

"Not Queen!" Zeke shouted when Brock turned on "Bohemian Rhapsody." "Ugh!"

"Be grateful I let you call shotgun," Susan added, humming to the music.

"But it's for old people," Zeke protested as his mother ruffled his hair and Kinsley laughed sweetly.

Brock found himself smiling the whole way to Darla's downtown address. Until he pulled up in the main driveway and noted the name of the apartment building: Washburn Lofts. He put the car in park, his mouth parting in shock. Who were these women? These lofts ran between four and six million dollars.

"Wow!" Kinsley hastily unlocked her seat belt and pressed herself to the window. *"This* is where Darla lives?"

"Holy—" Zeke caught himself.

"Now I'm really glad I came," Susan said, leaning over to look out the window with her daughter. "I thought you said they were analysts."

He looked over toward the back. "That's what Chuck said."

"I see." She mashed her lips together as if impressed. "I'd like to be an analyst like that."

Checking the address she'd texted to him, he confirmed it. His instincts were humming now. He'd always liked a good mystery. Had been reading the genre since his father had given him his first Andy Hardy and Sherlock Holmes novels as a kid. Now he leaned more toward James Patterson and Patricia Cornwell.

"Can we go inside?" Zeke swung his head around to look at his uncle. "I *love* seeing people's houses. Especially rich people's houses. Like yours, Uncle Brock. I want to be rich someday."

"You aren't supposed to talk about money like that, Zeke," Susan corrected. "But it *would* be fun to see where Darla lives."

"Wait!" Kinsley cried. "Does Val live here too?"

He realized he didn't know. "I asked earlier, before I left the arena, and Val said I could pick them both up here to make things easier for us."

He'd told her it wasn't a problem to make two trips, of course. Her usual reserve hadn't hinted anything, but he'd sensed her insistence wasn't really about putting him out. She hadn't wanted to give her address.

Now that prompted even more questions than he already had about her. Maybe the kids would be good investigators.

"Let me call Darla and tell her we're here." Maybe she would offer to show them up. "Hey, Darla."

"Brock! You're right on time."

"It was a miracle, trust me. Hey, I'm here with your eager sightseeing crew. Do you want us to come up and get you guys?"

"Does anyone need a potty break?"

He jumped on that invite and told himself not to feel guilty for being nosy. Taking care of business was smart. "Yeah, let's do that if you don't mind. Otherwise, I'll have to find a McDonald's later."

"Oh, fries and a sundae." She made a *mmm hmm* sound. "This mama could handle that. But please, come on up. I'm on the ninth floor. There's guest parking. I'll tell Val to meet you by the elevator. She just arrived."

One clue at least: Val didn't live here.

"Gotcha. See you in a minute."

He clicked off and turned toward his eager listeners. "We've been offered bathroom usage."

"Awesome!" Zeke jumped in his seat. "I wonder if they have gold toilets."

"Oh my God, you are so embarrassing," Kinsley moaned. "Try and act cool. Or some version of not an idiot."

"*Kinsley*," Susan warned.

"You try!" Zeke shot back with a backward glare.

"All right, that's enough," Susan said softly before his niece could reply.

"We'll *all* act cool and polite," Brock broke in, "because when people invite you into their homes, it's an honor. Got it?"

They both nodded and Susan sent him a smile of thanks. He headed to the guest parking, keeping his eyes peeled for Val, but he didn't see her. Soon, they were striding into the building with its lofty ceilings, country chandeliers, and funky rugs. Since Val wasn't in the lobby either, they took the elevator up to the ninth floor. When it opened, there she was—waiting for them with her hands calmly at her sides.

He schooled his expression. He hadn't known what to expect. But it wasn't this...

Even for a casual outing away from the office, she was wearing those ugly tan slacks. He'd dressed today like he did for team meetings, in a cashmere sweater with wool slacks and leather shoes. Apparently so had she. The black tennis shoes weren't much better than her white ones and fairly screamed old lady. Her baggy T-shirt was a forest green—not black like her usual uniform. The nerdy thick black glasses still cruised a face devoid of makeup, and her usual straight ponytail was fixed firmly in place.

Once again, he took notice of that sensual beauty mark beside her full lips.

So this was Val outside of work.

Susan shot him a veiled look of surprise.

"Hi, Val," Kinsley said softly when the woman before them remained still as a statue. "It's really good to see you again. Ah...do you live here too?"

He watched Val attempt to smile as she smoothed her hands down her sides, almost as if she didn't know what to do with them. "I...ah...it's good to see you too, Kinsley. Zeke. You must be Susan. It's very nice to meet you."

"You too," his sister said with a smile. "I've heard a lot about you and Darla."

"Yes, well..." God, was she as nervous as his niece?

Then she set her shoulders back as she turned to look at him, her posture almost queenlike. "Hello, Brock."

The way she said his name caught him. Her voice seemed dipped in honey, heavy and sweet, but she didn't meet his eyes. Turning back to the kids, she gave them a short smile. "Darla's place is just down the hallway. Welcome."

Brock watched the way she moved as she led his family. She had elegant posture and was capable of compelling stillness. He studied how people moved, and she had intention behind hers. He wondered if she'd had training, because the way she walked with her shoulders back and her torso uplifted reminded him of a ballet dancer.

A ballet dancer. Now that brought back memories. When he'd played for Chuck in Bean Town, Coach had hired a grizzled ballet teacher who'd graced the stage with the Boston Ballet forty years earlier to train them during a mid-season slump. She'd kicked their butts, this white-haired grandmother of six, and Chuck had gotten in one of his famous motivators: *even sixty-year-old ballerinas are better conditioned than you numbskulls.*

Coach had papered the locker room with Madame Markova's ballet photos along with the AARP logo. Brock had grunted every time he'd seen the posters. But he couldn't argue with results. They'd pulled out of the slump by doubling down and made it to the Stanley Cup finals that year.

He wondered again what Val and Darla were here to do for Coach. Only Darla was suddenly in the hallway, hugging Kinsley tightly enough to make his niece giggle as she clutched her back.

"Don't you look absolutely fine, girl! Oh, your shoes! I need me some of those. And you must be Susan. Hi, I'm Darla."

Brock did a double take as she hugged his sister, as much from the spontaneous act as from seeing Darla in normal attire. Jeans. A baggy red sweater. But it was the way she looked without the tortoiseshell glasses on, which he noted were pushed up into her straight long black hair. Not in a ponytail today. He was no expert, but he'd swear she was wearing gloss like Kinsley and light makeup, which made her light black skin glow.

She was gorgeous, he realized, with her big gold eyes dancing, a *just between us girls* smile on her face as she lightly touched Kinsley's hair with feminine appreciation.

He turned back to look at Val. What did she really look like? Because he knew he wasn't seeing the truth.

"I love everything about this, honey." Darla turned to give him a wink, drawing his gaze away from Mystery Woman. "She's going to be a heartbreaker, Brock. You'll have to beat the boys off."

"Boys are stupid," Kinsley muttered before Brock could

figure out how to politely say *If one of them so much as looks at my niece wrong, they'll wish they hadn't been born.*

He'd done the same for Susan when needed. Too bad he hadn't been able to keep Darren away.

"Yes, they can be," Susan replied in a subdued voice before shaking herself. "Of course, there are good ones out there like these two guys."

"No offense to present company, but I like to think there's just something about boys that makes the stupid parts worth it." Darla made a humming noise before Val cleared her throat, pointing to her friend's head. "Oh, excuse me. I forgot my glasses. And forget what I said about boys, Kinsley. Ignore them! As long as you can, girl, because once you open that box, you can't seal it back up."

"What Darla said." Susan had a broad smile now. "I knew I was going to like you."

Darla clapped her hands after giving his sister a wink. "Now...I hear somebody needs a potty break. Come on inside. I'll show you where the bathroom is, and then we can get this sightseeing tour on the road."

A few seconds later, Darla was leading Susan and Kinsley from the hallway through the airy loft. Brock appreciated the open floor plan and tall ceilings, and the view of downtown was incredible. Personally, though, he'd never liked high-rises. He was a home and lawn kind of guy. Susan sometimes teased him that all he was missing was a missus and a picket fence. He disagreed. Messing up with Erin like he had, he'd learned he needed to provide more than the basics. Next time he wouldn't make the same mistakes.

"I'll go too," Zeke said before Brock shot him a look. "Hey, I want to see. Besides, I drank soda when Mom wasn't looking."

That earned him a bona fide uncle look. "Do we need to implement a hockey nutrition plan?"

He scrunched up his face in horror. "I'm twelve! Can't I wait until I'm fourteen? I need pizza. It's like my life. See ya."

"A well-timed escape," Val said with a chuckle before she paused, clearing her throat again.

He'd never heard her do that before, but she'd done it three times since he'd arrived. Yeah, she was nervous. Usually, she sat completely still in their team meetings, watching intently or writing in that leather-bound journal of hers except for when she and Darla were clearly trading notes. Only then would he see a whisper of a smile break out over her face, transforming it into one he wanted to look at more. But when that happened, he'd drag his gaze back to hockey because that needed to be his sole focus.

"He wants to see if the toilets are gold." Brock made a face. "Kids. I remember being like him when I first started playing professionally. I began going to all these parties at swanky houses and apartments. For a kid from small-town Minnesota who shared a bathroom with his older sister, it was whole new world."

"Your sister seems very kind, but her fatigue and sadness are evident, if you don't mind my observation," Val said in that intent way of hers. "From the way Kinsley's dressed as well as her emotional expression today, she seems to be in better spirits at least."

God, she talked like a skull shrinker, but he liked the analytical quality. He'd been around plenty of women who prattled on about nothing. This woman said things that meant something, and after the miracle she'd worked with Kinsley, he'd hang on her every word.

"It all started with you and Darla, which means you

have my eternal thanks." He vaguely gestured with his hands. "Susan actually looked happier than I've seen her since the breakup, especially after seeing Kinsley dressed normally today. No humdinger T-shirts. Susan's struggling to help her too. She and I both feel like we owe you guys for the help you gave. A little sightseeing isn't even close to enough."

Val waved her hand. "Don't think anything of it. We're happy to have met Kinsley. And you and Zeke, of course, and now Susan. I worried I'd overstepped with the T-shirts, honestly. I was afraid to say anything to you about it this week."

She had kept her distance, giving him only a polite smile whenever they greeted each other at the arena. He'd wondered about that. But as he tilted his head to the side, studying her, he realized she wasn't simply nervous. She was shy. Maybe she wasn't so different from his niece. He already knew she and Darla had identified with her. Perhaps Val was hiding behind her thick glasses and outfits.

"I know I have a reputation for being fierce on the ice," he told her, "but I'm mostly a pussycat outside of hockey."

A finely arched auburn brow rose over the black rim of her glasses. "I doubt that, Mr. Thomson. By definition, a pussycat is a gentle, mild-mannered, easygoing person. As a competitor, you couldn't be successful if you had those traits."

"Well..." He could feel his mouth twitching at the professorial tone. "How about...I'm just a nice guy. Certainly someone you don't need to call Mr. Thomson."

She had used his first name before. He remembered that clearly. Why the change?

"And certainly not someone to be afraid of," he added.

"Off the ice," she pressed, that almost censorious look

really amusing him now. "I believe there have been media articles about your work with youth and your charitable contributions, so I will concede that point. Mostly."

If she'd been any other woman, he'd have sworn she was flirting with him. But she was Ms. Cool. Even her scent was crisp and clean, a contrast to many of the over-perfumed women he met.

He wondered what she looked like when she pulled those thick glasses off and put her hair down. His gaze went to the beauty mark to the right of her lips again. That part of her face, untouched by the oversized glasses, was more than pleasing.

She had full, rosy lips and a delicate, almost doll-like jaw. High cheekbones, too, and flawless skin.

He discreetly looked at her again when she turned her head, as if to see what was keeping Darla and the others. Her neck was long and elegant too, and he imagined her shoulders were, but the baggy T-shirt really cloaked her. Almost like she was wearing one of those black winter coats that some thought fashionable but looked like big garbage bags to him.

God, his curiosity was kicking in so hard it was almost laughable.

He was feeling the pull of wondering what it would be like to be Frank Hardy in the Hardy Boys series. Later, he'd have to ask Zeke if his grandpa had given him those books yet. Maybe he hadn't. Susan wasn't close to their dad. He'd always been a better principal than father, and Susan hadn't appreciated his ongoing desire to shape her.

Brock had definitely had it easier, knowing he wanted to play hockey. His father hadn't liked the violence in the sport, but he'd appreciated the discipline. So long as Brock kept his grades up and avoided penalties, his father had left him alone, so he'd easily followed the formula. It hadn't taken long to see it made him a winner both on and off the ice.

Reading books was a pleasure and one of the few things he and their father had in common. They still traded books when he visited him at his retirement community in Florida.

He looked around Darla's apartment, hoping for some personal mementos. Something that would give him more clues about Val since they were obviously good friends. But there were no photos of her parents or siblings even.

The space was full of high-end light neutral furniture in a style that screamed interior decorator. Brock knew first-hand that look. It had taken him six months to make his house his own after one of the best designers in the city had worked on it for him.

"Darla mentioned you'd arrived when we had," he said to Val, trying to keep his tone casual. "Do you live close?"

She went rigid before slowly turning back to him, biting her lower lip momentarily. "I'm..."

"Yes?" He leaned closer and noted the pulse in her neck was fluttering like a nervous bird. "You don't have to answer." He almost wished he could pat her on the back and tell her to chill. "I'm sorry I pressed."

"No, it's only...I'm private—about my personal life." She touched the long line of her throat, making him marvel at how beautiful her neck was—completely at odds with her nerdy persona. "I imagine you of all people would understand."

When she looked at him head-on, his vision went through the thick lenses to the heart of her. He found himself pinned by her vibrant eyes, so green they reminded him of the pines around his favorite lake up north, where he'd summered as a kid.

Darla had mentioned her eyes, he recalled, and Val had said her friend was joking. But now he could see why Darla had done so. They were compelling, arrestingly beautiful even. Was that why she wore those thick lenses?

He became aware that he was staring when she clenched her hands, so he finally made himself nod. "You mean because I'm the subject of a lot of media speculation."

"Exactly."

Their gazes met and held again, her pulse fluttering in that gorgeous neck of hers. His heart was pounding in his ears.

What were they talking about? Right. Him understanding privacy. Only he didn't really understand the comparison. Val was a normal person, supposedly, and he was so famous he had reporters going through his garbage when he was seen limping off the hockey rink after a hit, hoping to find out if he was on pain meds.

He wanted to ask her.

He also wanted to see what she really looked like—without the baggy clothes and thick glasses and rigidly tamed hair.

Because there was an interesting woman under there—a woman he wanted to get to know.

He liked how she carried herself and how she thought. How kind she was. Even in this moment, he admired how she kept her elegant poise and cool reserve. He knew about her fluttering pulse, but only because he'd been trained to pick up physical cues in people, ones that spoke of fatigue or distress or nerves. Sure, it was on the ice, but training was training.

She couldn't be more different than most of the women

he encountered. The stuttering kind who shyly asked for his autograph. The aggressive kind who'd shove their number or panties in his coat pocket if they got too close. Don't even ask him about the women who held up signs in the arena, saying they wanted him to be their daddy or wanted to have his baby.

Yeah, he understood the need for privacy. What had made her so eager to have it? Could it be about safety? God, some guy hadn't stalked her or hurt her, had he? He found himself clenching his hands as anger shot through him. He wanted to take that guy apart with his bare hands, and he wasn't a violent guy by nature. Not even on the ice.

"Personal lives are a privilege in my world, so you don't have to explain anything to me, Val."

He was aware of her name on his lips. Even the way he'd said her name had changed. His tone was deeper, richer, her name slower on his tongue. He set his weight against the feeling of being a little off-balance, similar to the way he felt after going without putting skates on for weeks in the off-season.

"Thank you for understanding." Again, he watched as she remained still as a statue. "You might not be a pussycat by definition, but you meet the letter of a nice guy."

His mouth quirked. And then she went and said things like that. Like a hot little librarian. Jeez, when had he ever had a hot librarian fantasy? Not even while attending Harvard. But all too easily, he could see her there, surrounded by stacks of thick, dusty books, her brow furrowed as she read some old tome through those horrible thick glasses. He studied that face again, taking it in without the nerdy spectacles and thought, she really is beautiful.

Beautiful.

Yeah.

Shit.

He probably shouldn't be noticing that.

"Ah, they've been gone a while, but Darla probably got excited showing your family her new closet." Her beauty mark shifted as she smiled softly. "It's the largest closet she's ever had, and she's gone a little crazy over it."

Her friendship with Darla softened her and made her even more appealing. He wished he could say something that would make her smile like that.

Yeah, he really shouldn't be thinking like this.

Except he couldn't stop himself from asking, "How long have you known Darla?"

A dreamy smile played over her face, lighting her up in a way that looked good on her. She wasn't so cool now. She was like a beautiful sunny spring day after a streak of dark winter. "A long time. We met at boarding school—which explains why we're standing in a multimillion-dollar loft. In case you were wondering."

He had to give her points for calling that out there, but since she was offering a clue, he sent her a conspiratorial wink. "It wouldn't be my business."

"Yet humans crave understanding, so a little explanation is often useful."

Again, she sounded like a sexy librarian, making him want to step closer and play with the ends of her ponytail.

He knew he was flirting with trouble, like speeding on black ice or goading a violence-prone hockey player.

But what harm could it do when it was just in his head?

He almost laughed at himself. Here he was *reasoning* away his strange attraction to this woman.

Her vibrant green eyes held his focus as she looked at him and gestured ruefully in the air. "To satisfy your curiosity..."

Her neck moved beautifully as she swallowed thickly and gave him a shy smile. He was suddenly holding his breath.

"I'm not usually one to share this, but since you're here... Our parents have money, obviously, but Darla and I both work for peanuts compared to them. Luckily, we both fell in love with the same profession, and we're best friends and close collaborators. We complement each other beautifully. I was so happy she agreed to come to Minneapolis with me to help the Eagles."

So Chuck had given her the invitation. Interesting...

She had walked bold as brass back into Ted Bass' office, he remembered.

"As analysts," she said with another soft clearing of her throat.

Somehow, he knew she'd offered that up so he wouldn't have the chance to ask her what profession she and Darla shared.

Ah, this woman. She kept her secrets well. Which only made him want to uncover them more.

"Uncle Brock! Uncle Brock!"

Brock held her gaze a beat longer before she looked off toward Zeke.

The little town crier was back, running toward them with an *I've eaten four funnel cakes* grin on his face before skidding to a halt. "Darla doesn't have a gold toilet, but she's got a sauna and a steam room, and her closet is as big as your kitchen. It's awesome! Although Mom and Kinsley have more clothes and shoes than Darla right now. It's practically empty. She said she's been living overseas and traveling light. Whatever that means."

Living overseas, huh? Another clue. Two, actually. Because Val had mentioned boarding school too. Only...

Why would Chuck have hired someone who'd been working overseas up until recently? What did these women do for a living?

"Traveling light means with few human staples," Val informed his nephew in that sexy librarian tone.

Brock ruffled his short curly black hair that always seemed to look spiky, similar to his hair at that age. "So you're ready to ditch my place, huh, and move in here?"

"Nah... But when I grow up, I want to live in a place like this. You can look out the windows and see the whole city and the Mississippi River. I'll bet when you order take-out, it gets here real fast."

"Zeke hates lukewarm pizza," Brock explained, wrapping his arms around his nephew and jostling him.

"I hate sweaty crusts!" Zeke practically bellowed, giggling when Brock tickled his ribs. "They're the worst."

"I couldn't agree more." Val was smiling, although she'd crossed her arms as if trying to keep her reserve. "Suboptimal pizza belies the reason pizza was originally created."

Zeke stopped giggling and regarded her with that puzzled expression again. "Be-lies... You talk kinda funny sometimes."

"Zeke!" Brock nudged him.

"I meant it as a compliment, Uncle Brock." He turned to Val and grimaced. "Sorry. You got Kinsley to wear normal clothes again. Mom almost cried today when she came out of the bathroom looking normal and not like some weirdo. Hey! Do you think I should go get them? They were laughing so much about girl stuff that I had to get out of there."

"Probably," Val said with a chuckle. "If we don't do something, who knows what scheme she'll create. Darla offered to throw a slumber party for us in her closet the other day."

"Cool! If it wasn't such a girl thing, I'd be into it. But only if there were video games—"

"And hot pizza with a crispy crust," Val bandied back, smiling down at his nephew with an ease that offset her previous shyness and reserve. "We would insist upon it."

Zeke held out his fist. "Hey, I like you. You're not like normal girls, who sigh and talk about their hair or their clothes or why someone doesn't like them. I'll go drag those crazy girls out of the closet. Just watch. Even if I have to say I saw a mouse. That always gets Mom and Kinsley moving."

Brock's shoulders were shaking as Zeke ran off. "I don't remember being that talkative or excited at that age about anything other than hockey maybe." Even then, he'd been more the quiet, studious type.

"It's a tribute to his mother and your family—you especially—that Zeke can love hockey with a pure heart and doesn't feel any pressure about being like you when he grows up. That kind of pressure can suffocate a child."

There was an oppressive stillness about her now.

Is that what happened to you? he wondered. He knew he shouldn't ask, but he couldn't stop himself. The words burned in his throat. "I'm sorry if you went through that."

Her posture stiffened and he knew she wasn't going to reveal more to him. "I should really go help Zeke. Darla probably is showing Kinsley and Susan every velvet-lined drawer and talking about what she'd fill it with, and trust me, there are hundreds."

He watched as she purposefully walked away. The afternoon sun caught the red and gold in her auburn ponytail, and perhaps her shirt shifted, but he could see the shape of her ass and legs through her black pants. She *was* slim underneath. He was sure of it. With honed muscles. No one could carry themselves like that without core muscles.

She was a puzzle, and one he found not only compelling but attractive.

He'd collected himself by the time she walked back in with a chattering Kinsley and chuckling Susan. But the soft smile and active way she was listening to his sister and his niece, who was practically dancing in her glittery shoes, grabbed him by the throat along with that fresh, clean scent of hers, which he was starting to pick out whenever she was near.

Darla and Zeke appeared behind them. She was laughing as he slashed at the air with an imaginary hockey stick, showing her his moves. He was trying to impress her, Brock thought. Like boys do with girls...

After a backward glance, Kinsley threw her hands in the air, shimmying her hips for some reason he couldn't hear. Susan joined in, announcing that these women had transformed her as much as they had Kinsley. Val gave a squeak of laughter before biting her lip to stop herself, enhancing the sexy beauty mark above her gorgeous mouth.

His heart beat a wild rhythm in response. All he wanted was to march across the room and take her face in his hands. Look deeply into her spring-green eyes. And ask, *Who are you really?*

Because I want to know.

I need to know.

This minute.

As if sensing his internal conflict, she looked up from his talkative niece and beaming sister. A riot of emotion filled his chest as they locked gazes. The pulse in her slender neck wasn't fluttering anymore. It was thudding in thick beats, and all he wanted to do was put his mouth there and feel the beat against his lips as she said his name in that hushed, sexy way of hers.

Shit... That thought was freaking crazy.

She was here to do God knows what for Coach and Ted Bass.

Wasn't his life filled with enough complications right now?

He had better figure out a way to control himself or keep his distance.

Stat.

SEVEN

What is it about men and their sticks?

VAL NEARLY CHOKED AT THE QUESTION WRITTEN ATOP a fresh page in Darla's field diary.

Not that she wasn't thinking the same. She couldn't yank her gaze away from the phallus-honoring ritual unfolding in front of them in the players' locker room. Part of her wished they hadn't waited until their third week with the team to schedule their observation of the taping of the hockey sticks. The other part was glad they'd waited to settle in more with the team because this observational study was going to be a doozy.

Chuck had found a mostly innocuous place for them to sit and watch the players conduct this mesmerizing ritual. Because it *was* mesmerizing. Giant, broad-shouldered men stroking, caressing, and tending to their...well, sticks.

She'd researched this ritual and knew it was intended to prepare the stick to the player's individual specifications and make them more successful on the ice. Rather like the warriors they'd seen whittle their own spears for the hunt. The variations from player to player were scintillating to watch, a virtual buffet for the senses.

She and Darla had done early research on what to expect, but seeing it...

She sat riveted, eyes unblinking, her pen poised to scribble notes. Some players made spiral or crisscross patterns with the tape while others used different-colored tape in the Eagles' colors of red, white, and blue to create a barbershop pole-like effect. They clearly favored a pretty, bright-colored phallic tool on the ice. Some layered the tape on thickly while others only partially taped their sticks.

And then there were the couple who only taped the shaft. The shaft! She'd traveled the world, and this was a global phenomenon: men and their fondness for phallus-shaped objects.

Darla elbowed her again and started writing excitedly.

> Are you seeing this???
> It makes me want to break into rhyme.
> I love his stick.
> It's my favorite to lick.
> It gives me a kick
> And never makes me go "Ick!"
> Did I mention we have THE BEST JOB EVER?

The effort it took Val not to laugh out loud equaled the effort she'd once seen an elephant employ to rise out of a muddy, swirling river. She leaned over and wrote her own thoughts down in response, trying to keep it academic.

Because they could not devolve into two teenagers in biology class laughing over human anatomy.

> *The human fascination with the male phallus is well documented.*
> *Men have been creating phallus-like structures for eons.*
> *Think obelisks like the Washington Monument and the Eiffel Tower.*
> *Cavemen both drew phalluses as well as sculpted them out of reindeer antlers.*

Darla's attempt to fight another smirk wasn't missed by Val as she scrawled back a response.

> Those caveman dicks must have been REAL hard.

Val bit the inside of her cheek. Darla never failed to make a study lively.

> *Perhaps not as hard as the broken bone rod found in La Madeleine in Dordogne engraved with the head of a bear facing a complex phallic form.*

Darla covered her muffled laugh with a cough before writing back.

> Most things were drawn to scale in cave art—EXCEPT male penises.
> Even cavemen exaggerated size.
> Hockey sticks sure are big and long.
> Do you see them taping the shaft with such care?
> It's like we're at the Hockey Dick Spa.
> Oh, I have another ditty:
> I really like his shaft
> It sometimes makes me daft.

This time Val had to muffle her laugh. She and Darla clearly had spent too much time in England. She leaned in with her pen.

> *Penile humor has been an entertaining pastime for eons.*
> *Do you remember reading Lysistrata?*
> *But we should focus.*
> *This is an important male ritual.*
> *Chock-full of one of the other areas of our study besides tools: superstition.*

Darla uttered a visible sigh before nodding and writing down one more thing.

> Did you notice that Brock doesn't tape his stick AT ALL?!

> He just runs his hands over and over it.
> It's like he knows his stick doesn't need any enhancement.
> Wink.

Val gulped as she stayed Darla's hand from writing anything more about Brock and his stick. She was having a hard enough time keeping her reaction to him professional. Her heart rate had picked up while watching his *bare-bones, no tape needed* ritual. Her eyes had practically zoomed in like she was a human microscope and he the most edifying glass slide in science.

The way he stroked his stick with his big, manly hands had her mouth going dry.

The wild electrical currents in her belly had worried her, making her wish for once it was indigestion.

She'd read Brock didn't use tape because he idolized the NHL Hall of Famer Bobby Orr, but she hadn't been prepared for her reaction to seeing it. Call it another speed bump in the ongoing battle she had with herself not to notice him as anything other than an Eagles employee and friendly acquaintance.

There was one lucky development there: Brock clearly had decided he needed to put their interactions back on more professional grounds after the sightseeing.

Which had been intense! A word she didn't use lightly.

She and Brock had continued to talk with those remarkable pauses and heated gazes at the various sights. Then Darla had volunteered to find everyone hot chocolate, with Kinsley, Zeke, and Susan agreeing to help, leaving her and Brock alone again as the mighty Mississippi rushed by at Boom Island Park.

Later, Zeke's stomach had groaned in the car, bringing up calls for burgers. Brock had suggested a place where he wasn't bothered too much.

She'd ended up next to him in a back booth after he'd signed some autographs, all too aware of his heat and scent.

By the end of the evening, she'd been clenching her hands, struggling with an attraction unlike anything she'd ever imagined.

The following Monday at work, Brock hadn't done more than thanking them for their kindness toward his family and greeting them with a *Good morning* or *Have a good afternoon* and *Kinsley says hello*.

His ongoing politeness had continued these past two weeks. Val was rather glad for the parameters. They had a job to do, and so did he. No one needed to get off track with any personal complications. Plus, if they spent more time with him off the ice, he'd likely ask more questions—like he had about how she'd met Darla.

She didn't want to deflect or hedge. He was a nice guy, although *not* a pussycat. The less interaction they had, the less personal investigation he'd be tempted to do. But she and Darla had missed spending time with Kinsley and Zeke as well as Susan, who had been so funny and sweet. She'd become almost girlish, but that was Darla for you. She always made you feel special. Val knew that magic firsthand.

She wouldn't say Brock was immune to that magic. He'd simply fallen into what she'd called "hunting mode" in past studies, blocking out everything but the game. She'd seen this with Pygmies and other hunting cultures. Some were eerily quiet and focused, like Brock, while others, like Mason "The Marvel," puffed out their proverbial chests and crowed like roosters about to mess with the hens in the henhouse.

Competition had a way of honing a person's entire mood and attention. It had created an atmosphere she felt too, making it easier for her to focus on her task as well. Thankfully, it had also kept her away from the ice so far. She told herself she didn't need the extra pressure of fighting with her feelings about the ice when she was already dealing with her unwanted attraction to Brock. So far, her logic was working.

Her gaze shot up, her reptilian brain sensing a change in the room. She found herself following Brock's progress as he slowly rose from his chair, looking larger and more powerful somehow, as if the ritual had added to his manhood. His shoulders looked more massive. His jaw harder. Those blue eyes of his seemed icier. And his scar...

Well, it seemed to announce his warrior-hewn toughness in a striking way.

He held his untaped stick reverently, his large hands still smoothing the length. Stroking it up and down. And then up again.

God, she was flushing with heat. Those hands. That stick...

She swallowed thickly.

His head lifted, his steely blue eyes locking on her. Her heart started to pound in her ears, rather like a tribal drum celebrating the ritual before her. Brock, the recipient of godlike powers. She, the blessed witness of sheer male power on earth.

Heady stuff.

A line of concentration appeared between his dark brows. Their eyes held. She watched his throat move. His hands grip the stick. She felt like a zebra must within the locked gaze of the lion. She couldn't move. Couldn't breathe. Then he tapped the stick to the ground, like he was breaking the moment between them, and he strode off in powerful, ground-eating strides.

Leaving her mind and body in an ecstatic state of wonder and longing, in tandem with a primal physiological reaction.

Completely uncomfortable.

Unnerving even. Usually this was when the women who'd witnessed a warrior-like ritual would take up dancing around the campfire, hands raised to the moon.

Val had never in her life wanted to dance more. Usually, Darla was the one to join rituals while she sat back and observed. But she understood the urge now. She needed to shake off this incredible current of energy rushing through her every nerve ending.

Her only salvation was to fall into researcher mode, like she had since she'd first noted her discomfiting reactions to the Eagles' captain. She reached under her baggy long sleeves to take her pulse. Elevated heart rate, she noted. Due to extra adrenaline in her system from her physical attraction to the subject.

Over the past weeks, she'd started another side study—one Darla was never to know about. She'd been monitoring her reactions to Brock Thomson ever since the sightseeing tour.

There was science behind her reaction to Brock Thomson, and Dr. Valentina Hargrove was going to document it, if only to herself. Documenting trends helped her understand them. So far, she'd noted down the reasons in another field diary:

One: his physical presence invoked a strong physiological reaction. He exceeded cultural norms of male attractiveness. Hadn't he been voted one of hockey's best-looking athletes? He was a healthy specimen, meaning he could procreate, something her primal female self had obviously noted. Even though she hadn't ever thought she'd have children.

Two: his pheromones were clearly potent to her. And his smell was something she could make out in a room full of other men. Pine with a touch of cloves. Along with a healthy waft of clean, hard-work sweat.

Three: He treated his niece and nephew with great love and affection, so her reptilian brain had catalogued he would be a good provider and father to his own children. Side note: she clearly was not the only woman who thought that, given how many women held up signs like *Brock, Can I Have Your Baby?* or *Brock, Will You Be My Daddy?*

Four: they had certain values and experiences in common. He'd gone to Harvard while she'd gone to Oxford. She'd been a professional athlete like him. She admired his work ethic, which she mirrored. He was grounded in his fame. She had never let hers go to her head. He was kind, which she valued in her relationships.

Five: he possessed a sense of humor. Darla's presence in her life had shown her she valued humor. The way he'd made Zeke giggle had haunted her sleep-challenged nights.

Conclusion: Brock Thomson was a very decent human being. She found him exceedingly physically attractive and liked and respected him, so it was only natural that she had a physical response to his presence.

Lastly, their forced proximity of seeing each other every day enhanced said response. She had no break from the items above.

She'd begun this particular study the night after their night on the town with him—having returned home, dressed in cozy blue fleece pajamas and comfy cream-colored UGG boots, and poured herself a cup of tea. With such comforting implements at hand, she'd pulled out her laptop and started researching human physical attraction and sexual desire. Her system had calmed down to where she wasn't smiling from the presence of Brock Thomson anymore, thank God.

One giant step for female kind, she'd thought.

Men's *maleness* could and did wear off.

She should take out a billboard in Times Square to comfort women everywhere.

Later that evening, it hadn't been Brock who'd put a smile on her face, but fellow researchers on human anatomy. Masters and Johnson had outlined "excitement" in their four-stage model of human sexual response while Helen Singer Kaplan's three-stage model spoke of both desire *and* excitement.

She was experiencing both. Her reaction went back to the first humans. Even before the cavemen.

Nothing to hyperventilate about...

Val was comforted by the academic parameters. Knowing the reasons for her unusual physical attraction to the Eagles' captain helped her better understand it. Observing her physical and emotional reactions and chronicling them over these past weeks had made her feel empowered.

Given their continued forced proximity and her need to study Brock as part of the greater whole, she imagined her reaction would be an ongoing issue. At least until he did something that was unattractive to her. Right now, however, she couldn't imagine him being rude to an elderly woman crossing the street or shouting at kids in his youth camp.

So she was counting on the forced proximity becoming

her new normal, rather like when she and Darla became used to riding in their Defender 90 and seeing lions and cheetahs only a few feet away, sometimes with blood on their mouths from their last kill. At first, her physical and emotional response had been high—Darla had frequently asked, *Are we crazy for sitting in that cat's kill zone?*—but after a month, their responses had plateaued to a passing glance as they drove by.

Val was looking forward to the same resolution with her attraction to Brock.

Right now, though, it was difficult. Sooo difficult.

Seeing him stroke his stick had her mind conjuring up images of what it would feel like to have him touch her with such care and intention. Or, worse, himself.

Oh God! Her body temperature spiked as the image catapulted through her mind.

Sometimes she needed to clench her teeth as his smell wafted over her or as he shot her that smile with a short uptick at the corners of his physically appealing mouth. Or called her name in that deep baritone, fertility-indicating voice of his.

When her heart rate increased or her focus zoomed in on his physically pleasing face with its curly black hair, square jaw, and steely blue eyes, she reminded herself it was the spike of adrenaline and norepinephrine coursing through her system.

Even the demands of traveling with the team for the three away games they'd won—Carolina, Detroit, and Dallas—hadn't diminished her response.

So she'd added a side question about who had it harder: hockey players or wildebeests? She was leaning toward wildebeests. Hockey players flew in private planes and had spa treatments and fine cuisine available, while the nearly two million wildebeests migrating in May and June from the Masai Mara plains in Kenya, all the way south into Tanzania's Serengeti and the edge of the Ngorongoro Crater, carried their newborn babies with them and crossed through spectacularly dangerous terrain.

There was no getting around it. Road games put her in even greater proximity with Brock. They'd ridden the elevator together to their rooms, his large body seemingly filling up the entire space. The enclosed air system of the private jet hadn't been any better. His scent had been as intense as walking through a department store at the holidays. Her body was like *sign her up for that sample*, God help her. Her nostrils had kept flaring so much to take in his intoxicating scent, Darla had found her some Kleenexes from her purse, suspecting a seasonal cold coming on.

So far she didn't think Darla suspected—the Kleenex offer had been sincere—but she couldn't be sure. Her friend knew her well enough to know this response would be both unwelcome and unprofessional. She wouldn't want to talk about it to her friend. She'd want to resolve it.

Only Val had to acknowledge there was no easy solution.

She was already looking forward to lunch today, the only time she was able to be away from Brock's presence other than the showers. So far, they hadn't scheduled their shower break. The primally affected woman in her wanted to flag Chuck down from talking with one of the assistant coaches in the locker room and demand a time to see Brock all slick and wet, but Dr. Valentina Hargrove knew studying male bathing rituals would only make her particular problem worse.

The weight of the upcoming hockey schedule settled

over her like this morning's fog. Her system had to calm down. It simply had to.

Chuck strode over toward them as the locker room emptied out, all of the players heading to the ice. Val snapped to attention.

"You two give any more thought to traveling for every road game? I talked to Ted, and he agrees with me. You should only do it if you have to. Because it's brutal. As you've already discovered."

She glanced at Darla, who gestured vaguely with her hands, a clear *I'm not sure yet*. "We're still debating the merits," Val answered.

She wasn't objective about this decision, and she knew it. They needed to observe the players in their regular environment, but was every away game necessary? She'd have to be around Brock, and his scent would be unmistakable to her even in a jet filled with other potent men. She still couldn't believe that was scientifically possible.

"Today's practice is open to the public." Chuck squatted down on his haunches next to their chairs. "The superfans love to come and watch the team before a game. It's part of the sport, but you should know I hate it. Fans fuel the sport, though, so we give them access. I think you'll find it fascinating."

"Having seen some videos and photos of other open practices," Darla said, "I can't wait. But I understand your feelings, Chuck."

His nod was a hard drop of his round face. "Glad someone does. Mason had been riding me for more open practices. Says the fans need to see him in action. I chewed his butt from here to Sunday about focusing on his game, but all he did was smile. I'm not getting through to him and that damn pack of his. But I will."

His voice was so rough-edged it could have sawed through the wooden cabinet behind them. "We're here to help."

"Yes, on that." He shoved his clear glasses up his nose and crouched down. "You mentioned the importance of studying my players' use of tools. Like their hockey sticks. Does their use of any tools count? Like if they need to improvise?"

Val could feel the stirrings of academic excitement. "Yes, the improvisation of tool use was one of the striking characteristics of cavemen as opposed to other early human species." She broke off her dissertation.

"Great! I talked to Ted, and I have an idea for something along these lines. Now, I need to go and kick some butts. You let me know if you need anything."

"We'd like access to the locker room after a game," Darla said in a crisp, lowered voice Val knew was designed to keep things professional. "After showers. We've heard some of your players come directly from the showers to the changing area to conduct interviews."

"Sky clad," Chuck ground out with a grimace. "Mason and his pack in particular. They like to show off their bodies like they're walking cologne commercials. Shit. I'm getting old. It's not like nudity and bare butts are new to hockey, but it's different with those kids."

"We're more interested in the locker room post-showers and dressing as a male bonding ritual." Val fought the urge to gulp even though she'd been to countless rituals where men had little or no clothes on. "Can you find a way for us to observe without it being against human resource policy or downright creepy?"

Chuck snorted. "The guys won't mind you being there. They know when we let the media in, and it's their choice how they present themselves, if you understand me. Some dress in front of reporters in the locker room simply to get out of the building faster as the interviews do take up time. But sure, I'll have you escorted into the locker room with the media if you'd like, although you have full access as employees on my coaching staff."

He paused then, and the way his searching gaze scanned her face had her stomach knotting.

"That includes you using the ice for some figure skating if you'd like in the early mornings. Ted mentioned he wasn't sure you'd used the facility yet, and he wanted me to mention it. No pressure. Just saying."

Had her father reviewed the security footage or something? She didn't want to know.

"Thank you." His timing couldn't have been worse since last night she'd dreamed about the feeling of taking flight in the air when doing a triple lutz, her favorite jump. "Like I told my dad, I'd rather keep focused on our work."

She heard Darla snort but didn't glance at her friend. Sometimes you had to battle the past the best way you knew how, and avoidance was an old strategy for her. That was why her skates were in the back of her closet, still in the box they'd been delivered in.

"As for the locker room," Val continued, "we really only need to see the full flavor once or twice."

"Anything you need. I'll see you inside." He was gone before either of them could respond.

Darla placed a hand on her arm. "He's really worked up. I was worried he might have a stroke or something. Is he on blood pressure medicine? Because from how red his face got when he was talking about Mason, he needs it."

"My father makes sure all his employees have an annual medical check, but I'll mention it to Dad."

She and her father hadn't seen each other again since he'd flown back to his corporate headquarters in Chicago, but they'd spoken over the phone. He'd wanted to know how the study was going as much as how she was, being back in the States. But the one topic he never addressed with her directly was her skating again. He always had other people who cared about her do that—except for Darla. Her father was a wily man and thought nothing of using the resources at his command when needed, but he knew best friends were off-limits.

She paused, considering, then added, "Only...what do you think Chuck was alluding to about other tools?"

"I suppose we'll find out." Darla rose after stowing her field diary in her satchel, prompting Val to follow suit. "You should take Chuck up on the offer to skate. You know you want to, and it's not like you need to tell a soul. Our badges are like Open Sesame cards."

So Darla had finally decided to mention it. Val shot her a look as she tugged on the lanyard holding her badge. "I'm a little restless around the ice. I can't deny it. It's hard for me to only do it for fun, and when I start feeling like I'm working at it, that's when acid fills my stomach. This place is for training. For work. I'm...not sure I can only skate for myself. For my love of it. That's why I prefer to do it alone, but even then, it's tough."

"I wondered if that accounted for all your extra energy these days." Darla opened the double doors leaving the locker room, and together they headed toward the arena. "You're a little at war with yourself."

Surely she hadn't noticed her attraction to Brock?

"Yes, and it's a new study in a new place with new people," Val said as her heart sped up. "You know how it is."

Darla shoved her glasses up her nose. "I wish these

would stay up. I don't know how people wear them for real. I'm still mad at you for insisting I wear them whenever I go out."

"You never know when you might cross someone's path," she told her as they entered the arena. "Oh, my! I believe our community interaction protocols are going to be tested today."

Val noted the massive group of fans seated together in the open stands behind the team's bench. They were wearing Eagles merchandise, some of which included tall hats in the shape of the mascot. A couple of people waved large orange Eagle hands while a few others waved those foam fingers she'd seen online.

But it was the signage on display that really captured her attention. Held mostly by cheering women, who looked like they'd done everything to accentuate their feminine attributes in hair, makeup, and dress, many of them were personal invitations to various hockey players. Mason had a few, of course, which would only feed his ego: *The Marvel = Hottest Rookie in the NHL* and *Mason, can I have your sweat towel?*

"This is going to be fun." Darla smacked her lips. "Superfans are observational candy for people like us. Do you see the one for Brock practically begging for fertility coding? *I Want To Have The Rock's Baby.* If I hadn't been exposed to my mother's fans, I might be shocked, but fans do all sorts of strange stuff."

Val wasn't shocked—people used to make signs for her, although not like *that*—but she did wonder at Brock's reaction. Mason would adore the attention, but how would Brock react to such an open invitation to procreate? "Like the time someone pulled off one of your mother's extensions as she bent over the stage to shake her fans' hands."

"Ripped it clear out, making her cry buckets." Darla shuddered. "One of the few times I felt bad for my mom. Come on, let's hurry to our seats. I want to watch this train wreck."

It wasn't so much of a train wreck as it was a massive community study, Val thought. The players practiced a little harder, she thought, but many were less focused and tended to showboat. Mason most of all. He blew kisses at the fans after scoring a goal, earning him one of Chuck's train whistle calls and a pointed finger to sit on the bench.

If Brock noticed the fans, he didn't give any hint. His locked focus was unshaken, and he practiced with both efficacy and poise, his skating both fluid and explosive when needed.

She hadn't been transformed into a hockey fan, but she was becoming a fan of the way he played and conducted himself.

When Chuck ended practice, Brock immediately skated toward the short door to exit the ice. Finn wasn't far behind him, along with a few others. But Mason and his pack skated to the bench to pick up white towels and wiped their faces down as they crossed to the wall in front of the fans.

People started to chant Mason's name. He blew more kisses, and then he threw his towel into the stands. A cluster of three women shot their hands out to catch it, vying for the object. The one who won screamed when she caught it and buried her face in it while the losers crossed their arms and sank down onto the metal bench as if they'd been robbed of life's greatest prize. Val realized they probably felt that way.

More towels from Mason's pack flew into the stands. More feminine jockeying and screaming ensued. Val noted the phenomenon in her field diary for later analysis.

Darla only made an *mm-hmm* sound. "I wonder if each woman is going to sell their towel on eBay or never wash it again and use it for...things I would probably shock you by saying."

Val was no prude, but prurient speculation was outside their realm of study. "I honestly don't understand what all the bother is about."

Darla gave her an exaggerated wink through her tortoiseshell glasses. "I know you don't."

A towel sailed toward them from one of Mason's pack, who clearly had no throwing arm. As her friend bent over to pick it up, Val put out an arm to stop her. "What are you doing?"

"Direct field observation." She held the towel up to her nose and gave a delicate sniff—and then another longer, deeper one, followed by an alarming groan. "Oh my God! I think I just ovulated."

"What?" Val grabbed her shoulders. "How could you know that?"

"Because I swear my right ovary just raised her pom-pom and said, *hey there, big boy."* She gave another sniff and then laughed at herself. "Not that I like the player who threw it our way. Jock Pagras is a total jerk in the Mason wannabes pack. But the man smell in his towel does something to me. I cannot lie."

Val yanked it out of her hands. "Stop that!"

"Just give me one more sniff," Darla pleaded. She tried to grab it back, but Val hurled it up higher into the stands, making some woman behind them squeal.

"Spoilsport, but my professional self thanks you." She nodded to the ecstatic woman behind them who'd caught the towel and was rubbing it against her ample bosom. "You can't deny the impact of male sweat and pheromones on the female body. Yum! It's like bottled sex."

"Bottled sex..." Her mind brought up Brock's scent of pine and cloves even though he was nowhere to be seen. "Make sure to add a footnote about that in our study."

Darla fanned herself as they left the arena. Chuck was waiting for them outside the locker room and crooked his finger toward them. They headed in his direction, and he opened the door before they could ask him what he wanted.

Only a quick peek inside told her what he had in mind: the hockey players were in towels and varying states of undress...with some not dressed at all.

She reminded herself of how much nudity she'd witnessed while studying tribes in Africa. Certainly, she'd also seen plenty of athletes change back when she'd been a figure skater in communal bathing and dressing areas, especially in Europe.

But knowing Brock was somewhere in this locker room packed with massively muscular men with little to no clothes on had her body flushing with heat. Darla sent her the teeniest of smiles that spoke volumes about her mindset. Probably more ovulating was going on, she'd say.

"I don't believe in waiting," Chuck said in his clipped, hard tone and practically pushed them inside. "Do your thing."

Val set her shoulders back as the Eagles' coach charged into the locker room. She reminded herself she was a professional. If she caught a glimpse of Brock, she would be fine. Not overheating or blowing a fuse. She wasn't an electrical appliance.

Only her heart rate continued to climb, and her mouth might as well have been filled by sand from the Sahara.

THE HOCKEY EXPERIMENT

Sighting the chairs she and Darla had sat in while they'd watched the stick-taping ritual, she crossed to them quickly and sat down, making herself as invisible as possible. She brought up her invisible wall for extra support. They were here to observe and study. Not to feed her clearly prurient reptilian brain.

Darla lowered herself next to her like she was alighting on a cloud. She pulled out her field diary along with Val, but she could hear her friend's shallow breathing. God, she didn't sound like that, did she?

Suddenly Darla started scribbling and then pointed to her field diary. *Here we go*, she thought, glancing over.

> We're in a locker room full of mostly naked hockey players!
> Best day of my life?
> Top ten for sure.
> I'm trying to remember I'm a cultural anthropologist and study their bathing rituals.
> But all I can see are DICKS!
> I can't even call them penises. These suckers are why slang was invented.
> Johnsons. Schlongs. The one-eyed snake.
> I might even understand for the first time why men—and women—give these appendages pet names like Mr. Midnight or Night Rider.

Val stayed her friend's hand when she started to write

more. Brock had just entered the locker room, his towel slung low across his narrow hips.

Her heart skyrocketed out of earth and into outer space, the propulsion so fast she was almost kicked back in her chair.

She tried to wrest her gaze away, but it was like fighting with her smart car when it took control of the wheel and wrested its way back to where it wanted to be. Her eyes slid down the water droplets still drying on his massive chest and washboard abs.

He immediately halted. His nostrils flared. His head turned, and the blue glint of his stare pinned her in place.

Heart racing. Heat rising. Muscles tightening.

She was aware of her reaction, but she could not stop it.

The sculpted muscles of his shoulders and arms made her hands tingle. Somewhere inside of her was a muscle memory of what it felt like to touch a man like him. It was primal. It was instinctive.

It had never happened to her before.

His sexy mouth tightened then, and he strode off toward his locker to dress. She lowered her head, like a dog in shame, and made herself study the blank page of her field diary. She needed to write something. Only what? *I want him* came to mind. She started shaking her head before she realized she was reprimanding herself.

"You okay, Val?" Darla leaned forward to get a good look at her. "Did you not eat enough again? You look peaked."

Peaked? Thank God she didn't look flushed. "I...don't know. It's stuffy in here."

"Let's get you out of here." Darla helped her out of her chair and took her field diary from her clenched hand. "We can always come back."

Come back? There was no way she wanted to expose herself to another round of Brock Thomson in a hastily wrapped towel. Her system could not handle it. *She* could not handle it. Her. Someone who'd won a gold medal with a stomach ulcer.

Mason entered the locker room with his arms out, completely naked, and gave a guttural impression of the Eagles' cry, the one piped in over the loudspeakers for a home game. A few other guys in his pack flew out of the shower area and joined in. The sound of six men crowing rather badly pierced her eardrums.

Other athletes dressing started laughing while a duo called out teasing comments like *that's how your mama sounded when we went home last night* and *don't quit your day jobs*.

Her gaze tracked to Brock. He was pulling on a long-sleeved gray sweater, a pinched frown on his face.

Thankfully for her haywire senses, he had pants on.

Whew! one part of her cried.

Boo! the unruly side of her jeered.

That second part needed to put a sock in it.

"One foot in front of the other," Darla said softly, putting a hand to her back.

Val realized she was standing stock-still, frozen. "I'm okay," she told her worried friend.

"I'm taking you to lunch." Darla moved her hand gently to Val's back as they started walking.

From the corner of her eye, she caught Brock moving forward. Toward them.

Her heartbeat turned into a jackhammer, and she fought for breath as he came closer. And closer.

"Hey!" His voice seemed to ping the hidden feminine muscles referenced in Masters and Johnson's sexual studies.

"Kinsley has been on me all week to tell you she's coming to our game tonight."

"Oh, that's great!" Darla exclaimed, ponytail bobbing in excitement. "I love that girl."

His luscious mouth moved, like it was working out a problem. "Zeke is the hockey enthusiast in the family. Susan can take it or leave it. But Kinsley... Well, let's just say she's coming tonight more to see you guys than me."

Val's fast-beating heart expanded in her chest, and she experienced a profound warmth. She was touched, she realized.

Darla's smile could have launched a thousand boats. "That's so sweet."

Except Val could tell Brock wasn't awash in the kindness of the action. He was uncomfortable.

"You don't need to worry, Brock," she found herself saying.

His entire focus locked on her, making any holdout neurons go haywire. "Are you a mind reader, Val?"

"You're concerned about us being Eagles employees and your niece becoming too attached to us." Darla's understanding *uhum* punctuated her point. "What you should know is that we'd never hurt her."

"Of course we wouldn't." Darla put a hand on Brock's arm before pulling back. "I know you don't know us well, but we'd never hurt a young girl. Hell, we don't hurt anyone really. That's traditionally what other people have done to me and Val. But we're so over that. Aren't we, Val?"

She made herself nod over the *rat-ta-ta-tat* of her heart. "We can keep things separate," she heard herself say, even though she knew the parameters of their study.

But this was a young girl they were talking about. Professional boundaries need not apply in this case.

"I can keep things separate too." He crossed his arms over his massive chest, his will and strength a tangible vow. "When I have to. Kinsley really wants to spend more time with you. Susan and I don't want to say no. She's different since meeting you. She even asked if she could sit with you for the game."

"Then have her sit with us," Val told him matter-of-factly. "In fact, if Zeke is coming with your sister, he's welcome to join us too. We can simply look on it as a wonderful evening with new friends."

He rubbed the back of his neck. "That's very nice of you. Now I have to tell you what else the women in my house are cooking up, so to speak. Kinsley asked her mom if she could ask you to come over to the house for dinner this Sunday. Susan was all for it, so it's falling on me. I told Kinsley I'd ask but you guys might be busy—"

"We're never too busy for a sweet girl like Kinsley," Darla said passionately, pressing a heartfelt hand to her chest. "Never. Right, Val?"

But she knew what he was saying between the words. "We aren't, and we genuinely like your family, Brock." Val was aware of the charge on her tongue as she said his name. "But if you want to keep our contact with your family to the arena, we can keep it here. Your choice."

Because what they were talking about was forging a personal relationship, one they'd started during the sightseeing, and one he'd ended, with her acquiescence. The greater their outside contact continued, the deeper the bond would become.

"I'd rather lose an arm or leg than disappoint my niece." He lowered his hands to his sides and looked off for a moment before turning that gorgeous face back to her. "Sorry, I'm new at this. The full-time uncle thing."

"You're doing great from my perspective." Darla leaned in and bumped his side, making him chuckle. "Growing pains are natural."

"Thanks, I needed that." His exhale was shot through with relief and good humor, and it made Val feel a tidal wave of dopamine so powerful she had to bite the inside of her cheek not to smile.

"So...game tonight and dinner Sunday?" he asked.

Darla looked toward Val, and they shared an understanding mastered in boarding school. "Perfect," her friend said. "What can we bring?"

"Another empowering girl's T-shirt? Just kidding."

But he wasn't, so she traded another look with Darla before saying, "We've got this. Trust me."

The narrowed focus of his gaze lasted for several long beats before he responded, "Oddly, I do."

A smile broke out above his hard, chiseled jaw, endearing and sexy at the same time, before he walked off.

Val stood there enthralled. Trust for a man like him didn't come easy, so she suspected she'd just received one of the biggest compliments of her life.

EIGHT

"Why do girls clean so much when people are coming over?"

Brock pulled Zeke out onto the deck as the vacuum cleaner roared to life again. For the eighth time today. His cleaning lady was coming once a week now that his family was living with him, and while she'd just come on Thursday, Susan hadn't thought the house clean enough.

Everyone had been given chores. Him included. Garbage duty was fine. He'd done it when married. But the biggest disruption caused by Susan's cleaning kick was incendiary, worse than the Flyers-Senators brawl in 2005, and he didn't want to get near it with a ten-foot pole.

Susan wanted Kinsley to take down her tent in the family room.

"I think they're trying to impress the other women coming over," he only answered.

Zeke gave a long-suffering sigh along with his signature eye roll. "God, girls are so weird."

Brock ruffled his hair. "Probably best to keep that thought to yourself, kiddo. Your mom—"

"Kinsley!" Susan's roar could be heard throughout the house. "I need to vacuum under your tent."

"I'm not taking it down, Mom," the girl shouted back from inside her canvas sanctuary, which she was physically defending from collapse. "It's my home."

"No, it's not, and you need to stop upsetting your uncle Brock. He likes to have order, especially during the hockey season."

"Mom's throwing you under the bus." Zeke winced and kicked at the floor. "She used to do that with Dad."

Brock crouched down in front of the boy. "Do you miss your dad?"

His nephew jerked his shoulder. "Maybe. But he doesn't miss me. He doesn't even call."

What kind of asshole didn't even call his kids? Brock had to tamp down the fire in his gut. He'd thought Darren would at least check in, but since he'd gone on tour, he'd made no effort with the kids. Susan had heard from his attorney, though, and that had pissed Brock off even more. The divorce was more of a priority than his children.

Darren didn't want custody, but he wanted spousal support. Susan had always made more money, and now he wanted his share. Of course, Susan's lawyer was horse trading about waiving child support if Darren waived spousal support. It was enough to leave Brock cold. His own divorce had been fast and easy. Erin hadn't wanted much from him, and he'd been happy to give her more than what she was entitled to in the settlement.

But Darren was a selfish prick, and Brock had visions of throwing the man as far as he could and eating a peanut butter and banana sandwich while listening to him cry.

"I can't change your dad's choices." He tipped Zeke's

chin up. "And I'm not your dad. But you can count on me. For anything."

Zeke crowded closer, his usual bravado gone. In that moment, he was a young vulnerable boy looking for an anchor. "I know, Uncle Brock."

Putting an arm around him, Brock held the silence. He knew Zeke was fighting tears. Truthfully, the boy wasn't the only one fighting unpleasant emotions.

"Do you think Mom would get mad if we did some hockey drills?" his nephew finally asked in a rough voice.

It would be good for the kid. It would be good for both of them. Still, they also needed some levity...

"Did you clean the grout in the shower?" he asked, raising his eyebrows.

"What?" Zeke jumped back with a shocked face. "I don't do that. I'm twelve."

Brock's shoulders stared to shake with laughter. "Got ya. Like I'd ever let you do that."

Zeke launched himself at him and pulled him into a hug. "You'd better not. You'd stop being my favorite uncle."

His heart rolled over in his chest as he hugged the boy back. "Can't have that. Go on and get the Green Biscuit and your stick. We can practice in the garage. I'll pull out my car."

"Will you tell Mom?" Zeke glanced surreptitiously over his shoulder as if looking for Susan.

"Not if I don't have to." The vacuum cleaner was still roaring. "She'll come find us if she needs us."

"You can count on that," Zeke said with an exaggerated huff.

He and Zeke worked on shooting drills in the garage until an orange Lamborghini Urus SUV pulled into his driveway. Through the windshield, he could see Val in her ugly black glasses in the passenger seat, her usual reserve in place. Darla was singing and moving to the beat, her tortoiseshell glasses nowhere to be seen.

"Whoa!" Zeke dropped his stick, pointing at their guests. *"That's* Darla's car? I want a ride like that."

"Zeke," he called as his nephew raced toward the driver's side.

As he was picking up the kid's hockey stick, he saw Val lean over and hold something out to Darla. The other woman frowned darkly and said something. Then she took whatever was in Val's hand and pushed it onto her face. Her glasses. Ones she clearly didn't need because she hadn't had them on for driving. Were they intended to make her look smarter?

Another fascinating clue, as was her ride. But what did it tell him?

He put the stick aside and walked over to greet their guests. Darla alighted in jeans and a baggy green sweater with boots, and he could see she had makeup on again. Zeke immediately started interrogating her about her ride, peeking his head in.

Brock turned to her companion, the woman who fascinated him in perhaps the most insane way he'd ever experienced. Val's ugly black tennis shoes appeared as she left the car, and when she shut the door, he noted she was wearing much the same outfit she'd donned for their sightseeing expedition. Still baggy and meant to conceal everything about her. Including an enormous black wool coat that seemed four sizes too big for her.

He had the sudden urge to strip her of that outfit and burn it in his backyard firepit.

"Hey," he called instead, raising his hand to Val, whose smile seemed strained.

Her glasses fogged up due to the change in temperature, but did she take them off and let him see her face? No, she just waited until they cleared. Then she was studying him in that focused way of hers, and after a few beats, he felt like she'd catalogued everything about him today. Including that he hadn't shaved. He rubbed his jaw, feeling the stubble. Did she not like a five o'clock shadow?

Then he wondered why he cared.

Only he knew why he did. If she wanted him clean-shaven, he could accommodate her. Her flawless skin had to be sensitive...

Thoughts he needed to veer away from like a deer on the highway.

"Hello, Brock," she said at last, clearing her throat quietly. "Thank you for having us over."

They both knew he hadn't issued the invitation. Seeing Kinsley hug the two women following the game the other night had actually made him smile after an incredibly frustrating game. They'd eked out a win, but just barely. Mason had racked up penalty after penalty, welcoming the cheers from the fans who loved blood sport.

Chuck had chewed them out in the locker room, but his rants clearly weren't working, and everyone knew it. Mason included. Brock was hoping for one of Chuck's famous motivators pretty soon, honestly. Which brought him back to the big question: how were these women involved?

He took a few steps toward Val, wishing she would smile and relax. Every time he was around her, she was nervous and a little shy. "Glad you found the house so easy."

She lifted her leather satchel over her shoulder. That was another funny item. She didn't have a purse. What woman didn't carry a purse? Erin, back in the day, had possessed an entire closet full of them, and even his niece had a collection of them.

"We're both good with directions." A short smile lifted Val's mouth, making her beauty mark more enticing somehow.

Yeah, he wanted to trace that mark too. Shit. It was going to be a long afternoon.

"Great," he said distractedly. What were they talking about?

The door leading to the house behind him opened and slammed, and then his niece was running past him in a blur. "Oh my gosh! I *love* your car."

"Darla said we could go for a ride," Zeke practically yelled, his chest puffed out. "Shotgun!"

"You always call that, moron." Kinsley hugged Darla, burying her face into her shoulder since they were the same height. "I'm so glad you're here."

"We are too, honey." Darla smoothed her hands down his niece's hair with a wide smile. "Did you cut your bangs?"

"Yeah." She twirled a finger around the ends of her straight black hair. "Mom was yelling at me, and I wasn't feeling pretty, so I decided to make a change."

Not pretty? And she'd just done that?

Brock studied his niece with concern. He couldn't tell the difference. They were still short and choppy and rested above her brows. He caught Zeke rolling his eyes and shot him a look.

"Well, they look great." Darla waved as Susan stepped out of the house and came forward. "Hey, girl! Looking good."

"Hah!" His sister winced and pulled her cream sweater

down self-consciously. "Maybe if you're going for an overtired, overworked look."

"Nah, don't be silly." Darla walked over and pulled Susan into a warm hug, which Brock noted his sister returned with equal affection. "We all have those times, but we get through them. Right, Val?"

His gaze swung back to her. She was still standing beside her passenger door. "We do, but we rise above them with self-discipline and friendly support."

He shoved his hands into his pocket. That was no regular answer. But it had the right effect. The women were sharing that look they got when women bonded over tough times. Next up: margaritas or cosmos. But he found himself fighting a smile. Susan apparently needed these women as much as Kinsley did.

Zeke pointed toward his sister accusingly. "Hey, Mom, Kinsley cut her bangs."

The little turd... He'd have to tell him later that you didn't ruin female bonding—or tattle on your sister.

"She did?" Susan frowned a moment before shaking it off and smiling. "Ah...it looks good."

Nice save, he thought. Kinsley's mouth parted in surprise before she smiled shyly and fluffed her bangs. Had she expected Susan to be angry? God, she hadn't done it for attention, had she? He instantly had nightmares of waking up to find a foot of her long hair on the floor.

"I was going to give the kids a ride in my car," Darla told Susan, patting the engine. "If that's okay with you."

Susan traced the hood as well. "You've got good taste. I love the orange. Ah...can I go with you guys?"

His conservative sister who drove a Subaru liked an orange car? The sky was falling.

"You betcha." Darla opened the back driver's side door. "Pile in. Brock, do you want to come?"

He spent as much time traveling as he did on the ice. No way he was spending his precious day off in a car. "Nah. I'll go put some wood in the fireplace."

"Take Val with you," Darla called. "One, she hates my driving, and two, she loves a good fire. Especially when it's inside. Right, Val?"

Brock sensed an inside joke. Val didn't say yes or no, or anything. She just stood with her hands held together in front of her. Moments later, they were staring at each other as Darla pulled out of the driveway with the rest of his family, music booming.

"Come on inside and I'll get you a drink," he suggested, acutely aware they were alone.

At his house.

With no one to interrupt them.

She glanced over her shoulder, her usual poise gone. Her shyness returned in the slight hunch of her shoulders. "Oh-kay."

She followed him slowly, and he swore he heard her exhale sharply. When they stepped inside, he led her to the kitchen.

"You have a beautiful home," she said in a halting way.

All he wanted to do was assure her. Help her relax. He turned at the kitchen island, noting how her hand was clutching her leather satchel. "Can I take your coat and bag?"

She nodded, and as she was unbuttoning it, he walked over to help her out of it. Standing behind her, he caught her clean, crisp smell and something subtly floral. Maybe her shampoo? He had the wild urge to press his head to her neck and inhale her.

His heart started to pound as he watched her smooth her auburn ponytail out of the way. He moved to help her, his hand glancing over her silky hair and the back of her neck. Her skin was as smooth as he'd imagined. God, he was getting hard.

What the hell?

He took her coat when she finally shrugged out of the giant thing. Slowly, she surrendered her satchel. Noting the large size on the tag as he took it to the coat closet, he realized she must have intentionally gotten something that didn't fit her. Like the rest of her clothes. But why?

He stored both the coat and the satchel and returned to find her standing where he'd left her in the kitchen. Looking shy and very unsure. Was that a red flush climbing up her neck?

"What would you like to drink? I have pretty much anything you could want except a piña colada."

The tips of her mouth turned up, making him want to squeeze another full smile out of her. "How about a Bootleg?" she asked. "I read Minnesota is famous for that cocktail."

That sexy librarian image of her rose up in his mind and stuck. Yeah, he could see her reading everything from Minnesota's history to cocktail recipes. "I'm fresh out of mint and frozen lemonade. Sorry."

"I was kidding." She absently traced his black granite countertop, another blush climbing up her neck. "But I'm not very good at it. Darla's the funny one."

She sounded almost sad about that fact. "I see you two joking and laughing while you're scribbling notes to each other. I'll bet you're funny too. Darla can't pull all the weight."

Her lighthearted laugh had her looking up at him. Her

shoulders seemed more relaxed now. They were getting somewhere. "You'd be surprised. Darla is a force of nature. I'll just have water. Or wine. Or juice. Really, I'm not picky."

"How do you feel about Châteauneuf-du-Pape?"

Her head tilted to the side and a small smile touched her unpainted lips. "Pretty good actually. But only if you're having some. I don't want you to open a bottle like that only for me."

"I'd planned on sharing it." He sent her a wink before he'd realized it, then walked over to the wine rack and pulled out the bottle he'd had in mind and began to uncork it. "I discovered wine when I played in Boston. I got dragged to a French wine tasting by a girl I was going out with. The wine stuck. The girl didn't."

Why was he telling her this?

He pulled out the cork with a pop and reached for two glasses in the cabinet. "Have you ever visited the region?"

"Châteauneuf-du-Pape?" She took the glass he'd poured her and swirled it around like she knew what she was about. "Yes, but it's been a while. Lovely country. You?"

"Not yet, but it's on my bucket list when I retire from hockey at the end of this season. That's not public yet, by the way."

Her fingers tightened on the wine stem for a second, and he knew she understood what a big confidence he'd shared with her. "Can I ask what you'll be doing after?" she asked hesitantly.

"I've got some business interests and endorsements, of course, but my main job will be coaching at St. Lawrence High School about an hour from here; it's one of the premier hockey schools for colleges and the NHL." He couldn't help the grin as he thought about standing amidst a bunch of boys in their uniforms, hunger and dreams flashing in their eyes. "Zeke is a strong candidate to attend in two years. It's going to be a joy to coach him."

Her gaze was instantly loaded with intensity. "Joy... What a wonderful way to put it. You'll be good at it. Zeke and the other boys will be lucky to have you."

While her praise was unexpected, it moved him all the same. "Thank you."

He watched the elegance in her motions as she took a sip of the wine. She made it seem oddly sensual, even with those silly glasses reflecting the glass in her hands.

"Darla said you like a good fire. Let's go into the family room. Only, be prepared for our new addition, courtesy of Kinsley. Her mother couldn't get her to take it down today. I'm hoping you and Darla might."

When they entered the room, he caught the sad look that crossed Val's face when she saw the tent. Walking to the fireplace, he poked the burning wood and added a fresh log. The rich smell of mesquite filled the room as it crackled. He'd always made sure to stock wood that had a good smell.

"Kinsley must be very hurt right now," Val said finally, coming closer to where he stood beside the fire.

He noted how her glance slid over the family photos on the hearth. There were photos of him, his parents, and Susan, as well as one of him holding a laughing Zeke's hand on the boy's first time on the ice. That was the photo her gaze seemed glued on, but before he could hold it out to her, she seemed to shake herself.

"She is." He put his boot on the brick ledge of the fireplace, touched by her empathy. "But she's been better since you and Darla appeared in her life. Like I said, Susan and I really appreciate your kindness."

"Please." She flashed him her first easy smile, and it nailed him right in the chest. "It's really easy to like her. Your entire family is wonderful. We enjoyed getting to know everyone more at the game the other night."

"I'm glad someone enjoyed it, because from my perspective, the game stunk since the team played like sh— Crap." He took a drink to offset the bitterness in his mouth.

"The team stats are playoff worthy, but it's the penalties and the consistency of play that seem to be a problem." She clutched her wineglass as she grimaced. "I'm sorry. Let's agree not to talk about work."

He knew when a wall had been raised. "Too bad you can't work the same kind of magic with Mason as you have with Kinsley."

She let out a shaky laugh, nervously wetting her lips, an act he knew wasn't intended to arouse him—but it did all the same.

"Kinsley is an easier subject in many ways, but again, maybe we should talk of something else. Umm...I see you like art."

He looked over to the couple of paintings he'd bought from a well-known local artist. The winter landscape especially made him want to head up to his cabin and ice fish and pond skate and just sit in front of the fire and read a good mystery. Looking at the landscapes helped settle him, especially when he got back from a game. Not that he'd ever admit that out loud.

"I was a little embarrassed about it at first—like I was about having a thing for good wine." He was sure his smile was almost sheepish. "I was raised pretty simply, not far from here. My dad was a principal, and my mom was the school nurse. Neither drank much except for a rare toast at a wedding. Ah...can we circle back to Mason for a sec?

Sorry, but it's been on my mind, and you seem to understand people well."

Plus, this time he was the one feeling a little weird. Shy wasn't a word he'd ascribe to himself. But talking about himself wasn't his thing.

She frowned into her wine before taking another sip. "All right. What would you like to ask?"

He rested his arm on the mantel above the fireplace, watching as she drew her guard up around her. Crossed arms. Furrowed brow line. Her green eyes turned practically flinty, even with her glasses.

"Mason clearly wants attention. To be seen, as you've said Kinsley wanted."

She nodded, her expression intent. God, she was a good listener, and very alluring with the firelight playing over the elegant planes of her face not obscured by her thick glasses.

"But he *is* seen. By millions of people. And he's still doing shit—sorry, stuff—that hurts the team. That's his chances as well as ours that he's messing with. What would change that behavior?"

She took a somber sip of wine, her long slender neck riveting him as he waited for her response. God, she was pretty under all that hiding. Clearly, *she* didn't want to be seen. So...what was it that made her want to hide?

"Mason presents a challenge because he does not seem to want to change his behavior. Unlike Kinsley. I expect Mason's behavior has also been going on much longer than your niece's. It's part of his identity now. It's even expected by some. Those items make it more challenging to change."

His sexy librarian fantasy started to roll even as he hung on her every word. God, she was smart. That was really sexy.

Now her posture was more confident. Her cool persona

was back. He marveled at the shift from guarded to commanding. "Keep going."

"In such cases, there are usually three options: punishment, humiliation, or exile. All are on the table for Mason, I imagine, if he fails to help the Eagles make the playoffs."

Total skull shrinker answer, and sexy as hell. God, he was salivating at the efficient way she'd listed out the options. So clearly and in a voice that said she knew what she was talking about.

He hadn't met too many women like that in his world, and it was arousing. He also liked being able to talk with her about work. That was something that had slipped away with Erin. She'd gotten upset enough about his injuries to the point where he'd had trouble setting his own emotions about them aside. After that, he'd decided to leave work at work.

Suddenly, his wineglass almost slid from his hand. They were *bonding*, much like he'd seen happening earlier between the women. Holy—

He picked up another log and laid it in the fire to cover his shock and then cleared his throat. "Not exactly great choices. Mason's been punished. He sits in the penalty box more than any player on our roster. He's been fined by the league. No change. He knows another team will be happy to pick him up if he's traded."

"Correct," was all she said with that crisp enunciation he wanted to hear more of.

"So that leaves humiliation." He watched her guard come back up. "Not something I relish as the captain."

"It isn't your job as captain."

He studied her. "It's not?"

"According to what I've read about team duties, that's a job for the owner and coach." She nestled her glass against that damn baggy shirt. "You have enough on your plate, leading the team to victory and modeling good behavior."

If she'd picked up a piece of firewood and knocked him in the head, he wouldn't have been more stunned. How did she understand all that? No one had ever described his role as captain so succinctly. Or with such empathy.

"You're a really good person, Val," was all he managed to say.

Tension settled in her shoulders again, although she gave him a polite smile. She glanced over at the kitchen as if wondering where the others were. "Darla loses track of time when she's out for a drive. Well... I hope that answers your question."

He gave a single nod, not knowing what else to say. He liked her insights, but he still wasn't sure what to do. And they needed to do something. Even if it wasn't his job to interfere. Because one of these nights, Mason's antics were going to make them lose.

"Sorry." He picked up the fire poker and stoked the coals to release some of his frustration. "I want to win, and the more I know, the better equipped I am to do that."

"Of course you want to win." There was passion in her voice that called to him. "You're a professional athlete. You work hard to maintain the highest levels of athleticism. Your mental focus must be absolute. You sacrifice in unimaginable ways—and yes, you are compensated—but your body endures great pain, especially in your sport, where aggressiveness and body contact are not only encouraged but part of a winning strategy."

He was oddly moved by her understanding. "You get it. Not many people do."

She flashed him a reluctant smile, and again, he felt the

strengthening of the new bond between them. "It's what I'm paid for, isn't it?"

He didn't know what she was being paid for. But he did know he wasn't done with this conversation. Watching her, he said, "The way you talked—about pain and sacrifice—it sounded like you knew from personal experience."

Her arms locked across her chest, the hand holding the wineglass fisting around the stem. "Do I look like a hockey player to you? Maybe I should tell Chuck to put me in next time you guys are behind."

Again, her humor was dry, but he sensed her discomfort. She wanted to move off this subject. Immediately. "I'd pay to see that."

The amused smile on her satisfied face was downright sexy, and again, he had the urge to put his wineglass down, close the short distance between them, and remove those thick glasses so he could look into the vibrant green eyes staring back at him.

That wouldn't be enough, though.

He'd want to take her over to the couch, cover her with his body, and then frame her hips in his hands as he took her mouth. God, how he wanted to feel exactly what was going on under those baggy clothes.

An idea struck him, one so brilliant he lifted his hand to his mouth to cover his pleased smile. Never say he wasn't a brilliant strategist, on and off the ice.

He would dangle out an invitation to use the hot tub to their guests. Both the kids and Susan loved it, although they howled about the cold until they were nestled in the warm water. Darla might bite. He hoped Val would. Otherwise, he might have to orchestrate a more enticing invitation.

The thought of finally seeing what was under her clothing had his palms sweating.

"Uncle Brock! Uncle Brock!" Zeke's thudding could be heard throughout the house as he raced into the living room. "Darla can sing like *nobody* you've ever heard."

He watched Val close her eyes, her lips pursing with frustration. Interesting.

"I thought that her voice had musical quality," he replied as Zeke hugged him and then looked up at him with big eyes. "Are you thinking what I'm thinking?"

Zeke wiggled his little hips and executed a pretty good spin. "Karaoke night!"

The kids had brought the machine Susan had gotten them for Christmas, and while sometimes it drove him nuts, today wasn't going to be one of them. "Maybe in the hot tub?"

His nephew jumped up in the air with a delighted cry. Val only snapped her parted lips shut after a momentary loss of composure. She turned away, walking slowly toward the sound of happy feminine chatter coming from the kitchen.

"I'm telling the others!" Zeke cried.

More thudding footsteps sounded as he raced off.

When everyone returned, Val looked pale as milk while Darla was doing a little conga line step with Zeke.

"I hear someone's got karaoke and hot tub in mind." She took Kinsley's hand and spun the girl around, causing her to giggle. "I can't think of two things I love more. Hot water and singing. But I'll need something to wear."

Val cleared her throat. Loudly. Darla looked over, and again, her lips took on the same pinched quality they'd had when Val had handed her the tortoiseshell glasses hanging on the end of her nose.

"Let's go see what we can find for you," Susan said,

putting her arm companionably around Darla's waist. "I'm sure we have something that will work."

Val cleared her throat again, toying nervously with her wineglass. "I don't think I'll go into the hot tub."

"Oh, come on." Kinsley ran over to her, a pleading look in her eyes. "It will be so fun!"

"Yes, Val, it will be." Darla's voice held an edge. "You don't want to be the only one sitting out in the cold by yourself."

Val bit her lip, which only made his mouth water. "I could read or something…"

God, her agonizing was difficult to watch. He almost called off the plan. But then she straightened her spine and nodded briskly. "Very well, but I'll need something baggy. Because you know how shy I am, Darla."

A snort of laughter erupted from her friend, who put a conspiratorial arm around Kinsley. "She really is, you know, so don't let anyone shame you for being shy either. Being shy is like being loud. It's just how you were made."

Huh. How did women come up with things like that? But the radiant smile on Kinsley's face was full of hero worship. He thought it was downright cute.

"Don't worry, Val," Brock decided to add, unable to contain his grin. "I have just the baggy thing for you."

She beamed then. Because she'd heard baggy. Inside, he was doing the two-step.

Which of them would be happier if she agreed to put on the outfit he had in mind?

NINE

"Why do men's clothes smell so good?"

Val stepped forward to stop her friend from taking another sniff of the clothing Brock had found for her to wear: his practice jersey.

Wearing his worn jersey, knowing it had been against his skin and smelled like him, would send her to her death. Her heart rate was dangerously fast. The organ would implode if she didn't drop the object in question. Then Darla would be putting her in an early grave, crying beside her tombstone.

Her friend went in for another sniff.

"Will you stop that?" She finally had to wrench the jersey from Darla's hands and then promptly dropped it because her skin tingled at the contact. "And no ovulating."

Her friend's chortle only had Val glaring.

"I mean it, Darla. I don't like this whole hot tub idea one bit. You should have known I wouldn't like it. How long have we been friends?"

"Val..." Her friend tugged Susan's oversized T-shirt over her head, wearing only a bra and panties under it—a combo

Val was terrified to mirror herself. "You love hot springs—and you love to sing. Stop being so uptight about everything and start changing. You can relax here. This sweet little family is not a threat to our cover. Have we talked once about our jobs?"

"I did while you were gone." She sent back her own fish-eyed look. "You could have come back sooner."

"I was having fun." Darla sat down hard on the bed in the guest room where they were changing and kicked her feet happily. "I like to have fun, and you know I love kids. So do you. If you'd just let down your guard a little, there are some really good things waiting for you here. Kinsley loves us, and so does Susan—even though they just met us. And Zeke is a total charmer. We're good."

"We are standing in the guest room of the Eagles' captain, about to go out in practically our underwear." She put her hands on her waist, her insides rolling with adrenaline at the thought. "This is probably a complete conflict of interest."

Her gaze shot to Brock's jersey. Wearing his jersey certainly would be. It would be imprinted in her mind for life—a tangible memory she could unpack anytime, mixed with warmth and scent and sweetness.

"You didn't think so before or we wouldn't be here." Darla drew off her glasses as she tucked her hair up into a bun and secured it with them. "Look, this is no different than knowing Chuck—or your father for that matter. Do your personal interactions with them change your academic protocols in any way?"

Dammit. "You know they don't. But we aren't studying *them*."

"Oh, for heaven's sake. Chuck is technically the chief of the group we're studying. It's totally parallel. But it's not an issue because we decided it wouldn't be. So we spend extra time with Brock and his family outside work. I happen to love it. Val, I need more people in my life. You know that. Usually we socialize with the tribe or group we're studying. We haven't been doing that here, and it's isolating. I can't just hole up in my loft the whole time we're here. I get lonely sometimes."

Emotion backed up in her throat. She did too, but then she'd turn to work to fulfill her. Or Darla. Usually it was enough. "I know you do, and I'm sorry."

Darla pushed off the bed and wrapped her up in a tight hug. "Honey, I know it's hard for you to open up, but you can trust me on this. These people are worth opening up to. In fact, we might even have a long relationship with them."

She darted back, unease shooting up her spine. Did Darla suspect her feelings about Brock? "What do you mean?"

"You and I are going to do our job, and then Chuck is going to do his job. With your dad. So is Brock. If all things work out like we all hope, your daddy will keep this team, and we will probably be coming back to watch them play. You might even see Brock at one of your dad's parties—not that we ever go to those. But we might now. Because we have a stake here. That means seeing these wonderful people again."

She had the sudden urge to take her glasses off and press the heels of her hands to her stinging eye sockets. Too many emotions were sifting through her, and it was frankly unnerving.

She'd already felt her heart lurch in her chest when she'd seen the photo of Brock with little Zeke on the ice. God, that image had reminded her of everything good about the ice. The pure joy of it. Brock's face had been lit with that joy as he held the laughing toddler's hand. She'd gotten so affected she'd almost choked on her wine.

"Val, Kinsley asked me if we could come to her birthday party next month."

Val's head shot up, unease and delight arcing through her.

Darla put her hand to her chest, her gaze liquid. "I told her I'd talk to you, but honey, it would mean the world to her. And honestly, it would mean a lot to me too. I really love that girl. Did you see the tent she pitched in the living room with that sign taped to it? That's something I would have wanted to do at her age. You too. It about broke my heart, Val."

When Val had seen it, she'd been aware of Brock's regard. He'd wanted to know how she felt about it. He'd hoped she and Darla might be able to fix it. She had wanted that too. "Do you want to know what I thought? I thought it was ingenious of her. To put it all out there where everyone could see what she was going through. And do you know what else, Darla?"

Her voice was strained, and she knew Darla was aware she was struggling by the way her friend's face softened. "What, honey?"

"I thought how incredible it was that no one had made her take it down." She pressed her hand to her aching throat. "Not that you or I would have dared to pitch a tent like that and write those signs, but if we had, both of our mothers would have dismantled it before our eyes and thrown it away."

"Mine would have kicked it down in a rage and stomped on it." Darla laid a comforting hand on her arm. "Your mother would have summoned the butler and given you a haughty glance that sent you into therapy."

Therapy, the bane of her childhood existence, along with her mother. Her shyness had been something to be corrected. She *had* to smile for the cameras and on the ice. She *had* to exude warmth and emotion when people asked her questions. When all she wanted to do was hide under the covers and read a good book or simply skate all by herself with the cold air on her face.

"Our mothers sucked," Val choked out with a laugh. "Susan doesn't."

"No, she's having a tough time, sure, but she's great. Funny. A little goofy. And really sweet. Like her kids. She'll recover. They all will. And Brock's a big source of sweetness, wrapping them up in his house and his love."

Like she needed any reminders of how great he was. He was smart. He was funny. He respected her and listened to her. And when he smiled at her, she felt like taking to the ice and spinning through the air, dreaming that she'd never come back down to earth.

"Now..." Darla put her hands on her hips, that scary determined gleam in her golden eyes. "Are you putting on that jersey and hanging out with us or what?"

She knew they'd come to the end of their conversation and it was time to decide. "All right. I'll put on my mock swimsuit. But I'm leaving my glasses on. I need them to see."

They were prescription, although they certainly weren't her usual. She wore contacts and occasionally fashionable cat-eyed glasses.

"Well, I'm not!" Darla tossed them onto the bed with a little hip wiggle. "And neither should you. The hot tub will only fog them up anyway."

Val nearly gulped. She hadn't thought of the steam rising from the water, working its magic around Brock's bare chest, which she'd seen in the locker room with only an inadequate towel wrapped around his hardened, muscular body. When she couldn't sleep, that was what her mind served her, the traitor. "I'm getting cold feet again."

"Get dressed, hon." She grabbed Val's glasses off her face and ran for the door. "I'll be right back."

She was gone before Val could yank her to a stop and demand her glasses back. Everything was blurry. How in the world did Darla expect her to see? Had she stowed a seeing eye dog in the back of her SUV without Val knowing?

The door popped open. "Here you go, babe. I'm throwing your contacts on the bed. I always keep a spare set for you in my satchel, remember? See you shortly."

A small object flew through the air in a blur. Val walked toward the bed and rummaged around until she found it. Of course. Since that time in South Africa when she'd lost a contact while swimming in the hotel's pool, Darla had kept a spare set. Sometimes it came in handy.

God, she might as well get dressed too. Brock's red and white practice jersey was soft from use and multiple washings, being cotton and not the usual polyester he wore for games. His number and his last name were displayed in bold red, and she found herself tracing them.

A whiff of his scent, pine and cloves and something earthier, reached her nose, along with the undercurrent of laundry detergent. She was lifting the jersey halfway to take a sniff when she realized what she was about to do. Appalled, she threw it down on the bed.

But she could still smell him. Man. Forest. Spice. Her nose wanted a good solid whiff. She turned around to face the opposite wall. Clenched her fists. She was not going to do this.

Taking a sniff of his jersey was ridiculous.

But she needed to put it on, didn't she? Well, she would just have to hold her breath. Stripping quickly to her underwear, God help her, she tugged it over her head and felt it touch her knees. There. Mind over matter.

Holding her breath still, she grabbed the black travel case and used her hands to guide her to the adjoining bathroom. After washing her hands and putting her contacts in, she surveyed herself in the mirror.

Her mouth dropped at the sight.

The jersey enveloped her slim form, sure, but without her glasses on, she looked like that tiny doll-like girl who drew too much attention. One reporter had even said she was Clara come to life in the *Nutcracker*. She was no longer a young girl, but a woman. Except she still looked a little too doll-like for her own comfort. Her vibrant green eyes lit her face, as captivating as a fully lit crystal chandelier. They always had. And her beauty mark was more visible somehow, a flirty punctuation to her rosy lips.

From the time she was young, her mother had commented on how lucky she was not to need lipstick to enhance her already perfectly tinted lips.

She let out her breath in a rush, forgetting she'd been holding it. What would he do when he saw her like this? Her brow furrowed. She didn't like thinking about it. Would it change how he perceived her? Worse, did she want him to? Vulnerability crawled up her throat. She wanted him to find her pretty and that unsettled her. Fine, it also excited her, making her heart beat faster, but she didn't want to focus on that.

"*Val!*" Darla's voice preceded a flurry of knocks. "Come on. Last one in has to sing first."

That threat had her moving.

She ran down the hallway in her bare feet toward the family room. Through the patio door, she could see everyone was piling into the hot tub. Zeke and Kinsley were giggling as Darla dropped in with a heavy splash of water, falling playfully back against the side, her entire face lit with joy. Susan ran to the edge and climbed in, ducking down under the water.

Her eyes scanned the deck. Where was Brock? Gooseflesh broke out over her arms, and instinctively, she knew he was behind her.

The low rumble of a throat being cleared had her heart rate taking off at a Pimlico gallop. She swore she could hear him gulp.

"*Val.*"

The way he said her name wasn't a question. It was a command somehow. To turn around and face him.

Because she knew he was waiting for her...

Instantaneously, she was both sensually aware of her bare skin under his jersey and terrified of him seeing her without her glasses on. God, how was she supposed to explain her new look? *Umm...my crazy friend stole my glasses and brought me the spare contacts she keeps for me. So my glasses wouldn't fog up.*

She'd sound like an idiot. People with doctorates from Oxford didn't do mortifying.

The seconds ticked by, and the quiet presence behind her was making her system crazy. She could feel the cold air on her bare calves. Her hair was still up in her ponytail, but now she wanted to take it down and use it to cover up as much of her face as she could.

Because he was about to see her as she usually was.

And God, she realized she didn't want him only to like what he saw.

She wanted him to like the whole package.

Dr. Valentina Hargrove, PhD. The doll-like form she'd been born with. The walls she'd built.

She wanted him to *see* all of her.

More laughter from the deck reached her ears. People were waiting for them. She made herself turn to face him and felt like a hot wave of jungle air was knocking her back.

He was shirtless. In fitted black swim trunks. His muscles were the kind that had been celebrated by master sculptors since the beginning of time. Hard. Defined. Ridged.

Complete male perfection.

When she finally met his gaze, she felt rooted to the floor under her bare feet. His blue eyes were bright and filled with the same primal heat rolling through her system.

His nostrils flared, and God help her, his mouth parted in shock.

"You... Uh... Mm..."

Guttural, monosyllabic sounds.

Totally primal.

Completely arousing.

Adrenaline continued to flood her system. Her body seemed to burst into flames on the inside as his massive hand rose, his fingers so close they were seemingly tracing her skin as he gestured to her. All of her.

"You're...beautiful."

His rough voice pinged something deep within her belly.

"I knew it." He sucked in a huge breath before his exhale rushed out audibly. "Sorry, I'm... It's only... You and the nerdy glasses and the clothes. They didn't...suit. I thought it from the first time I saw you."

She was shocked. He'd concluded that from the beginning? That meant he'd watched her. Studied her. Analyzed her features.

My God, he *did* see her.

The professor in her knew what courtship involved. What he'd just listed sounded like key components. Her chest was rising and falling under the softness of his jersey. Another conclusion rocked her back on her feet.

He *liked her* liked her.

Her mind started to spin like the wheel of death when a computer froze, but her body's instincts, honed over thousands of years, knew what to do.

Let him look.

While she looked back.

Her gaze took in his massive shoulders and the sexy trail of hair cruising over his rock-hard abs to the root of their primal differences as man and woman. When she lifted her eyes, he was still staring, his pupils slightly dilated now. That meant adrenaline was coursing through him. Because she'd admired his body?

Dear God, she was facing the stirrings of male arousal.

Don't look down. Don't look down.

"I...ah...didn't want any of the players to notice us." Her speech was a whisper of its usual strength, as if her voice box had up and fainted. "Our job is our *raison d'être*."

She was speaking French now?

His nod was slow and emphatic and *off-the-charts* sexy. "I get it. You would have stopped traffic."

She shook her head at the turn of phrase. "No, I'm—"

"Yes. You. Are." He swallowed thickly, his Adam's apple moving now. "I like you as you are. Val."

The shot of dopamine was as heady as homemade jungle hooch, and it had her smiling despite herself. He liked her, and she most definitely liked him. Her entire being felt like everything was good in the world. Global peace was possible. Poverty would be eradicated.

She'd read about the roller coaster of male-female courtship, but she'd never felt it until now. A female shyness stole over her then. "Oh, I—"

"I didn't mean to make you uncomfortable." His gorgeous mouth worked like he was searching for words. "I'm just... Shit. I'm usually better on my feet."

"Maybe it's because you're not on the ice," she joked and then winced, feeling the cringe of an awkward boy-girl interaction. "Sorry, I told you I'm not funny."

"But you are." He opened his hands in a helpless gesture. "And you talk like a librarian, which I like. Ah...I'm about to completely step over the line I'd drawn."

She stepped back from him as he took one powerful step toward her, his allusion becoming a physical reality. "Wait!"

"I can't." He stopped in front of her, inches away, his gaze searching her face with the hunger of a lion who'd gone too long without a meal. "God, I knew your eyes were green. But they're even brighter when you're not wearing those glasses. And your skin...it's even more flawless without your glasses taking up so much of your face. Part of me can't believe you hid all this, but then part of me can. Don't even get me started on your beauty mark."

Lifting her hand to her mouth, she made a nervous sound somewhere between a giggle and an audible cringe. "It's only genetics at work."

A crook of a smile made him completely adorable. "There you go. Talking like a sexy librarian. Which is why I'm stepping over that line I mentioned. Will you have dinner with me? Because I haven't felt like this in a long time, and I promised myself I would do something about it if I did."

Her heartbeat pounded in her ears like large hail on a tin roof. "We work for the same organization."

"We can keep it separate." He swallowed thickly, his throat so totally masculine and sexy. "Like we did today."

She gestured to the jersey she was wearing, smelling him on her all of a sudden. "This is keeping it separate?"

His low, toe-curling laugh had her insides tightening. "Yes. Do you still believe you can do your job tomorrow?"

Outrage at any other suggestion surpassed her physical response to him. "Of course."

"So can I."

His mouth broke out in another sexy grin, and she wondered if later she would try and count them for her other field diary, with the heading "The Number of Times Brock Thomson Smiled at Me Today."

"Val, I want to know you better. Because I don't think I've ever met a woman who intrigues me more."

She blinked before a huge surge of happiness flooded her system. Dopamine, she told herself, but she couldn't fight the desire to smile. Nothing on earth could stop her from smiling at him right now. "Then I'll go. But we *have* to keep it separate, Brock."

Neither her father nor Chuck could ever know...

He grunted, a one-note sound of satisfaction. Totally sexy. She probably was going to count those sexy sounds he made too.

"Say my name again," he said, tilting his head to the side, a teasing glint in those devastating blue eyes of his.

A part of her wanted to chant it, to offer it up to the gods like she'd seen at a naming ceremony. But sheer mortification stopped her. "I think you know your own name."

"I like the way you say that." He bit his bottom lip, making her thighs clench. "Val, I'm really glad you decided to come out of hiding. I was getting pretty tired of it, honestly."

"You were?"

"I had compulsions about pulling those glasses off your face—along with other things."

Her mouth was going to be sore from all this gaping. "Darla took my glasses and gave me my contacts. It's her fault."

"Then I'll have to thank her." He crossed his arms over his bare chest, causing her mouth to go dry. "We should get out there. The others are probably wondering what we're talking about."

She glanced over her shoulder. Darla raised her hands and twiddled her fingers playfully at her.

That was when she knew for certain.

Darla had suspected the whole time that she was attracted to Brock Thomson. Today she had decided to do something about it. God, she loved that girl.

She thought it only fair for him to know. "We've been set up."

"If you only knew the half of it." He lifted his hand and playfully waved back, a really funny act for a large man like him. "I might have suggested the hot tub to see if you'd unmask yourself. I hope you don't mind. You look really good in my jersey."

Her insides liquified, as if his gaze had put them in a blender and flipped the ON switch. What she wanted to say was, *You look really good without a shirt on,* but she said instead, "I find I appreciate the sheer brilliance of your strategy."

Another wave of heat filled his gaze, and her internal

temperature rose in response. "Good. Because I'm feeling like I won the lottery, seeing you like this, all woman, wearing only my jersey."

She couldn't stop her dopamine levels from surging or her physical reaction to him. Human anatomy was outcompeting her usual good sense. Leaning closer, knowing it would bring her an avalanche of his addictive, sexy scent, she said, "Know what? Right now, I feel the same way about looking at you."

Another earthy grunt of satisfaction. "So tomorrow night? You and me?"

Dr. Valentina Hargrove knew all the reasons she should say no. But she wasn't driving the primordial bus right now.

"Perfect. It's a date."

Outside, the first karaoke song began to swell, a sweeping intro of strings before Darla began to sing Etta James' "At Last," about how her love had finally come along.

Only the knowledge that her friend was singing it for her could make her look away from Brock. She turned around and crossed her arms, trying to look stern. Darla just continued singing, throwing her kisses as the kids laughed in the hot tub next to her.

The dopamine flooding her system was the only explanation for the sweet urge she had to run to her friend and throw her arms around her. Darla always knew. Thank God.

"We seem to be missing the party," Brock said in that deep *make her skin tingle* voice, drawing her to face him again. "Shall we?"

His warm, curved smile, twinned with the sexy look on his face, gave her the answer to Darla's initial research question when they'd first arrived.

What is it about men?
This.

TEN

How was it that one woman could overtake a man's usually laser-sharp focus?

Brock was known for being locked on one thing: hockey. He'd worked on the mental aspect of the game as much as the physical since he was a kid playing on hand-me-down skates with a used hockey stick.

But with the intriguing Val, he was facing off-the-charts levels of infatuation. God knew he thought about sex as much as any guy, but his fantasies were like a constant weekend of binge-watching a gripping TV show. He couldn't stop hitting the Next Episode button to another captivating fantasy.

The way she'd looked in his jersey last night—dry and later wet. The garment had clung to her lithe body, confirming what he'd guessed. She was sleek and toned under those baggy clothes she wore to work.

Then there were her eyes. Green. Captivating. Radiant when she was laughing with Darla and the kids in the hot tub as steam rose up around her.

He hadn't been able to stop thinking about the sexy

little auburn curls that had sprung up around her nape once wet.

Or how his name and number had clung to her hot little body.

She was a total knockout.

As he unlaced his skates after their afternoon practice, he tried and failed not to look for her. But she wasn't in the locker room. When he'd seen her this morning at the team meeting, her usual outfit had been in place. Baggy clothes. Thick glasses.

The brief greeting she'd given him had been like other mornings, polite and professional, like she had her walls up. If his blood hadn't been throbbing in its vessels, his mind conjuring up images of how she'd looked yesterday, he might have thought he'd dreamed the whole thing.

Only Darla had pursed her lips like she was trying to hold back a smile when she'd given him a warm *hello*. She was pleased with herself, and he still owed her some thanks. But as far as he was concerned, they were the only people who could know about his interest in Val.

Not even his family could know. Kinsley, Zeke, and even Susan had chatted nonstop before school this morning about how much fun they'd had with the two women. If they found out about the date, they'd get even more excited than they already were, and he didn't know where this was going to go or for how long.

Truthfully, though, he wanted it to mean something. He couldn't remember fantasizing this much about Erin or anyone else. His thoughts kept cycling back to their date. To getting to know her. Seeing her out of her usual disguise. Hearing that sexy librarian voice talk about things in her very smart way. And seeing more of that toned, sexy body of hers...as her big green eyes locked with his own.

He wanted her like he wanted to win their division, and the drive he had to reach that goal was an inferno of fire inside his belly. He knew what he had to do to win.

Now he was wondering what he had to do to win *her*.

This mysterious, fascinating woman.

"You're a little off today." Finn plunked down his gear and started to unlace his skates. "More trouble at home? Please tell me Kinsley didn't hang up a new killer sign?"

Brock didn't make a habit of lying, and he wouldn't start today. "I know I need to get my head back in the game, and no, Kinsley has stopped hanging up her signs, thank God."

She hadn't taken down the tent, but she'd shown it to Val and Darla. He'd heard them tell his niece how cool her pad was, so he figured their instincts told them Kinsley wasn't ready. Pushing the girl wasn't the way. Even Susan had backed off.

"Maybe we should go out." Finn slapped him on the shoulder. "Away from the rink. Away from the house."

"It's not a good time." He rubbed the back of his neck as his friend raised a bushy blond brow at him. "Don't ask me any more questions, Finn."

His friend nodded slowly before pulling his jersey off and tossing it in a heap on the floor. "Fine. I won't. But you know where I am."

They shared another look of understanding fostered by their long friendship. "I do. Now get yourself to the showers, man. You reek."

"Like you don't." He sniffed his armpit. "Okay, that's ripe, but we're paid to sweat, so I'm good with it. See you in the showers."

"In a sec." He picked up his phone to make sure he didn't have a text about the kids coming to the arena last minute. They'd both asked when they were going to see Val and Darla next. He and Susan hadn't been able to answer, saying they'd have to play it by ear given everyone's schedules.

"I owned you today, old man." Mason sauntered over to him, fresh from the showers, totally naked. "You feeling your age today? You were a little slow out there. I hear it happens with hockey vets."

Brock cocked a brow even though the kid was right. "Enjoy the moment, Mason. I don't have many off days."

"Oh, I plan to." He rolled his shoulders, sticking his junk out in a lame attempt to show his size. Brock wasn't the only one who was fed up with the kid's blatant exhibitionism in the locker room. Of course, some fans loved it. He'd been photographed naked holding nothing but a stick in a major magazine and had racked up a huge following for showing off his tattooed body on social media.

"For God's sake, Mason, put some pants on." Chuck stormed over and set his weight. "We all know what kind of a package you're carrying. No man likes having it shoved in his face."

"Is that what I'm doing?" But Mason backed away with his arms up, a cocky smile on his face. "I'm air-drying, Coach."

"Air-dry somewhere else," Chuck barked before turning to Brock. "You were off today. I could have outskated you. Whatever it is, clean it up. You know how much I'm counting on you."

The first glimmer of shame covered his skin. "It won't happen again."

Chuck nodded and marched off. Brock sighed and headed to the showers, ignoring everyone around him as he turned the tap to the coldest setting and did some breathing exercises to get focused. Finn and the other guys knew to leave him alone.

By the time he was dressed and ready to head out, he was feeling more grounded. Checking his phone one last time by the lockers, he found a message waiting for him. But not about the kids. This was one he'd been waiting for since the beginning of the season. He clicked on his agent's text and read:

> *Congrats! I just got the call. Reebok wants you. They like that they know what they're getting. No off-ice surprises or personal meltdowns. Nearly a million with other benies I can tell you about when we talk.*

He wanted to punch the air and let out a *Yes!* His agent had approached the shoe and apparel company for what he thought might be Brock's final big endorsement in hockey before he became a prominent high school hockey coach. Icing on the cake, they'd agreed, and the doorway to more profitable opportunities in the business world.

Brock had worked with his agent since he was sixteen, when he'd pulled in a major endorsement with a beverage company. Harold Griffey had convinced his parents of the long-term benefit of Brock having a selective but lucrative marketing strategy, focusing on only three brands to endorse and waiting to pursue the others until after his rookie years so he could make more money.

Brock's interest in business had been set after that, and going to Harvard had been the ideal way to continue to learn how to make good investments and create a wealth portfolio for when he retired from hockey. He'd learned the ins and outs of owning everything from shares in Kentucky Derby winners to award-winning restaurants.

Being a sound businessman was something he liked being known for, even though it wasn't as broadly discussed as his work on the ice. He planned to continue his business interests after he retired, but with this endorsement, he was hoping to move to the next level: he wanted to be on the board for a major business like Reebok.

That kind of cred would make him a mover and shaker in business. Not just a retired hockey player and high school coach. Plus, that kind of shit really helped recruit good players. Not only could he teach them hockey—he could teach them how to be a successful brand. That was becoming more and more important in the sports industry.

"You look like the cat who got the canary," Finn said, opening his locker beside him after coming back from the showers in a towel.

He wasn't the kind of player who danced on the ice after a goal, but he felt that urge now. "I got Reebok!"

"You did?" Finn chest butted him. "Of course you did. You have the proverbial nice guy image with the competitive drive everyone is looking for."

"So do you," Brock shot back, toning down their celebration when other players in the locker room looked over. "You need a better agent."

"You keep telling me that." Finn twisted his usual lumberjack face into a scary pantomime. "But can you see me grinning as I huck a soda pop or protein bars to aspiring hockey players? People would turn off the TV."

"You're an idiot," Brock said, shoving him playfully. "But you know I'd be happy to hook you up with Harold."

"You've been saying it since college days." Finn fist-bumped him. "But it's not me. Although Mason is going to shit a brick when he hears about it."

Brock scoffed. "Why? He's got a million endorsements."

"But not Reebok." Finn leaned in. "Plus, it's something you have and he doesn't, and you know the kid's competitive."

"He's a moron." He fought the urge to roll his eyes like Zeke. "I'm so out of here. See you, Finn."

"Later, man," Finn said, inclining his chin.

When Brock left the locker room, he spotted Darla talking with the Eagles' facility manager. As he neared, she broke off the conversation and started walking beside Brock, her face seemingly buried in her phone.

"Val realized you two didn't discuss the date venue," she said in an undertone, "so I'm here to ask for the place and time you have in mind so she can meet you there. Understanding, of course, that you both don't wish to be seen. I assume you have a low-profile location in mind."

He thought about stopping to talk but since she was pretending to text, he kept pace with her. "First, I don't date often. Second, I plan to pick her up since it's a date—"

"That's a no for her," Darla countered, pushing random buttons on her phone. "I told her you wouldn't like it, but she won't budge. She talked about the secrecy protocols needed until I wanted to plug my ears."

Usually, he would appreciate her wish to keep things low profile. He was a public figure and some of the women who'd gone after him wanted him to parade them through a crowded venue so they could be seen or post about it. But he wanted to be a gentleman, and he also really wanted to see where she lived. "Why don't you give me her number so I can call her?"

"Can't." She didn't look up as they turned the corner. "She didn't even like me giving you my number for the sightseeing. And before you argue, you should know I get both of your points of view here. You're going to want to do the man thing for the date. Like you should. But she's going to toe the line on secrecy, which protects you and her and even me, to some extent."

He uttered a heartfelt sigh. "So a public place is out. It's too cold to picnic. I can't invite her to my house—"

"You can have dinner at my place," Darla offered, still clicking away.

Fighting the urge to scowl took some doing. "That's nice of you, but why not hers?"

Darla's hands stopped tapping on her phone. "She's not ready for that. Look, she's already wigging out about how to dress tonight."

He did growl this time. "Call me old-fashioned, but I *was* hoping for a normal date."

"Oh, good Lord, you two. You make me want to bash my head with my phone. Now I'm the date mediator. Great. How about this? You come to my place for dinner, I convince her your goodwill gesture should be met with normal Val. No glasses, baggy clothes, or ugly tennis shoes."

Thank God they could agree on the shoes. Not that he would ever say that out loud. "Fine. This time."

"We're building trust here." She shot him a look. "Val doesn't really date much either, so don't mess up my dating machinations with piddly list items."

"Piddly? Who says that?"

She shushed him. "Keep your voice down. In the real world, I shouldn't even be walking with you. You're a hockey god, and I'm a piddly little assistant. Hence why I'm pretending to work on my phone. There, I used piddly *again*."

"Darla—"

"Now, hush." She went back to tapping on her phone.

"Do you want to bring dinner or have me arrange something? I'm fine either way."

He fought his frustration. The simple act of him grabbing takeout caused a media frenzy. "It would be easier if you arrange it, but I'll pay."

"If you fish money out of your pocket," she said, stopping him from reaching for his money clip, "I'll be tempted to knock it from your hand. You cannot be seen giving me money, Brock. Hello! It could be construed—"

"Jesus. Fine. This is getting complicated. All I wanted was to go out with a great girl—"

"Woman," she corrected, "and she's better than great. She's the best in the world. So, in sum—you come to my place, dinner will arrive. What time works for you?"

His brain brought up Miss Sexy Librarian in bed by nine with a book, in matching pajamas he'd want to rip off. "Seven?"

"Perfect." She stopped when they reached the door to the parking garage. "When Zeke was bemoaning eating Susan's pot roast yesterday, he mentioned that you're a pizza guy. Pizza would work for Val."

He appreciated her giving him some context for that detail, but then again, Val had already talked about pizza with Zeke. The kid talked to everyone about pizza. "Make sure it doesn't have a soggy crust. Val told me she doesn't like it."

She glanced up sharply. "She told you she loves pizza? Honey pie, you are ahead of the game."

Since no one was around, he gave in and winked. "I got her to go out with me, didn't I? And wear my jersey in the hot tub?"

Her laugh was low and slightly hair-raising. "Brilliant, I grant you, but that was one hurdle in a 110m hurdle race.

Stick with me. I'm on your side. I like you, Brock, and I like you for my girl. Don't prove me wrong. People have been known to disappear."

His low chuckle had her grinning. "I have a pretty good idea of what you're capable of."

"You think you do, honey, but let me assure you, Val and I have stories that would curdle your blood."

"I have no illusions, Darla. Chuck hired you."

They shared a look. "Right. No questions on that either —if you want to see Val again."

"We agreed to no work talk." He stared her down. "Anything else I need to know?"

She worried her lips before saying, "Expect to talk about yourself more."

He pointed at himself. "Me? But aren't men supposed to ask women interesting things about themselves?"

"Not tonight." She waggled her brows, making her tortoiseshell glasses slide on her nose. "Now, shoo. I've got a lot to do in a very short amount of time. Tell your family we had a ball yesterday. Also...don't mess this thing up with Val because we really love them. I am not going to stop seeing Kinsley. Got me?"

He knew the stakes. "Do I look stupid?"

She pulled her glasses down and studied him over the frames. "No, and I have high hopes for you, but your gender has a strong track record of messing good things up. Be above that. You're a winner, right? See you later, handsome."

He scowled at her as she hustled away. "My gender. Jesus. Is that librarian speak?" It didn't sound as cute when Darla did it.

Pulling open the door, he headed to his Rover. He probably should be insulted by her man jab. Hell, he should probably cancel the date after how he'd played in practice. He was distracted, off. Everyone had seen it.

But there was no way he was going to cancel. No, he was going to get his head on straight and go out with Val. Last time he looked, he could walk and chew gum at the same time, so to speak. He would find out a new balance in his life. He'd done it with his family. Now he would do it for her. Because she was worth it and then some...

He brought up an image of her standing in his jersey, her big green eyes locked on him. Cataloguing his body and his every reaction to seeing her.

She was complicated—she'd talked about secrecy protocols, for God's sake—but all he wanted to do was dive into the deep end with her. He didn't doubt it would feel good. Be fun even.

A dopey smile started to spread across his face as he strode across the parking lot. Fantasies of seeing her in something other than his jersey played in his mind. A dress... A lacy little teddy... Nothing at all...

His body voted for all three.

He pulled the car door open after the locks disengaged. Focus, he told himself. Before dinner, he would go home and watch tape. Play with Zeke maybe.

But he knew where half his mind would be.

On the mysteriously sexy Val.

And what she'd be wearing tonight.

Among other things.

ELEVEN

"Why do men make us lose our minds?" Val gestured to her navy blue dress after asking her question.

"Because they can." Darla picked up the brush Val had brought over to her loft and started gently combing out Val's hair. "What's wrong now?"

She tugged on the scoop neckline. "I'm doubting this choice. Doesn't it say too much? Like *hey, I never wear a dress and I'm really uncomfortable but trying to look nice.* Darla, I don't like this. Wanting to look nice for him. It's not me."

"Honey, with the right man, it's *all* of us." She sighed as she set the brush aside and cupped Val's face. "I know this is new territory—"

"*New?* Darla, this is the Matterhorn."

A gurgle of a laugh flirted out of her friend's mouth before she resumed brushing Val's hair. "As in the hardest mountain to climb until Edward Whymper conquered that bitch?"

"*Yes.*" Val took her hand before Darla could fluff her hair. "I can't be with a man like this. I don't feel like myself.

In fact, I feel almost sick. There's a pit in my stomach. I feel slightly nauseated. I had trouble keeping track of what Chuck was saying in the team meeting today because I could smell Brock. My notes suck. I didn't have a single interesting thought for our study today other than my ongoing thesis that Mason wears a fur coat much like the cavemen of old because he has an affinity for primal man."

"Do you think that's where Chuck got the idea?"

"Maybe." She smoothed down her hair with both hands because her hair didn't do bounce. "I don't know. I don't feel like I know anything right now. And stop fluffing my hair. I'm not a dog competing in the Westminster Kennel Club."

"You kinda are, honey." Darla bumped her. "Let's put on our PhD hats for a minute."

She tugged up the neckline of her dress and nodded briskly. "Yes, please. Lay it on me, Dr. James."

Darla flicked up one finger. "One, we've observed plenty of courtship rituals. A date is part of a courtship display, which is—"

"A set of display behaviors in which a person, usually a male, attempts to attract a mate. Except where a female has a choice in the courtship. Then she is also interested in sending messages to the male that she is interested in him physically as well as socially."

"Because the getting to know you phase gives each party the knowledge they need to determine whether they would make a strong union, leading to a successful mating, which leads to—"

"The contract of marriage—or reproduction." She clutched her stomach as SEX flashed in garish Vegas Strip lights in her head. "God, I'm going to be sick."

Darla heaved her up and anchored her hands on her shoulders. "No, you aren't. Because one, this is a first date.

A simple and easy getting to know you to determine if there will be another. It's a critical data gathering point, which is why there are so few second dates after a first."

Val frowned as a pain shot through her chest. She liked Brock. She wanted a second date with him. "Oh God, I really like him. Like really—"

"Yes, I know, honey." Darla resumed brushing her hair and twisting her locks into loose curls, like she was a Pekinese at a dog show!

She spun away, making the brush pull her hair, causing her to yelp like said bitch. "I wish you would have told me you knew how I felt so we could have discussed this rationally. I think I could have talked myself out of it."

Darla brushed her cheek, Dr. James gone, her BFF completely in command now. "I wouldn't have let you. Since I've known you, you have never once looked at a guy like you look at him. You haven't stumbled over your bag after a guy talks to you. You have never turned a cute little pink from having a guy look at your body like you did when you two came outside to the hot tub. And you have never laughed like you did with him when I made you two sing 'Islands in the Stream' for karaoke yesterday."

"That really was terrible of you." She could already feel a silly smile cruising over her face as she remembered how their voices had blended and their eyes had held. "But he really does have a great voice, doesn't he?"

"And there it is!" Darla turned her toward the mirror, standing behind her with her arms suddenly hugging her from behind. "That's why we walk down this path even though it makes us lose our minds. *That look.* Val, he lights you up inside. This Val—she's like the first sighting of a comet to me, honey. And I've been studying Valentina Hargrove's sky since the day we met. I thought I knew her every constellation and planet. I'm rooting for him. Because I love seeing you like this."

"Crazy for a guy?" Her silly smile faded. "Like I usually see you."

"No, honey." Darla laid her cheek next to hers. "Happy. Because you've achieved so many things. Done so many things. I've been there for most of them. But I've never seen this look. This Val. And I'll do everything in my power to keep her shining bright."

Her heart was full, like how it had been when she and Darla stayed up late watching movies in boarding school, their feet tangled together as they giggled like little girls. "I kinda like this Val too, even though I don't know her. Which leads me to wonder. How can Brock like this Val if I don't even know who she is?"

"That's the beauty of courtship, I imagine. When you happen upon a worthy mate—and Brock checks those boxes as healthy, attractive, smart, witty, and kind—then you go on a journey together to find out who you are together. Because being with someone—the right someone—brings out the best facets of us. Even when we didn't know they were there. Or so I like to believe, but you know me. I'm a sucker for happily ever after."

Val gave in to the unusual urge to hug her friend, and Darla wrapped her up in a tender embrace. "When you talk like that, I want to screen courtship candidates for you until my eyes bleed so you can have your HEA."

"That's why you're my bestie." Darla pulled back and twirled her hair into a wave. "Just be the Val I know. Because she's the best. Which is what I told Brock when I acted as your date mediator. Speaking of which. I need to get going so I can pick up the pizza and be back here in time for the crust not to get soggy. He told me he knows how you hate soggy crusts."

Her mouth did an arabesque into a smile. "He remembered that?"

"He did." She grabbed her diamond earrings from her jewelry case and held them out. "Before you protest. Courtship displays are important. We dress up for men to look good, yes, but we also do it to show him he means something to us, that he matters. I think you want Brock to feel that way when you open the door."

She did, she realized, as she put the earrings on. Her hands fell to her sides as she looked at herself. The navy color of the dress really did wonders for her skin while the modest neckline accentuated the slight curve of her breasts. Her hair looked rich and luxurious down and loosely curled, and the slight makeup Darla had insisted on accentuated her features, making her eyes seem bigger, her lips and cheeks rosier.

As a figure skater, she'd been expected to be beautiful all the time, to the point where it had held no meaning for her. It had become a means to an end for her mother, and ultimately, she'd hated the porcelain-doll routine.

But that wasn't the image before her.

She was a woman.

About to have her first date with the most compelling man she'd ever met.

"You look beautiful, Val."

She turned toward her friend. "I do, don't I? Thank you for helping me. And for listening to me getting a little crazy."

"I figured it was your turn after all the years you've listened to me." She tapped her nose playfully. "I'm off to be your take-out minion. Freshen up your lip gloss. Brock should be here shortly."

After blowing her a kiss, Darla left the bathroom. Val studied herself. She looked her best. Now she had to figure out what her best was when she was with Brock Thomson, because no other man had brought it out in her.

Her stomach heaved. The lead-up to this date was more terrifying than waiting to compete for Junior Olympic gold.

She turned away from the mirror and went to find herself the ginger ale she'd bought at a local grocery on her way over to settle her stomach.

When a playful knock sounded on Darla's door sometime later, she jumped in her chair. Her hands gripped the armrests as her controlled breathing shattered.

He was here!

God, did she need to check the mirror again? Was her lip gloss smeared from the glass of ginger ale?

"I'm losing my mind," she mumbled, forcing herself up. "Be calm, composed, and collected. Just like old times."

But this wasn't her figure skating days, because when a melodic pattern of knocks sounded, reminding her of a jingle she couldn't place, a smile started to tug at her mouth. *Elevated dopamine levels*, her academic side told her while another new side of her practically sang, *Isn't he cute, knocking like that?*

When she opened the door, she felt as if she were floating off the floor in pure joy. Brock was holding a bouquet of white calla lilies, and he'd clearly spent time on *his* courtship display. He was wearing a sexy blue suit with a white dress shirt—no tie—and he looked clean-shaven. His usual scent of pine and cloves was stronger tonight, combined with notes of musk and lime.

All sexy male, and for tonight, all hers.

Maybe courtship wasn't so bad.

"Hi there." He tilted his head to the side as he held out the flowers. "You look beautiful."

She wanted to duck her head in shyness as she took the flowers, fighting the urge to bury her face in them and sniff until her nose couldn't take any more. Like a teenage girl. Calla lilies didn't smell, so it was a perfectly illogical impulse, but she told herself to be patient with herself. "You look very nice too. Come in."

He walked in slowly and closed the door. The way it slicked shut was somehow erotic, and her mind called up the image of him shirtless in the hot tub with steam rising up around him. "I want to go on the record that I wanted to take you out. Pick you up. Help you take your coat off. Pull out your chair. Take you home. All of it. But I understand why we needed to do it like this."

She fell back into the ease of studying him. He was becoming her favorite subject, after all. "Darla mentioned you weren't sure why we weren't having dinner at my place."

He winced but lifted a broad shoulder. "You're a private person. We discussed that before. Like Darla said, we're building trust."

But she did trust him, she realized. And she trusted very few people. "It seemed better to start at a neutral site, of sorts. Maybe next time." Then she grimaced. "I'm so sorry. I'm not assuming—"

"Val..." He crossed and laid his large hand on her arm, sending her nerve endings to the moon. "I knew the moment you opened the door that I'd want to do this again."

She blinked. "Why then?"

His mouth tilted to the side in another spellbinding smile. "Because I'm finding myself obsessed with seeing you like this—the real you. Although I like seeing the old you too. I just knew something was off. You're gorgeous and hot and mysterious, and I'm intrigued by you so much that I blew practice today. In case you didn't notice."

The amount of carbon dioxide fighting to be exhaled could fill up a tank, but she tried not to exhale sharply at his very alluring opening. As a courtship opener, he was in a class all his own. "I might have realized something was up when Chuck blew his whistle and yelled at you. I've never seen him do that with you."

His face seemed to darken. "That's because I usually don't give him cause. It's had me worried. All this thinking about you."

The honest assessment of his behavior was clinically comfortable and emotionally assuring. "I had trouble paying attention in the team meeting, and I didn't have a single creative thought today. That's rare for me."

He angled closer to her, his sexy, skin-tingling scent making her knees feel like she'd done a thousand leg lifts. "So we're both feeling distracted."

"Darla—and Masters and Johnson—assure me this is a normal biological reaction to the opposite sex."

He looked to be biting the inside of his cheek. "Masters and Johnson... The scientists who wrote *Human Sexual Response*. I caught the TV series about them on Showtime when I was on the road once. It was interesting, to say the least."

Hearing the way his deep baritone voice said *sexual* from his full lips had her belly tightening. "Yes, that's them. They outlined the biological essence of male and female interactions as related to sexual attraction and relations."

His blue eyes speared her with a heated glance, and her

brain cheered the attraction indicator. "Is this light reading after you finish up at the arena?"

She became a little self-conscious. "Are you making fun of me?"

"Never." He took a step closer and lifted his hand to play with the hair resting against her right shoulder and breast. "I like it when you go into sexy librarian mode."

Her mouth went dry. Her heart rate cantered. She lost track of what she was saying as she stared into his warm blue eyes. "Ah...where was I?"

"You were telling me about sexual attraction and relations—and essences."

His voice was velvety soft, igniting an inferno of desire in her core regions. Belly. Thighs. Even her breasts felt tight. She'd never experienced this level of arousal before— with any of her three partners. Before, she'd looked on sex as a human act to be explored as much for the scientific miracle it was as for the personal experience.

The miracle hadn't been obvious with her partners, and as a personal experience, she'd been more excited to dissect her first frog. A vibrator—courtesy of Darla for her birthday—had given her a glimpse of the miracle. But she'd never hungered for it.

Not like she hungered for the man in front of her.

"Val..."

Brock's use of her name brought her back. "I...umm—"

"Maybe we should get ourselves a drink and sit down while you tell me more. Before I give in to the urge to kiss you. Right now."

Kiss her?

This soon? "But I thought that came at the end of the evening on a first date in most cases."

He fought what looked like a grin. "Usually... But we're in new territory."

"You realize that too?" She nearly slumped in relief that it was out in the open.

"I do. Didn't you hear me mention my focus issues today?" He took her elbow and gently led her through the open family room to the kitchen.

"Exactly!" She tripped a couple of steps in the heels Darla had insisted she put on before he capably righted her. "My attraction indicators for you are at extreme levels, Brock. Scientifically compelling. Personally alarming, honestly."

God, was she saying too much? "I don't mean alarming like it's completely bad," she continued, pausing to glance outside. Snow was falling now amidst the bright lights of downtown. Her body was so warm she wanted to rush outside and let it cool down her heated skin.

"That's good to hear," he said, amusement lacing his voice. He was so large he was almost taking up as much space as the refrigerator, she realized. "What are you drinking tonight?"

"Ginger ale." She pressed a hand to her stomach. "It's snowing, and I'm driving. I'm not used to driving much anymore. Especially in a big city. Oh, I'm talking too much. I'm not even making sense. Usually, I'm composed."

"I know."

"I'm practically babbling like a gray mouse lemur."

The rumble of a chuckle escaped him, kicking up her desire levels. "It looks good on you."

She glanced up into his understanding eyes, as blue as a clear sky. "I'm not myself. I mean, I was prepared for the elevated heart rate and the increase in body temperature.

And the high dopamine levels that make me want to keep smiling at you."

"I do like seeing you smile." He was leaning against the granite countertop, his casual pose like a tidal wave of potent masculinity.

She waved her hands. "But this frantic mental activity, where I can't keep a calm thought in my head, is completely unacceptable and so not me. I *always* know what I'm going to say. In school I was a lead debater. I'm acclaimed for my lectures."

She slapped a hand over her mouth.

"Oh, God, I wasn't supposed to tell you that! We weren't supposed to talk about me or work or anything important. This was the getting to know you phase. First date. A light dusting of facts and engagement around topics of mutual interest."

"A light dusting of facts, huh?"

"You *are* laughing at me!"

He stood and walked over to her like a jaguar who'd only just awoken from a long, restful nap. "Val, if you knew what was going through my head right now, you'd know laughing is the furthest thing from my mind. The way you're acting is downright sexy and adorable. I'm doing my best not to kiss you senseless."

She wanted to kiss him too, she realized. *Leap up and wrap her arms around his neck* kiss him. "Do you think it would help? Stop you from thinking about it, I mean, and me from babbling?"

The look he leveled at her, filled with heat and amusement, had her smiling at him. For no reason. Goodness. She was setting smile records for the *Guinness Book of World Records*.

"Are you asking me to kiss you? Because I pretty much

repeated *end of the night* over and over to myself as a mantra all the way from my house so I wouldn't move too fast."

"Too fast? Did you not hear me talking about alarming rates of physical attraction indicators?"

"I did—and the whole lemur comment." He put his arm around her waist and drew her to him so slowly it made concepts like physics' debunking of time and space become credible. "Which I kinda imagined you saying wearing those thick glasses with your hair up. I might need to hear the daytime Val say something like that. But only for me."

She stared up at his towering physique, the angles of his rock-hard jaw and face shadowed by the overhead lighting. "Only for you... Proprietary urges in males are common indicators of physical attraction."

He cupped her cheek in his hot hand, making her want to curl into him. "Are they? Well, truthfully, I seem to be having a lot of proprietary urges when it comes to you, Ms.... What is your last name, by the way?"

Oh, God! The moment she'd been dreading. She squeezed her eyes shut. "I can't tell you. I told you—work and this have to be separate."

"Your last name is off-limits?"

She opened her eyes when she heard him utter a harsh sigh.

She bit her lip. "I'm sorry, but it's for you as much as for me."

"What are you? In witness protection?"

Her brow rose of its own volition. "If I were in witness protection, I wouldn't be concerned about you knowing my last name, as it would be a fake name."

His shoulders started to shake. "Okay, so you're going to remain a woman of mystery, down to your last name. I can live with that for now, but that might need change. I'm only warning you."

"Duly warned and appreciated."

"So, in moments like this, I'll have to call you...Miss Sexy Librarian." His blue eyes seemed to twinkle like the Milky Way. "If that doesn't offend you."

A shiver went down her spine. "Since I admire librarians, I will not take insult. And no one has ever called me sexy before, so it may take me some time for it to sink in."

He zoomed back. "No. One. Has. Ever. Called. You. Sexy? Where in the hell have you been living?"

"I can't tell you that either," she blurted out, the urge to start laughing at her own ridiculousness rising within her. "Oh my God, before I ruin everything, will you please just shut me up and kiss me?"

"With pleasure," he growled as he yanked her to him and lowered his head.

His lips touched hers, and the heat and roughness of them shocked her already electric senses. She didn't know what to do or where to put her hands. His maleness was overwhelming. The heat of him, the scent, and the taste. *My God, the taste!* How did she not know a man tasted like this?

But instinct, primal and primordial, kicked in. She rose on her tiptoes to better meet his mouth and wrapped her arms around his strong neck, knowing she would be supported. Their bodies brushed at the contact, igniting a wall of fire down her torso. The large hand around her waist tightened while the other threaded itself into her hair, tugging at her nape in the most delicious way imaginable.

He kissed better than anyone she'd ever known. Not that she'd kissed many men. But his skill shouldn't have been surprising, perhaps. He was a professional athlete, and he gave his best to everything he did.

Including kissing her—slowly and with so much thoroughness every thought evaporated from her mind as her body took over.

Her belly contracted as their shared heat slid down to her thighs, where she was pressed against his front. She could feel his arousal against her, and the urgent press of his manhood had her tugging her mouth free so her head could fall back. She took gulps of air as his mouth pressed kisses to the side of her neck, where her pulse beat strongly against her skin. A moan erupted from deep inside her, a shocking sound, woven with a torrent of longing and temptation. She wove her hand into his thick black curls, the silky texture sending shivers up and down her spine as his scent filled her senses—pine, cloves, and aroused male.

She cupped his smooth jaw, feeling the strength of his bones, and guided his mouth back to hers. Together, they tumbled down the rabbit hole of lust, urgency, and desire.

His tongue slid between her lips, something she'd never fully understood and enjoyed, and for a moment she froze. He slowed down then, beckoning her with long strokes of skin-on-skin rubbing that had another moan tumbling up her throat. This was French kissing? Now it all made sense.

Soon, she was pressing her tongue between his lips, matching him, arousal climbing a steep peak inside her. Matterhorn peak.

The lock to the loft turning reached her and had her springing back, her hand pressed to her tingling mouth. "Darla," she whispered harshly as her friend entered the loft.

"Oops! Did I catch you two kissing? I'll just leave the pizza here on this table and take my pretty self off. Val, I'm staying at your place tonight, so if you need to stay here... Ta-ta, sweeties."

Val looked frantically at Brock, who let out a long, agonizing breath. The door clicked shut. The silence in the loft was somehow audible—even over the pounding of her heart in her ears. Horror at how far she'd almost gone had her mouth gaping in shock.

"We almost—"

"Don't go babbling again for no reason," Brock said, pulling her gently to him and cupping her cheek tenderly. "We were barely to first base."

Given her lack of experience—and the fact that all of her three partners had been British, scientists, and more inclined to follow space travel than baseball—she didn't feel she could debate him properly.

She knew what had happened to her—a lifetime of restraint had shattered in moments, her understanding about what constituted kissing and physical contact between men and women ripped asunder.

She'd read discourses on sex and physical attraction. Pored over volumes by the greatest experts in the world—only to discover she personally hadn't known or understood anything. Copernicus must have felt this way when he'd discovered the earth circled the sun and not the other way around.

"You should know I'm a little unclear about the base metaphor. I understand penetrative sex is the home run, and I think kissing is first base, but—"

He laid one tantalizing finger over her mouth, a sexy smile lighting up his rough, desire-stamped face. "We were running to second base maybe. A little faster than I'd told myself to go tonight. Val, I don't want you to think I'm rushing you."

She felt her mouth drop. "*Rushing me?* You aren't rushing me. This—" She gestured to their bodies. "This is primal physical attraction. It's textbook, Brock."

"*Textbook.*" He started to laugh, wrapping his arms around her. "I love how you talk, Val, whatever your last name is. And yes, this is primal physical attraction. Stronger than I've ever experienced."

"Me too!" She laid her head against the soft wool of his suit, smiling when she heard his heart pounding. "It's like you're facing your greatest competitor in some ways."

He leveled back, his gaze heavily lidded but curious. "What do you mean?"

"Well, a competitor brings out new and unexpected facets inside of us. They challenge us, which can either take away our focus or hone it. Like you challenge me."

A provocative glint appeared. "I love it when you talk like this."

"That's why I found my focus dropping in and out during the team practice this morning. All I could think about was you and how you looked without a shirt on. Oh my God! See! There I go again."

She dug her face into his suit again.

"You thought about me being shirtless today, huh?" he asked, his voice husky.

"Yes, of course, and last night." She lifted her head, staring at him like he'd grown two heads. "Did you not hear me when I was talking about physical attraction indicators?"

"I'm catching on. So…one of those indicators is thinking about the other person's body?"

She nodded over a gulp.

"Then you should know, I have that indicator too. In spades."

She was immediately breathless, imagining the arousal on his face as he thought about her body. Nostrils flared. Heat in his eyes. Like yesterday. "Good to know. Elevated heart rate is obvious. I could hear it when I pressed my face to your chest. What about raised body temperature?"

He gave her a slow, toe-curling once-over. "Val, we're talking white-hot levels here. I feared I might melt the ice today because I was thinking so much about you."

"Goodness!" She put her hand to her chest. "That *is* hot. Because the ice is twenty-four degrees Fahrenheit."

Another dark chuckle made her skin electric. "You would know that, and all I want to do is kiss you again."

All Dr. Valentina Hargrove, PhD, could answer was a banal, "Okay."

He tipped her chin up and kissed her slowly, so slowly, she felt her heart roll over in her chest, even though that was physically impossible. When he angled back and caressed her cheek, all she wanted to do was gaze up at him. And never stop.

"Our pizza is getting a soggy crust," he said in that low, husky voice. "I know how much you hate it. I'm going to reheat it for you."

The sweetness of such a gesture was shocking. Was this a courtship display? If it was, the act was better than receiving flowers. Homey, comforting, and thoughtful in a way she'd never imagined. She rather liked it.

"I don't feel hungry for food." She leaned into his touch. "All day I was slightly nauseous. I even bought ginger ale to settle my stomach."

His hand caressed the line of her belly, making her fight off a moan in the back of her throat. "Are you still feeling that way?"

She made herself take a clinical inventory. It was either

that or have him demonstrate more of the baseball bases metaphor. "Not nauseous, but my belly feels tight. Masters and Johnson would say that is likely an indicator of need. In the excitement level."

"Need, huh?" He kissed her again, his tongue slipping inside her mouth to drive her mad before breaking the contact, his breath hot on her face. "Tell me more about the excitement level? Wait, better not. This is a proper date, after all."

Proper date. She couldn't help smiling.

He kissed her once again before stepping away from her, backward, with the same kind of grace he could skate backward. He was a pleasure to watch. In all the ways.

Most especially in the excitement level.

"I'm going to grab the pizza." The finger he pointed at her held a coach-like authority. "You turn on the oven. We'll eat. Have a beverage. Talk. And then do whatever you want to do. Ideas?"

Her head turned to the windows. "How about we watch the snow fall?" Then another thought came, not from a list of academic courtship rituals but from her. "And hold hands. Maybe— No, it's silly."

"Tell me."

She heard the hope in his voice, and it gave her the courage to share. "Ah...how about we make hot chocolate and then walk through the snow, holding hands. That seems...nice."

His mouth formed another devasting, almost boyish smile. "It does, doesn't it? Consider it our post-meal activity, then."

He turned around and started toward the pizza. She moved to heat up the stove. It felt good to fall in this simple pattern of working together. The opening steps in a partnership.

"Hey, Val."

She looked over.

He'd stuck his hands in his pockets.

"What?"

"You remember how I said I knew I wanted a second date the moment you opened the door?"

Her throat grew tight, emotional longing overwhelming the previous physical sensations. "I remember."

"I just want to be sure we're on the same page..." He looked her straight in the eye, the tough warrior shining in his gaze. "I really like you. And I know you have your reasons for keeping things from me, but I need to know. None of those reasons can hurt me or my family, right?"

She thought of the contents of their study. Her father or Chuck planned to use it to motivate the team, if needed, which meant she and Brock shared the same goal. They all wanted the team to succeed.

Satisfied that she'd done her internal due diligence, she shook her head and smiled. "No, like I've told you all along, this sexy librarian—and her best friend—are here to help you and the team. When you hear more about it, you're probably going to laugh or maybe you'll be interested. Since you like the way I talk. Because it really is fascinating."

The initial findings were heading toward an expected conclusion: hockey players *were* modern cavemen. Textbook, really.

"Good." He suddenly was shrugging out of his jacket and rolling up his sleeves, stealing her breath. "And you're right. I do like the way you talk."

"I'm probably going to talk like that more."

His brows rose to his forehead. "I can't wait. Oh, and

pour me some ginger ale too. I'm feeling a little queasy myself all of a sudden."

"You are?" She would need to note his physical reactions in her private field diary, the one she should probably simply call WHAT BROCK THOMSON DOES TO ME.

"I most certainly am, Miss Sexy Librarian."

As he headed for the pizza, she found herself prancing the rest of the way to the stove, the melody of Vivaldi's "Spring" playing in her head. They were both nauseous, experiencing the same unpredictable and utterly compelling indicators of physical attraction. Wasn't it wonderful? Darla was right.

She couldn't be happier.

TWELVE

"Why do girls beat around the bush and not tell us what the issue is and then get mad when we don't figure it out?"

Brock swung his head over to look at his nephew. Zeke's big brown eyes seemed even bigger as he tugged on his seat belt, his backpack resting in his lap.

"Are you talking about why Kinsley slammed the bathroom door shut on you this morning and is now making us wait?" he asked mildly.

His nephew balled his fists up and set them to his forehead. "All I said was that it was nice that she looked normal again."

Brock eyed the clock on the dashboard. He needed to get these kids to school, and this morning's altercation was threatening to put him behind schedule. "Let's be honest. You poked the bear for no reason. Kinsley has been dressing normal since Val and Darla came over."

"So I wanted to encourage her."

As if. "You said, 'Hey, moron, you look almost normal

again.' When she let out an aggravated scream, you asked why. Then she slammed the door."

Had he ever been this clueless with women? Probably.

"Girls are the worst!" His nephew let out a feral cry and put his fists to his eyes. "Uncle Brock, you have the best job ever. You hang with guys all day. I've decided that's another reason I want to be a professional hockey player."

"Because you won't have to deal with girls?" he asked, trying not to laugh. "But that's not completely true. Val and Darla work for the team."

"Yeah, but they're not *weird* girls like Kinsley and my mom. Last night, Mom started huffing at me for no reason and when I asked her why, all she said was, 'you know why.' Like I'm a mind reader. I'm twelve!"

Having his family live with him was showing Brock the ins and outs of their family dynamic. Right now, he was trying to be a sounding board and help out when he could. He was not the kids' father. He was the uncle, and uncles were better loved to his mind, because they didn't have to do shit like laying down the law.

He made sure to keep his voice un-accusing. "I think she was referring to the mess you'd made in the dining room."

"I was going to clean it up this morning." He sighed heartily. "I can't please anybody right now. Except for you, Uncle Brock. Can we go away and do some ice fishing or winter camping on your next day off? I need to get away from these women!"

Brock frowned, wondering where Zeke had gotten that idea from. Then it hit him. He'd bet the kid had picked it up from Darren. The asshole who'd told his wife that she and the kids were an inconvenience. Although he didn't think Zeke fully meant it.

"Your mom and sister are pretty great, all things considered, you know. You're lucky to have them."

"Maybe," came the reluctant reply.

The door to the garage opened, and a very pissed-off Kinsley gave it whiplash. As she walked to the car, her open coat displayed their worst nightmare. She was wearing the Eagles jersey Val had written on, the one that said SEE ME.

"Uh-oh," Zeke groaned.

Brock tapped the steering wheel. "Didn't I say you poked the bear?"

Kinsley pulled the back passenger side door open and then gave it a proper slam behind her. Terrific. He had a boy poised on the threshold of becoming a man, asking questions men had been asking about women since time began, and a teenage girl still trying to find herself and her place in the world.

"Everyone ready to go?" Brock asked conversationally, slowly backing out of the driveway.

The silence in the car might as well have been as loud as an air horn. Zeke jerked his head back toward Kinsley. Brock shot him a look. Was the kid really thinking he would try peacemaking now? His nephew scrunched up his face and continued to slouch.

By the time Brock pulled out of the neighborhood, Zeke's fists were pressed against his thighs, and he looked like a bottle of shaken soda ready to pop its top.

"Anyone care for some music?" Brock asked, putting a toe into the fray.

"Kinsley, you pick," Zeke offered, craning his neck to see if she'd take the peace offering.

"I am not talking to you, moron!" she yelled.

Zeke let out an aggrieved cry. "Look, I'm sorry. I didn't mean to make you mad. All I was trying to say was that you looked like you used to. That's not a bad thing, and if you weren't being so stupid, you'd know it."

"Okay, that's enough name-calling," Brock said with a wince as he realized he sounded like his father. "Kinsley, Zeke is sorry he hurt your feelings. You can stay angry if you want. But I won't have you both continuing this fight. Got it? Tell me instead how we can turn this morning around so you can have a good day."

"I want to call Darla and Val."

His gaze tracked to his niece, staring mulishly ahead in the back seat, her face a complete return to misery. She looked small again, like a tire someone had let the air out of. Then he winced. That terrible kind of analogy was how Zeke had poked the bear this morning. "If you want, I can give them a note."

He thought that a fair compromise. Kinsley was looking for connection and understanding, but he didn't want to give his niece an all-access pass to the women. Especially when one of them, namely the woman now entered into his phone as Miss Sexy Librarian, had been reluctant to give him her number.

Even after he'd kissed her senseless and shown her what second base meant.

"I don't want to send them a note, Uncle Brock." She leaned forward, her big hazel eyes pleading. "I want to *talk* to them. On the phone."

"Kinsley—"

"No!" she cried out, her eyes glistening now. "I know what you're going to say. Mom told me too. They work for the Eagles, and that's where you work. We need to keep things professional. But I don't work with them."

She had him there. "You're right—"

"They understand me!" Her voice choked on the end.

Pain shot through his chest at her anguished plea. "I know they do, Kinsley."

He paused—because he didn't know what to say. *I'm starting to date Val, and keeping that professional and secret from work is hard enough?* He certainly didn't want to say he didn't want his niece to get even more attached if things didn't work out between him and Val.

"Please, Uncle Brock," she whispered when he remained silent.

"I'll talk to them, Kinsley." He could feel a headache starting at the base of his skull. "That's all I can promise. Okay?"

She flounced back in her seat, crossing her arms protectively around herself. Zeke slumped forward in his seat, head bowed in what looked like defeat.

Brock hated that look. Defeat wasn't in his vocabulary. When he played and lost a game, he didn't say the other team had defeated them but that they'd played better that day. So he was struggling with what to do and say, knowing his niece and nephew were trying to understand the fallout of their parents' marriage, their new place in the world, and a new reality of living with their uncle and not seeing their fucknut of a father who hadn't really loved or appreciated them and was supposedly "off" doing his music and wouldn't be coming back.

He needed counsel, and he knew who he needed to go to for it—the same people Kinsley wanted to call.

And did that make him a hypocrite or what? He wasn't sure, and the thought sat like undigested steak tartare in his gut.

By the time he got to the arena after dropping the kids off, he was sporting a massive headache and an uncomfortable ache in his chest. He didn't know how to help them, and that kind of powerlessness made him feel like he was skating on thin ice.

Worse, the happiness he'd felt at the thought of seeing Val today, knowing how she tasted and felt like in his arms, was completely gone. He left the car, slamming his door shut because it felt good.

Mason zoomed past him and swerved into his parking spot two spaces down, honking the horn of his 1969 convertible hugger orange Camaro, another homage to *Fight Club*. Brock didn't want to deal with the kid today off the ice, so he strode toward the door to the parking garage, prepared to take the stairs to the main floor so he wouldn't be caught waiting for the elevator.

"Hey, Brock!"

Mason's rough voice resonated in the lot as much as on the ice. Brock increased his pace.

"I heard about the Reebok deal! You should just stick to coaching snot-nosed kids at St. Lawrence when you retire."

Rushed footsteps sounded behind him. Mason was running him down. Shit. He pulled the door open and took the stairs two at a time.

"That deal was mine, motherfucker!" the kid shouted.

Brock stopped a floor above him and looked down over the railing. "Then why did they give it to me? Jesus, kid, grow the fuck up."

He didn't wait for a response, but he caught Mason's middle finger slashing up in the air.

That made him pause. "You need to back down and remember what's important here. Petty squabbles with me aren't going to get us the Cup. If you're not here to win it all, you should find another team."

When he reached the main floor, he headed to the

locker room to change, never more grateful for an off-ice individual training day.

Finn was already warming up when he hit the gym, hands pressed against the wall as he stretched his hamstrings. "Whoa! You practically reek of sulfur today."

"What?" he snapped, filing next to him against the wall and taking the same pose.

"You look like hell, man." Finn stood and stretched his hands over his head, tipping from left to right.

"I had a bad morning." He blew out a full steam of frustration. "Kinsley and Zeke got into it. Then I ran into Mason, who apparently heard about the Reebok deal even though it hasn't been announced yet."

"You know those deals don't stay secret, man," Finn reminded him. "Plus, you've looked happier than usual. As well as distracted. It was an easy guess."

That happiness and distraction had to do with Val, but he wasn't planning on sharing that. His dating life was no one's business. Not that he was sure Finn would see it that way, since they'd been friends since college. But he wasn't ready to spill yet.

"Let's get to work." He signaled to their trainer that they were ready to start.

He and Finn were in the same training group, each one based on the players' specific needs, with consideration to both movement restrictions and injury histories. Mason liked to joke Brock and Finn were in the Geriatric Squad.

With that thought to motivate him, he dug in. The speed, power, and strength exercises gave him a good burn, and by the time Mason entered the gym and shot him a nasty look, he was in his zone.

Brock "The Rock" couldn't be touched there. He was locked. He was focused. He was completely in control.

The routine anchored him. He was doing the squat rotation—goblet squats, front squats, box squats, and asymmetrical squats—when he caught a clean, crisp scent in the air. His breathing went from slow and even to deep, lusty inhalations.

Val.

He could feel his focus slip, like a towel falling away from his neck after a hot shower. His head swung to the right, and his eyes zeroed in on her, standing next to Chuck and Darla at the edge of the gym.

His heart went to triple speed as he lowered his body, keeping up the rhythm of his squats. But he lost the count as his skin prickled with awareness. Even through those ugly thick glasses, he knew those beautiful green eyes were watching him.

A low guttural sound rumbled around in his throat as he went lower in his squats. He liked the idea of her watching him. Seeing how strong and powerful he was. What his body was capable of.

Because it was only a preview of what his body wanted to do with hers.

The pumping of his heart grew louder in his ears along with his harsh breathing.

"Slow and steady wins the race, Brock," his trainer reminded him.

Idiot.

Didn't he know when a man wanted to impress his woman?

He growled as he continued the reps, his muscles burning.

"Jesus, man," Finn called out, standing up in the group along with the other players who'd been doing the exercises with him. "You're killing it today."

He only grunted, his eyes locked across the room. Chuck had stopped speaking, and so had Darla. But even from the distance between them, he could see the faint pulse in Val's neck, the one he'd kissed and licked and tasted last night.

"Shit, man!" one of the players from another group shouted as they came over to rubberneck. "You go!"

"Yeah, old man," Mason called, appearing on the edge of the gathering crowd. "Show us how the Geriatric Squad does it."

He glared at Mason. Call him that shit in front of his woman? He'd show him. A ripple of shock flickered in Mason's eyes as he stared him down. The men around him began chanting, "Brock, Brock, Brock."

By now he was used to it. Didn't even hear it. But when Val's mouth formed his name with her lusty, unpainted mouth, he wanted to roar in triumph.

Yes.

Her.

Watch.

She was all he could see as he kept up his pace, over and over again, muscles screaming, sweat dripping, heart racing.

He felt like a god, and all he wanted to do was offer up his body and take her when she said *Yes*.

"Okay, that's enough!" Chuck called out. "Nice to see you're more focused today, but save some for the ice, Brock! But you other bozos could learn from him. That's dedication to your sport. That's what I need from you to win the Cup."

Brock slowed his pace so he wouldn't strain anything and was aware of a wave of fire running up and down his legs. Leg burn, the good kind that only came from a no-holds-barred workout.

Finn pressed a towel into his hands, and Brock used it to wipe the sweat dripping from his face and the back of his neck. Knowing Val was still watching had his skin prickling with awareness again.

He had never felt more alive, knowing she was here, watching him at his best.

A tornado couldn't have stopped him from meeting her gaze head-on. His heart pulsed in deep, throbbing beats in his chest. His blood raced through his veins.

All he wanted to do was cross to her, pick her up, and carry her to the nearest surface, covering her with his length.

She stood taller moments later, and he knew she was pressing her shoulders back and standing tall in that baggy black T-shirt. Calling on that cool composure that so fascinated him—and made him eager to strip it away.

Val swallowed slowly and then stiffly turned, muttering something to Darla, before the two walked out.

But his mouth tipped up even though she'd disappeared from view.

Because he knew how he'd affected her.

He knew where they were heading.

And after today, from both of their reactions, they needed to head there soon.

THIRTEEN

"How is it you tell a man one thing and he does the opposite?"

Val was glad few women used the female bathroom in the Eagles' facility as she pressed a cold, wet paper towel to the back of her heated neck.

"I think it's because they excel at putting their wishes ahead of ours." Darla sank back against the vanity, crossing her ankles. "You're in pretty bad shape, aren't you?"

"Did you not just see what happened in there?" She couldn't stop panting after seeing Brock in the gym. "He— Oh God! I almost moaned in there! After I expressly reminded him to act like nothing had happened between us."

"Yeah..." Darla only agreed, picking at her fingernails.

"What was he thinking? Doing that and staring at me?"

"I hate to tell you this, sweetheart, but he did it because you *were* there. All his good intentions went by the wayside seeing you."

"What?" She nearly dropped the towel down her back. "Why would he do that?"

"Val, how many times have we watched male warriors try and impress females in their tribe?" Darla asked, cocking her brow over her tortoiseshell glasses.

She fanned herself with her free hand. "But I'm not— He's not— God, I can't even speak coherently."

"It's the man virus, honey." Darla grabbed another paper towel and wet it before handing it to her. "You can't stop it. It gets in your blood. It takes you over. It makes you—"

"Crazy! I could barely sleep last night. All I could do was replay our date and smile. That's it. Replay and smile. Like a stupid lovesick girl."

"You've never been that girl, Val." Darla stroked her chin thoughtfully. "Like I said, I really like her."

"Well, I don't right now." She pressed her hand to her heated forehead. "I wanted to cheer him on and shout his name back there, Darla."

"You want to shout his name in another setting too, and that scares you," her friend told her with her usual candor.

She clenched her eyes shut and tipped her head toward the ceiling. "I didn't know it was like this. All these years. Even when I watched you go through this, time after time, I didn't get it."

"I know you didn't, honey," she said softly.

She opened her eyes and gazed at her friend. Darla didn't have her usual sassy radiance, and Val hated that she'd thrown a blanket over it. "I'm sorry. If I ever did or said something that wasn't understanding. Because I'm sure I did. I was so practical about it. I was so academic. I...didn't understand."

"You were the voice of wisdom when my inner goddess was raging." Darla took her hand and squeezed it. "You did what a best friend did. I needed that. Like you need me to do for you now."

"I don't know what to do with all of this... It's like extreme weather events got sucked inside me. I'm an earthquake and a hurricane and a tornado. I want him, Darla. More than maybe anything I've wanted in my whole life. Somehow even more than you, because you were so easy. You were just the other part of my heart when I met you. With him— It's like—"

When Val faltered, Darla slung an arm around her and pulled her closer at the sink. "Tell me."

"It's like I want to spend every moment with him. Know everything there is to know about him. Devour him from head to toe. Make him smile. Make him laugh. Make him... Call me Miss Sexy Librarian in that rich, velvety voice of his."

"He does that?" Darla fanned herself. "Whoa, mama, you've got a hot one on your hands. Which I saw in spades in that gym back there. Whew!"

"I know!" She turned and gripped the sink, studying her flushed face in the mirror. "God, if my dad saw me like this. But maybe he will since he seemed to know I hadn't been ice skating yet."

"Hey, now, let's calm down." Darla took her by the shoulders. "You are so not yourself if you believe that about your dad. Now, listen to me. You are falling for a really good man, one who makes your body scream with lust."

The thought of screaming sent her arousal indicators through the roof. *"Oh, God!"*

"Hush, honey. Because like you said, I have more experience with the man virus than you do. Right?"

She nodded stiffly.

"And you trust me..."

"I do."

"If I thought for a second that you should run from this, you'd trust me, wouldn't you? If I told you this man was not worth your time—that he was only going to break your heart and ruin you for other men for a while—you'd pack a suitcase and we'd blow town, right?"

"You know I would." Her practical reasoning hadn't completely deserted her.

"You've done it for me plenty of times." Darla gave a little snort of laughter. "Do you remember that charming cartel leader with the cocky smile and the great hair? You got me out of Bogota the day after I met him, when I was on the verge of accepting his invitation for the long weekend up at his estate in the mountains."

Val bit the inside of her lip. "You even talked about learning how to dance the cumbia and improve your Spanish while searching for bulletproof clothing online from one of the cartel's haute couture shops downtown."

Darla burst out laughing. "Tailor-made bulletproof clothing like it's from Fifth Avenue. God, I was a mess. Only in Colombia... But I still kinda have regrets about not getting that one red dress. It *was* stunning."

Val could feel an answering laugh welling up inside her. "You would have had Jorge—"

"It was Juan," she corrected.

"No, Juan was in Mexico City when we went to study the Nahua people."

Darla counted on her fingers. "You're right. He's the fifth J in a long line of Js. Why am I so bad with men whose names start with J? God, Freud would have a field day with me."

Val shrugged. They had long debated this question.

"The best theory remains that your father's name starts with a *J*."

"Love is the worst," Darla breathed out before she smiled softly, wonder stealing over her face. "Except when it's the best. And honey, I think Brock is one of the best. You should go for him. All the way."

Her throat went dry. She clenched her fists to her sides as the mere thought sent desire flooding through her system. "I can't control what I feel for him."

She touched her cheek tenderly. "I know it's scary, honey. But that's how it is for all of us. Him too, I imagine. Because he couldn't stop trying to impress you in the gym when he knew better, and even in his prime condition, he's going to be feeling that burn in his backside for a few days. Maybe you could rub some tiger balm on it for the poor fella."

Val tried and failed to stop chuckling. "Tiger balm? Really?"

"It's a thought." Darla twirled the ends of her hair playfully. "Action and practical assistance are where you excel, Dr. Hargrove."

She gave a mocking bow. "Why thank you, Dr. James."

But the image of Brock's rock-hard butt popped into her mind, and all too easily she could smell the menthol of the tiger balm, a balm she was all too familiar with from her figure skating days, on her hands as she imagined running them over his beautiful glutes.

"You need another date with him. Soon. I know it's tough with the game schedule, but on his next night off, you have him over to your house. Because you'll want him in your bed. Besides, I suspect that man is going to want to stay after, and you'll be more comfortable there. Plus, cuddling."

The floor dropped from her stomach. "*Cuddling?* What do I know about cuddling?"

"You did it with me when we were in boarding school. This just involves a big hulky man and his joystick."

"You were waiting to make a stick joke!"

"Honey, it's all about the stick—and the man it comes with. The trick is to find a man you want and a stick you want in the same person. You've got that with Brock."

She did, and she knew it.

Her secondary field diary—now titled BROCK—detailed that experience in precise, academic terms.

"My house, huh?" Although it didn't feel like her house yet since it was a temporary furnished rental.

Darla turned the sink on and flicked water playfully toward her. "You need to cool down, Val."

"If I sleep with him, will it make me feel like my old self?" she whispered as vulnerability rocked her.

Darla shut off the sink. "Sometimes it goes away instantly. Itch. Scratch. Basic causality. But in your case... It will likely strengthen things. When you make love with a man—really make love to him, and he you—you come away stronger. Inside. I don't know how better to say it. I only know it's true."

Emotion clogged her throat. "You're thinking of Tony."

"Always." She got that dreamy smile on her face as she inhaled richly, as if the air was scented with roses instead of bathroom cleaner. "He was my first. And best. Maybe being so young made it all the more intense and beautiful. But it also meant we didn't stand a chance. Neither one of us really knew who we were or what we wanted. Well...that's not totally true. After I'd made love with him, I remember thinking that I knew something about myself, something that could never be taken away from me."

This was new, and Val leaned closer with excitement at the wistfulness in her friend's voice. "What exactly?"

"That I could love a man like that. Share myself. It was like touching the heavens, Val."

Her heart, the one that had been swaying like a seesaw inside her since the moment she'd met Brock, seemed to sigh in her chest. "I want that, Darla. Even though part of me is scared and another part of me thinks it's flat-out impossible. I've never felt like this before. Maybe my wiring won't..."

"Translate into the bedroom?" Darla suggested. "Trust me. It will. But most importantly, you need to trust yourself. In here."

She laid a gentle finger against Val's chest.

"So my house..." She brought up the hockey schedule in her head. "The team has St. Louis, Pitt, and Buffalo, all in the next three days."

"Brutal, but doable. I say you pick this Saturday since the team is flying home after the game on Friday. They have two full days off. That way you can savor your time together. Because I don't think Brock is going to want to be anywhere but with you."

"Right now, that seems like the distance between our first day at Oxford and our PhD ceremony."

Darla gave a low murmur. "Yes, it does. Look on it as anticipation."

"Masters and Johnson talked about that," Val said with a resolute nod. "The higher the excitement levels, the greater the— Well, you know. Likely a vaginal orgasm."

Her friend looked to be choking on laughter. "There's nothing like it. I wouldn't say it's the unicorn—"

"What do you mean? Is that a phallic horn reference?"

"No, I'm saying it's not as rare as seeing a unicorn."

Darla tugged on Val's baggy shirt. "You need better underwear. I saw what you were wearing that day you wore Brock's jersey, and girl, those bits are old. We have time now. Good thing we're not traveling with the team for every away game, right?"

No, they'd decided to be selective and focus on their writing while the team was gone, working on it in pieces, their usual practice, as their research came together. "What am I supposed to do with him in the meantime? Clearly, I can't be in the same room with him without wanting to—"

"Yank his clothes off and take a bite?" Darla offered with a sly grin.

Her thighs clenched at the mere thought.

"You text each other," Darla informed her. "Later, if you need support to be in the presence of the man who makes you want to scream to the heavens, we can hang out with Kinsley and Zeke, and Susan, if she's in town."

Val clasped her trembling hands, wishing Darla would stop mentioning the screaming. "Keep it to a group experience. Like chaperones for a courtship. I see the appeal even more now. You will be my guard dog or hen sister. Making sure I don't do something too soon. I want to get to know him better. This is a big step for me."

Her nerves rose up as Darla took her hands. "I know, and I've got you. Like you've always had me."

"When you listened," she managed with a shaky laugh. "I still remember how we saw that guy in the parking lot, and you told me he was making you shake all over but asked me not to let you go home with him because you'd just met."

"We know the rest of the story. It was a wonderful weekend, though. No strings. Lots of pleasure. But you're not like me, Val. You've had three men, one every three years, and all rather clinically chosen for a controlled experience. I admired your dedication to creating a risk-free environment to see what all the fuss was about, as you called it."

"I didn't want to become my mother," she whispered, pressing her hands to her chest. "She used to be so strong. On the ice, she was invincible. But afterward, without a purpose, she lost herself, and men couldn't fill the void." It hurt to say the last piece but she knew she must. "*I* couldn't fill it."

Darla gently touched her arm. "But we're not our mothers, honey. Despite how much I like to blame my mom sometimes for my actions. It's probably something I should stop doing. Victim-perpetrator crap is so tiresome."

Indecision still pounded at her like cold sleet. "But I'm... completely obsessed with Brock. Past reason. Past all sense."

"Because you're human, Val." She hugged her then. *"Human."*

Human. What a funny thought. "You do realize the irony here, don't you? We study the origins of human beings and try to make sense of the way people behave."

Darla squeezed her sweetly before pressing back with a lopsided grin. "I study what I do not understand. The truth is, Val, we humans really are a mess sometimes. Except when we're being completely exceptional. As a species, we're either in the heavens or the shitter. I doubt either of us will get bored with our chosen profession."

No, that was the one certainty in her life right now, besides Darla and her father. Brock wasn't a certainty: he was a variable. She needed to remember that. "So let's work. Distract me. The away games will give us a chance to hone our initial findings." The very idea of work was like a cup of chamomile tea through her system. "We do have a report to complete."

"Yes, we do, Dr. Hargrove, and it's going to be a damn good one."

They shared a secret smile. Brock said he loved it when she went all sexy librarian.

He was going to go crazy over her work.

FOURTEEN

"Why do women change their minds so much?"

Brock hated asking his friend for insight into the female mind, and given Finn's immediate glower, he looked like he'd rather drop and do a thousand push-ups than answer. Then again, they'd just suffered an agonizing defeat on the ice to a lesser opponent because of a Mason penalty at the end of the game, which had allowed the opposing team a penalty shot.

The loss—and the reason for it—made him livid, so he'd decided to focus on Val instead of crossing the locker room and taking Mason by the shirtfront and reading him the riot act. That was Chuck's job, and he'd already given the kid a blistering sermon after the game, in front of an eerily quiet team. Even Mason's pack were eyeing him with veiled anger after the hole he'd put them in with his recent penalties and selfish play. Everyone suspected the kid was in a sulk because he was still pissed over Brock's Reebok deal.

Brock had done his best to rally the team and put them on his back on the ice, trying to score enough goals to beat the opposing teams, but the Eagles had come up short.

They'd lost all three away games, putting them in what Chuck called "The Skids"—that horrible place when the playoffs can start skidding away.

If they lost another game, they likely wouldn't make the playoffs. They'd have to rely on someone else losing to get a wild card, and that wasn't how any winning team did things. You controlled your own destiny.

One of his infamous motivational strategies would be popping up soon, and Brock was more than ready for it.

"What is it this time?" Finn asked, referring back to Brock's question. He rolled his right shoulder where he'd taken a hard hit on the ice. "Kinsley sneak out of the house and get a nose ring?"

That sent a full-body shudder through him. "No. Jesus. What I mean is...when you think you're on the same page about something and then that changes."

Finn leaned against his locker after pulling his suit jacket on. "Care to give me a 'for instance'? Because I know this is about a woman."

He felt the pull to share but remembered his agreement with Val. He could tell no one. Hell, he'd almost blown it in the gym the other day, and he knew it. "Forget I said anything. I was only venting after that loss so I wouldn't grab Mason by his short hairs."

"Get in line. I'll see you on the plane, then."

He watched Finn walk away, feeling a growl forming in his throat. Keeping Val a secret had become challenging. His moods were about as steady as a ship at sea, swinging from raging lust to sweet tenderness. He couldn't wait to see her tomorrow...

When she'd told him she and Darla wouldn't be traveling with the team for the grueling away games, he'd understood. She'd mentioned it was for the best since they needed to keep cool, and both of them had nearly given themselves away at the gym. His fault, he'd said, before she'd knocked him for another loop.

She'd wanted to text.

Not talk on the phone.

Text!

Something he hated. First, there wasn't a phone big enough for his hands, which made any message he sent a grammatical nightmare. Second, he had enough paperwork and email awaiting him from business and his publicist after a long day that he hated having to type more. That made him sound like an idiot, but it was true. He preferred to talk. In person. On a date. Which, sure, wasn't possible right now given his travel schedule. But he'd felt like she was pulling back.

Because...

Texting?

Susan had jokingly suggested sending her emojis when he'd asked for advice. A few days before, he'd asked Val if he could tell Susan after his sister had mentioned inviting "the girls" over again while he was gone.

His sister didn't need to be blindsided again, certainly not by him and his choices. Val had understood his reasons and agreed, although her tense voice had translated her reluctance.

Kinsley and Zeke were really becoming attached to Val and Darla, and Susan was as well. So her reaction to the news hadn't surprised him—she wasn't a hugger, but he'd caught her pleased smile.

He'd been pleased, too, but not right now.

The away games had been a huge, epic bust. He'd missed Val like crazy, and he'd hated not being there when she and Darla had hung out with his family.

He was also pissed off from frustrated lust.

And schoolboy longing, which *really* pissed him off. He wanted to listen to her talk and hear her laugh and watch as she laughed while Kinsley and Darla sang a *Barbie* song in the hot tub while Zeke plugged his ears and pretended to make gagging sounds.

But the worst reason he was pissed about the texting situation was because he wanted to hear her voice, that sexy librarian voice, because it made him smile and filled his chest with hopes and dreams he hadn't had in a long time.

He wanted her.

More than that, he was falling for her.

So what had he done?

He'd texted her.

Every freaking day.

Between breaks.

On the plane.

In the locker room.

At the hotel.

He'd spent hours going over his texts before sending them, even correcting badly spelled words. Because she was smart and he wanted to impress her. Like he had in the gym when he'd burned his glutes to the point of pain where Finn had joked about getting him one of those donuts people with hemorrhoids used. Haha. Thank you very much.

His friend. Who knew that he was involved with someone.

He should have known Finn would guess. Did anyone else know? Chuck? God, his stomach flipped at the thought. Brock hadn't let himself be distracted after Chuck had called him out in that one practice, and certainly his recent stats proved he was locked. Being back on the road and not seeing Val every day had helped him focus—there was no denying that—but now he felt defeated and more than ready to see her.

He wanted to feel her intent gaze on him. Feel her slender, toned body against him as she surrendered to him before she stepped back from the edge she feared, one he understood. See that shy smile of hers and that other one... the one that was recent, the one that immediately sprang over her gorgeous mouth the moment she saw him. Unreserved. Like the woman she was becoming with him.

Control and poise were her North Star, the same way intensity and laser-sharp focus were his on the ice.

When he boarded the plane, he closed his eyes and thought of her. Wet and tangled around him. Rolling on the bed with him. Looking up at him as he loomed over her, taking her.

He had two free days coming up, and all he wanted to do was spend them with her. But he was torn. He'd missed Zeke and Kinsley and Susan too, even though he'd video chatted them up briefly.

Zeke had a hockey game at ten tomorrow he wanted to attend. Somehow, he would have to balance his time off. These two days were his last consecutive ones until the season ended. If they kept winning, he wouldn't have this kind of time until May.

If they kept winning...

And who knew where Val would be then?

He didn't know her plans.

He knew nothing about her really.

Except he did, and he wanted her more than he'd ever wanted another woman. Yes, even Erin. When the thought came as the plane started to descend, he searched himself for guilt and found none.

No fear either.

Only the certainty that this was the opportunity that he'd always wanted: a woman to love and make a life and a family with. One he respected. One he could discuss his ideas with, his career with. Who gave smart, informed observations. One who held herself with respect and confidence and understood him and his family and life. A true partner, friend, and lover all in one.

How she felt about that he had no idea.

He could only control his own part, but when an opportunity came his way, he always gave it his all, knowing his commitment would give him what he wanted.

They were like a new team, a team of two, and there were always intangibles you couldn't control with new teammates. Still, he knew Val was the kind of woman who gave her all as well. She was already doing it with Darla, much like he had done with Finn on the ice.

Settled, he took a cat nap, knowing he wanted to be refreshed for when he saw her tomorrow. Because they were taking things to the next level. He thought she was with him on that. God, he hoped so...

When they deplaned, he tipped his hand to Finn as they walked to their vehicles.

His friend clapped him on the back. "You know...I've been thinking about your question. As for why women change their minds, they usually have a reason. That's all I've got for you. Have fun. If you need me, you know where I'll be."

"House slippers on your coffee table watching *Fast and Furious* movies?" he teased.

"Beats *Fight Club*." He looked over his shoulder. "Maybe something will happen to force our team's yokel to get his shit together."

He thought about Val and Darla. They were here to

help Chuck. He just didn't know how. But he had a feeling they were all about to find out. The Eagles could not drop another game. Chuck would pull the trigger on his strategy soon if past history bore out.

"Hope isn't a strategy, man. But I'll take it. See you in a few."

Picking up his stride, he was already pulling his phone out of his coat pocket to text Val. Sure, it was nearing one in the morning, but he couldn't wait a moment longer. They hadn't made definitive plans, except to check in when he got back. Well, he was back. If she wasn't awake, she could answer him in the morning.

Hey, Miss Sexy Librarian! When am I seeing you? Like what time tomorrow? I missed you.

The ellipses immediately appeared, and he stopped short. She was up! He waited, his heart rate picking up instantly.

Soon.

He waited for her to continue, his breath visible in the cold. But nothing came. He wanted to growl.

Soon? Cute. Want to be more specific? Zeke's got a hockey game in the morning, but after... I'm all yours.

He saw the ellipses appear again, and he gripped his phone as he waited for her text.

Soon, Brock. And I missed you too. Have a safe drive home.

Then nothing. He wanted to shake his phone. The infernal woman! If he were wearing one of Kinsley's T-shirts, the word DYING would be on the front in all caps. Had their time apart helped her return to her cool-as-a-cucumber self? Well, he would melt that.

He yanked his car door open and tossed his bag inside. "Soon! Women! Why the hell do we let them do this to us?"

God, he was starting to sound like Zeke.

Turning on his car, he took a few deep breaths to calm himself down, cued up some Macklemore, and drove home.

When he was three houses away, he noted an SUV parked in front of his house on the street. Pulling into his driveway, he looked in the rearview mirror and watched as a woman left the vehicle and started toward the house.

He knew that elegant posture, that determined walk. His heart might as well have dropped out of his body and slid across the ice he was so shocked. Then he was grinning as he killed the engine quickly and got out of the car, striding toward her.

"You're here!"

"Shh!" That pointed finger touched her gorgeous lips, the ones he couldn't wait to kiss. "The kids! Your neighbors."

Right now he didn't care if anyone heard him, and that smacked him as totally reckless. Only she had a wide, unreserved grin on her beautiful face. No glasses. Only her. All he wanted.

He had her in his arms a moment later, picking her up off the ground and spinning her around, making her squeeze his neck tightly as she fit her body to him.

"I *did* tell you soon."

"God, Val!"

Then his mouth was on hers, pouring all the longing and wild new feelings into a kiss that went on and on. She held his head in her hands and surrendered, matching his urgency.

Finally, she tore her mouth free, sucking in gulps of air. "I thought it might be good to see a familiar face after being on the road and having a tough run," she whispered, tracing his stubbly jaw. "It can get lonely and frustrating."

Her understanding always touched him. She seemed to know things he didn't have to tell her, and he fucking loved that. "It was lonelier and more frustrating this time than it's been in a long time," he found himself saying quietly. "Val, every moment away was..."

"Awful," she finished, kissing him sweetly again. "I know. Even work didn't completely satisfy me, and it usually does."

"I hear that." He pressed his face into her warm neck, inhaling that clean, crisp scent of hers. "God, I'm so glad you're here. I just... Val." Emotion swamped him, and he squeezed his eyes shut.

"I know, Brock." Her grip tightened. "I thought about you all the time. My usual tools didn't help. You wouldn't stay behind my wall. I can usually do it to anyone."

He lifted his head, because her voice was rough and shaky, and it felt like she was confessing the hardest thing of her life. "But not me."

She shot him one of her sexy librarian looks. "Don't look so pleased with yourself."

"Can't help it." He took the sides of her face in his hands tenderly. "I can't shut you out either. But Val, the truth is, I don't want to."

Her hand rose and settled softly over his heart, and any lingering weight from the recent losses lifted at her touch. "I don't either. Brock, I want what's next, even though I'm nervous and scared and excited."

"All that?" He kissed her again, savoring the feel of the silky strands of her hair between his fingertips. "You need to know I thought about this. About what's next between us. All I feel is certain."

Her green eyes seemed to flash even in the dark night, he knew he'd touched someplace deep inside her with his admission. "I like knowing that. I'm certain too. Which is why I texted Susan and asked if it would be okay to wait outside the house for you once you landed. I didn't want to risk scaring her."

Her thoughtfulness for his family didn't surprise him but it moved him all the same. "How long have you been out here? Are you cold?" His hands caressed the sides of her arms, calling to him even through her warm wool coat. Not the baggy one she'd worn to his house last time, thank God.

"No, I'm feeling rather warm actually, and I haven't been here long. I started over after you texted, judging the time of your arrival."

"Now that's my sexy librarian," he said, his voice low and rough. "I missed her. A lot."

"She missed you. A lot." Her hand came up and feathered a lock of his hair off his forehead. "And tomorrow after Zeke's game would be fine for another *rendezvous*."

"*Rendezvous*, huh? That's the sexiest thing I've ever heard you say."

She ducked her head shyly. "Stop. We're in your driveway."

"You could come in." He nodded to the house. "The kids are asleep. We could make out on the couch."

He didn't like that she started shaking her head. "We both know it won't stop there. Brock, we need to be smart."

That studious voice was so damn sexy. "Smart... Val, I just finished three away games. All losses. It's nearing two in the morning. I'm exhausted, but I'd stay up all night with you if you let me. Smart took a vacation days ago."

"Then I'll start walking away since you need to rest." Her playful tiptoeing had him wanting to chase her around the front yard. "Text me after the game is over and we'll meet up."

Texting was about to take a vacation too, but first he had another matter to settle. He tapped the place where his watch rested, over his frantic pulse. "Where? You've been dodging that question."

She paused and seemed to lift her face up to the night sky. The moonlight caught the graceful angles of her cheeks, and for a minute, she looked like a snow queen out of one of his boyhood storybooks his father had read him. "That's because I thought the answer would distract you."

"Babe, I'm already distracted."

The word flowed out so easily he didn't have the urge to snatch it back. She was a babe. His babe. And he planned to show her so in as many ways as she let him. Clearly, she liked it because she was grinning now.

"You used an endearment. That usually comes later on in courtship. How totally...wonderful."

His whole world seemed to settle when she talked like that. Then she started to walk away. "*Val.* The place."

"Oh, right." She spun around in a circle before landing gracefully. "I got carried away. My house."

His balls dropped to the floor. "Your. House."

"You see why I didn't tell you? You should see your face. You look like a lion ready to eat."

He could feast on her at this point. "Then you'd better run because I have the wild urge to chase you."

"You couldn't catch me." She flashed him a grin before dashing to her car.

"Oh, yes, I will," he whispered as she took off. He indulged himself by thinking of what it meant that she'd invited him to her house. She trusted him. Deeply. They were going to have sex, he'd had no doubts about that. Only the timing had been in question. But now...

She'd told him her privacy mattered deeply to her, and

she'd invited him in to another part of her life. That was big time.

A stupid grin broke out on his face.

He waited until her headlights disappeared to go inside, aware he was acting a little lovesick. When he reached the kitchen, he jolted at the sight of two silhouettes moving beside the refrigerator.

Like they were hiding.

He flicked on the lights. "I know you two are up. Might as well come out into the open."

Zeke appeared first, dressed in his Eagles pajamas, hair standing up in tufts, before Kinsley stepped up behind him wearing pink fleece pants with a new black flannel T-shirt he hadn't seen, one he imagined was from "The Girls." The word scrawled in silver glitter across the middle caught his attention: PERFECT.

"I like your shirt, Kinsley. Now why are you two up at this hour?"

They exchanged a look, and Kinsley pointed to her brother before he violently shook his head and thrust his finger at her. "Ah...Zeke heard your car drive up, and then he woke me. Because he thought he saw something and wanted me to see too. Umm...Uncle Brock...are you and Val dating?"

Jesus. He felt rooted in place. What the hell was he supposed to say? Should he get Susan up for this? But that seemed crazy. "How about we all hit the hay and discuss this in the morning?"

"But it is morning," Zeke pushed back. "Technically. And you *were* kissing her."

Instantly, he felt his exhaustion. "I'd really prefer to talk about this in the morning when your mom is up."

"Why?" Kinsley took a few steps toward him, her eyes

angry. "Because we're kids? We know things. We just saw you and Val. Why can't you be honest with us? I thought you..."

The unspoken phrase punched him in the gut. "Were different?"

She nodded before her younger brother did. God, they looked like the two lost kids Susan had shown up with months before after their home had broken apart. "I am, but I also promised someone I'd keep this to myself."

"Val, right?" Kinsley fingered her shirt. "Because she wouldn't want to get anyone's hopes up. Mine especially."

A blow to the back of the head wouldn't have been so shocking. How old were these kids? "We also work together."

"Which complicates things," Kinsley summarized as she and Zeke shared another nod. "We know how the real world works, Uncle Brock. We won't say anything. Right, Zeke?"

His nephew made a zipping motion over his lips. "Not a peep, Uncle Brock. To anyone at school or anything."

He hadn't imagined they'd spread the news. Terror had a new form, and it was his relationship with Val going viral because some teenage kid posted about it on his Snapchat account after hearing about it in the lunchroom.

"That's good to know because it could hurt me and Val —and maybe even the team," he answered honestly.

"We know when to keep a secret," Zeke told him with way too much authority. "Hey, Uncle Brock, sorry about the losses. They totally sucked. I'll bet you wanted to knock Mason's block off."

He stared his nephew down. "You don't hit another teammate. You let Coach talk to the team, and then you figure out a way to win the next game."

"That's what you're supposed to say." Zeke whacked his forehead with his palm. "But even the sports announcer after this last game said he imagined you and the other players wanted to bash Mason's head in since he pretty much caused your last three losses with his stupid penalties. He's becoming a... What did he say, Kinsley?"

"He called Mason a liability. I think he's a jerk."

He bit the inside of his cheek as they turned into angry fans right before his eyes. "We were mad, yes, but—"

"Everyone online was going *crazy*." Zeke threw his hands in the air. "You guys can't lose another game, or you might not make the playoffs."

Kinsley walked over and nudged her brother in the side.

He grimaced. "Sorry, Uncle Brock. By the way, if you and Val are dating, we're cool with it. We like her. And Darla."

"Zeke!" Kinsley elbowed him. "But there's no pressure, okay? You just get to know each other. We won't say a word."

"Not. A. Word." Zeke raised his hand to his mouth and mimed throwing away the key.

Their little agreement was cute, but it was fraught with hellish scenarios—the kind that made people agree to secret relationships in the first place.

"Of course Kinsley can't wait to talk to Darla about it," Zeke blurted out. "Because if you and Val hook up, that means Darla will be around all the time too. I mean, if you guys get married in a couple years, I might even be able to drive Darla's car."

Brock didn't balk at the projected timeline. Val showing up tonight confirmed his confidence in her—in *them*. But where did these two get their ideas? Was he ever this crazy as a kid? "Let's do what we do in hockey, Zeke. One game at a time."

"But this is *life!*" His blue eyes widened to saucers. "How does that even make sense?"

"There's no way Darla will ever let you drive her ride," Kinsley haughtily informed him in a voice mirroring Val's.

"Wanna bet?" He grinned. "I can be charming."

"Okay, that's enough for tonight." Brock gestured to the digital clock on the stove. "You are up way past your bedtime, and your mother will probably shoot me for not shoving you both back into your beds. Someone has a game tomorrow. If you fall asleep at breakfast—"

"I'll just say I stayed up late watching sports highlights of your game," Zeke offered. "That's what I usually say when it happens in school."

Brock leveled him a glare.

He lifted his shoulder. "Hey! Some of my teachers are huge Eagles fans. They get it. We're all rooting for you, Uncle Brock."

That reminder brought the reality home. He wasn't the only person who wanted the Cup. His family did too, as did the entire Eagles community.

Chuck had better work his magic quick.

FIFTEEN

"Why do men always expect you to drop everything and come running when they call?"

Darla practically moaned the question. She had her hand covering her eyes as Val drove them to the arena where Chuck had summoned them for an eight a.m. meeting. Val had been awake to receive the summons, but Darla preferred to sleep late on weekends. Especially after a night on the town, which they'd had last night before Val had left to meet Brock. Her friend hadn't returned her text or picked up her call. So Val had gone over to her house. She'd had to pull her friend out of bed and then stuff her into her hated work outfit in order to get them out the door so they'd be on time.

"Well, Chuck is our boss, and this isn't a nine-to-five kind of job. Plus, the team is in trouble." The kind where Chuck brought out the big guns, as her father had called them.

"Yes, they are, but it's still a little annoying, especially how he ordered us to his office with not even a word of politeness." Darla gave an indelible snort. "Mama says men do it because it shows they have power over you. Of course, when she did that kind of thing, they called her a diva. God, my head hurts. I thought I'd be fine having that extra margarita with that cute firefighter I met last night. But they were so good—"

"Plus, we hadn't had a margarita since our trip to Dallas for that anthropology conference four years ago. Isn't the aspirin kicking in yet?"

She whimpered. "Yes, but the tiny bats in my head are still banging around, trying to find a way out, like they did in that cave we stumbled into when we were looking for those cave dwellings the locals told us about in Tanzania."

Now that had been a great find. The bats, not so much. "You ran out screaming when one buzzed your head."

"Which awakened hundreds of those little suckers." She moaned and dug her face into her seat. "I can still hear their high-pitched screech. I almost peed my pants. You were unfazed."

"When you grow up with people screaming and cheering as you perform, you learn to tune it out. If it makes you feel better, it did startle me."

"It does, thanks." Darla slid up higher in the passenger seat. "So, let's talk more about you. I was dying too much to ask when you picked me up, but I'm rallying. You went over to see Brock last night, right?"

Val didn't look away from traffic. That would be totally irresponsible. But she did give a happy nod. "He was really glad to see me. Like you'd guessed."

"Of course he was! Have I not been helping you with all your texts while he was gone? We had a plan. How did he take the news that you were inviting him over to your house?"

She gave a girlish chuckle, the kind she'd given way too

often lately. "Like one of those cartoon characters who gets knocked in the head and loses a tooth but still can't stop the dopey grin on his face. He was adorable. Oh, and he called me babe! If it hadn't been so late, I would have called you."

"I was still up but tipsy. The firefighter put me in my cab after kissing me good night and giving me his number. What is it about men who use a hose for a living?"

"A question for another time..." She clenched her hands as she pulled into the arena lot and parked. "We have our hands full this morning. I'm guessing Chuck wants to talk about Mason."

"You heard the bar crowd last night." Darla dug out her mister and sprayed her face, something she swore helped with jet lag and hangovers. "They wanted his blood after the other team won on the penalty shot. I know we didn't intend our girls' night to be study session, but that restaurant bar was gold. The natives are getting restless, as they say. I can't count all the people who were debating whether the Eagles should keep him or cut him after these recent losses."

She'd seen Mason pull the move that had gotten him that final penalty—he'd hit the player from behind into the boards and gotten a five-minute major for boarding and a ten-minute misconduct. This was after he'd racked up ten minutes of penalties earlier. He was one of the most heavily penalized players in the league. His fans usually liked his aggressive play. But not when it put the team in playoff jeopardy.

"Chuck will be looking for answers, especially with only four weeks left to win the championship and make the playoffs," she told Darla as they got out and started walking into the building. "Let's give him what we can."

Darla finally slid her sunglasses off, substituting them

for her costume glasses, as they walked to his office. Val knocked softly.

"*Enter!*"

When she opened the door, the sight of her father had her rushing toward him. "Daddy!"

He caught her up in his arms against one of his Italian blue suits. "Val." His grip tightened. "I flew in this morning to talk with Chuck after the game last night. I thought I'd surprise you."

"You did! In the best way."

He turned to Darla and swept her up in his arms. "Hey, sweetie! You taking good care of my girl?"

"You know it," Darla playfully responded with a twinkle in her eye.

A harsh clearing of a throat had everyone freezing and turning to face Chuck.

"Sorry to interrupt, but can you guys catch up after we talk? I have a million things to do after the Mason stunt last night."

"Of course!" Val broke out, a bit mortified.

She and Darla hustled over to the two chairs in front of his desk while her father loitered at the end.

"I'm still waiting to hear if the league will suspend Mason, and I'm dealing with an onslaught of pissed-off fans. I had one drop a note in front of my house this morning along with my newspaper."

He held it out, and Darla took it and started reading. "'*Hey Coach! Why don't you do something about Mason? He's going to kill our playoff hopes. I'd hoped you were going to get him under control, but he's doing the same stupid shit. Fucking trade him, you moron. Grow a pair.*' Ouch."

"I've heard worse." Chuck grabbed his stress ball and started squeezing. "I was awake much of the night thinking.

I need to get Mason in hand. The team is pissed at him and looking to me, and we can't afford another loss. We've arrived at 'The Skids.' I need a status report on the caveman study," Chuck ground out. "Thoughts on how to handle Mason. Anything."

Val glanced at Darla before kicking off. "Our study and our knowledge of human group dynamics suggests a few courses of action in this situation. Punishment. Exile."

Chuck threw his stress ball in the air before catching it and resuming his squeezing. "So he gets suspended by the league or we do it. If not, we bench him. Or we trade him. Like the wise Eagles fan suggested in his note to me. God! Why can't the kid change? Any caveman wisdom there?"

Darla gave her a nod indicating she wanted to run with this one. "Chuck, we've been watching the players since we arrived, and while we aren't sports psychologists, we have seen this kind of archetype before. In our studies, we'd call Mason a next-generation warrior. He's clearly a gifted and revered individual within the group—the league and your team—but he's not top dog yet. Either in age or in kills. Kills are victories in this sense."

"He's still trying to prove himself to his elders," Val added, picking up the thread. "You as his coach. But also to veteran teammates like his captain. He wants the older warriors' respect, and he knows he doesn't have it."

"But why the cheap shots when he's so talented?" Chuck stood up, his fist slamming onto the desk. "If he wanted, he could score us five goals in one game."

"So could Brock." She glanced at Darla. "He had three last night. The only points scored."

"So he's jealous of Brock Thomson. Tell me something I don't know, and Brock's Reebok deal only made it worse.

Dammit, I'm sorry. I don't mean to take my frustration out on you, but I'm—"

"Pissed," Ted answered. "We all are."

"Wait!" Darla leaned forward in her chair. "Mason watches *Fight Club* before every game, right? Maybe someone needs to help him focus on the deeper meaning of the story."

Val turned to her. "How do you know that film's meaning?"

"Please, my father is J-Mac. He and his guys love that movie. He sent it to me for my thirteenth birthday with the note, '*All you need to know about men. Love, Dad.*'"

Her father barked out a laugh. "Good God! And I thought I had parent moments to make up for."

"Anyway, since I wanted to understand my father when I was a teenager, I looked up the meaning. Sorry, Val, before you can tell me the movie is based on a book, I know, and I didn't read it. So, there are a million different interpretations of the story online, of course. But I like this one. *Fight Club* is really about fighting with yourself. Your fears. Your image. And the destruction that happens when you let it run you. I think you might have someone tell Mason that. And punish the jerk as a follow-up. My two cents."

"I agree." Her father stood up from the desk and cocked his head to the side. "Chuck? I can give Mason the whole *Do you want to be part of this organization* speech with a little *Fight Club* aside and then send him down to you for punishment. Thoughts?"

"Let's do it." Chuck lowered himself into his seat. "If the league handles it, fine. If not, I want to suspend him for three games. Fitting since that's the number of games we just lost. You good with that, Ted?"

"Can we win without him?" her father asked, crossing his arms.

"Like Val said, Brock scored three goals—our only goals—last night. He's our lead scorer, and he's put the team on his back. Right now, he's making up for Mason on the ice. I think everyone will play better without him unless he shapes up. But there is no guarantee."

"Then we suspend him if the league doesn't." He and Chuck shared one of their looks before her father turned to face Val and Darla. "I think we're done here."

"Yeah, thanks for coming in today," Chuck told them as they rose. "The *Fight Club* insight was rock-solid stuff, as was the younger warrior shit. I appreciate it."

"We're here to help, Chuck." Val only wished they could do more.

He nodded and picked up his phone. Her father led them through the door, and they all stopped in the reception area. "So how's the study going? I know you've kept me up to date by email, but I can't wait to hear more about it later. I was hoping you and Darla would have dinner with me tonight at the penthouse."

Her smile faltered. "Oh!"

Her alone time with Brock had just gone up in smoke. She certainly couldn't tell her father she had plans with his team's captain, and she couldn't imagine ever lying to him. Keeping something like this from him wasn't perfect either, but it was practical. Still, her face began to flush. "Of course. That would be great."

"Val... Don't tell me you forgot?" Darla hugged her around the waist and gave a *tut-tut*. "How about breakfast heading to brunch? Nowish? Ted, Val wouldn't want to hurt your feelings, but I finally talked her into going to

Paisley Park with me. We're doing the whole VIP Experience thing—"

Paisley Park? She had no idea what Val was talking about, but when her friend stepped softly on her foot, she forced a smile. "It totally slipped my mind in the moment."

"Sure, we can do breakfast." Her father's laugh lines deepened. "I know how much you love Prince, Darla. Your mother's duet with him is still one of my favorites."

Prince! Right. "Yeah, sorry, Daddy. She's so crazy about him I had to give in. Best friend duty, you know. If I had a dollar for every time she made me listen to 'Pink Cashmere,' I'd be as rich as you."

That had him practically guffawing. "That rich, eh? I'll have to give that song a listen. I don't think I know it."

"It's not as well known as some of his other hits," Darla practically preened. "So we'll see you at the penthouse, then? In the interest of keeping things under wraps?"

Val's brain was still buzzing from the near immolation of her plans with Brock. The secrecy she'd been living with felt like it had just mushroomed. They were keeping her relationship with her father from the team. Now she was keeping her new relationship with Brock from her father.

Because how would he react to the news?

"Yes, I'll meet you there after I let Lavinia know my change of plans." He kissed her on the top of her head and then did the same to Darla before heading off in the other direction.

Darla hurried her away. When they were out of earshot, Val sagged against her friend. "Thanks for saving the day. I didn't know how to get out of it."

"I figured." She slipped her sunglasses on as they continued toward the garage. "For a moment, I thought you were going to blow it. Val, after being my BFF since we were teenagers, how can you not know the name of Prince's house?"

"Hey! I knew it was in Minneapolis. That's more than most people."

"Some days I can't believe we're friends." She snagged her arm around Val's shoulders. "But I'm glad we are."

"Me too."

"Damn right, and we are so listening to 'Pink Cashmere' on the way over to your father's penthouse."

Of course they were.

"While we talk about your hot date with Brock," her friend continued. "Which your daddy cannot know anything about." Val gulped. "Because while Ted is a very smart and sophisticated man, he's never had to face that ugly emotion some fathers experience when their little girl finds a big, strong man in her life. Especially when said big, strong man works for him."

She made herself ask the stink-bomb question. "How do you think my daddy would react?"

"Honestly, I have no idea, but he's a man. When that's the case, you know my M.O."

They shared a look.

"Say nothing," she muttered glumly.

For what was supposed to be a simple academic study, things were really getting complicated.

SIXTEEN

Why did women make men wait when they knew how horny they were?

Brock stared at his phone as Zeke made *pow-pow* sounds at his video game next to him on the couch. Val had texted that she was running late because something had come up. He wanted to tear his hair out. None of the hours and hours of mind training he'd done had helped him stop the flood of images rocking his brain.

Val: naked.

Val: wet.

Val—

"Uncle Brock?"

He jumped in place. Zeke gave a war cry and uttered a *Take that* to the poor kid from school he was beating in a hockey video game, eyes glued to the TV. He'd racked up a hockey win this morning in a real game, and now he was gaming. His nephew was having a better morning than he was so far.

Turning his head, Brock spied Kinsley standing shyly behind him wearing a pink T-shirt with STRONG in blue glitter. "I like your top. Another new item from 'The Girls'?"

"Yeah, they get me," she said so softly his heart clutched.

He realized Val mostly got him too. And here he was complaining about being horny. He should be grateful she was in his life.

Good. New perspective. He liked it. "I'm glad. It's nice to be understood."

She ducked her head again and thrust something out. When he took it, he realized it was one of those friendship bracelets she sometimes wore. Rainbow beads with letters on them that formed a message. He held it up and read: YOU MATTER. Whoa! Even he felt the punch.

"That's for Val. For when you see her."

"Girls," he heard Zeke mutter before yelling another *Gotcha* into his headset.

Brock sent him a stern look, which his nephew ignored, but Kinsley looked down at her feet. He wanted to take her gently by the arm and sit her down between him and Zeke. "Why don't you wait and give it to her yourself?"

Twirling her finger in her hair, she lifted a slim shoulder. "I kinda...wanted her to know I like you two dating. I thought you could tell her so I wouldn't embarrass her. Darla says she gets embarrassed easily."

She did? Then he thought of how she'd blushed when he'd admired her in his jersey. "That's very nice of you," he said, tucking the bracelet carefully into his jeans pocket.

"She's my friend." Her hesitant smile as much as her tone tore at his heart. "Ah...since you're going to be with Val, can I call Darla?"

His warm, bubbly niece feeling was gone. He knew a

setup. "You know what your mom said. You let Darla and Val check in with you."

"But I don't see why." She gave a giant huff, blowing up her bangs. "I should be able to text or call who I want to, when I want to. I'm not a baby."

Here we go. "No, you're not. But Val said privacy means a lot to her—"

"You have her number. And she's my friend too."

He almost called for Susan, but she was upstairs doing laundry. "Kinsley, I know it's a little complicated—"

"She's just mad because she can't find them on social media," Zeke broke in while tapping the keys of his controller. "They're like ghosts."

"Can't you tell me their last names, Uncle Brock?" his niece asked, all big eyes and teenage angst.

How was he supposed to tell his niece that he didn't even know their last names? He rubbed his jaw, which he'd shaved after they'd gotten home from Zeke's hockey match. Because Val had smooth skin, and he was not going to give her beard burn. Plus, that kind of thing could be awkward at the office. "Like I said, Val likes her privacy."

"But they're not even on social media, and usually the only reason—" Kinsley's eyes were really wide now. "Was she like...stalked?"

He stiffened. "How do you know about that kind of thing?"

"Please, Uncle Brock, it's like in all the movies," Zeke told him in the long-suffering voice of a twelve-year-old burdened with clueless adults.

"Your mother went through her rules when you guys moved in, so I happen to know those kinds of movies are off-limits."

Neither kid responded. Not that he'd expected otherwise. He'd been their age once, eons ago. He knew about watching those kinds of movies at the houses of friends with lax parents.

"You didn't answer my question," Kinsley finally said, lifting her chin with a determined glint in her eyes. "Was Val hurt?"

This was getting out of hand. "As I told you, it's early and we're still getting to know her, but she must have a good reason for her privacy. We will respect that."

"So don't ask her if she was stalked, moron," Zeke prattled on, not seeing his sister had moved behind him and was poised to climb onto the couch.

Brock held her back before she could jump on her brother. "How about we not fight?"

"But he called me—"

"Zeke, apologize to your sister," he ordered as he set the girl back down.

"Sorry," he muttered, tapping his console. "But you really shouldn't ask people personal questions like that."

"I know that, moron," Kinsley fired back.

"Enough!" Brock wanted to haul them both into the showers like his boyhood coach had done when two of his teammates had started fighting at hockey camp. But girls hated to get their hair wet, and that seemed like too steep an intervention.

"Kinsley! Zeke!" Susan's crisp tone had both kids freezing in place as she came into the living room. "Are you driving your uncle Brock nuts?"

They both looked at him, so he couldn't nod. He gave his sister a tight smile.

"Zeke, that's enough video games for today. You have a room to clean up. It looks like Godzilla rolled through it."

The boy groaned. "I hate cleaning."

"Then keep it cleaner." Susan came over and put an arm around Kinsley. "Since you don't have a room yet because you still want to stay in your tent, how about you and I go through your books and put some of them up in the bookshelves your uncle ordered? I told him you probably miss them."

They shared a look. Susan had hoped it might lure Kinsley into moving into her room if they started to outfit it with some of the things she liked. First up was a new set of white bookshelves.

"Okay," she said in a muffled voice.

He wanted to high-five Susan for her brilliance. She sent him a quick wink. "Why don't you head upstairs with your brother?" she told the kids. "I'll be there in a jiffy."

Zeke said goodbye to whomever he was playing with and restored the living room back to order before following Kinsley upstairs.

Brock started laughing. "Were we ever like that?"

"Not really." She rested back on the couch, tired but looking younger somehow in an old Soul Asylum sweatshirt. "Mom and Dad were stricter than I am. I'm not the perfect parent by a mile, but I didn't want them to be punished as frequently as we were growing up. A few squabbles aren't the end of the world."

"You're doing good. I always thought so."

"Well, you're picking up a lot of slack with Darren gone." She inclined her chin to cover up the sheen of water in her eyes. "Thanks again for the bookshelves. I would have ordered them."

"It was two clicks on my phone," he told her, aware of her discomfort. "I keep telling you that you don't have to do everything on your own."

"I know." She righted the couch pillows like she hadn't heard him. "Old habits die hard. No word from Val yet?"

He picked up his phone and his heart pinged, seeing her text from five minutes ago.

Hi! So sorry again about being late. I'm home now. Address to follow.

"Just in. That means I'm outta here. Until tomorrow. Think you can cover for me?"

She reached over and tugged on his ear. "Well, I am your older sister. Although the kids seem to be up to speed on why you'll be gone tonight. God, why did they grow up so fast? Go! Have fun."

He fought a smile. This *was* his sister. "If you need anything—"

"I'll call Finn," she said with a laugh. "He is your backup as we agreed. Now, get your stuff and go."

He didn't need any further encouragement. "Already in the car." He walked over and called up the stairs. "Zeke. Kinsley. I'm taking off. See you later!"

An answering chorus of young voices called out *Bye, Uncle Brock, have fun,* and *Tell Val I said hi.*

Waving to Susan, he jogged to the garage. Inside, he pulled up Val's address to get directions and sat back in shock when he noted the estimated time. *Five minutes.* Shit, she lived right around the corner in the Rolling Green neighborhood, close to his own Parkwood Knolls.

How had she not said anything? Right, privacy. He started the car and decided to be grateful she was so close. Saturday traffic could be a nightmare.

But all the way, he wondered about her privacy and why she was staying in a luxury home in Rolling Green.

Maybe the Eagles owned a few furnished homes in case they acquired a new player and his family during the regular season. Out of his scope. Still, when he arrived at the modern two-level split house, he was impressed. The large yard was covered in snow, but he spied water to the side. Nice. He'd wanted a waterfront property, but none had been on the market at the time.

The front door opened as he pulled the car to a stop, and his breath stopped when she stepped out in a navy blue sweater and dark jeans and boots. Her auburn hair was down in loose waves, and her green eyes seemed to glow mysteriously while a pinkish hue cruised her cheeks.

She was nervous, he realized, and he told himself to slow down. They had the rest of the day and tomorrow. He'd assumed he would be staying over, but he decided he wasn't going to rush her—no matter how wild he was for her. They'd barely dated. They'd only had one evening by themselves, he'd reminded himself. They'd have another date today and then...

Her wave was also a little stunted, but her smile took his breath away. God, she was so beautiful. He waved back.

She mimed rolling the window down, so he hit the button. "Hi! Why don't you pull around back and park in the garage? I thought it might be...smart."

Smart. That was the word she'd used last night. "Sure thing."

The house had an underground three-car garage, and he noted the impressive view along the water as he pulled in next to her Defender.

Opening the door, he pulled out his bag and then thought better of it. Maybe he should wait. Slamming the door shut, he spied the exits and headed to the one he hoped led to the house, his shoes slapping on the concrete slab in the mostly bare space. The door he'd been going for popped open, and she stood in the threshold, a smile flickering on her lips like in old movie footage. The garage door closed as she hit the button by the door.

"Again, I'm so sorry I was late," she repeated, waving him inside. "The main floor is up this way."

He didn't pull her into his arms since she seemed a little skittish. So he followed her up the carpeted stairs after noting she had a full gym on the lower level. When they reached the main level, he glanced at the tall white walls and open floor plan with the large windows showing bare trees out back, a snowy yard, and a deep blue lake, choppy from the wind and iced at the edges. The house was furnished with a baby grand piano, a state-of-the-art entertainment system Zeke would go crazy for, as well as neutral furniture underneath soaring modern art on the mammoth walls. None of it seemed to quite suit her. Much like he'd originally thought about her clothes.

"Welcome," she said, clutching her hands together. "Can I get you something to drink? I have—"

"Val..." He crossed and put his arms on her shoulders, waiting until she looked up at him. "Hi."

"Hi." Her sigh cruised out as she gave him a tight smile. "I'm a little nervous. I keep telling myself not to be nervous, but facts are facts. I don't...do this. Have men over for the weekend."

He wanted to ask more questions, but he only rubbed her shoulders up and down to assure her everything was all right. "Then I'm honored."

"Honored." Her brow knit. "Right...male codes about women's sexuality."

"There's my sexy librarian." He pulled her to his chest slowly and kissed the top of her head, wrapping his arms around her. "I missed her—and you. Val, my time away from you felt like an eternity."

"For me too."

Her stiff frame took a moment to melt but it did, slowly, like the best kind of ice. She needed more time. He racked his brain for what else they could do. Movie? Lunch? He'd have to block the image of wild, hot sex like he did a puck. "What do you normally do on a day off? Is there anything special we can do?"

Her muscles went tight again, and she eased back with a veiled look in her eyes. "You mean besides sex?"

The way she said *sex*—in her almost studious tone—had heat shooting straight to his groin. "I mean we don't have to rush anything. I'm here to spend time with you—"

"You mean you don't want to have sex?" She almost sounded panicked. "Because that completely throws off *everything*."

The puzzlement in her narrowed green eyes had him pulling her back to his chest. "I do want to have sex. Very badly. But you're nervous, and we can sit and talk—"

"*Sit and talk?*" Her hand pushed against his chest again as if she were outraged. "I don't have anything planned to talk about."

God, he was going to lose his mind. "So what did you have planned? Spell it out for me."

Her shoulders went back as she stood up a little straighter. "I'd thought you'd kiss me when you arrived, and things would take off from there. When you kiss me, I... Well, it creates the first stage of arousal, and that's what we're going for."

First stage of arousal... God, he was so hard right now. "Then come here."

"Orders in the bedroom are common arousal flashpoints," she commented, stepping toward him. "I can see why. Your voice dipped lower than usual."

He'd done his fair share of talking in the bedroom but never like this. And yet, it was pretty hot. "Shall I say it again?"

"Yes." She fiddled with the wool of his sweater. "If it pleases you, of course."

She was going to be polite? He was going to love making her scream. "Come here, Val."

She shivered this time and laid both hands against his chest. "If you insist."

He wove his hand into her hair and tugged gently on her scalp, making her gasp. "I like it down like this. So I can wrap my fingers around it."

"Men like women with long hair because it's a sign of health and fertility," she informed him as she pressed closer.

"What do women like?" he asked, realizing this might be his biggest entry point into the female mind as he lowered his mouth to the side of her neck. "You, especially?"

She jerked when his open mouth touched her skin. "Oh, I like that. Ah... Statistically speaking, women like their erogenous zones touched. Repeatedly. For stimulation purposes."

He closed his eyes, feeling way too stimulated himself, as he kissed the fluttering pulse at her neck. "Tell me more about these erogenous zones."

She tilted her head to the side to give him better access, clutching his sweater when he bit her lightly where her shoulder and neck met. "Depending on who you read, some focus more on the genital area, but that is widely seen as too myopic."

Her breath shattered as he pressed his open mouth to

her neck. "We don't want to be myopic here, do we?" he whispered into her skin.

She hastily shook her head as her hand curled around his nape. "We both strive for excellence."

He rather loved that. "So we're going for thorough. *All* the zones." Her audible swallow made him smile as he inhaled her clean scent. "Let's review them to make sure we're on the same page."

"Right. A focused, logical plan. The zones include ears..."

He nipped her lobe, making her utter a short moan.

"Umm...fingertips and palms."

He brought her hand off his nape and pressed his lips to the center of her palm before taking her index finger into his mouth and biting down gently.

"Yes, I see you have a good working sense of things." Her green eyes were turning slumberous. "Darla assured me you would. You're a heathy male, so it follows you would have a strong sex drive."

He could feel laughter tickling his throat. "You bring it to new heights."

She rocked back, shock widening those generous eyes of hers. "I do?"

His slow nod had her mouth curving. "But we were talking about you and your zones. So I don't miss any."

"Yes," she said, her smile cresting in that new, easy way he loved seeing. "Let me see. The bottoms of the feet are widely discussed, especially in Asian cultures. The inner thighs and the backs of the knees, of course. Then there are the ones everyone agrees on: nipples, clitoris, A- and G-spots, and the vagina, as you well know. Did you know that women have the capacity for multiple orgasms because they have a wider range of erogenous zones?"

God, he could listen to her in her sexy librarian mode all day. "I didn't. We'd better get serious here. We have a lot of area to cover."

He picked her up in his arms, making her gasp. Her hands twined around his neck as he headed for the stairs on the main floor. Since he couldn't kiss her and find her bedroom at the same time, he did the next best thing. He caressed the backs of her legs as he carried her, eliciting a squirm and a sigh.

"Darla assured me you would be as committed to any sexual activity as you were to regular hockey practice," she informed him. "She is rarely wrong about these things."

He knew women talked about guys like guys talked about women. "Val, I'm as committed to this as if it were the championship game."

"That committed?" She was a picture of delighted shock in his arms as he took the stairs. "Then let me equally assure you that you will have my best. I expect you have more practical experience than I do, but I am well versed in the *Kama Sutra* and many other sexual texts. I do not think you will be displeased."

No, she was going to totally rock his world and make this one of the most unforgettable moments of his life. "You've actually read the *Kama Sutra?*"

"Of course." Her tone was almost put out that he would suggest otherwise. "Human sexuality is not so very different now in terms of actual coupling. What has changed is—"

He covered her mouth with his since he'd reached the top of the stairs. Her hand curled around his nape as her lips met his in urgent, wicked passes. He gripped her to him, savoring the slender, taut lines of her body. His tongue pressed deep. She opened to meet him, and they got down to some serious stroking, her body turning into an inferno in his arms.

When his lungs demanded air, he broke away from her mouth, causing her to moan, her fingers tugging his hair to bring him back. "Tell me where your bedroom is."

"To the right at the end of the hall," she whispered, guiding his mouth back to hers for another impatient kiss.

He did his best to walk down the hall with their mouths joined. Because she was not letting go. He wasn't complaining. All her nerves were gone. When he reached her suite, he closed the double doors behind them, sensing she might like the privacy, and crossed the high-ceilinged room to lower her to the massive king bed. He stretched his frame out beside her and kissed her again, feeling heat at his back. The sound of a crackling fire reached his ears.

When he broke the kiss again, he looked over at the white marble fireplace and then traced her soft, pink-tinged cheek. "You made a fire for us?"

She smoothed her hair back as she nodded. "The rituals of romance are equally important to the actual sexual joining. I also lit candles, as you can see. There is a bottle of champagne in the bucket of ice beside the bed in case that would please you."

He felt like a jerk. "I didn't bring you anything. Jesus, Val, I'm sorry."

"Why?" She propped her head up with an elbow. "You were on the road for three away games. You had Zeke's hockey game to attend this morning. When were you supposed to shop? Besides, I didn't expect anything."

But she should. He would do better next time. "I'll make it up to you, I promise."

Her green eyes veiled. "Let's agree not to make promises. We're here now, and that's where our focus stays."

She was talking like a guy now? His arousal was shifting as his own frustration rose. "How about this? I'd like to make you feel special, so if I do something, it's my choice. Okay?"

"If you'd like," she answered crisply.

Why was she so wary? He should never have opened his mouth. "I believe there are a few erogenous zones I need to attend to."

Turning on the bed, he took her foot in his hand, marveling at how tiny it seemed. Slowly, he slid off her socks, running his finger up the middle of her foot.

She giggled, and the sound was too cute for words. "Sorry. I'm a little ticklish. In fact, I'm not sure whether this one will work for me as an erogenous zone."

He was a competitor. They'd see about that. Rising to stand at the foot of the bed, he tugged her to the edge and brought her foot to the center of his chest while his other hand ran up her leg from the back of her thigh to the back of her knee to her calf to her foot. Her green eyes fired. "I think it's a combination play," he told her.

"Yes, I see," she managed in a husky voice as he did it again. "Combination. I'll make sure to note that."

He lifted her other leg to his chest and then ran his hand up between the middle of her legs. She squirmed in response. "How about that?"

"There is some arousal...so I believe you are right about the combination play."

He knew what else might cause Miss Sexy Librarian to lose her mind. Tugging his sweater off, he tossed it aside. Her bare feet rested against his naked chest. Her eyes greedily took in his body, and he let her have her fill.

He'd been admired for his body since he was a teenager, and he worked hard for the physique. But he'd never had an ego about it. In fact, he was turned off by the women who threw themselves at him because of it.

But pleasing her with the way he looked? It mattered more in this moment than it had in a long time. He wanted her to want him. Burn for him. "Like what you see?"

She retracted her feet from his chest and rolled until she was kneeling on the bed in front of him. "I never imagined I was the kind of woman to be swept away by a man's body—there are so many other things I like about you. But you are very beautiful, Brock."

Something hotly emotional pressed against the back of his throat. Her praise. That she liked him. That this was more than a simple weekend of sex. "There's a lot I like about you too, Val, and God knows you take my breath away."

Her hand hesitantly touched his chest. "But not with my ugly work uniform."

He snorted. "It didn't stop me from noticing you, but yeah, I prefer you like this. With your gorgeous hair down. Looking up at me with those big eyes of yours. Wanting me."

She swallowed thickly. "I do want you. More than I've ever wanted anyone else. It's rather...disconcerting sometimes."

He put his hands around her tiny waist as she knelt in front of him. "And why is that?"

Her sigh was filled with regret to his ears. "Control, I suppose. I feel easier when I'm at my best. Not that you don't make me feel...good. You do."

The quick caress of his jaw was supposed to assure him, but he waited for her to continue, sensing he was learning more about the real Val.

"It's easier to live up to a certain standard when the

variables are known," she continued in that sexy librarian voice.

They had so much in common. Did she see it? He cupped her cheek. "I know we bring out new variables in each other," he said, remembering their conversation. "But you can trust me to help you through it in the same way I'm trusting you. Because Val, I also love control. I embody it on the ice and off. It's a key to my success."

"Brock 'The Rock,' right?" She touched the scar on his jaw.

"Yeah." He traced her beauty mark and then touched her lower lip. "But I'm willing to give up a little control to feel the other things you make me feel. Crazy with lust."

Her satisfied smile was the kind that had owned men for centuries.

"Distracted by your beauty as much as your sexy librarian mind."

She beamed.

"And emotionally tugged when you're sweet, especially with my family."

"I like them," she admitted. "Zeke makes me think of what you must have been like as a boy, and Kinsley... Well, she's very familiar to me and Darla, as you know."

"You might tell me the rest of the story sometime."

Her eyes lifted and locked with his. "Sometime. But not now. I believe we let our excitement level lower due to our talking."

He oddly didn't care. "I told you we have plenty of time."

"You did." She leaned up and kissed his jaw. "Besides, extending excitement usually leads to more powerful orgasms."

There she went again, destroying all his control. He

pulled her to him with a growl. "Let's get to those orgasms then, shall we?"

He lowered them both to the bed and rolled over her, careful to withhold his full weight. Her mouth locked on his, her tongue pressing inside this time. He swept her up in a dance that had them both gasping. When she broke free to take her sweater off, he was there to help her. Only to have his insides sizzle like they were on the fire across the room when he saw what she was wearing underneath.

The lacy teddy was a forest green and made her skin glow like marble—only marble was cold, and Val's skin was warm and inviting as he traced the neckline hugging her breasts.

"Another ritual I thought you might like," she whispered. "Darla helped me pick it out."

Thank you, Darla. "I like these romance rituals of yours. This one especially."

"The male preoccupation with lingerie is well established."

He fought laughter. "Yeah, we're pretty basic."

Leaning down, he ran his mouth across the line where lace met skin and loved hearing her sigh. But it wasn't enough.

"Is this one of those snappy things?" he asked, reaching for the buttons on her jeans and undoing them.

He had to see all of her. Or die.

"Yes, there is a set of snaps holding it together," she whispered, her hips arching into him as he teased the exposed skin at her V before tugging her jeans down her long, bare legs.

Now there was a sight. He'd thought she had strong legs before under those baggy clothes of hers, and certainly, he'd gotten a better sense when she was wearing his jersey. But upon closer inspection—because he was a thorough man—he noted the definition in her upper thighs as he traced his way down to strong calves.

For good measure, he tickled her feet again, wanting to hear that cute little giggle, so unlike her usual serious reserve. Then he slid his hands all the way back up her body, making her restless, and cupped her sweet little butt in his large hands.

She made another soft little groan and bit her lip. He was lost. Taking her mouth, he plied her with deep kisses and long strokes of his tongue, loving as her hands started to roam. Over his back. Up his chest. And then down to his jeans.

When she made no further move, he released her and stood to undo his jeans, taking them down his legs before toeing off his socks. He stood naked before her, feeling proud of his body in a way he never had before as her gaze raked over him.

"Oh, you weren't wearing any—" Her big luminous eyes locked on his cock. "Very practical of you."

"Easy access has its benefits." He picked his jeans up and tugged a few condoms out, glad he'd brought more in his duffel bag—because they were going to need them. "Are you good with this?"

She swallowed thickly. "Yes, I forgot to mention... I have my health tests for you showing I am clean, as they say. I know you have regular health checkups with the team, so I'll take your word that you are clean as well."

He'd never talked about sexual health or safe sex in such clinical terms. But that was his Miss Sexy Librarian for you. "I am clean, but I value you taking my word about it. I want you to trust me, Val."

"You wouldn't be here if I didn't," she told him quietly, her gaze soft yet filled with seriousness.

The moment was fraught with meaning. He slid back onto the bed, rolled to his side, and cupped her face. "You are the most amazing woman I have ever met."

Her smile was so bright, the sunshine might as well have come out and rained its glow right onto her beautiful face. "That might be one of the best compliments I've ever had. Thank you. I think you are certainly one of the most exciting men I've ever met, and certainly you are interesting, although I meet very interesting characters in my work—"

He shut her up with his mouth.

Their hands soon were roving over those erogenous zones they'd agreed to be thorough about. He couldn't get enough of her breasts, he discovered, as he undid the teddy and drew it off her body. He lowered his face into the valley and inhaled. She was soft and clean and hot under his touch, and when he took her breast into his mouth, she arched in one sexy line off the bed that had him growling in his throat.

His other hand found the sweet little auburn triangle between her legs, his thumb pressing for that other zone she'd almost primly mentioned. Her loud groan filled his ears, and he slipped a finger inside her, loving that she was hot and wet and very much his.

She widened her legs, urging him on with a thrust of her hips, and it didn't take long to bring her to the first peak. Panting, she laid a hand over her forehead. "Well, that was... I might say I've reached a new arousal level with you."

He loved hearing that as much as they way her entire face was tinted pink. *"Babe..."*

She lifted the hand from her eyes and smiled. Just

smiled. Even though he was hard and ready, it blew over him like a summer wind on the lake.

"You ain't seen nothing yet," he promised her as he lowered his head between her thighs.

She was slick and ready under his mouth, and soon her hands were gripping his head as she rose up, her cries more urgent, louder. He knew she was close, and all it took was a deep stroke to her core to have her lose all her hard-fought control.

He wanted to beat his chest in victory.

SEVENTEEN

What is it about men that makes women lose complete control of themselves?

She lay there, panting.

Panting like a wild animal.

But she couldn't feel bad about any of it. She hadn't stretched the truth when she'd told Brock he'd brought her to new arousal heights. Her orgasms before might as well have been mere champagne pops compared with the Mont Blanc avalanche she'd just experienced.

He was a man of his word.

When she opened her eyes, he was lying beside her, his face flushed with arousal, his incredible gorgeous male appendage a glorious study of hardness and compass-like intent, pointing upward the way it did. She'd never seen a more gorgeous penis in her life.

"You should be commended for your thoroughness," she finally managed, her voice husky from all the harsh cries she'd uttered.

He seemed to smirk in response. "You ready for another arousal level? Because I am."

Even though he must be highly aroused—all the indications were obvious from his heated eyes, rapid pulse, and fast breathing, not to mention his erection—he didn't seem in a hurry.

She found she wanted to do something about that.

Rising up on her side, she reached out a hesitant hand toward his erection. She hadn't touched many, and when she had, there had been urgent demands immediately thereafter, which hadn't led to the most pleasing of intercourse for her. They'd been ready. She hadn't been. Afterward, she'd wondered about the fuss people made.

She'd waited to touch him until now, wanting to be further along. He hadn't disappointed. But even so, as she gave him her first stroke, she made sure to watch his face. His eyes closed, his face a mask of agony.

"Do you want me to stop?"

He wrapped his hand around hers. "God, no. Don't stop. I need your hands on me. Your mouth too, but maybe later for that. I want to be inside you."

She wanted that too. Her hand felt bold with his hand commanding it, giving her permission to stroke his length and run her finger over his shaft to the tip of his erection. Then he pressed into her hand and uttered a long, harsh, lust-inducing cry.

She eased back, feeling his sensitivity to her touch—it was rather academic—and proceeded to repeat her moves. Long strokes up his shaft. Swirls at the top. Then back down again. She marveled at the heat and hardness of him in a way that was both scientific and womanly. When he pressed her hand to his balls, she explored there too, feeling the skin tighten up.

"You're perfect," she said, her voice soft as he pressed urgently into her hand again.

His blue eyes opened, and the glitter of male lust, heat, and intent in them ignited an inferno in her belly. "You're about to find out how much."

He reached for the condom and put it on, his need for control obvious. She waited to see what he was going to do. Take her this moment? The idea was glorious.

When he turned that heated gaze on her and gently pushed her back down on the bed, it felt like a river of liquid lust had been unearthed inside her. She was hot and breathless as he studied her with those glittering blue eyes.

Then he lowered his mouth to the V between her legs again and set her to screaming. This time his kisses weren't easy or gentle. No, this was complete and total possession. With tongue and fingers and the heel of his hand. She flew into a lust-filled craze under his mouth, urging him closer, her hips pressing into his mouth as she uttered hoarse words. *Yes. Please. More. There.*

The madness was almost painful in its urgency. She whimpered, her nails grazing his skull. She was going to die. Couldn't take any more.

And then she exploded.

She felt him gather her up, her legs around his waist, and then he was coming into her in one deep stroke that made her urgent all over again. He pumped into her, his hands gripping her hips. He was on his knees, his body like a plank over her. She latched her hands onto his shoulders and thrust up and up and up. His breathing blew heated air on her face. His grunts were the kind legends were made of. She tightened her legs around him, squeezing him because she wanted to crush him inside her somehow to stop the agony of need.

But she didn't want to stop looking at him. Not when it was the most beautiful sight she'd ever seen.

If he could take it, so could she.

He pumped into her all while she kept her gaze focused on him, her nerve endings screaming for release.

Then he punched up his speed to an almost inhuman level, his hips levering down in uncontrolled thrusts. Hoarse words. Demanding thrusts. He arched into her as he came, gripping her hips with such urgency she felt the molten lava resting in her inner belly swirl before flying straight up her middle.

She came in a series of whispered cries and hoarse shouts, her entire body filled with him and her pleasure. Her eyes squeezed shut as she rode out the wave with him, and then she was catching him as he partially fell onto her, his hot moist breath rasping hard in her ear, his entire body slick with hot sweat against her. His head came to rest on her shoulder, and she slid her hand into his wet black curls and held on as pulse after pulse after pulse rocked her system.

When he finally rolled them to the side and dealt with the condom, she kept her arm around him. Every nerve ending was still buzzing. Her ability to speak was gone. All she could do was hold on to him and wait for things to settle.

Maybe in the next century.

His heavy arm was over her, and she was aware that he'd tucked her against his chest, tangling his hand in her hair. He couldn't let go any more than she could release him.

"You alive?" he finally rasped.

"I'm certainly not dead."

This caused him to chuckle, except it came out as more of a rasp. "God! Woman, I had no idea you had that in you."

Woman... The primal invective seemed perfect right

now. She felt like a woman. Darla was right. She had learned things about herself, ones she would reflect on later. "Neither did I, actually. By myself, I've done pretty well, but never like this."

He grunted. "Pretty good by yourself... You trying to kill me with that line?"

"No. Why?"

"Because it's hot, thinking about you taking care of yourself." His harsh exhalation raised the hair on top of her head. "Jesus, Val."

Crude language often took the place of deeper sentiments according to her research. "I take it you're pleased."

He laughed wickedly. "I can hear the pleased smile in your voice. You destroyed me, and you know it."

She finally could give a languorous stretch. "We did promise to give it our best. Oh, no!"

He shot up. "What is it?"

"I forgot to take my heart rate."

"Is that all?"

She nearly laughed at his scowl before he tucked her close again.

"We will have to try again later," she told him, tracing the drops of sweat on his gorgeous chest, her new favorite Greatest Wonder of the World site.

"That's a given." He grunted again as he traced her back. "Tell me your romance rituals involve steak and a baked potato."

This was her moment to chuckle. "I know something about the kinds of foods the body requires after strenuous physical activity. Red meat is one, so yes, you're in luck."

"You might be the ultimate woman," he said, nuzzling her neck.

No one had ever said so before, and she found that it

sent her dopamine levels even higher. She'd worried about any awkwardness after sex. But all she felt was a happiness she'd rarely felt with anyone other than Darla—and for very different reasons, obviously.

"Are you hungry now?" She didn't want to leave the warmth of his body, but she would, she realized. Because if he were hungry, she wanted to see him fed. Goodness. Talk about primal instincts.

"You're thinking again," he said, doing that very sexy nuzzling thing she'd seen wild horses do to each other. "Anything interesting? Did I miss any erogenous zones, by the way?"

She went back over their list in her head.

"What are you doing?" he asked in a deep rumble.

"Counting."

"Eleven," he answered flatly.

She revisited her list again. "I believe we listed ten."

He leveled her back. "Listed what? I was telling you how many orgasms you had."

Sputtering out a laugh, she pushed a black lock of sweaty hair off his forehead. "I had more than that, but we won't quibble. And you're preening like a rooster."

"Damn straight I am. I just had mind-blowing sex with the most beautiful woman in the world. And soon, I'll be having steak. It might be the perfect day."

"Men are known for having simple needs," she commented, watching as a sexy smile played on the mouth she'd just kissed so much she'd made it a little swollen. Talk about pride.

When had Valentina Hargrove ever kissed a man senseless?

"What do *you* need?" he asked suddenly.

Her eyes flew to him. No sexual partner had ever asked

her that. "I...ah...I'm good. Happy. Satisfied. It was a complete experience."

He leaned in and kissed her slowly, so slowly her breath caught and her heart turned over in her chest.

When he eased her back, he tucked her hair behind her ears. "Let me try asking that a different way. I want to eat steak as I watch you sitting across from me. What would make you happy to do with me?"

One image rushed into her mind—the photo of his happy face as he held Zeke's little hand on the ice.

Then another one rose up. The two of them holding hands and skating side by side as he looked at her with that beautiful smile he had only for her.

She sucked her breath in. *No, not that.* She could not do that. It would only beg more questions she couldn't answer...

But the image stuck, like a fossil to a stone. Ever since she'd first seen him on the ice, she'd been entranced. She'd wondered what it would be like to skate with him. Flow with him as their skates scraped the ice. For him to watch as she danced around him. God, she wanted to share the love she had for the ice with him—because he loved it just as much.

She could find the pure joy of skating with him, and deep down, she hungered for it.

"Are you planning to tell me what's going through that sexy mind of yours?" He gently tapped her temple. "Or are you going to make me guess?"

She looked at his bare chest, trying to formulate another answer. But all she could see in her mind was her skating around him, his wickedly sexy smile inviting her to smile back. "I'll have to think about it."

He lifted her chin up until their eyes met. "Afraid to tell me?"

Naked and warm in his arms, she found it difficult to call on her reserve. She didn't want to put up a wall between them to get past this moment. Not after the beauty they'd just shared together. Besides, she didn't want to blow him off. She wanted to draw him more deeply inside her, like she had with her body.

"Yes, a little." She paused, gritting her teeth, and then added, "Maybe another time?"

Something flickered in those warm blue depths before falling away.

She'd done something to dampen the light that had been there, and this she couldn't bear. "All right. I'd like to go skating with you."

His brow shot up so fast, another sweaty lock of black hair tumbled down. *"You skate?"*

If she weren't so nervous, she would have laughed. He sounded like she'd confessed to having six fingers or claimed to have the answer to wormholes. "I have been known to, yes, although it's been a while," she said, feeling even more naked now as she toyed with his chest. "But you skate all the time, so you don't—"

He laid his finger to her lips in the gentlest of motions. "I'd love to skate with you, Val. How about after we eat? I know this fabulous little pond we can use up north. It's about an hour away. Hot chocolate comes with the deal. Does that work?"

She blamed her beaming smile on the soaring dopamine levels. "That would be perfect."

EIGHTEEN

WHY WAS IT THAT WHEN A WOMAN SMILED LIKE THAT, A *man wanted to give her the world?*

Brock couldn't look away from her. Her green eyes glowing, her mouth a picture of pure, complete happiness.

All because he'd agreed to skate with her.

He knew some women wanted more—credit cards, shopping sprees, and trips to island getaways. Sure, Val had her money, but he'd known plenty of hockey players who'd dated wealthy women who still asked for the world.

She'd only wanted a simple date involving skating.

That she might love skating like he did had never dawned on him. But why would it? He didn't know much about her. Except he did. He knew her mind and her heart, and now he knew her body. Every piece of her was a new revelation, and with every unfolding, he only wanted more.

He was falling for her. Hard. And he had no desire to stop the descent or put on a parachute.

"You take my breath away when you smile like that," he told her, lowering his face and kissing her until they both sighed.

"Elevated dopamine levels," she answered between sips of her mouth.

He snorted out a laugh. "You didn't answer me before. Did I miss any erogenous zones?"

When she scrunched up her heated face, he knew she was thinking. "No, I believe you experienced all of mine. I, however, did not experience all of yours."

Was she talking about his G-spot? Because that was certainly unexplored territory. "We can go for that later. After we eat. I'm starving, and I need a couple of gallons of water."

"Food and hydration are suggested for successful bouts of prolonged sexual activity."

"I'm glad you're up on the perfect system." God, she was wonderful.

She touched his chest with a tenderness that filled his heart before she rolled to the side of the bed and rose. The sheer beauty of her backside had lust rushing through him again. Acres of creamy porcelain skin. Sweet little tush. Long, slender but toned legs. Her back was lithe with elegant muscles, the kind that came from training. Hadn't he suspected she had a strong core to be able to carry herself the way she did?

"I like you naked," he told her honestly.

She looked over her shoulder, her quirky smile telling him she was a little shy, a little amused. "I imagine that's a good thing given our sexual attraction for each other. I find you equally pleasing."

Pleasing...

Her formal tone made him want to haul her back to bed, but she was padding to the bathroom. When he heard the shower turn on, he was off like a shot. Now, *that* they could do together.

They found a few more of his erogenous zones.

Once they were able to crawl off the shower floor, Val insisted on dressing. One, she told him, they needed to subvert temptation in order to eat. Second, it was dangerous to cook with few clothes on. This she knew firsthand from Darla, who'd gotten burned one time while cooking for a beau in the nude.

That had made him laugh.

In the kitchen, they found a good rhythm. She insisted on making a salad to go with the steak while he washed and scrubbed the potatoes and stuck them in the oven. The steaks she unveiled from the butcher paper had his mouth watering. His was larger—a T-bone—while hers was a small rib eye.

"Now that's meat," he commented.

"I thought you'd like a steak with the bone-in." She pointed toward the back patio. "Would you like to grill or shall I? I have good experience with fire if that concerns you."

He leaned against the counter and watched her bustle around efficiently. "Not a bit, but can I ask why you have experience with fire? You didn't say grilling."

She paused briefly after taking two plates out of the glass cabinets before setting them down slowly. "I...ah...have cooked on a campfire many times."

He almost slid off the counter. He loved to camp. In the off-season, he couldn't do it enough. *"You camp?"*

Her nod was perfunctory. "I do, as does Darla. Speaking of...I should check in. She was...anxious for me. I'd like to tell her all went as hoped."

Again, her use of words had him wanting to snatch her up. But he was touched her friend had been concerned. Not that he was surprised, he supposed. Another girl thing. No guy would think to check in and tell a friend the sex he'd had with the girl had gone okay. A good guy didn't talk, for one.

When she came back in, she was smiling softly. "I started the coals while I was talking. They should be ready soon." She walked over to check the baked potatoes.

He crossed the kitchen to where she stood because she was too far away for his liking. "How is Darla?" he asked as the heat of the oven escaped, enticing him with the smell of baking potatoes.

"Good. Shopping. She's making up for lost time, it seems."

Her sigh was a puff of air before she closed the oven door. He touched her back as she walked past him, and he felt her surprise. She wasn't used to being touched. Well, that was going to change.

"Why does that bother you?"

She stilled from lifting her water glass to her mouth. "Well, because normally we travel light, as I believe we discussed with Zeke on our sightseeing trip. I'm concerned we need a little more certainty to... Well, things. Filling up her closet will make it more difficult for us to pivot if we have need to."

What the hell did that mean? "I have a whole bunch of questions, Val, but I have a feeling they're off-limits."

Her cool reserve was back but coupled with an assuring smile. "For now. Do you want to talk about the away games?"

This time he shook his head. "Not really. It'll only make me angry. Truthfully, I don't bring work home with me after Erin. My ex. We married young and only lasted two years. My injuries really upset her, which affected me. So I decided hockey is business, and when I'm off the ice, I'm off." Even though he remembered being able to talk to Val very easily about work when she'd been at the house that first time.

"That's part of your mental training and very wise of you," she replied, sipping her sparkling water with lime.

He could only stare at her. *Wise?* No one had ever called him that.

"The constant pressure and competition can take over your life and hurt your well-being if you don't have defined boundaries."

He stared at her in wonder for a moment, because she understood the depths of him in a way no other woman ever had. "You really are the perfect woman, you know."

She gave a surprised laugh and set her glass down. "I'm far from perfect. But there are some things that are obvious. This is one of them. Shall we grill the steaks?"

"You bet." This he wanted to see.

Used to the cold, he didn't don a coat like she did, but she kept her hands free of gloves as she checked the coals. They were glowing and must have satisfied her because she gave an absent nod to herself and then carefully positioned his steak on one of the grill racks after adjusting the heat.

"It won't be the same as a cook fire," she told him, the sun washing her smiling face as she looked up at him. "But I believe it will do for our purposes. Yours will take longer, I imagine. Although I forgot to ask...how do you like your steak?"

He wrapped his arms around her, fingers playing with her waist. They were trading little details like how they liked their steaks while the bigger ones—why she camped and knew how to cook over a fire—remained a mystery. But he wasn't ready to press her. "Medium rare."

"Of course you do." She rested her hand on his chest,

like she was getting used to the newness of touching him. "Better iron content and flavor."

"How do you like this place?" He gestured to the man-made lake behind the house.

"It's suitable, I suppose." Her face was a study in peaceful repose as she turned her head. "I like nature, and I appreciate the space. The quiet. I could go weeks without seeing another person here."

There was a wistfulness in her voice. He'd sensed she was shy, but maybe she was a loner as well. "Darla is the social butterfly, huh?"

Her enormous smile had his heart turning over in his chest. "Darla loves to tell me about the people she meets in the elevator." Her laugh was infectious. "Everywhere we go, she talks to people. She's a magnet. It's always been that way. I'm grateful for it most days. If she weren't so outgoing, I don't think she would have become my friend."

He sensed a story, and because he couldn't resist, he tangled his hands in her long hair. "Why do you say that?"

Her green eyes darkened for a moment as she looked off. "When I met Darla in boarding school, I was in a rough place. I've always been shy, but I'd grown mistrustful and reserved to the point of numbness. She…kept at me until I came out of my shell."

Like they were doing with Kinsley. "I'm sorry you had a rough time."

She lifted her shoulder. "We all do at some point. If we're lucky, we have someone like Darla come into our lives. I would have gotten through it. I'm too disciplined and determined a person not to. But I wouldn't have been as happy. Darla brought that into my life. Laughter for no good reason other than making a face over a boy. Staying up late to watch a bad chick flick while eating too much popcorn."

Simple pleasures. "That sounds special. It's funny. When I went to boarding school for hockey, that's when stuff like that fell away from my life. All that was left was hockey and school. The pressure took away everything."

She caressed his chest in comfort—her warmth moving him deeply. "I've had my own experience with such matters. Pressure can steal your childhood and your life. I hope you've gotten your sense of fun back, Brock."

He traced her cheek, watching as her big eyes looked up at him. The whole world was in those eyes. "It's still a work in progress, but yeah. Camping does that for me. Being with Zeke—Kinsley too, when she's being easy with herself. Maybe we should stay up late and eat too much popcorn together."

"I'd like that." She laid her head against his chest, and for a moment, the pure peace of holding her felt like what he'd been looking for his whole life. "Oh, I should check your steak."

He let her go and watched as she poked it with another absent nod before turning it with her usual proficiency. She laid her steak on the grill next to his and then shot him a smile. "I don't think I've been this hungry in a long time. It feels good."

Did it? He ate food for fuel, and sure, he enjoyed it. But her admission felt different. "I noticed you don't eat much."

"I don't burn as much..." She trailed off. "Great physical activity is the key for working up a good appetite. Do you want to check on the baked potatoes?"

He didn't. All he wanted to do was stand beside her. He simply didn't want to be away from her. Her fresh clean scent. Her sweet little smile. The pull of her green gaze. But it was madness, and he nodded slowly. "I can do that."

Soon, they were sitting across from each other at the

dining room table. He dug into his steak like a man who hadn't eaten in days while she cut and ate her steak in an orderly fashion, like a lady. She laughed when he served himself three baked potatoes, but she didn't seem surprised. Erin used to marvel at how much food he could eat.

Again, he noted he was thinking about Erin and comparing her to Val and vice versa. He'd never done that with any of the other women he'd dated after his divorce.

The reason was obvious.

He could see long-term with Val.

Perhaps he was getting ahead of himself, but he felt a certainty he'd rarely experienced in a relationship. When he felt that kind of certainty, he pursued it. She fit him. They understood each other—even without all the details of her past. And God, they were insane in bed. Cataclysmically good.

"Do you want dessert?" She set her fork and knife aside and dabbed her mouth with her napkin.

God, that sexy librarian thing was going to kill him.

"I remember reading you liked peanut butter pie," she continued, "so I arranged for some." Flashing him a smile, she added, "I don't have a sweet tooth, as a rule, but I'd try a piece."

He couldn't take the distance anymore. Sliding his chair back, he stood up and stalked to her side of the table. "You got me peanut butter pie?"

"From Rolands." She leaned back as he loomed over her. "It's your favorite, yes?"

God, her thoughtful touches were destroying him. "Another romantic ritual, Val?"

"One does wish to please the person one is attracted to." She laid her hands on his forearms. "It's not like the acquisition of a peanut butter pie was difficult. I had it delivered."

"It's more than that, and you know it."

He wanted to drag her back up to her room and show her how much it mattered. He wasn't a sentimental guy, but this was like her building them a fire. Or her being in his driveway when he'd gotten home from those brutal road games. Little acts that said she cared about him, and honestly, they didn't feel little at all.

She fiddled with her napkin, touching him with her shyness. "I hope this particular ritual was not an overstep."

That had him hauling her out of her chair and against his chest. "An overstep? Val, it's one of the nicest things anyone has ever done for me. Now come here."

His mouth was on hers in an instant, his need for her growing thick and fierce. She wrapped her arms around him, her hands digging into his hair. His heart thundered in his chest, and in an instant, all of his good intentions were gone. He was setting her on the edge of the table and tugging her leggings and lacy undies off before undoing the button of his jeans and letting himself free.

She fisted her hands in his sweater as he rolled on a condom, her breath coming in pants now. He slid inside her only an inch. The green eyes that slayed him looked up at him as he lifted both her legs in his hands and thrust in deep.

She arched against him, an urgent cry erupting from her sweet little mouth. He pumped into her as he held her behind the knees, controlling the tempo. Her hands were fisted in his sweater as she strained against him. Then she gave a loud cry and lay back against the table, pushing the china away from her. He swept his hand beside her, making sure she didn't hit her head on anything, and continued to pump into her, feeling her clench, feeling her reach for him.

His hands joined hers on the table, their fingers twining together. Their eyes met, and time seemed to stop.

She was so breathtakingly beautiful, and right now, she was his.

He leaned down and kissed her, driving deeply into her as his tongue rubbed against hers. Their breathing grew harsher, as did her cries. She was close, and he was going to make her come.

"Come for me," he ordered, watching as her eyes closed. *"Right now."*

The explosion rocked him back as she let out a high-pitched cry, bowing back with a strength guaranteed to take him with her. He went willingly, coming hard into her, and gave a guttural cry of release that left him spent.

When he managed to open his eyes and lever himself up, she was laughing as she moved a fork away from her mass of hair. He cupped her shoulder and helped her up, sliding out of her and cleaning them both up.

"I believe we've both had dessert." He kissed her swiftly, loving the sweetness of her soft mouth.

When he released her, she looked down at her shoulder and grimaced. *"Oh my God!* Is that steak juice?"

He bit his lip to keep from laughing as she hauled her hair over her right shoulder and let out a cry.

"Looks like," he said. "Now that my head is back on, I seem to recall your hair landing on my plate."

"Dear God!" Her horrified expression was as funny as her grabbing a clean napkin and dabbing at her auburn tresses. "This is mortifying. I have never done anything so..."

"So sexy?" He leaned in and gave a sniff. "You smell like steak, woman, and sex. Bottle that."

Her haughty expression had his lips twitching. "Steak, woman, and sex. Of course you'd love it. You might as well beat your chest, it calls so primally to you as a man."

His shoulders started to shake. "Damn straight. It's a scent I'll always remember."

When she threw the napkin at him, she started laughing. "This is one time I wish memories were not so tied to smell. God! You've made me completely lose my mind. On the dinner table!"

He did want to beat his chest, hearing he'd just given her a first. Instead, he slid his arms around her and smoothed her hair for her with another napkin. "You were beautiful before, but this might take it over the top. If other men saw you like this, they'd all worship you too. Of course, I'd have to beat them senseless—"

"With steak juice in my hair!" She sputtered out a laugh. "God, you're easy. Another guy might have cringed and lost all interest in me. But you... You crack jokes."

He wondered about the kind of jerks she must have been with in the past. Idiots. Fussy, to boot. "It's no joke, Val."

There was a gleam of vulnerability in her green eyes. "I'm glad you didn't find it funny—or me. I...you make it easy for me to be with you. I didn't know how it'd be beyond the sex. I'd hoped—"

She broke off, leaving his heart throbbing painfully for her. He framed her face. "I like you. A lot. With all your baggy outfits, mysterious background, and simmering sexuality."

Her long throat moved as she swallowed. "I like you a lot too."

As the team captain, he knew when someone was the

best person to blaze a trail, and for the path he wanted them to take, he had to be the one. "I happen to have fallen totally in love with you, Miss Sexy Librarian."

Her mouth parted before she laid a trembling hand on his chest. "Without knowing everything about me?"

He grabbed her hand and squeezed, sealing the pact. "I know when I'm certain about things, and I'm certain about this. About you and how I feel with you."

"That's...an incredible amount of trust." Her voice held equal parts awe and warmth as she drew his hand to her cheek and sweetly pressed it there. "You're brave to tell me. I will have to meet that." She looked him straight in the eye. "I happen to like you a lot more than the paltry word 'like' conveys. The truth is I've never felt this way about anyone else."

Ah... He couldn't contain the slow smile breaking across his face or the urge to lean in and kiss her softly. "Good. Then we're on the same page. Also, since I'm still loving the scent of sex and steak radiating from you, I want to go on record as saying that I happen to like you uninhibited. I like having you on the dinner table—or anywhere else we want."

She fought a smile so hard she bit her bottom lip, which only made her more achingly sweet. "Darla always says sex is messy business when done right. Appears she was correct once again. At this rate, she's going to be insufferable."

"Another sexy word from Miss Sexy Librarian. Come on. We can have the peanut butter pie later. We need to get on the road—before I decide to strip you, rub steak juice all over you, and lick it off."

Her gasp had his shoulders shaking. "You'd do that?"

"In a hot second." He kissed her swiftly. "Now, get cracking. We have skating to look forward to. Also, pack an overnight bag."

"All right." She surveyed the dishes. "Let me clean up."

He stayed her with a hand. "Go pack. Skating is more important."

When she gave him that once-in-a-million smile again, he knew he was totally in love with her.

NINETEEN

How had a man made her lose all her senses?

The moment Val was out of the room, she picked up her phone and dialed Darla, climbing the stairs to her bedroom.

Her friend picked up immediately, appearing on FaceTime, and pointed to her watch. "Right on time. You're freaking out."

"I don't know what I am. I have steak juice in my hair because I had sex with Brock on the dinner table, and I think we might have just said we've fallen in love with each other."

"*Hold on.* You have what in your hair?"

"Steak juice," she said, lifting one of her damp locks.

Darla's guffaw was not unexpected. As her friend wheezed from laughing so hard, Val headed into her closet. Picking up an overnight bag, she stuffed a few items into it.

Wiping her eyes, Darla said, "My BFF, the restrained, disciplined Dr. Valentina Hargrove has steak juice in her hair after having sex on the dining room table. Oh my God! The day has finally come. Sweetie, I am so proud of you. To think, this is bigger news than you and Brock being in love with each other. I knew you had it in you, girl."

"Wait!" She dropped the bag on the bed. "Why is the news of us being in love not as shocking? It's steak juice, Darla!"

Her friend shrugged as she peered into the screen. "You and Brock look at each other like you love each other." She shook a finger. "I know looks, and this is more than the *I want to tear your clothes off* variety. This is a *let's make a fur-lined cave together* variety."

Her knees gave out, and she dropped onto the bed. "You are not talking about marriage. *Tell me you aren't talking about marriage.*"

"Honey, you know I don't care if you put a ring on it—although a good man would want to—but yes, I am talking about the possibility of you and Brock making a life together. Here. In Minneapolis, a town I'm really starting to love, meaning I'll be here too as we move forward with the next stage of our career."

Even after that assurance, her heart was thumping against her ribs. "But I'm terrible at long-term. I like my space. Darla, my parents. My mom..."

"Val, you are the steadiest, most loyal person I have ever met." She put a hand to her heart. "As someone who has lived with you for most of my life, let me assure you that you are completely able to do the long-term with someone. You did it with me. Beautifully. Now you can do it with a hunk of a man with a big, huge dick to keep you satisfied."

Val nearly dropped the phone.

"Honey, this is an upgrade."

"But, but... We aren't talking about *marriage.*"

"You will," Darla singsonged, "and since I know you,

I'm giving you plenty of lead time to analyze and think things through. Now, before you make yourself so sick you'll need a paper bag to breathe in, I want to remind you of one thing."

She sucked in her best impression of slow and steady breaths, because Darla was right. Hyperventilation was a possibility. "I think you're being a little optimistic. Brock and I just met—"

"I was going to go first." Darla held up another professorial teacher finger to stop her from jabbering back. "Brock wouldn't spend two precious days off during a hockey season to be with someone he's only infatuated with. Val, I popped over to see Kinsley after I went shopping because I found this cute little shirt for her, and Susan pulled me aside and told me how happy she is that we came into their life. Like *tears in her eyes* happy."

Val's eyes started to burn.

"Susan said she's never seen Brock this happy or eager to be with someone. Not even his ex-wife."

Okay, she was going to drop the phone. "But he doesn't know anything about me! Darla, this is awful!"

"No, it's not." The phone zoomed in close on her friend's face, Darla's golden eyes intent. "You listen to me. This is not a man who waffles or plays the field. You're the same way. Do I need to start quoting study after study about how humans find their best match? He's yours, honey."

"I can't breathe." She clawed at the shirt at her neck. "He can't feel like that this soon. What if he freaks out when he finds out who I am? Why I'm here?"

"Calm down. Honey, I knew you'd need some time to wrap your mind around this. It's a big change for you, and you're more emotional than I've ever seen you."

"I'm a yo-yo, Darla." She breathed shallowly. "Me! Dr. Valentina Hargrove."

"So tell him the truth."

"What?"

"You have the rest of the weekend to talk to him and find out I'm right."

Did she? She looked down at her feet, not sure she was feeling them right now. "But we promised—"

"Your dad and Chuck." Darla waved her hand. "Yes, I know. It would be a breach, but your relationship is more important, isn't it?"

She rocked in place. "This is too much to take in right now."

"So you start wrapping your mind around it. Now, if I know men, Brock is probably prowling around downstairs waiting for you to come down."

Her hand touched the bag next to her. "I need to pack—"

"Pack? You're going somewhere?"

"Yes, skating. I—"

"You told him you wanted to skate?" Darla's eyes filled with tears before she brushed them aside. "Together? Oh, honey, you love him *so* hard. I'm hanging up now. Remember this moment. I'm popping some champagne myself."

The screen went blank. Val fell back on the bed.

"Are you finished packing or am I going to have to come up there?"

Brock's yell had her levering herself up. "I'm coming."

She flew into action, stuffing more things in her bag, including her skates, which she finally removed from their box. Then she was banking the fire in the fireplace.

Hustling down the stairs, she found Brock prowling around the kitchen, just like Darla had said she would.

"You cleaned up," she said in shock.

"I am somewhat domesticated. Plus, you were taking a while. Darla, I assume. Or was it the steak juice? Come on. You can tell me in the car."

He crossed to her, grabbed her bag, and headed to the lower stairs.

She raced after him. "I'm a little off-balance at the moment."

"You can tell me about it in the car," he repeated, opening the door leading to the garage. He let her go ahead of him before pushing the button to raise up the big, jointed door. Looking very much in charge in a sexy way.

She raced over to the passenger side where he had the door open. Her bag was already in the back. When he shut the door, she fumbled to put her seat belt on before twisting in her seat as he got settled in the driver's seat.

"Ah...when you say you've fallen in love with me," she said slowly, "do you mean it in poetic terms or in the more long-term definition of the phrase?"

He started the car and began backing out, his mouth crooked in a sexy, off-center smile. "I don't do poetic. Probably should work on that. But if by long-term you mean that I can't imagine my life without you, then we're headed in the same direction. Although I know it's early yet."

She pressed back in her seat. "Oh my God! She was right."

"If we're talking about Darla, she's always right." He put his hand on her knee. "According to what you've told me, at least. Val, this is not a weekend hookup. Did you think it was?"

"No, I—" Where was her brain? Her logical reasoning? "I'm having trouble putting it all together right now."

He squeezed her knee and then released it, focusing on holding the wheel responsibly, with two hands. "You take all the time you need. We have an hour. Do you have any musical preferences?"

Her neurons were surrounded by fog. That had to be why she couldn't make rational sense. "Driver chooses the music."

"That's what I always say," he said, shooting her a clever wink. "Just sit back and close your eyes. You'll calm back down. You're just overly stimulated. All that sex and steak juice."

He thought this was funny? She wanted to clobber him. And her, a believer in nonviolence. She did her breathing exercises while he drove, taking note of her pulse. Observing her physical reactions helped bring her back in control of herself. She might not have the answers yet, but she was aware she was beyond her normal setting of physical stimuli.

By the time he pulled up to a rustic cabin in the middle of a forest of bare trees, snow and ice coating their branches, she was calmer, if not completely sure of the way forward. Brock didn't seem concerned. They hadn't spoken much on the way—he'd simply driven and sent her scorching smiles.

Now, as he came around the Rover to open her door, she was once again sure of one thing. She might not be poetic either, but she didn't want to think about not being with him.

The mere idea...hurt. Worse than having a shoulder dislocated or a bone break. She'd had both, so she knew.

"You good now?" he asked, tracing her cheekbone softly.

"Yes, thank you. I appreciate you not pushing me to... get back to normal."

He snorted. "That's not me, babe. Come on. Let's get you some hot chocolate and find you some skates. I think Susan's might work, if not Kinsley's."

Her heart shot to the moon as if from a cannon. This was it. She was going to skate with him. She could already feel his hand in hers as the cold air tickled her face. "I have my own!"

Her raised voice had him leaning in and kissing her softly, so softly her heart did another impossible somersault in her chest. She really must look up how that phenomenon happened since the heart couldn't physically move around in her sternum.

"I'm even more eager to see you skate than I already was." He tapped her nose playfully. "A woman who travels light. With her own skates. This is going to be good."

She followed him up the stairs onto the house's porch, loving the rustic atmosphere created by the exposed timbers. "When you mentioned a pond, I expected a public place. But this is a private residence."

"Mine." He took her hand and led her inside after unlocking the door. "And I've never brought anyone here besides family—and Finn, whom I've known forever. In case you need more proof of my intentions. Look around. Make yourself at home. I'll start a fire and the hot chocolate."

All she could do was touch her neck, where all her emotion was clogged.

"Oh, by the way." He drew something out of his pocket and held it up. "I forgot to give this to you. Got distracted. It's a friendship bracelet. From Kinsley."

A friendship bracelet? Her heart melted as her hand

curled around it. She pressed it to her heart. No one but Darla had ever given her something so dear. Her eyes burned when she saw the phrase on it. "Oh...that's so sweet of her."

"Well, that lit you up like fireworks." He cupped her chin and gave her a swift kiss before heading off. "Kinsley wanted you to know she approves of us dating."

Her hand fell to her side. *"She knows?"*

"Yep. I walked into the house last night to find her and Zeke in the kitchen. They saw us kissing in the driveway."

She raced after him, absently slipping her friendship bracelet on. "But this is terrible!" He was filling a copper teakettle with water, but he glanced over with a half smile and shrugged.

"Isn't it?" she pressed.

"It is what is it," he said practically, turning a knob on the stove and igniting the gas. "But I told them not to say anything at school. Susan had a talk with them too. Who would have imagined I'd get to sneak around like a teenager again with my girlfriend?"

Sneak around.

Teenager.

Girlfriend.

"I've never done any of that." She found herself nearly floating off the floor, thinking about being his girlfriend. "I like that perspective."

"Good!" He opened more cabinets, taking out two mugs and a gourmet hot chocolate mix. "Marshmallows?"

When he waggled the plastic bag stuffed with the white buttons, she decided to look past the sugar content and go for it. "Sure."

"Get on your skates and whatever else you have to put on. Only, make sure you're warm. The wind's high today."

She looked toward the back of the house, where a large, natural-stained deck was tucked amidst the bare trees with a smashing view of an iced-over lake with snow-covered edges. God, she couldn't wait to get out there. "You don't need to worry about me. I know how to dress warmly."

"Too bad." He shot her a look filled with heat. "I'd planned to take extra care to warm you up afterward."

This kind of flirting was new to her. When she'd had sex in the past, the encounters had been almost transactional—arranged for the convenience and pleasure of both people, even though she'd truthfully gotten little pleasure from them. True, her three partners had all been scientists. One had even forgotten where she'd lived on his way over. His reason had made Darla chortle: he'd finally solved a mathematical equation about prime numbers that had been troubling him for some time.

"You can still warm me up." Forcing herself to stand tall instead of giving in to shyness, she raised a challenging eyebrow. "That is if you think you'll have enough energy after we skate."

Ah, that sexy lift of his gorgeous mouth made her glad she'd gone with strength. "Don't worry about me. I'm a professional athlete. You, however, sit around watching the team all day and making your sexy librarian notes. You're the one who should be worried."

Little did he know how rigorous her exercise regimen was. Sure, it wasn't anywhere near what it had been during her career as a professional figure skater, but she was still in tip-top shape because it made her feel good. She couldn't wait to prove it. "We'll see."

She sauntered out of the kitchen and headed to her overnight bag, where she'd tucked her skates. Her shoe size had been the same since she was twelve, so she was fortunate. If she were going to go all researcher on herself, she might note her lucky skates were about superstition and mystique. Perhaps that was why she understood hockey players and their rituals so well. She'd had her own set of parameters to follow before a competition, and she'd felt like she was skating on clouds in these particular skates.

The teakettle blew, and the clinking of a spoon sounded moments later. She pulled the rest of her gear out. The pink one-piece thermal suit with the fake fur-lined black hood and belt would be perfect for the outdoors, along with her fake fur bandeau to protect her ears. The fit gave her the mobility and fluidity she'd want. Pulling it on over her jeans and sweater only took a moment.

Brock caught her wiggling into it as he came in with their mugs. He paused and smacked his lips. "You look good enough to eat. Maybe we need a warm-up before we brave the big, bad cold."

She thought about it for a second, seeing the flash of heat in his eyes. Now that they were having sex, the heat was always there for her to see. Certainly, her desire for him hadn't abated. Not like it usually did after a sexual encounter. But she'd never had an explosive sexual encounter before, had she? Her belly was still achy with want every time he looked at her that way.

The knowledge that she could have him whenever she wanted was intoxicating. The time it gave them. The freedom... "If we have another sexual interlude, it will probably be pitch-dark by the time we're ready to go. While I want one very much, I think it would be wise to capitalize on the daylight for skating." Listen to how calm she'd managed to sound even though she was already imagining the first jump she wanted to try.

"Sexual interlude...capitalize...you're only making me

want you more." He made a humming sound. "But I see your point. I'll grab my skates."

He set her hot chocolate in front of her on the coffee table, touched the fur on her hood in an ever-so-sexy way, and then walked off toward another double doorway. Alone, she picked up her hot chocolate and sipped, the flavor making her eyes pop open. Strong, dark, and rich with the punch of melted marshmallows to make her lick her lips.

Oh, the memories it brought back. Of her father taking her skating for the holidays at the community skating rink in the town where she'd grown up in Connecticut. The twinkly lights had added an extra dose of magic, and with the holiday music playing over the loudspeakers, she'd imagined she was acting in *The Nutcracker* but on ice.

Of course, her mother hadn't gone with them, saying she didn't waste her talent skating at a community ice rink. Another reason they'd never bonded over skating. Her mother hadn't shared her love for the ice because she had never possessed any. Whether she had earlier, before all the hard years of training and competition, Val didn't know. Not that it mattered now.

Brock came back in, carrying worn hockey skates in one hand. He was dressed in a suede thermal jacket with black thermal ear protectors on. His shoulders looked even larger in his outerwear, and in a quick second, she was thinking about doing something she'd never considered before: putting sex before skating.

Was the sky falling?

He took a healthy sip of his hot chocolate before setting it back down with a *thwack* and grabbing her hand. "No changing your mind."

"You could tell?" she asked, matching his quick pace to the patio door.

Pulling her to him, he gave her a slow, toe-curling kiss that had her gripping his jacket. "If I hadn't seen it in those liquid green eyes of yours, I'd have known by the flush of your cheeks. Besides, this is all you wanted to do other than have your way with my sexy body, so I'm reminding myself of that."

When he opened the door, a sharp cold breeze slammed her in the face. "I'm cooling off now," she told him with a laugh as he dragged her playfully outside.

The stairs from the deck led down to the lake. Off to the side of those stairs was an enclosed fireplace with cozy cushions protected by the wind. He headed that way.

"It's a nice place to spend time when the weather is warmer." Resting on the end of the outdoor couch, he undid his shoes and put his skates on with practiced ease.

She matched him in speed and facility and beat him onto the ice by a few seconds. The moment her skates touched, her heart might as well have been in a trebuchet because it shot up in her chest with pure joy before settling back into place. She closed her eyes and let the feeling fill her.

This.

Yes.

It was always so right.

She savored the bite of her blades on the ice for a few moments before she opened her eyes. The view before her had her thinking this might be the best day of her life. Her body was loose and limber from sex. Her mind and heart were happy from being with Brock. And now, she was on the ice for the sheer joy of it all—on a pond they had all to themselves.

"You're pretty good," he called out, skating a few yards away, taking her in with his clear blue eyes.

"Pretty good, huh?" She laughed. "You just stay in your lane, and we'll be fine."

He gave her a sexy wink. "We'll see. I have the urge to chase you. One of the reasons I love this pond is that it brings out the boy in me, the one who loved to skate—even when temperatures were below zero. I always felt happy and free. Like the whole world was mine."

She understood. They'd had a frozen pond on their property as well before her mother had insisted she practice inside on "better" ice. But she'd liked the uneven surface of the ice on the pond. It had given her a little challenge.

"Anywhere I need to be careful of?" she shouted over the wind.

"Nope. It's all solid. I have it checked with an ice meter to be sure. Skate away. Only...stay in your lane."

That he threw her words back at her only made her grin. Oh, she had the urge to impress him. She took a little longer to learn the ice and feel her skates. The circle she made of the pond brought her into a good rhythm. Brock was skating backward now, watching her from a distance, a boyish grin on his now cold-reddened face.

She knew the moment she was ready for more. Her bones seemed to settle into her body, as though they were floating on water. She hit a spin and extended her arms to the sky, turning three times before easing out of it and continuing to skate.

"Oh, ho!" Brock's voice was a deep rumble. "Someone's had some figure skating training."

Her chuckle was mostly for herself. She didn't feel any pressure to perform. He didn't know what she could do on the ice. She had the freedom to do whatever she wanted, and that was like liquid silver through her veins.

The trees were a blur as she increased her speed, and

then she was taking an easy single Salchow jump. She landed flawlessly, and while it was the easiest of jumps, she lit up inside when she heard Brock clapping.

She looked over and blew him a kiss.

"So my sexy librarian doesn't only keep her nose in a book." He skated closer to her, waggling his dark brows. "God, it's no wonder I love you. You're an entire book filled with twists and turns—the kind I grew up reading."

I love you...

Were there any more powerful words in any language? She knew them in at least ten—had worked extra hard to learn them in languages with a different alphabet, painstakingly writing each letter again and again so the phrase would stick. Why she'd thought to learn the phrase *I love you* in so many languages she'd never given much consideration.

Until today.

Those words had never struck her like they did now. She wanted to lift her arms into the air in pure joy. Skating close to him, she ran her fingers along his arm before skating backward so she could see his face. "What I am is someone who's completely head over heels in love with you too," she answered.

He might have uttered a healthy male grunt of satisfaction. "Good. I didn't think I was the only one feeling like that."

Maybe it was time to tell him more details about herself. Darla had suggested telling him everything, but she wasn't ready for that yet. It might destroy this moment, and she couldn't bear to lose it. "Is this when I start to share things about me? I can't tell you everything—"

He skated closer. "Actually, I'm pretty happy with the current question. Who is this beautiful woman I've fallen in love with? The one who knows how to figure skate and who walks around with a set of encyclopedias in her head. Who went to Swiss boarding school. Let's wait until you can tell me everything. When that happens, it's going to be like unwrapping gifts at Christmas."

The metaphor had her flowing into a simple loop jump, because she agreed entirely—all at once would be so much better, and it wouldn't be much longer. *"This* is like Christmas to me," she called out over the wind as he skated until he was beside her, matching her movements. "Skating with you. Being out here like this. Brock, meeting you is the best thing that's happened to me since I met Darla."

"Same goes for me." He reached his hand out to her.

She took it easily.

His blue eyes were as warm as her heart, and seeing the happiness and tenderness in them filled her with a new certainty—yes, she could imagine being with him like this as the seasons changed.

"Care to hold my hand for a little while as we skate around the pond?"

She knew she was beaming with her cold-roughened cheeks. "I'd love that."

Someday she hoped to have a picture of them doing this so she could tuck it to her heart when she needed a happy memory on a tough day.

They held hands and skated easily together. Their connection felt as strong as it had during sex, and Val marveled at that. Before, she'd always skated alone, and preferred it that way. Today there was happiness and romance in the air. Maybe it didn't matter what she was doing with Brock. Whether sex or skating, they were connected. Deeply. From the heart.

Every once in a while, she'd look over to find him gazing

at her, a smile tugging at his mouth. Her heart would do another leap, like her feet wanted to, and she'd tighten her grip on him as they continued another lap around the pond.

Finally, he skated close and wrapped her up, taking her feet off the ice as he spun them around. She was laughing when he finally put her down, and then he cupped her cheeks in his cold, gloved hands and pressed his even colder lips on hers.

She twined her hands around his neck as his mouth plundered, his tongue pressing deep into her mouth and stroking her until she was breathless.

The skating hadn't made her breathless.

Brock did.

Val never wanted it to end.

When he finally eased back, he set her away and let go, flashing her a cocky smile as he skated backward. "Think you can catch me?"

The challenge fired up all her competitiveness. The likelihood of that happening was hard to know until she tried. He was a professional athlete. She wasn't now. But she was lighter than he was, had a few tricks up her sleeve, and she knew how to use the wind to her advantage.

"How about you try and catch *me*?" she volleyed back.

"You're on," he called, and then he was off like a shot, his arms pumping at his sides as he tore across the ice toward her.

She took off, loading up on her pushing foot and using her body with opposing slashes of her arms through the air. Even bending with her knees low to the ice and driving for all she was worth, she was barely ahead of him. When she was sure he'd have her, she sailed to the right and turned sharply. He went into a wider arc to turn and follow her, and then he was back in pursuit.

Her heart was beating madly now. Adrenaline poured through her like a waterfall. She was conscious of her rapid breathing as she darted across the ice, not making it easy for him.

"Not bad," he called out as she used her toe-pick to do a 180-spin and took off in the other direction.

When he'd get close, she'd push and drive off as fast as she could. But soon her heart rate was out of control and her legs were screaming. She knew he was enjoying the chase, and so was she, but she didn't want to risk injury.

So she slowed and flipped around to skate backward so she could see his face. "That's about all I can do without being reckless."

His pumping arms slowed and soon he was skating right in front of her, their actions perfectly choreographed. "You're faster than I expected. There's no way you could do that—or any of those jumps—without training. Your body makes more sense to me now. I'd wondered about ballet, but you figure skated, didn't you?"

What harm could it do to share this part of her past with him? "I did a long time ago. Ballet too. I haven't skated in a long time before today."

He was studying her intently now, his warm blue eyes avidly taking her in as he skated a short distance away from her. "All that traveling light? And yet you had skates."

"A family member sent them to me," she told him honestly. "I knew I'd be working close to an actual ice rink every day."

"So you've worked out on the ice?" he asked, extending his hand to her again and falling in beside her. She accepted it, and they skated like a pair again.

"No, I hadn't."

Three words. None of which could convey what she was feeling.

He scanned her face. "So you haven't skated until today. Clearly, you love it. Certainly, you're good at it. I'm no expert, but your jumps looked impressive. Was this more than a hobby?"

Her insides started to tighten up. Talking about all the painful and stressful years as a young figure skater still gave her anxiety. It was like melting a block of ice inside her and finding bits of the barbed wire fence that had kept her caged in so long. Someday she could tell him. "Yes, it was more than a hobby. Can we just skate?"

He only remained silent, tightening his grip on her hand. "Sure."

"It brings back some tough memories for me," she felt compelled to add.

"None of those today," he said, skating close to her and effortlessly picking her up off the ice again. "Today is about having fun."

Yes, it was.

With their faces only a few inches apart, she wrapped her hands around his neck and leaned forward to kiss him. He continued to skate easily with her in his arms, and when she lifted her mouth from his, she realized she'd trusted him to hold her and keep her safe. She kept trusting him, more and more; surely that meant something.

"Thanks for skating with me, Brock," she whispered, meeting his gaze. "Thanks for bringing me here."

He drew them to a stop and lowered her to the ground. His hand rose and traced her cheek. "Val, don't you know it yet? I'd give you anything you want. Especially when you smile at me."

Hadn't her heart had enough exercise? It executed a

triple Salchow in her chest. "Shall we go back? I feel like I might need to be warmed up. By a professional."

That warm glint appeared in his clear blue eyes. "You've found your man, then."

They skated for the outdoor fireplace area, hand in hand. She rolled his words over in her mind. Darla was right, she decided.

She had found her man.

TWENTY

WHY DO WOMEN ALWAYS ASK SO MANY QUESTIONS?

Zeke sent him an aggrieved eye roll, and Brock could almost read his mind. They were in the car on their way to school, and Kinsley was full of questions about his weekend with Val. He loved his niece, but right now, he wished he could quiet her with a piece of candy. But she was much too old for a bribe like that, and he'd never stooped to such behavior when she was younger.

"You're sure she was happy when you left her house?" Kinsley pressed as he steered the car. "Like smiling happy?"

Zeke put his hands to his neck, pretending he was choking. Brock fought a laugh. "Yes, she was smiling."

Beaming like the sun, he might have added, but that would be downright corny. Then he'd have to make a gagging motion directed at himself because God knew Zeke would.

"So what are you going to do when you see her at work?" Kinsley was practically out of her seat belt she was leaning so close to his seat.

"Probably nod at her and say hello." Of course, he'd want to say more, but that was ill-advised.

"That's a good plan since no one can know you two are dating. But you should give her a present. To tell her that you like her."

Zeke's gagging sound filled the air. "Come on, Kinsley. Leave the man alone. He knows what to do."

"Does he?" Kinsley leaned her head in and glared at her brother. "Because sometimes guys forget you exist after they say they like you."

He heard a quiver of hurt in her voice, and instantly he wanted to kick some kid's butt for making her feel like this. It was the same protective impulse he had with Susan. "Did that happen to you, Kinsley?"

"Like all the time," she told him with heat. "But they're idiots, and I'm better off without them."

"Even Kale?" Zeke taunted. "Because you sure looked like you still wanted to suck face with him last week after school."

Suck face with some guy named Kale? Like the salad green? Not on his watch. "Kinsley, I was once a boy your age, and I can tell you firsthand that we don't improve much until we're in our late twenties. I would give up on guys until then. Save yourself a lot of heartache."

Because he didn't want her to be hurt, and it sounded like she had been. By idiots named after vegetables who didn't deserve her.

She sighed. "That's what Darla said when I told her about Kale, but she also told me that I should trust myself. That's the best thing a woman can do. Because a real woman knows herself."

"Oh, brother," Zeke moaned, pantomiming banging his head repeatedly against the window. "Uncle Brock, can you drive faster? I'm dying with all this woman talk. As if you're a real woman, anyway, Kinsley. You're only fourteen."

"Enough, please!" He raised his voice only when he knew things were about to get out of hand between them, something he'd gotten good at judging. "Kinsley, you listen to Darla. She's right about a lot of things."

Hadn't Val said so repeatedly this weekend?

"But when a boy doesn't treat you right from the start, it's a sure sign that he's a—"

"Dick," she finished. "Yes, I know. But sometimes they don't seem like that in the beginning."

"That's because they want to get into your pants," Zeke answered, blowing Brock's mind. "Right, Uncle Brock?"

God, how could he take the fifth when it was true? "Yes, with most guys, but—"

"That's not all you want from Val," Kinsley pressed like a pushy sports reporter. "Darla said she's never been happier, which makes Darla happy. I'm happy too. So what are you going to get her? Oh, and when are you two going out again? You should take her someplace special. Somewhere that means something to you, Uncle Brock."

Zeke gave a pitiful moan, the kind you'd hear someone give when they had the flu. "I just took her to my mountain cabin. I've never taken anyone there but family and a few hockey friends."

"But you have more special places," Kinsley pressed, leaning up again, her black hair falling down over her shoulders.

"He'll figure it out, Kinsley." Zeke sent him a pleading look that said *stop the bleeding, please.* "He's got this."

She sat back, and he watched in the rearview mirror as she fisted her hands in her lap. "I know. I'm just nervous. I like Val so much—and I love you, Uncle Brock. I'd like someone to be—"

When she broke off and looked sadly out the window, he had to do it. He sent a grimace toward Zeke as an apology. "Be what, Kinsley?"

Her chest lifted with a serious sigh, the kind he feared would make her break out more T-shirts with words like MISFIT or MISUNDERSTOOD scrawled on them. He'd been grateful to see she was wearing Darla's newest gift, a baby blue T-shirt with BRAVE written on it, this morning.

"Well, I just want someone to be happy." Her throat sounded scratchy, making his hands tighten on the wheel. "Like when they're in love. Because you love her, don't you, Uncle Brock?"

Even Zeke turned from the window and stared at him. He wasn't used to expressing his feelings, but somehow it felt right to tell them the truth. So he tightened his hands on the steering wheel and said, "Yes, I do."

"Like a picket fence kind of love?" Kinsley asked, but the chick-flick term didn't make Zeke gag for once. "We were really little when you got divorced before. It had to be awful that it didn't work out."

Zeke only stared up at his uncle as if his whole life could turn on the answer.

Brock realized why. These kids needed a win. They needed to believe two adults who loved each other could be happy together and create a stable family since theirs had been blown up. He knew they wanted him to be happy and not get hurt like their mom. But they also cared deeply about Val and Darla, who were a package deal. They could imagine being happy with them, and that meant a lot to these kids who had to have trust issues.

He took a moment again to search himself. It *was* early,

THE HOCKEY EXPERIMENT

and he didn't know if Val wanted a picket fence or any other kind of fence. He didn't know much about her really. Except somehow he knew everything. "Yeah, like that."

"Good," Kinsley breathed out, fidgeting with her hands again. "I want that for you, Uncle Brock. And I want it for Val too. Darla said they both didn't have a lot of good stuff happen to them growing up. That's why they're so close. They've been like us against the world. We can be there for them. Like they can be for us. We get each other."

His gut trembled with a new kind of pressure. "Kinsley, do you have any ideas about what I can get Val? To make her happy," he added uncomfortably.

For the rest of the ride to school, she brainstormed gift after gift as Zeke plugged his ears beside him. But Brock listened. Because she was a girl with good insights—and making Val happy had become his number one new goal besides winning the conference championship and getting into the playoffs so they could win the Cup.

After dropping the kids off, he made a few calls. Ordered a few items Kinsley had suggested. It helped that he had Val's address now. When he arrived at the facility, he headed inside, eager to see her.

She was wearing her nerdy outfit like usual. All he wanted to do was cross the distance between them and put his hands on her. Kiss her senseless. Make her moan into his mouth.

Instead, he did what they'd agreed. He inclined his chin and gave her a professional good morning. She did the same. So did Darla, but he caught her biting the inside of her cheek as he headed to the locker room to change.

Chuck had already texted everybody to go straight to the ice. When he joined his teammates, everyone had one question on their minds:

Where was Mason?

Their coach walked out onto the ice in front of them and crossed his arms over one of his ill-fitting polo shirts. His round face looked ten years older, and from the way his thin gray hair was sticking out, he'd clearly been shoving his hands into it in frustration.

Everyone shifted, sensing Chuck was about to boil over. No surprise. He shoved his glasses up his nose and smacked his hands together. "Do I have your attention?" When the team nodded, he gave a terrifying grin. "Good. Because after the shitty play I've seen from you jokers, we're at my magic number. We've had twenty-three losses, and statistically, teams with those kinds of numbers don't make the playoffs. We're going to have to win every single game to control our destiny."

A few other players grunted along with Brock. His assessment was no surprise.

"So today we're starting to pave a new path to success. To that end, you're about to have the hardest, toughest practice of your life. Mason is suspended. Not by the league, but by me and Ted. He's going to be away for three games, contemplating his life, his career, and his place on this team. Fitting for the three games we lost."

Brock rolled his tongue at the news. Chuck had never suspended a player for that long to his knowledge. He watched a few of Mason's packs shift their feet in response. Finn only elbowed him in the side and gave him a look that said *about time*. Brock couldn't have agreed more. Clearly, Chuck didn't think an elderly ballerina was going to cut it this time.

"Don't think Mason is the only one on my shit list." Chuck readjusted his glasses before raking them with a once-over. "One player does not make a team. And this is not a team. We've got all sorts of camps here, don't we? The old guard. The young guard. Well, I'm sick of it. You will be too. I'm going to push you past your limits and then some."

When he flicked his hand toward a few of the Eagles' arena staff patiently waiting at the exits, the sound of garbage cans being brought in reached his ears. *Oh, shit.* Brock braced himself. He knew what was coming, and as a motivational strategy, this one really sucked.

"If you need to puke, use one of the cans." Chuck cracked his knuckles. "We're about ready to have an old-fashioned 'bag skate.' For those of you who are barely old enough to tie your own shoes, let me educate you on this singular gem in hockey. The 'bag skate' means the puck won't be leaving the bag today. We're talking about a practice designed to change your bad behavior and make you more motivated to win. So we won't have to go through this again."

No one groaned, although Brock caught a few of the younger players with sweat on their brows. They were right to be afraid. He'd only had two "bag skates" in his career, and both times he'd barely fought off booting up his insides. Finn had been with him for one in college, and he'd upchucked so hard he'd been hoarse afterward.

"The lore of the 'bag skate' isn't bullshit," Chuck continued. "The Edmonton Oilers had a 'bag skate' when they hit a slump in their 1986-87 season. Sound familiar? Even good ol' Wayne Gretzky puked. But if you know your history, you'll remember the Oilers won the Cup in '87, and two more times after that. So think about that when you want to kill me. When you want to lay down and cry on the ice. When you're bent over the garbage can. I want you to remember that this skate is going to motivate you to travel the rest of the way into the promised land."

Brock could feel himself readying to go. The promised land was where he wanted to be. If they had to do this to get there, so be it.

"We might not be the Oilers, but we *are* winners." Chuck stared every one of them down. "When you leave the ice—alive—you'll know that about yourself. You'll respect yourself more. And your teammates. *Winners* respect themselves. Now, let's get to it. Line up."

Everyone got positioned on the ice, and when Chuck blew his whistle, Brock was ready. They sprinted from one goal line to the other and back, over and over again. Brock's focus became reaching the end. When his legs started to protest, he had to double down. When his insides wanted to come up, he had to grind his teeth. It continued and continued and *continued*, and he had to close out everything but skating.

Other players started puking around him, but he didn't take his gaze off his goal: getting to the end and then doing it all over again. Finn left his side at one point, the only time he was aware of another player. When he returned, Brock made himself turn his head, although it took effort, and nod at his friend and teammate. Finn nodded back, but barely. He wiped his mouth and hunkered down as Chuck blew the whistle again.

After two hours, grown men were moaning, hands on their knees. Brock could barely feel his legs. He had his hands on his waist, telling himself he could do another round. *More* was the mantra he said over and over again in his head. Because you got nowhere if you focused on the pain.

You told your body it wanted more.

After another series of punishing sprints, Chuck finally blew the whistle. "Okay, that's enough. Hit the showers.

And then buck up. Since you didn't have breakfast, you're going to eat lunch. The team cooks prepared something memorable for you since you don't have a 'bag skate' every day."

Brock forced his legs to skate toward the exit. He was there before anyone else, and he watched as Val rose to her feet in the stands. Her face was pale, and when Darla tugged on her hand, she slid back into her seat. He knew she was upset, but he couldn't focus on that right now. This was hockey, and the sooner she saw the tougher parts, the easier it would be for her to support him.

In the shower, he was barely aware of the hot water. Other teammates filed in with him. No one spoke. Guys lowered their heads under the spray, as if praying to God to be put out of misery.

Brock was the first one dressed, as a team captain should be, and the first one in the lunchroom. He scented Chinese food immediately. Ginger, garlic, and something tangy. Even though every part of him was hurting, his stomach growled. He trudged over to the long table filled with chafing pans and started dishing up food, hunger grabbing him in her claws.

There was kung-pao chicken and beef and broccoli and piles of egg rolls along with hot and sour soup and oodles of pillow-shaped dumplings. An acre of freshly spiced rice lay at the end.

He started piling food on his plate with one goal. To feed the beast inside begging for nourishment. His plate heavy, he headed for a table, noticing Finn and a number of the other guys were trailing behind him, loading food on multiple plates.

Sinking down, he looked around for silverware. There

was none. No napkins either. He glanced back at the buffet and didn't see any. Nor any staff to ask.

Brock looked down at his plate and found he didn't care. Hunger was a raging need as the scent of ginger and beef rose to his nostrils. His body needed fuel. He couldn't wait for silverware. Picking up an egg roll, he bit in.

His teammates filled the tables, and over the high-pitched noise in his ears from the "bag skate," Brock heard other people muttering about the lack of silverware before they dug in with their bare hands.

He looked around. His teammates were tearing their food apart and stuffing it into their mouths. Some were lifting the bowls of hot and sour soup to their mouths. Others were using their hand like claws to feed themselves rice.

Then it hit him.

Chuck had said the staff had made them a memorable meal. Only he'd gone a step further: he hadn't included any silverware.

There had to be a reason. Chuck didn't do anything without cause. Was this designed to strip them down to the bone? Remind them of their base hunger to win?

He glanced over to where his coach was standing. In the corner. With Val and Darla—and Ted. They were all watching the scene before them. Val was white under the gills. He turned back to his food.

He could trust his coach.

Chuck's motivational strategies never failed.

TWENTY-ONE

Why didn't men seem to know when they'd gone too far?

Val wanted to turn to Darla and ask her friend the question, but she couldn't do so in front of her father and Chuck. Both men were glowering as they watched the scene in front of them.

It was a buffet of animals.

Grown men using their mammoth hands to shove food into their starving mouths.

Food strewn across tables like kindergartners had supped there.

Beards and mouths smeared with everything from rice to fish sauce.

Val couldn't help but be shocked by it. This, on the tail end of the "bag skate." More than once, she'd told herself cavemen had also used painful rituals for warrior training and punishment. She'd had a coach push her like that once, and yes, she had puked. But once her father had gotten wind of the man's harsher training drills, he'd fired him.

Her feelings for Brock were clearly affecting her. She'd

been one long line of agony as she watched him use every ounce of his strength to keep skating sprints over and over again.

That he'd been one of the few not to vomit was a testimony to his willpower. She'd seen the way his jaw had locked. Watched the way his eyes were almost unfocused as he skated up and down the ice. She knew he'd had to go to a special place inside himself to keep going.

Turning toward Val and Darla, Chuck said, "I'll need your initial findings by tomorrow morning first thing. Don't worry about it being perfect. I only need bullet points."

She traded a look with Darla before saying, "We'd like to compile our full report—"

"Plenty of time for that." Chuck took off his glasses and cleaned them with the edge of his polo shirt. "I need what you have now. The time for the big guns has arrived."

They'd suspected this day was coming, but the confirmation made her throat constrict. "I suppose we all wished this day hadn't come," she said woodenly.

"That's an understatement," her dad agreed, putting a comforting hand on her arm. "I know today's practice was hard to watch, but it's well documented in the league that 'bag skates' lead to success."

Success at any price, Val thought. She'd been in that world, and it had been a hard place for a young girl. She was glad Brock and the others were grown men, but the path to victory was still not an easy one.

"You don't think we're *squeamish*?" Darla patted her father's arm this time. "Ted, we've seen people mutilated, burned, pierced, and tattooed in rituals and rites of initiation. We'll get you our initial findings."

Darla's smile was picture perfect, the kind she used to

give her mother when she came to the boarding school for a rare visit.

"If you don't mind," Darla continued, putting her hand around Val's waist companionably, "we're going to head back to my place and get going."

Another flash of a beauty-pageant smile had Chuck nodding. "Fine. You can email it to me when you're finished. I need to talk to the photographers."

Val had seen the Eagles' PR staff discreetly documenting the "bag skate" and the subsequent meal. Their job was to record everything, she knew, but this seemed different.

"We'll see you two later, then." Darla put an urgent hand to her back. "Come on, Val."

She forced a short smile for her father's sake, and even though she knew not to, she looked over to where Brock was sitting as she walked out. He was an island by himself, one large hand clutching an egg roll as he tore off another bite. He had to be starving after two hours of that kind of practice.

The rest of the players around him weren't in much better shape. They were using every means they had to feed the hunger cutting their insides up, everything from forking up food with their hands to lifting their plates to their mouths. She didn't envy the cleanup crew. The lunchroom looked like a downright massacre.

When they'd arrived at the lunchroom, Chuck had quoted them, saying cavemen were creative in their use of tools. He'd told them to watch. She had, but she hadn't felt like she was observing an academic study. She'd felt like she was watching a setup. One photographers had been brought in to document.

That didn't sit well.

As they exited the double doors, her inner worry was mounting. Something didn't feel right. She grabbed Darla's wrist. "I really think—"

"Not yet, Val," Darla hissed under her breath. "Not until we're back at my place."

Right. Because if she was overheard losing her cool, it wouldn't be good for anyone.

Darla sent her a compassionate look. "I'd drive you, but you'll want your car."

She did. She wanted to see Brock later. All she wanted was to put her arms around him.

The drive back to Darla's didn't appease the tension wreaking havoc on her stomach. By the time she arrived at the parking lot, she was taking slow and steady breaths to calm down. Cutting the engine, she dug out her phone in her satchel and texted Brock.

Hey! I don't know what to say about today, but I wanted you to know I'm here.

She stared at her phone, feeling a strange burning sensation in her eyes. That was what mattered. She wanted him —needed him—to know she was here for him. Especially after a day like today.

How many times had she faced days like that all alone in her youth—the aches of the body warring with the desolation of the spirit? Because you knew your chance of winning depended on you being able to get back up again and do better. Be better.

Even though she understood tough training regimes as a former competitor, it had been hard to watch. She knew how badly Brock wanted to win, and because she'd been the same way, she knew what today had been like for him.

Brutal. The kind of day that could crush you if you let it. She rubbed her eyes, feeling way too emotional. But she needed to finish her message.

I have to finish up some work things, but if you'd like, you could come over for a bit. If you're too tired, we can do it another time. I totally understand. Okay? I...

She stared at her screen, her breath coming in shallow pants. The press to say what she really felt finally made her type it out.

I love you. You stood up today, and it was incredible. You're an incredible man, and I'm so grateful you're in my life.

She sent the text before she could chicken out and then fell back against the seat.

God, this was working her all up. Love. Him. *Them.*

Is this how it felt when you really loved someone?

She hurried up to her friend's apartment and knocked. When she opened the door, Darla wrapped her arms around her and pulled her inside.

"I feel so upset." She pressed her face into her shoulder. "I hate this! I felt like I was coming apart as I watched what he had to go through. Darla, I have zero objectivity. I'm no use to our study. I—"

"Shh," her friend only said, hugging her tightly. "I know it was tough. I had half a mind to jump up and yell, *Toxic masculinity should be a crime.* God knows we've seen young male boys' bodies mutilated as part of initiation rights. We've seen girls pressed into marriage at fourteen and pregnant soon after because that's the group's culture. Don't get me started on female genital mutilation. This is hockey culture, and we have to step back and remember that."

Val angled back, finding she was sniffing now. "I know all that, but I love him. Watching him drag himself across the ice again and again, forcing himself to go on and not puke like the others, hurt me too. Loving him changes everything. Is it always like this?"

Darla gently smoothed her black ponytail consideringly. "Yes, and it should be, because when you love someone, it's hard to see them suffer. I'm not telling you anything you don't know, but Brock is a grown man, as are the others. Hockey is their chosen profession. And apparently this 'bag skate' thing produces results. You can bet I looked it up the minute I got home. Val, you know some people respond with success after being pushed beyond their limits. You were one of those people."

"I know, and that's another reason I'm not objective here. Darla, a practice like that can break your spirit if you let it."

Darla framed her face, tension knitting her arched brows. "But it won't break Brock's. You saw it. He was the captain today as much as he ever was, and everyone noted it. The way he carried himself. The way he pressed on. He looked like a god out there, and while I don't fancy ever seeing anyone pushed like that again, he stood up. Now, we're going to do what we were hired to do."

Her diaphragm clenched, constricting her breath. "Right."

She stroked Val's arm. "Like Chuck said, the big guns are here. That's us. We all want to motivate the team to victory. So we give him our complete set of findings. Honey, we've got this. And so does Brock and the others. Your dad too."

"But to not give them silverware..." Val pulled her glasses off finally and rubbed her eyes. "I don't like that. He's setting them up for something. You saw the cameras."

"Honey, you need to trust your dad here." She shook her gently. "And Chuck. Let them do their jobs while we do ours. Now, come on. I'm going to open a nice bottle of red wine and start a fire. You want to change into your contacts and more comfy clothes? Because we have a lot of writing ahead of us."

She nodded, sipping in more calming breaths. Focus on the study. Finish the work. That had to be her goal now. Everything else was out of her control.

She only hoped Brock knew he could count on her.

Because he'd somehow become more important than this study—her work—and that was a first.

TWENTY-TWO

How do you assure a woman when the shit hits the fan?

Brock sat in his SUV in the arena parking lot after reading Val's text. Everyone had finally dragged themselves away after being dismissed by Chuck. Putting one foot in front of the other and heading out had taken his every effort. He'd told himself all he needed to do was summon the energy to drive home responsibly.

All the way to the parking lot he'd thought about what he was going to say to Val. Not in a million years would he have told his ex-wife about the "bag skate." But Val had seen it and the ensuing silverware-free lunch. Although she'd done her best to hide it, he knew it had upset her.

But then he'd given in to temptation and checked his phone and read her *reach into his chest and rip out his heart* text.

He wasn't a sentimental kind of guy. The thing was, neither was she really, his Miss Sexy Librarian. Emotionally, they were both pretty even keel. He'd been called Brock "The Rock" for his steadiness as much as his play.

She embodied a cool-as-cucumber persona that fit well with his own approach to life.

But reading that she loved him and was proud of him...

What the hell was a guy to do except feel like he had a hockey puck lodged in his throat?

She'd been emotional, something that wasn't easy for her, and the punch had hit him hard. But her reaction had been different than Erin's. Val was proud of him for having endured the training exercise because she got it. Erin would have berated him for putting his body on the line and getting hurt. He started typing because he couldn't wait another minute to reach out to her.

Hey! It wasn't so bad. I've done it before. The lack of silverware was new.

He paused. Jesus, what the hell was he doing? The lack of forks and spoons weren't what was stuck in his throat.

Your text meant a lot. More than I can probably ever say. I like knowing you're here for me, because showing up is what you do when you care about someone. And I love you too. Your text today only shows how well we fit and why I fell so hard for you.

He reread it, the fatigue starting to fill his body. Yeah, that was better.

Why don't you hit me up when you finish work? If I'm not passed out asleep, I'll come over. I'd like to. Good luck with the work, Miss Sexy Librarian. I'll see you soon.

Satisfied, he started the car and drove home. Susan was picking up the kids today, so the house was empty when he arrived. He did what his body needed. He collapsed on his bed and fell asleep, not even bothering to take off his shoes.

When he awoke, his room was dark. His mouth felt like he hadn't drunk anything in days. Rolling to his side took effort, but he caught the time on his bedside clock. 10:45 p.m. Terrific. He'd slept way past dinner. His stomach rumbled with hunger.

Grabbing his phone, he smiled when he saw a text Val had sent around eight o'clock.

I just left Darla's. I hope you're asleep if you need it. Sometimes that's all your body can do after that much training. I'll be up for a few more hours, so if you want to come over, please do. I would be happy to see you—even for a little while. Nothing else, if you understand me.

Was she implying he couldn't get it up after today? He supposed maybe some guys wouldn't have the energy. But they didn't have his motivation. Miss Sexy Librarian could wake up a dead man. He picked up his phone to text her.

Hey babe! Just up from a dead sleep. I'm going to grab some food and then head your way if that still works.

When she didn't immediately respond, he heaved himself out of bed. He was aware of the stiffness and aches in his body as he headed downstairs to eat and hydrate. God knew how many calories he'd burned today. Eating again would make him feel better.

"Hey, sleepyhead!" Susan called softly from her spot at the counter when he walked into the kitchen after he'd tiptoed past Kinsley's tent. "I figured you guys trained hard today, so I told Zeke and Kinsley you'd probably zonked out."

"Yeah, so hard my stomach is eating me from the inside out."

"I put your plate in the refrigerator, knowing you'd be hungry," she said, closing her laptop.

"You're the best!" He studied the shadows under her eyes as he pulled out the plate, hungrily eyeing the fried chicken, mashed potatoes, and green beans before popping it in the microwave. "Had a 'bag skate' today for motivation. Never fun. But always effective, and God knows we can't lose another game. How are things with you?"

"Not bad." She organized her scattered paperwork as he grabbed some silverware with a renewed sense of gratitude. "I've got to go to Cleveland at the end of the week. Couldn't get out of it."

He set his plate on the counter in front of him as he slid onto another barstool. "I've got an away game then."

"Don't worry." She tucked her hands into a navy sweatshirt that said BOSS on the front, making him wonder if "The Girls" had given it to her. "Darla volunteered to stay over if we ever need help. I called her earlier tonight to ask, and she said she'd be happy to come. Val too. I said I'd talk to you and confirm tomorrow."

He knew what she was asking. Was it okay for his girlfriend and her best friend to take care of the kids when he wasn't around? "I'm good with it. Plus, it will make the kids happy, Kinsley especially."

Hell, maybe the tent would finally come down.

"Yes, I caught her at the doorway of the room you

offered her," she replied, reading his mind. "She had a dreamy expression on her face. I think she's close to giving up tent life."

"Thank God!" He rolled his aching shoulders as he dug into his chicken, a meal he realized she'd prepared with him in mind—like Val had—which meant he had two of the best women in the world looking after him. "That girl has the Thomson streak of stubbornness."

"Like you." His sister gave a laugh as she picked up an orange from the red fruit bowl and started peeling it. "I never had that kind of spine. But I'm getting there. When my boss told me he needed me in Cleveland, I told him the timing wasn't good for me. He didn't change his mind, but I was proud of myself. I'd never have done that three months ago."

"Good for you." He shoveled in a few more bites of crispy chicken and buttery mashed potatoes. "I'm going to see Val for a while. Maybe stay the night. Can you get the kids to school in the morning if I'm not back?"

Her mouth worked like she was fighting a smile before she popped in an orange slice. "Sure thing. Brock, I say this with love. You'd better marry that girl because she's a keeper. I'm not saying right away, but in the future. You two fit like bread and butter."

"I know." The certainty hadn't come in a flash—it felt like it had been there all the time, since the first moment he'd laid eyes on her. "We get each other."

"Plus, there's Darla." Susan grinned over the fatigue on her face, looking younger. "I want to be her when I grow up. You know she gave me this sweatshirt this weekend, and I...finally decided I could do it. Be boss. I need to be now."

There was a warmth inside him that hadn't come from a

home-cooked meal alone. "We're doing pretty good, aren't we?"

"Yeah," she said rather wistfully. "I'm finally starting to feel like everything is going to be okay. For me and the kids. And for my baby brother. Not that I ever worried about you. Even after you and Erin got divorced. I knew someday the right woman would fall into your lap. Your life always went that way. I was the one who had to work at things. But I'm a boss now. *A boss!*" She ran her hands over her sweatshirt.

"God bless Darla," he said with a smile.

"Yeah." She rose and walked over to hug him lightly, like she used to when he was a young player and his body was aching. "You finish up eating and then get yourself to Val's. I'll see you tomorrow after work. Don't worry about picking the kids up. I've got them."

"I'll call them in the morning before they go to school," he told her.

"They'd love that." She kissed him on top of his head, much like their mother used to. "Good night."

"Good night."

He ate slowly, his thoughts a rumble of pure contentment. Inviting his sister and his niece and nephew to move in with him had been one of his best decisions ever.

So was being with Val.

Checking his phone, he saw that she'd texted him back a couple minutes ago.

Hi! I'm still up so please come over. I also made you dinner since I thought you'd be hungry. Second dinner? See you soon. 🩶

He traced the heart for a minute. Val's texts didn't run

to emojis. This was the first she'd used. His heart seemed to expand in his chest. Jesus, they were a pair. He sent her a heart back—his first too—and then went to pack an overnight bag before heading over to her house. Once they'd talked and made love, he was going to be out. Hard.

The outdoor lights were on. The garage door was open for him to roll into. She appeared a moment later in dark purple pajamas with black fleece slippers and ran across the garage to him after hitting the garage door button on the wall.

God, that did funny things to him, seeing her running to him, and even though he was fighting off massive fatigue, he was smiling as he opened the car door and pulled her close. He pressed his face into her shoulder, inhaling her clean scent, as she ran her hands soothingly over his shoulders before pulling back and studying his face.

"How bad are you hurting?" Her voice was whisper soft, but it was her strained face that slayed him. "Don't sugarcoat it. You don't have to. I saw."

He worked his mouth for a moment. Hadn't he said he'd have to figure out a way to make her feel okay? "I've had a couple 'bag skates' before. They're not pretty, but I know how to handle them. Seeing you is part of the recovery process. Now come here."

Cupping her cheek, he lowered his head to kiss away the stress on her face. Only she gave him so much back, tangling her fingers in the hair at the base of his skull as she opened her mouth to him and let him have everything he wanted. Her fingers gave a pressure point massage as he devoured her mouth, groaning audibly.

"I could take you right here," he said hotly, gently biting her bottom lip.

"Would you be able to move afterward?" she asked in

her serious sexy librarian tone. "I'm all for being on top and doing most of the work since you have to ache everywhere, but sleeping in your car wouldn't be comfortable."

His laughter spurted out. "I love you so hard when you're being practical. Car sex would probably be really stupid today."

"Another time, then." Miss Sexy Librarian was in full control now. "Did you bring a bag?"

He nodded toward the back, and she opened the door and hefted it out, moving out of his way when he tried to take it from her.

"Don't piss me off, Val. I can carry my own gear."

"You can probably feed yourself too," she quipped over her shoulder as she walked toward the door leading to the house. "And bathe yourself. But I *am* prepared to feed you and scrub your back in the bath I ran for you. Menthol salts will take most of the aches away. Trust me. And then I'm going to massage arnica oil into your muscles. After a good night's sleep, you'll feel like a new person."

She knew her stuff. More mysterious information about this incredible woman. "Have I told you how much I love you?"

She spun around like she had on the ice, her green eyes large. "You have, Brock. Do you have a head injury? Have you forgotten? Because I know today was rough."

He found himself laughing, a miracle after this afternoon. "No, I don't have a head injury, Miss Sexy Librarian, and yes, I know I've told you I love you. I only meant, have I really told you? Because every day I seem to love you more, and that is pretty damn incredible if you ask me."

Her mouth transformed into a smile and then retracted an inch before stretching to the corners again. "I rather like that. I feel the same about you."

He took his bag from her shoulder and grabbed her hand so she couldn't reach for it. "Good. I'm fully committed to you. To us."

She paused, the harsh glow of the fluorescent lights unable to detract from her cool beauty. "Me too. And when I commit to something, I give it my all. Always."

Her resolve punched through him, straight to his heart. "We're so alike in the best ways, Val. I'd go through another 'bag skate' if I had to for you."

She swallowed thickly. "That's a pretty big gauntlet, Brock."

"After seeing it today, you should have no doubt about my feelings, then."

"I don't." She looked him directly in the eye. "Do you have any about mine?"

"No, not a one." She was smiling softly as he opened the door to the house. "Let's get inside somewhere so I can hold you *and* lie down at the same time."

"Bath first," she insisted, heading up the stairs to the main floor. "I ran it when you texted me. Why don't you get in there while I heat up your dinner? You're still hungry, right?"

He reluctantly nodded. "I burned maybe six or seven thousand calories."

"I'd estimate closer to nine with the two-hour timeframe," she said like the sexy librarian she was. "You can eat in the bath."

"Thank you." His stomach rumbled at the mere mention of food. "But hurry up. I'll be missing you."

"Turn the steam shower on before you get into the bath," she called as she headed to the kitchen. "It will help."

God, she had this whole *taking care of him* thing down to a T. "Yes, Miss Sexy Librarian."

His legs felt like anvils as he climbed the stairs, slower than he'd like. When he reached her bathroom, he sighed at the comforting smell of menthol. Turning the steam shower on, he rid himself of his clothes and then climbed into the tub. The water was perfect, and he immediately closed his eyes and laid his head against the back.

"Good, you're already relaxing," he heard a while later. Had he fallen asleep?

He pried his eyes open to see her sitting on a stool beside the tub with a plate piled with another T-bone steak —cut into perfect bites—on a bed of lentils and steamed kale. The latter made him think of the jerk Kinsley had mentioned, but he decided he wouldn't hold it against the vegetable. "Lentils? Really?"

"After the massive amount of calories you burned as well as the adrenaline your body produced to get you through it, you need some complex carbs. Lentils are loaded with fiber, vitamins, minerals, and plant-based protein. They are a must after a serious workout, and you certainly had that today. Shall I feed you?"

Her tone was playful, but he scowled at her. "I'm tempted to see if you would, but no, I can handle it. Just tell me you brought silverware."

She had a napkin wrapped with cutlery under the plate, he realized, as she set it down on the flat marble lip surrounding the tub. "I do. That was rather odd, wasn't it? The lack of utensils today."

"Chuck has his reasons, I'm sure, but I don't want to waste any time talking about it. Unless you need to."

She tucked her foot under her as she settled onto the stool beside the tub. "Why would I need to? You were the one who experienced it."

"You were upset."

"So? I'm an adult. I can handle my own emotions."

"You really are the perfect woman." He popped the first forkful of steak in his mouth and groaned. "God, this is good. I might get used to this. Susan made me dinner too."

"She's a sweetheart."

Her soft smile and the warmth in her green eyes grabbed his heart. "How do you know about the menthol and lentils and stuff? More from your mysterious past? Maybe when you were figure skating?"

"Yes," she said with a little heat. "Are you wanting to dive into that tonight?"

"When I can barely keep my eyes open to eat?" His laugh was like an old car trying to chug up a mountainous hill. "All I'm saying is that your past fits me perfectly, whatever it is. Even Susan—who's been around hockey with me most of her life—doesn't know to do this stuff. We had chicken."

She laid her hands in her lap in that still way of hers. "Chicken has its place, but not after an extreme workout."

He couldn't help but grin as he continued to eat. She really was perfect. Then she took perfect to a new level, pulling his leg out of the tub and massaging the muscles of his calf and thigh before digging her fingers into his foot.

"Is this male erogenous zone stuff?" He didn't so much chew the lentils as swallow them. "Because I remember it feeling differently."

"You're a massive line of aches right now. Of course arousal will feel different. And like I told you. We don't have to do that tonight."

He snorted. "Babe, you might know about menthol and lentils, but you don't know shit about my sex drive. I could make love to you even if I had a dislocated shoulder or a torn hamstring."

She leveled him a stern glance. "That would be exceedingly unwise. Fair warning, I will not be game for such a thing—hoping against hope that it doesn't happen, of course."

"God, is it any wonder I'm head over heels in love with you?" He chuckled as he forked up some steamed kale. "Laying the law down on sex and injuries."

"I am trained in many areas. While orgasms can boost the metabolism and help heal the body, sex is ill-advised at certain moments. If such a moment occurs, we will discuss it. Practically."

He loved the steel in her voice. "This is me discussing things." Pointing to his ever-growing arousal because of her massage, he met her gaze with a pointed look. "Is that proof enough that my body has some energy for you?"

"We shall see about its endurance," she informed him in that same practical tone, one he didn't take issue with. "Finish up eating. Massage next."

"Yes, drill sergeant," he called, but he was too tired to salute her.

He finished the meal quickly and carefully climbed out of the tub. Grabbing a towel from the heated towel rack, he wrapped it around himself and turned off the steam shower. Heading into the bedroom, steam pouring out behind him, he found her arranging a crude makeshift oil warmer. She'd set a candle under a tin bowl.

"Industrious too? This is my lucky day."

"Lie down, please." She pointed to the bed, making him note the soft lights in the room—like spa mood lighting. "And lose the towel. Your glutes must be sore, so I plan to give them some attention. Face down first."

He was almost giddy from fatigue now as he threw the towel on the floor and lay down. Suddenly all he wanted to do was laugh. "You're wonderful. Val, if I could have picked the attributes of the perfect woman for me, I still couldn't have come up with anything as good as you."

She knelt at his side after filling her hands with massage oil, the scent strong and comforting. "Certainly not someone who looks so incredible in baggy clothes and atrocious glasses that she could command *your* attention."

He started laughing. He couldn't help it. "Yeah, that was a pretty big surprise. But I couldn't stop looking. Now I'm thinking I have a hidden talent for finding diamonds in the rough."

"I can personally assure you that finding a diamond in the rough is a difficult, back-breaking proposition that yields hours of labor with few if any results."

If she hadn't started massaging his shoulders, he'd have lifted to look at her. "You've diamond prospected? My God, woman, what have you not done?"

"Many things, of course. Life is a rich course, and the world is a big place. Now, be quiet and relax."

"I like hearing these little details about you." He groaned as she hit a particularly sore spot under his shoulder blade.

"Another detail you should know." Her hands made magic on his throbbing lower spine. "I'm thorough. So be quiet and let me do my work."

Oh, she was so hot when she took charge. He finally closed his eyes and let her have her way.

God, she *was* thorough. Front and back. As thorough as any trainer he'd ever had. There wasn't a muscle group she didn't hit. She probably came close to massaging the more than six hundred muscles in the body. He groaned. He moaned. He jerked when she hit a painful spot. With his eyes closed, his world became her magically strong hands and the way they moved over his body.

When she finally removed her hands and told him, "Sleep now," he opened his eyes slowly.

She was exercising her fingers. On her face was a look filled with so much love, his heart started to thud thickly in his chest.

"No—I want you." He knew his voice was a whisper of itself after the bath and massage. "Even if for only a little while."

She knelt beside him and cupped his jaw, studying his face. "All right. But you'll let me do most of the work."

"Ah, Val," he said quietly, caressing her cheek. "This isn't work. You're pure pleasure. Thank you, by the way. No one's ever taken care of me like this."

He watched as she undressed quickly, her movements practical. "On days like today...I'd imagined care like this would help."

There was something in her voice, but then she was gently climbing onto his thighs and taking his semi-erect cock in her warm, slightly oiled hands. He immediately grew hard. She kept her strokes long and easy, as much of a massage as what she'd done before. He lay back and enjoyed it, eyes closed, straining toward her with every stroke.

"You can come," she told him softly.

Opening his eyes was like wrenching up a stuck window. "No way." His hand lifted to the soft curls between her legs, his fingers seeking her core. "You're coming with me."

"Stubborn even when tired." She laid her head back, surging against his hand as his finger slipped inside her to rub. "I'll have to remember that."

He chuckled darkly, pleasure and fatigue a heady drug. "Babe, you seem to understand me inside and out. That can't be a surprise. Now, lean back a little farther for me so I can get you hotter."

She gave him one of her sexy librarian looks but did as he asked. Her surrender was sweet, the way she opened her legs wider to let him stroke in deeper. When she started rocking against his hand, he couldn't wait a moment longer.

"Now, Val," he ordered. "It's got to be now."

She fitted him at her entrance, a sensuous smile on her face.

"Whoa," he grunted. "Condom."

"I went on birth control," she responded in a hushed tone, sliding onto his length. "I wanted us to be like this. With nothing between us."

With nothing between us...

Her words echoed in his mind as she moved fluidly. She placed her hands lightly on his shoulders, her breasts tickling his chest in the hottest fucking way, and started to ride him. Slowly at first, concentrating on the rise and fall of her body. She was too much in her mind, he realized, being careful with him, and he fisted his hand in her hair. Her gaze flew to his.

"Be with me." He pressed up quickly with his hips, thrusting in deep.

She cried out, her green eyes going wild with lust. Yes, that was the look he wanted from her. He wrapped his other hand around her butt and dragged her toward him as he thrust up again. Her moan was an agonizing sound of unfulfilled desire, and he knew the antidote.

"Kiss me, babe."

When their mouths met, he tangled his tongue with hers, stroking her deep as he thrust off the bed and deeper inside her. Her guttural sounds mingled with his before she tore her mouth away and angled her body up, arching her back as her hips rolled over him.

"Yes! God, yes, Val. Lean back."

He drew up his legs so she could rest against his thighs. Tangling his fingers at her core where they were joined, he rubbed and pressed. She started keening, her body moving faster over him. He knew she was close, her muscles tightening around him. He grabbed her waist and thrust up, pressing in deep.

She cried out, her spasms destroying the last of his control. He groaned, holding her against him as he came, hard and hot. His vision went dark. She pulsed around him, taking him higher.

When she curled over him, he wrapped his arms around her and rolled them to their sides. He pulled her to him and lowered his head into her hair, breathing her in. The fresh clean scent of her, menthol, and the sweet smell of sex.

"I love you," he whispered as she tunneled into him, her breaths coming in shallow pants against his neck.

"I love you too." She kissed him softly, soothing his hair back from his forehead. "You'll sleep now."

His eyes were already closing and then he was out.

When he awoke, the sun was streaming through her windows. She was sitting on the bed, a cup of coffee in her hand. Her hair was slightly damp, but she was dressed.

Even with her so-called work uniform on, she was the most beautiful woman in the world.

"Good morning," she said quietly. "I let you sleep as long as I thought sensible. We have about an hour before we need to be at the arena. How do you feel?"

He stretched his lower back as he sat up. "Only little stiff, and that's a miracle. You were magic last night."

Her smile might as well have been morning sunshine, it was so welcome and bright. "Why don't you shower? I'll have breakfast ready when you come down."

He took the coffee and set it aside before pulling her down toward him. "I think you forgot something."

Her green eyes seemed to glow, even behind the atrocious glasses. He laid his mouth over hers softly, kissing her with all the love he had for her. When she sighed, he gently nipped her bottom lip and released her. "That's better, don't you think?"

"Much." She looked down at her hands, almost shy now. "Thank you. I was already in work mode."

"Understandable." He stroked her arm until she looked at him. "But let's be here. Until we have to be *there*. If you understand me."

She nodded and leaned forward to kiss him, her lips a delightful press of warmth and sweetness. "I do. How was that?"

"Better," he said with a grin. "I wish we had time to take that further this morning. What time is it?"

When she told him, he laughed and hauled her up onto the bed, swiftly unbuttoning her ugly tan slacks.

"Really?" She didn't protest but her gaze held that stern look he loved. "I'm going to smell like you, you know."

He grunted. "I can think of worse things. Come on, slip those slacks and panties off. We've got time."

She slid off the bed, her brow furrowed, but chucked her bottoms down, leaving her tan wool socks on. Which he thought was rather hot.

"Now what?"

Grabbing her under her forearms, he lifted her onto the bed and rolled on top of her. He was a little sore, sure, but he was far from dead, and she was soft and warm, and he wanted nothing more than to have her again. "You need to get used to this being our morning routine."

"Is that so?" She cried out when his fingers found her core. "I suppose we can add this into the schedule. Oh, God, Brock! Yes. Like that."

She was pudding in his hands. He was smiling as he took her mouth in a rough kiss. "Let me walk you through the schedule I have in mind."

When they were both satisfied with his plans, he hit the shower, shaving quickly. By the time he descended the stairs, he could smell bacon. God, she was terrific. He found her standing at the stove. Creamy yellow eggs dotted with herbs were simmering along with the bacon and a pan filled with bubbling oatmeal. A fruit plate stood to the side, filled with bananas, raspberries, oranges, and apples. Again, he was touched, knowing she'd probably chosen everything for his body as much as his tastes.

"I like this part of our morning too," he told her as he walked over and wrapped his arms around her. "Feel free to add it to the list."

She laughed. "I'm glad this works for you. We'll need to eat fast though if we're going to be on time."

"I can be a few minutes later than usual this morning," he told her as she dished up their plates.

"You might be able to, but I can't." She headed to the kitchen table in the corner. "Although I think our time with the team might be..."

He followed her and sat down across from her, noting the sudden stiffness of her shoulders. "What?"

She picked up her fork, her brow really knit now, as if she were struggling with something. "I plan to ask for clarification, but I think it's plausible to assume our time with the team is coming to a close."

He reached for her hand and squeezed it. That meant she'd be able to tell him more about herself. "Good. So we'll be able to put everything on the table. I can't wait."

Nodding almost absently, she picked at her eggs. "Yes, that's a good way to look at it."

"Val..." He tilted his head to the side until she looked up at him. *"I love you.* Beyond reason. You don't need to worry about what's next. I'm not."

Her exhale was audible before she started eating. He dug into his food, finding he was still starving. When it came time to leave, she handed him a paper sack.

He gave her a questioning look.

"I read you love peanut butter, honey, and banana sandwiches, so I made you a couple for lunch." She was flushing. "Or whenever. You need to keep your body fed."

Laying a soft kiss onto her mouth, he felt his heart roll in his chest. "I've got no words for how sweet you are."

"Good thing," she said with a rough chuckle, "since we need to get going."

When he tucked her into her vehicle, attaching her seat belt, she lit up with another heart-tugging smile. Leaning in to kiss her, he gave in to the urge to taste her lips one more time. When he pulled back, she gripped his coat.

"That's going to make this morning's drive to work very distracting," she told him in that tone he loved.

"I needed it." He kissed her again swiftly. "So do you. I'll see you soon, babe. Drive safe."

She seemed to purposefully keep her distance from him on the road. He would have loved to keep her within sight, but he let her fall back. One, he probably drove faster than she did—when the kids weren't in the car—and two, she probably was all practical about them not arriving together.

He dialed Susan's number when he hit the interstate

and smiled when Zeke answered, "Hey, Uncle Brock! I saw Mason got suspended this morning. For three games. That's insane! Maybe it will push him to get his stuff together."

So the news was out. "Here's hoping. Hey! You guys headed to school yet?"

"Yeah, Mom's got us in the car." He sounded like an aggrieved twelve-year-old. "Are you going to be home tonight?"

"You should be with Val!" he heard Kinsley yell.

"Kinsley, I'm talking here." Brock could practically see his nephew rolling his eyes after that comment. "Girls! In case you didn't know, Kinsley is going cuckoo over you and Val. When Mom told her you weren't here this morning because you were with her, she almost did one of those herkie things cheerleaders do."

"Did not, moron!" he heard yelled.

"Zeke, I'm going to be home today," he told the kid with a smile.

He missed seeing them. Maybe Val could come over for a while. Kinsley would be over the moon. Susan too, probably. He could see about Darla coming as well.

"I'll see you later, man," Zeke said. Brock almost laughed at his nephew's grown-up tone. "Uh... Kinsley is tugging on my shirt because she wants to talk to you, so here."

"Hey, Uncle Brock. Did you and Val have fun?"

What the heck was the right answer here? Telling his niece how much fun he'd had wouldn't be appropriate. "She's the best. Look, I've gotta run. You have fun at school. I'll see you guys later, okay?"

"Sure. See you."

The line went dead. He wondered if Zeke was calling

her a moron again for hanging up. Susan probably had her hands full.

When he arrived in the parking lot, Finn was dragging his body out of his Porsche like he was a corpse.

"Jesus, how are you so limber?" his friend snarled, walking stiffly across the parking lot toward him.

"I had a lovely helper take care of me last night." He couldn't help but smile at the memory.

"I'll bet." He groaned as they walked to the elevators. "I told myself all night that this isn't me getting old. The rookies are going to be groaning today. Chuck had better not be planning an intense practice."

Brock shrugged. "He knows how hard he can work a team. Always has."

Finn grunted as he hauled his bag up higher on his shoulder. "I'm only sorry Mason missed it. I would have loved to see that kid puke his guts out."

"Yeah, too bad about that." He punched the button to the locker room floor. "But a 'bag skate' is better than a suspension any day."

"True that." They left the elevator together, trading covert looks as they passed shuffling rookies on the way to the locker room, coming down from the breakfast area.

When Brock opened the door for Finn, he heard Finn's "Fuck me."

Entering the locker room, Brock stopped short.

A four-foot sign in the center of the locker room asked: *Are you a caveman?*

Under the bold, black letters was an illustration of a trio of animated caveman characters beating one another with clubs. All three were wearing a Flintstone-like animal print. Under them was a life-size cardboard cutout of Mason wearing his massive fur coat and one of his snotty little smirks. The resemblance of Mason to the cavemen couldn't be more obvious.

But Chuck hadn't stopped there.

Full-size renders of their team eating like animals papered the walls. There were even two giant cardboard cutouts of two Eagles players in full caveman grotesque mode lining the path to the showers.

"Oh, Jesus." Brock winced as he spotted a horrifying photo of himself tearing into an egg roll with his teeth like an animal. "Chuck's outdone himself this time with his motivational humdingers. Mason must have given him the idea with his fur coat. Man, this beats the geriatric ballerina to hell."

"To hell," Finn muttered. "Fucking Christ. If my mother saw a picture of me eating like a baboon, she'd be horrified."

"How about having your girlfriend see you like this?" one of their teammates muttered as he walked past, head hung in shame. "Wait until you see what Coach put on our lockers."

Brock headed over, knowing that avoidance wouldn't solve anything. When he reached his locker, he noted another particularly unflattering photo of himself ripping apart an egg roll with his massive bare hands. But it was the simple piece of paper taped under it that had him leaning closer.

Cavemen: early humans with physically dense, highly muscular bodies; known for aggression and territorialism; capable of using tools like a bat; with simple linguistic capability

Hockey players: modern humans with physically dense,

highly muscular bodies; known for aggression and territorialism; capable of using tools like a hockey stick; with simple linguistic capability

Popular slang describes cavemen as ignorant.
Stupid even.
Rude.
Reckless.
Unwilling to change.
Unable to form or execute complex thoughts or plans.
Outcome: Unsuccessful.
ARE YOU A CAVEMAN?

He bit the inside of his cheek, feeling anger rising up inside him, hot and potent. The unsuccessful part really dug in. God, Chuck had outdone himself. Brock couldn't wait to put on his skates and prove his coach wrong.

"Fuck," Finn mumbled harshly. "I'm trying not to take this personally, but I've been called a dumb jock most of my life. I hate being called stupid. Call me an asshole. Call me a jerk. But don't call me stupid."

Brock clapped him on the back. "This isn't personal, and you're not stupid. Chuck did it to get a rise out of us. So we get angry and play better."

"I'm so there." Finn opened his locker with a bang. "I hate that it came to this. Why couldn't we all just play like fucking professionals and get the job done? You caught how Mason looks like Caveman Number One in the cutout, right?"

Brock nodded. As he got dressed for the ice, he read the caveman manifesto, as he'd decided to call it, over and over again until it didn't bother him.

The locker room was dead silent around him other than

a few muttered curses. Everyone was dealing with it in their own way.

He stared at his own picture and the rest of the photos in the locker room until they had no power over him. Rising above the anger was how he wanted to play. Not from this place, anger clawing at his guts every time he walked into this locker room. Because Chuck would have this shit up until the end of their season if past experience was any indication.

He was reading the manifesto when the words suddenly struck him in a different way. He read the opening lines again. The definitions...

The back of his neck tingled.

He knew someone who talked in definitions. Who used this kind of clarification in daily conversation.

This manifesto sounded like the work of Miss Sexy Librarian.

He wanted to sink onto the bench in front of his locker and put his head in his hands. *Oh, Jesus, Val.*

This was what she'd been working on for Chuck?

His stomach soured, because he knew it must be true.

He told himself what he told Finn. That it wasn't personal.

But he couldn't completely shake it off.

He was as proud as the next guy. Her opinion of him mattered—maybe too much.

Is this what she thought of him?

That somewhere, underneath everything—Finn would make a loincloth joke probably—he was a *fucking caveman*?

He stewed as he laced his skates up, his heart hammering in his chest.

When Chuck entered the locker room with Ted Bass at his side, Brock turned around to give them his full attention like the rest of the team. Ted's eyes were practically flinty, narrowed to the point of disgust. His disappointment in them radiated like harsh stadium lights. Like he wished he'd never bought this team with its band of cavemen.

Coach only gave a challenging smirk and crossed his arms, his narrowed gaze raking each of them in the locker room.

"Do I have your attention now?" he barked loudly.

Brock nodded amidst a chorus of grunts, all the while looking around for the woman he'd fallen in love with.

The woman whom he feared might think some of these things about him.

TWENTY-THREE

Why do men think humiliating other men will make them perform better?

Val clenched her teeth together when she entered the empty locker room, pain flaring up in her stomach as if she had another ulcer.

Darla hissed quietly, "Oh, no! This is bad. Bad, bad, bad. Oh God! This is not *at all* what we discussed. The whole tough, dominant, smart caveman stuff was supposed to motivate the team. Not the stereotype about them being stupid ignoramuses. Chuck is one devious man."

Devious wouldn't be her choice of words, but he certainly did enjoy using old-school tactics to motivate people. Punishment had been the key to the "bag skate." Now he was adding humiliation. She hated it when men used these tools to motivate others. Of course, she'd seen women use them too, but this was going too far for her liking. Worse, it subverted their study.

"You've gone gray," Darla said, taking her arm gently. "Maybe we shouldn't have come in here."

Chuck had told her and Darla *not* to go in. So had her

father. Guess what? That had only made her and Darla want to go in more. Hadn't they heard of reverse psychology?

"I had to. This affects Brock. I had to see how our initial findings were used. We both did."

Darla patted her arm before strolling over to the first locker. "Well, Chuck didn't give each player a copy of what we sent him, that's for sure. He twisted our words, Val."

"He didn't twist them."

Val turned at her father's voice. He stood just inside the locker room with a frown on his face.

"I saw you on the security feed, so I cut my call short and ran down," he continued, a worry line stretched across his brow. "I told you two not to come in here. I knew it would upset you. I was planning on talking to you the minute I finished my call with Mason's agent, who is threatening all sorts of crap to get us to undo his suspension."

"Upset is an understatement." She wagged her finger around the locker room, glad Brock was on the ice so he wouldn't see her shame. "We're respected academics. We knew the caveman question was going to be used to motivate the team. We signed up for that. But I never thought you and Chuck were going to twist our findings and use them to humiliate the players."

Brock especially. But she couldn't say that.

"Val, Chuck and I did everything we could not to arrive at this moment." Her father walked over to her and put his hands on her shoulders, his brown eyes sincere. "We both wanted to motivate this team positively. You know me, Val. I don't like to tear down other people. I fired anyone who did that with you."

She wanted to believe him. "I know you did."

He raked a hand through his short white hair. "Thank

you for that. We *had* planned to use the caveman analogy as a more positive motivator, the way we originally discussed. The whole *dominant and territorial* angle, along with the phrase, *So tough they survived the Ice Age.* But Mason went too far, and he had too many of the younger players going along with his crap. We can't lose another game. Chuck and I felt we had to take a tougher tack. He's the coach, and he knows how to get things done. How to get a team to win."

She hoped so. Because when Brock realized she'd been a part of humiliating him...

She didn't know how he'd feel or if he could let it go. Could she? If he'd done something like this to her, she'd be hurt.

"All right, Ted." Darla put her arm around Val's waist, clearly in best friend mode. "We know this isn't easy stuff. These are grown men. Professional hockey players. Being called cavemen is just another blip in a long career full of name-calling. But I don't think we need to be around on-site after this."

Val could only nod despite the ache in her throat. She liked to end fieldwork on a high note, but they were not going to have that here. "Darla's right. I assume you don't need to see our final report."

Her father's brow furrowed deeper, and he laid a gentle hand on her arm. "I always read your articles. I read your initial findings. I think they're brilliant and full of insights into humanity and what makes us tick as a species. Your articles always make me think. I'm proud of the work you two do."

She knew he meant it. Right now, his praise put a bitter taste in her mouth.

"I know this isn't ideal," he continued, tension lining his

eyes, "but I'm grateful to you two for coming here and doing what I asked of you."

"Hell, Ted, you know how much we love you." Darla warmly hugged him. "From the moment I met you. You were different than the other parents at boarding school. You actually loved your daughter."

His mouth worked before he could say, "I have from the moment I first held her in my arms." When he turned to her, his heart was in his eyes.

Her heart might as well have been cut in two. She loved her father, and she'd been so happy to support him. But she'd been part of a strategy to humiliate the man she loved.

How was she going to make that right?

"Let's have dinner tonight." Her dad gave her one of his slightly goofy smiles, so not in keeping with Ted Bass, the Corporate Mogul. "Is there a cuisine you really miss while you're out in the field? Name it, and either my chef can cook it up or we can fly to the city with the best restaurant and make a night of it."

Normally, she and Darla would be on board for this, but not tonight. She knew what she needed to do without even looking to Darla for guidance. "Dad, I can't. I wish I could. But I need to talk to someone important to me."

Darla shot her an unguarded look before smoothing out her features.

Her father caught the moment, and his brows slammed together. "Hang on. This is why you're so upset. Because of a person..."

His gaze seemed to look into the core of her. "Yes," she only answered.

Realization flickered in his eyes. "You're dating someone on the team. I can't believe it."

She swallowed thickly, not in the least bit surprised

he'd guessed without more to go on. He'd made his first million reading the face of a man with a supposedly tapped-out mine in the lower Sierra Madres. "I never imagined it might happen, Dad. You know me." She cast a pained glance at her friend. "I'm usually immune to men."

He scrubbed a hand down his face. "He must be very special."

"Ted, she let him skate with her," Darla added softly.

His brows flew to his forehead. "My God! I'd hoped when I bought this team that you would skate again but this—"

Emotion clogged her throat, as much from realizing her father's hopes as from an image of her and Brock holding hands on his ice. "It's Brock Thomson, Dad, and I'm in love with him."

His mouth tugged to a smile before he smothered it. "I see. Harvard grad. Family man. Known as one of the nicest players in hockey. Val, I'm happy for you. Knowing Darla approves makes it even better."

Relief had the weight on her shoulders easing a little. "I'm glad you said that, Dad."

"He knows you, Val." Darla nudged Ted companionably. "So he knows this must be the real deal for you."

Ted muffled a curse. "Now I get it! You think our strategy here will hurt your relationship with Brock? He doesn't know about—"

"I promised you I wouldn't say who I was during the study or why we're here. At first that seemed practical. Later, it was essential. He knows I have secrets."

"Then you'll tell him everything you need to." He squeezed her shoulder, paternal concern in his gaze. "I release you from your contract. If he has a problem with it, he can come talk to me. I won't let our actions hurt your relationship, Val. Count on it."

They shared an old look of understanding, one they'd mastered when they'd had to manage her mother during her figure skating days. "I hope it won't come to that, but thank you. I'm going to text him about coming over to talk after he's finished here."

She would not obsess about his possible reaction while she waited, she told herself. Counterproductive.

"I'll hang with you until then." Darla put an arm around her and bumped her hip. "Ted, thanks for showing me again what a bang-up father you are. I was worried you and me were going to have to have a 'Come to Jesus' talk about Val being in love with the Eagles' captain."

He choked out a laugh. "I can't remember the last time someone was brave enough to have one of those with me. Might have been fun. But you might call me later, Val, to tell me everything worked out. I don't worry much about anything—I taught you why I think it's wasted emotion. But I still have my moments, worrying about you."

She hugged him, and his arms came around her, strong and true. "I'll call you."

"Good." After kissing the top of her head, he gestured toward the door. "Let me escort you out."

She looked around the locker room one last time. When she'd first arrived here, she'd thought this study would be like all the others. Different only in that it was taking place on her home turf. She'd follow her academic protocols. Rely on her training. Study. Observe. Conclude.

Nothing had gone according to plan.

And yet...if she had it to do over again, she wouldn't do anything differently. One of the reasons she'd fallen in love with Brock was that he'd been so accepting of her despite not knowing who she was.

Her personal finding beyond their academic study was simple: if another Ice Age was coming, she'd want Brock by her side, trusting he was the best mate to survive it with.

But her attachment to him went deeper. Together, she believed they'd find that elusive concept Darla believed in, one she hadn't until now: a happily ever after.

Because in some ways Brock answered the question that had plagued women since the beginning of time: *why are men so irresistible?*

She knew the answer. It was because of the strength that permeated both his body and spirit. He cared for the people in his life, protecting them if needed and taking care of them when he had to. He looked at her like she was his everything, making her believe anything was possible.

She only hoped Brock was still able to look at her that way after today.

TWENTY-FOUR

Why did men dread having "the talk" with the woman they loved?

Brock clicked out of Val's text, having checked his phone as soon as he'd taken off his skates in the locker room. He could feel every muscle in his face tightening into a glower.

If he hadn't put two and two together and noted her and Darla's unusual absence from the building after Chuck's caveman motivator, the uncertainty in her message would have tipped him off.

> *Hi! I'm at home and hoping we can talk. Finally. I know you've had a rough day, but there are things I need to explain. Come over anytime.*

No heart emojis this time. Straight to the point. It was time to reveal who she was and what she'd been doing here. Like he didn't already know.

God, he didn't want to do this.

"Oh shit! Shit. Shit. Shit. Mother—"

"Jesus!" someone else exclaimed.

He turned around as Kirkpatrick hurled his phone into his locker, breaking it apart. "Oh, fuck no! He did it. That mother—"

"What the hell are you talking about?" Brock's voice was harsher than usual from fatigue and built-up frustration.

"Mason is tweeting out pics from the locker room and putting music to them like 'Jungle Boogie' and shit, and it's gone mega-viral." Kirkpatrick lifted his hands like he was choking someone. "I'm going to kill him. This was supposed to stay in the locker room."

Brock had hoped the unspoken understanding of the locker room would hold. You didn't talk about a 'bag skate' to the media, and you certainly didn't share photos like that on social media.

He should have known better.

"Who the fuck sent Mason these photos?" Kirkpatrick stood on the bench in front of his locker, looking like an outraged giant. "When I find out—"

"The locker room is sacred." Finn hauled himself up on the bench alongside Kirkpatrick. "You younger punks just crossed a line you don't cross with your teammates. Did you not understand anything Chuck was trying to drill into your thick skulls? Sending those photos to Mason and having him make fun of us—his own team!—makes us look stupid. Ridiculous. Like we don't even have control of our own locker room."

Brock decided it was time for him to speak up. As captain. He crossed his arms over his chest and regarded the pack of younger players who ran with Mason. Most were shifting uncomfortably on their feet.

"Not only do we not have control of this locker room, but we don't respect each other."

A few people grunted in agreement.

"You know I'm not one for big speeches as captain. I let my actions speak for themselves. But we're not just on 'The Skids.' We're at a crossroads."

He walked over to the manifesto and started to read. "'Popular slang describes them as ignorant. Stupid even. Rude. Reckless. Unwilling to change. Unable to form or execute complex thoughts or plans. Outcome: Unsuccessful. ARE YOU A CAVEMAN?'"

He made sure to look at each and every player in the locker room.

"I guess that's what we all need to decide," he said flatly. "I hope you join me in saying 'fuck that' and winning every game we have left, heading to the playoffs, and winning the Cup. Because that's what I plan on doing."

He picked up his bag, not even bothering to shower and change, and walked out.

On the way to his car, his phone rang, and when he dug it out, his diaphragm tightened.

Why was the outgoing coach of St. Lawrence calling him right now? He picked up the call with dread.

"Hey, Coach Adams!"

"Brock!" He sounded surprised to have reached him, which only had Brock's stomach turning more sour. "Heck of a thing going on over there with you and the team."

He knew the feeling of when something was about to blindside you on the ice. Right now, that feeling was overwhelming. He paused and pinched the bridge of his nose. "Yeah, you know Coach Collins and his famous motivators. This might be his best yet."

"Yeah…" The pause was like taking a stick to the knees.

"Listen, Brock, I've already had a few calls. There's concern about you taking over the team with this caveman stuff all over you."

He dropped his bag to the floor.

"Maybe it will blow over in a while, but the administration doesn't think parents are going to want to send their five-star players to play for someone who's been seen eating like an animal or starring in one of Mason's caveman reels. At the school, we teach boys to become responsible young men as much as successful hockey players. Brock, this is ugly business. I know you'd be a great coach—"

"But I look like a fool right now," he ground out through clenched teeth, "and I'm a liability to St. Lawrence and the program. I understand, Coach."

The man's heavy sigh filled the space. "We still hope Zeke can join us at St. Lawrence. Good luck to you."

With that, the call ended.

Just like that.

The future he'd wanted for himself, the one he'd planned, was gone. Like someone had snapped their fingers and made it vanish.

He thought of Zeke, his guts spilling out onto the floor. What was he supposed to tell his nephew? The kid was going to be devastated.

Like him.

God. He bit the inside of his cheek to stop himself from hurling his bag against the wall. He had the urge to throw things. Rage around. Anything that would make him feel better.

But it wasn't going to go away.

Mason had done that, proving he'd never wanted this team to succeed. His pack of followers had put the final nail in the coffin by sending him those photos.

His goal of winning the Cup seemed even more out of reach. All that hard work...

By the time he arrived at his SUV, he had a call from his agent about Reebok, informing him that they were pulling out of their agreement with him. Brock wondered if Mason had intended for that to happen. He didn't care about the money. But his reputation was another thing, and it was taking the kind of hit some people didn't get up from.

Well, he wouldn't be staying down.

He buckled himself into the car and gripped the steering wheel, torn between heading back to his house to talk to Zeke before he heard the news about St. Lawrence from outside sources or going over to talk to Val and see what role she had in all this.

Because if she was involved like he feared, he didn't know how they could have a future now.

She'd ruined the one he'd planned to ask her to join.

TWENTY-FIVE

Why did a man simply stare at you when you were ready to pour your heart out?

Val watched Brock walk stiffly across the garage toward her, staring at her the entire way. His mouth had a tightness to it she'd never seen, not even in hockey games. He also hadn't changed from practice on the ice, save for his shoes. His black curls stuck to his head from wearing his helmet. So he'd run out without even showering...

"You've guessed some things," she made herself say through the dryness in her throat.

His nod was almost robotic. "That you were here to help Chuck with the caveman comparison? Yes, it seemed obvious when I read what he'd put on our lockers. It sounded like you."

God, that hurt. She wanted to rub the ache around her heart, but she gestured for him to come inside. He hustled up the stairs, not bothering to let her ascend first. That worried her, as he was always courteous.

"I can't stay long," he told her, stalking into the family room and stopping in the center, hands on his hips. "I have to get home and talk to Zeke before he finds out that St. Lawrence just rescinded their offer for me to be their next hockey coach."

She sucked in her breath. "No! That's ridiculous."

"Mason got pics of the locker room and has been making us into a complete joke on social media." His voice was a harsh slap of sound. "We're cavemen, and we look like animals."

She could feel herself start to tremble from the inside out. Their study had been used to hurt a good man, *her* man, in ways she never could have imagined. "I never meant for that to happen. No one did."

His mouth worked before he said, "I believe that, but it doesn't matter now. St. Lawrence doesn't think that I would be a good representative of their school or the kind of coach parents would entrust their kids to. When I step back and consider the situation from their perspective, I can't say I disagree. If Zeke were my kid and I was a parent, I'd choose another school in a heartbeat if the school had Coach Caveman."

She knew the sharpness of his voice masked a greater pain, and when she thought about Zeke and how he would feel, she had to bite the inside of her cheek to keep it together. Susan was going to be so upset. And Kinsley... They'd hurt his family—a family she deeply cared about— the one thing she'd promised never to do.

"Will you..." She took a shallow breath, feeling anxiety clawing at her. "Let me explain. Darla and I are cultural anthropologists who study—"

"Val, I don't have time for an entire recitation." A tic appeared in his hard jaw. "My entire world just exploded. Give me the basics."

She squeezed her hands at her sides, trying to find the

right words in the riot of shouts inside her head. "All right, Brock. We were hired to study whether hockey players are the modern cavemen for the Eagles' management team to motivate the players if needed. Our findings were twisted."

Like his features, she thought, as her heart beat painfully.

"What you need to know is that cavemen were terribly smart. They could take down woolly mammoths. Their use of tools advanced the nature of man. They multiplied and thrived. They were dominant, and so tough they survived the Ice Age. Our comparison was favorable. Not what Chuck made it out to be."

He raked a hand along his nape before letting his arm fall. "Well, that's something at least. I thought you might have— Never mind. Anything else?"

The tremble took over her lower lip, and she had to will it to stop shaking. "Besides the fact that I love you and I'm so sorry that I was a part of something that hurt you? *Especially* when I'd told you it wouldn't." Because that was vital. How could he trust her again?

His jaw popped audibly, and from the cold way he was looking at her, she knew how she felt didn't matter.

She'd hurt him.

She'd cost him something precious and hurt his family in the process.

The look he'd given her, the one that made her feel like she was his everything, was gone for good. So...she might as well pull off the last Band-Aid.

"You should also know that Ted Bass is my father, and that's why I helped," she said, lifting her chin.

That news cracked his hard expression. *"Ted Bass is your father?* You didn't think that was important? He owns my team, Val. He's my boss. You're his daughter. Does he know about us?"

She wanted to wrap her arms around herself. Instead, she called up her old protective wall and surrounded herself with it. She had to get through this. She owed him that much. "My relationship to my father had nothing to do with us or our study, and no, he did not know. Until today, when I told him how upset I was over the way he and Chuck used our findings and that it had hurt someone I cared about. He guessed then."

"Jesus." He raked his hand through his hair. "Could things get any worse?"

The agony in his voice stole her breath. "You don't need to worry about my father. He wasn't upset—"

"Well, good for him, because I am!" His voice broke for a moment before he stalked off toward the windows, tilting his head toward the ceiling before turning around and pinning her with an icy gaze. "Dammit, Val, I asked if anything could hurt me or my family, and you said no."

"I meant it!" She took a few steps toward him, her eyes burning, before she halted, concentrating on her wall. "I didn't know this was going to happen, Brock. I love you! And I love Zeke and Kinsley—"

"Don't." His voice broke as he held up his hand. "I can't bear to think about how upset they're going to be."

The wall she'd tried to create fell to the ground as if it were shattered glass. "Tell me what I can do to make this better," she pleaded.

Even though she wasn't sure anything could get better after this.

"I don't know, Val." He heaved out a sigh. "I believe you didn't mean to hurt anyone. I do. I just... Everything is different now. I..."

His shoulders fell, and she could see that what she'd feared might happen after the "bag skate" had come to pass. His spirit was destroyed.

"Without the coaching job at St. Lawrence, I'm going to have to stay in hockey. Jesus! I don't even know if it will be with the Eagles after this. The team's falling apart. Your dad knows we got together… I need to find a way to restore my cred. I lost Reebok too today."

She clenched her eyes shut at the news. "I'm so sorry, Brock."

"Yeah." He sucked in a breath. "It's not about the money. I used to stand for something. That seems to be as much in jeopardy as my goal of winning the Cup. I have a lot of work to do."

Nodding, she dug her nails into her palm. "I'll help in any way. Talk to anyone—"

"No, you should…go back to whatever it is you do."

"But I love you…" she whispered, trying not to cry. "I want to help."

When he met her eyes this time, the pain she saw in his gaze cut her open. "I know you do, and that means a lot." He took another moment, his jaw ticking with emotion. "I love you too, but it's too hard right now. I need to protect my family, Val. And my future is a mess. With everything I'm fighting to get back, I won't have time for anything else."

He paused, and it was worse than those seconds in the air when she knew she'd taken a jump wrong and was going to fall to the ice.

"And honestly, I don't know how we get back to what we had."

She wanted to argue with him, and she hated arguing. She wanted to cross the distance between them, grab his jersey, and make him figure it out. With her.

Up until now, the only person she'd ever wanted to force to do anything was her mother. She'd wanted to make her mother love her. And right now, that was all she wanted with Brock too.

But that was a no-win proposition. You couldn't make anyone love you or want you, and right now, he didn't want any of those things because of what she'd done, even if unintentional.

He didn't want her anymore.

"I'll say it again," she said, retreating to that quiet place inside herself. "I'm sorry for everything that's happened."

His mouth clamped into a line. "Me too."

The silence between them made her want to scream. She wanted to run from the room and find Darla upstairs. She wanted to get on the next plane and forget she'd ever come here and opened herself up to all this possibility and pain.

He rubbed his jaw and started for the exit. Then he turned. "You know...I'd thought we'd have forever."

Pain pushed up her ribs and into her throat. She fought back a cry, wrapping her arms around herself. "So did I."

"Good luck, Val." He stalked a few more steps away before looking over his shoulder. "Ah...don't reach out. To Kinsley or anything. I'll talk to Susan, but I think it's better if we handle things with her from now on."

She felt the cut of that in her heart, as if he'd just sliced away another precious part of her. "I understand. I'll tell Darla. Will you tell Zeke and everyone else how sorry we are?"

He was quiet a moment before he nodded crisply.

The silence between them sounded like someone screaming. Maybe it was the sound of her heart crying. "We...really enjoyed getting to know your family."

Something flickered in his eyes before he veiled them. "Yeah."

Then he walked out.

She listened to his footsteps and the closing of the door to the garage. She thought about running to the window to catch one last glimpse of him. That was how far gone she was. How much her emotions were controlling her.

She hated feeling like this. The pain was unimaginable. She should never have let herself feel like this.

Darla appeared at the edge of the family room, her face a study in sadness and worry. "I saw Brock leave. What happened?"

Pain was rushing up inside her. She fisted her hands tighter to hold it back. "He lost the coaching job at St. Lawerence. His Reebok deal. Probably his goal of winning the Cup given where the team's at."

Darla only pressed her lips together, her eyes bright with tears. "What else did he say, Val?"

The words hurt, the finality of them stealing the last pieces of hope inside her. "He's going to be staying in hockey, and he's not even sure it will be here. There's so much for him to fix that he doesn't think he'll have time for...anything else."

Her.

She pressed on, her voice cracking. "And even then, he's not sure how we could get back to how we were. Darla, he doesn't think there's anything more for us. And he doesn't want us to get in touch...not even with Kinsley."

Val started to cry then. Pressing her hands into her eye sockets, she couldn't hold back. A moment later, Darla's arms came around her, holding her tight.

"Oh, honey," she said, rocking her gently. "We're going to figure out something. This isn't the end of things—"

"Yes, it is!" She pushed back and gestured to her face. "Look at me. Look at how I'm acting. I knew better. We ruined things, even if we didn't mean to, and this is the outcome. Darla, I almost begged him to stay. To listen to me. To figure things out. To love me."

Her last words should have been a scoff, but they lodged in her throat.

"Of course you wanted all that," Darla said softly, wiping her tears and then Val's. "You love him, and he loves you. All of this stuff that happened is really bad, but that doesn't change how you feel."

"But I don't want to feel like this!" She pressed her hand to her chest, tears raining down her face. "It hurts, Darla! I was better off studying things. Observing things."

"I know, honey, but that's not living. That's not being human."

"Then I don't want to be human." She took a few steps away, almost tripping over her feet. "Humans are fragile."

I'm fragile.

"Yes, you feel like that now." Darla walked over and smoothed back her ponytail before cupping her wet cheek. "But like you always say about humans, we must be pretty strong. We survived the Ice Age."

"Oh, you shouldn't quote me." She raked her hand through the air. "I'm not even a good professional. Look at the mess we helped make with this study. Our work is supposed to illuminate things. Uncover truths. Make sense of—"

"Life?" Darla interrupted. "Human behavior? *You have.* This team's and your own—in your personal field diary, which I hope you'll let me read someday."

No way in hell that was happening. She was going to turn the gas stove on and torch it the first chance she got. "I was shortsighted. Who was I to think we could study cavemen and hockey players? Their lives are completely different."

"Are they?" Darla pressed, brow arched. "We might not have the same living conditions, but we still face the same stuff. War. Poverty. Environmental disasters. And on the personal side, we survive personal loss. Broken bones. Broken marriages. Broken hearts."

She wanted to put her hands over her ears so she wouldn't have to listen to this. "We don't even have that much direct knowledge of cavemen—"

"Bullshit!" Darla cried out. "Are you really going to go back on years of study? On purpose? Val, I know you're hurting, and so is Brock, but if there's one thing I know about humans, it's this... Brock will survive this. So will you."

"But I don't want to survive this!" She pressed her hand to her heart, the one breaking inside her. "I want to fix this. And that's so not like me."

"Welcome to the wonderful and awful world of being in love," her friend said gently. "I know you called our study here 'The Hockey Experiment,' but I wondered if your side study should be called 'The Human Experiment.' It doesn't sound so sexy, does it? And yet, it's kind of true. This experiment we're on is filled with risk. We try and put containers around them, like I imagine you tried to do with Brock when you imagined a glass wall between you."

Her friend knew her way too well. She could only nod and rub her eyes.

"Val, we all have those kinds of walls to prevent disaster from falling on us. But sometimes it doesn't work. Sometimes we have to live to the fullest expression of ourselves.

We fall in love, because it's one of the best feelings on the planet, and even when it hurts, we do it again sometimes."

Tears were falling steadily from Darla's eyes now, the hurt of old loves returning like ghosts from the past.

"The human existence is a perilous, fragile one, yes," her friend continued in a rough rasp, "but it's also so heartbreakingly wonderful sometimes that it makes everything seem worth it. Even when you want to curl up in a ball and die."

How many times had she watched her friend do that? Fall in love. Open herself up. *Live...*

Every time, she'd thought she was foolish. But now she understood why Darla had done it.

"Darla, I made his voice break." She pressed her hand to her mouth to fight off another cry. "I did that to him. How am I supposed to live with that?"

"One day at a time." Darla came over and led her to the couch, taking her hand. "You asked him for forgiveness, right?"

She nodded, now swiping at her runny nose. "He knows I didn't do this on purpose, but I've hurt him. Zeke too. I played a part in ruining his plans and his credibility. How could *anyone* get past that? God, I'm a complete mess! I've never been like this."

"No, you've always played life pretty carefully after your figure skating highs and lows." Darla gave her arm a comforting stroke. "But I think Brock is a better bet than a gold medal."

"I lost him today, Darla," she said, leaning over from the pain. "I have no answers for this."

"Good thing you have a friend who is really good at puzzles." She hugged her tightly. "Want to know someone else who is?"

She blew Darla's hair out of the way. "Who?"

"Your dad."

"Yeah, Brock wasn't thrilled about that either. I screwed up everything."

"Stop that now." Darla's hands ran soothingly over her back. "Together, we're going to figure this out, because while I fall in love often and somehow recover, you aren't built that way."

"Another truth I wish we hadn't unearthed."

"You're going to be wearing invisible widow weeds if you lose Brock. Hell, I wouldn't put it past you to buy an old nineteenth century house in New England and hole up, teaching at Harvard with no personal life, and Val, *I won't allow that.*"

She let her friend raise her chin.

"I love you too much to let this make you retreat. I happen to like seeing you happy from being with a man, and Brock is one of the best guys out there. I'm not going to let the light inside you die out again. It was almost out when I first met you in boarding school. Do you hear me? We aren't giving up!"

She felt the urge to cry for a different reason. "You're the best friend in the world."

"Damn right." She kissed her cheek and then guided her head onto her shoulder, wrapping her up like a mama bear. "Now, cry yourself out, and then we'll get serious."

She was good at serious.

She just wasn't sure it was going to turn anything around.

TWENTY-SIX

WHAT DOES IT TAKE FOR A WOMAN TO BELIEVE THAT when a guy says "Nothing" after they ask, "What's wrong?," it means he doesn't want to talk about it?

Brock stared at his sister, who was blocking his path to the stairs. "Susan, I don't want to do this right now. I need to talk to Zeke."

She stepped in front of him, wearing her BOSS sweatshirt, as if he wasn't Brock "The Rock," who could make rookies look down at their skates with one icy look.

"I sent Zeke over to a friend's house along with Kinsley because Darla told me you were likely planning on giving up on the St. Lawrence job. Like you gave up with Val."

What the fuck?

His hands clenched. Darla had called his sister? After he'd expressly told Val not to reach out?

Emotion he'd carefully topped with a cork rammed its way to the surface, threatening the control he'd cultivated since leaving the woman he loved. The woman he no longer had a future with. The woman who'd unintentionally broken his heart and destroyed his future and his nephew's dream. The woman who was his boss' daughter. He was lucky Ted Bass didn't cut him from the team for that, because Brock had trouble believing the man would simply be okay with one of his players secretly hooking up with his daughter.

Especially since Brock had broken her heart...

He'd seen the anguish and tears in her beautiful green eyes. Pain sliced through his already mangled insides.

"Susan, you need to get out of my way now. First, you shouldn't be talking to Darla—"

"Forget that." She laid a finger on his chest like his mom used to do when he'd come in angry after losing a game. "She *is* speaking sense right now, and she has your best interest and this family's best interest at heart. You're the one letting something slip away again. Like you did with Erin."

He clenched his jaw and heard it crack for the second time today. "What in the hell are you talking about? Erin walked out on me."

"Brock, you let her walk out." She screwed up her face like she was fighting with herself over what she was about to say.

Only he already knew what she was going to say. He *had* let Erin walk out, because he'd thought she would be better off—happier—if she weren't married to a hockey player. So he'd pulled back from his marriage, knowing it would drive her to do what he couldn't. Leave.

Susan's forehead smoothed out, and he knew she was going to go for it. "You two were so happy when you first met, but the moment she got upset, you thought it was your fault. Since you couldn't see a way to fix it, you let her go. Brock, I know my relationship track record sucks, but I can see your patterns easily. Probably the same way you can see mine. What is the one thing you wished I'd done differently with Darren?"

He blinked for a moment before checking whether he should be so honest. "Not married him."

"Exactly!" She shoved him a little as if she were trying to cheerlead him up, her own inner fire overcoming the usual fatigue in her face. "I couldn't agree more, but I couldn't say no to him at the time. I thought settling down would make him want the same things as I did. I was wrong. I'm glad I have Zeke and Kinsley, but I understand how I got where I am today. Do you trust my take on you?"

He heaved out a sigh. Part of him wanted to shove past her, but he knew he would be choosing avoidance, and that was what cowards chose. He wasn't a coward. "Yes, you were right about Erin."

Her smile was the same now as it had been at fifteen, after she'd schooled him about something. Always his big sister. "Good. And now I'm telling you Val is the best thing to ever happen to you. You *cannot* let her go."

Another sharp pain flared in his chest. He'd laid his head on the steering wheel in her garage and felt a dark place calling—one where hurt and loss defined him. It had shaken him.

"She didn't really fight me, and there's Zeke to consider. How is he going to feel when he hears I won't be coaching him at St. Lawrence? Susan, Val might not have meant to cause trouble, but it doesn't change the result. How can Zeke ever look at her the same way again?"

Her hands went to her hips and her expression turned cross. "What kind of talk is this? When I told you Darren was leaving us and that he'd hurt the kids with his 'inconvenience' talk, you had a plan. Move in with me, you said. We'll fix it, you said, and we've made a good start, haven't we? Kinsley is pressing me to let her go shopping with Darla and Val for a comforter set for her room."

He rubbed the back of his neck, fighting off hard emotion. "It's too complicated with the kids. They're going to be hurt by what Val and Darla did. To me. To the team. To this family. I can't protect them from that. But I can protect them moving forward. They aren't going to feel the same way about Val and Darla after this. I don't!"

Her gaze softened, making his heart throb more painfully after his outburst. "I think you underestimate my kids. And yourself."

His core, which he'd always thought would stand strong and solid in the face of anything like "The Rock" he was named for, shook. "Things have changed, Susan."

She gave her chin a thoughtful stroke. "I don't think less of them for what happened. They did the job they were supposed to do. Chuck used their work to fit his purposes. They didn't intend to hurt you."

"I know that, dammit!"

It struck him that if he had to join another team and move, it would impact Susan and the kids directly. What the fuck were they going to do? Was he really going to ask them to uproot themselves and move with him?

"Brock." She took him by the arms, her hands gentle. "Let's remember that Mason made this the problem. He's been the problem all along."

His mouth curled when he thought about that little shit and the rest of his gang. "Doesn't change anything."

"Bull! Listen, Val and Darla are as much victims as you are in some ways. They're certainly as upset as you are. Did you know some people in the academic circles where they work might think less of them as professors for being involved in this convoluted study and the ensuing media circus? Did you know they have doctorates from Oxford?"

He rubbed the back of his neck. God, his Miss Sexy Librarian's unique way of talking and seeing the world made so much sense now. "No, we didn't get into that."

"Darla mentioned they were hoping this study might lead to more management analysis for other sports teams or even corporations. They're both tired of peeing in a bucket and having to run baboons out of their tents. Can you imagine?"

He really couldn't.

"They were hoping to stay stateside," Susan pressed. "Darla mentioned she loves it here. Val does too."

He stalked over to the window because he couldn't stand still any longer. Not while he was thinking about her and what she might be going through. Because he couldn't fix that either.

"But Val didn't tell you any of that," his sister continued. "Darla didn't think she'd realized the future implications yet, because she was so focused on how *you* were feeling."

"You're showing me a pushy big sister side I haven't seen in ages," he shot back, skewering her with a look over his shoulder. "I'm not sure I like it."

"Tough."

But he felt her rush over and wrap her arms around him, pressing her face into his back. "If Darren had been a good guy and we'd had a chance of making things work, you would have pushed me to try. Like the sweet baby brother you are."

His scoff didn't come off too harshly given the emotion trapped in his throat. "Don't try and butter me up. I'm all out of good humor."

She smacked him gently on the back of his head—again, a mother move. "Of course you are. Your heart is broken. So is Val's. Darla and I made a pact to fix that. So you can stew, but afterward, you'd better get on the program. Because I will sic Zeke and Kinsley on you, Kinsley especially."

He spun around. "You wouldn't."

She grinned like a jack-o-lantern. "I'll not only buy the T-shirts—I'll paint them myself. The first one that comes to mind is... TAKE VAL BACK. And maybe I'll have Kinsley leave the tent up too with pictures of Val on it."

A feral-like growl erupted in his mouth. "That's fighting dirty."

Her wink was downright annoying. "I learned from my baby brother. He practically spews fire and brimstone on the ice."

His breath seemed overloud when he exhaled. "So you and Darla are playing dirty. What is Val doing?"

"Crying probably," she said with an arched brow, going in for the kill. "Then Darla will try to put her back together like I'm doing with you. After that, Darla promised me she had a plan cooking. With Ted Bass' help. Ah...I about swallowed my tongue when she told me Val was Ted's daughter. I imagine that was a shock."

"You think?" he scoffed.

"I loved hearing that she was a Junior Olympic figure skater!" Susan made a pirouette. "A gold medalist too! No wonder you two fit. You're both relentless competitors."

He stared at his sister. "Wait! She won the gold?"

Susan clocked her head to the side. "Did you let her tell you everything?"

No, he'd cut her off, thinking what did it matter? They couldn't be together anymore, and learning anything more about her would have made it hurt more. "You know the answer."

Her face went all maternal again, making his heart throb painfully. "So you go stew, but if you're interested, Darla told me their names. Val's professional name is Dr. Valentina Hargrove. Her mother was a gold medalist, too, and thought she should use her name professionally since it still carried weight in figure skating. Also, I know it's not really on topic, but I've been bursting to tell you about Darla's background."

Jesus, women and their love for gossip. "What is it?"

"She's the love child of Regina Eastman and J-Mac! When they were both married to other people. Isn't that the craziest?"

He shook his head as more shock knocked him flat. "It certainly explains her voice. And her love of fast cars, penthouses, and—"

"Bad boys." Susan locked her pinkie fingers. "Darla and I are like this when it comes to men. We've vowed to break our patterns. I hope you're going to help me with that. Because I might need a responsible younger brother looking out for me in the scary dating world when I finally decide to jump back in."

A reluctant chuckle rumbled up his throat. "Susan, you know I'll be there. Now, I'm done talking. I'm going to go stew. I might even find the green puck and whale it into the net about a thousand times."

Susan worked her mouth before saying, "Or...you could simply go over and make up with Val."

He gave her the stink eye.

"What do you want, Brock?" she shot back. "Because I've never known you to let anything other than you dictate what you can or can't have."

Jesus, she'd nailed him dead center with that one. "Fine, I hear you, and you're right."

"Good." She started backing out of the room. "Here's something to think about while you're stewing. If you don't come to your senses soon, I know Darla is going to get Val out there again right away so she can get her mind off you."

The mere thought of another man seeing what a gem Val was had him wanting to pick up the nearest piece of furniture and hurl it against the wall.

Get her mind off him, would she? He wasn't on board with that.

Stewing could wait.

TWENTY-SEVEN

Why do men have the power to reduce a strong woman to tears?

Val scrubbed her face and looked in the bathroom mirror. She didn't like the ravaged, red skin she was seeing. Worse, she hated the doubts swirling inside her, like she'd been shoved into the Nile River and was turning in circles because of the strong current.

"'The human experiment.'" She mimicked Darla's sultry voice. "Well, the human experiment sucks."

"Are you talking to yourself in there?" Darla called from Val's bedroom. "Get a move on. Your dad just drove up. We're about ready to start turning around this runaway train. Ted is *mega-pissed* at Mason and the jerks who leaked this to the media. You don't think he's going to let a team he owns be the laughingstock of the sports industry, do you? He's in mogul fix-it mode. I'm so psyched. See you downstairs."

She pressed her hands to her cheeks, hoping to draw some of the heat out. Apparently, that's what happened when one bawled their eyes out over a guy. Her first experience was not something to write home about. She would prefer to forget it had ever happened.

But then she thought about Brock losing the future he wanted—and Zeke too—and she found the strength inside herself to get up and stop wallowing. If they could fix this, she would be at peace.

No, her heart wouldn't be any less broken, but the spaces around the broken edges wouldn't feel so sharp. She could maybe look back on this time as a good learning experience in which she'd grown as a person.

She wanted to throw the washcloth at herself for spouting all that personal transformation bullshit right now when she was so raw.

But she knew it was the only way forward. Bitterness and regret weren't her way. Not even when she'd retired from figure skating at fifteen. She'd been a husk of herself, but she'd risen from that, so she knew someday she'd feel like herself again.

Except she wouldn't be herself again, would she? She hadn't before. This new Val would be carrying around a broken heart and the memories of a love affair that had made her feel...

She squeezed her eyes shut as tears welled. Yeah, best not bring out those memories right now.

When she finally arrived downstairs, her father was sitting on the ottoman across from Darla with his ankle over his knee, listening intently. The moment he caught sight of her, he was up out of his seat and wrapping her in his arms.

"Mason kamikazed his own team," he spat. "Chuck and I didn't think he'd ever stoop that low. But how are you? Stupid question. Hurting, huh? Well, you let your dad and Darla figure a way out of this mess. Because I don't like owning a team that's become the mockery of professional hockey."

"Ted was just telling me someone at a rival corporation who hates his guts tweeted out a photo of him wearing nothing but a loincloth," Darla told her, making Val lift her head up to see her father's face transform into a snarl.

"I don't look very good as a caveman," her father bit off, his eyes flinty.

Darla tucked her foot under her bottom and patted the seat beside her. "Val, come sit. I was about to share an idea with Ted. It's a little unorthodox, but it's like my mama always says about the media. You've got to give them a bigger story to cut their teeth on or entertain them so hard they forget everything else."

Val grimaced. "Don't tell me we're going that route."

"We're throwing it down old school, honey." Darla looked a little ill herself, her normally radiant skin anything but. "Ted, do you remember the Chicago Bears and the 'Super Bowl Shuffle'?"

"Of course I do." He leaned forward on the edge of his chair after loosening his tie. "That song and the fabulous video they made came out when I'd started my first company. It was 1985. Mike Ditka was the coach. Their quarterback was Jim McMahon. But who could forget Walter Payton? They made it before they won the Super Bowl. I remember thinking it was a ballsy move."

Val's already sick stomach turned even more sour. "I don't like where I think this is going..."

"It's still considered one of the most successful collaborations between sports and pop music." The scary gleam in her golden eyes was familiar to Val. "And with your permission, Ted, I was going to call J-Mac about coming up with a caveman song for your players to sing. Because you need to *own* the caveman analogy. Otherwise, you and your players are going to keep popping up in viral tweets looking like idiots in loincloths and get eaten up, so to speak."

Her father pressed his hands into his knees, giving her a considering look. "You could get him to do that?"

She twirled the ends of her long black hair. "I could ask J-Mac for both his kidneys and he'd say when do you need them. He feels terrible about how I came into the world. He's always wanted to make it up to me. I've decided I'm going to let him."

Val was shaking her head. "No, no, no, no—"

"Hush!" Darla put a hand on Val's thigh. "I'm doing it. But Ted, you're going to need to get your star players on board. J-Mac knocks hit songs out in a day when needed. But we're going to need buy-in from the team to get out of this humiliation. Chuck included."

Her father turned grim. "I've heard from Chuck. I won't tell you his current mood after finding his motivational strategy backfired because of, and I quote, 'some snot-nosed, punk-ass kid.' He's not thrilled to be photoshopped wearing a loincloth either. Clearly, the team didn't take his motivational strategy seriously."

"Some did," Val said quietly. She thought of Brock losing his coaching position. Sighing, she added, "The 'bag skate' might have worked, but the public humiliation was a game changer. Everyone needs to be on the same page to get out of this mess."

"Mason seems to find it amusing to be a caveman." Darla bared her teeth. "Ted, I think you put him front and center in the video—and then make him sit the bench and watch his team win without him. Because I think they will win if you play things right. Men want redemption at all costs after public humiliation."

Darla's concise tone had Val feeling the first glimmer of hope. "As usual, Darla is an expert on human nature."

Her father steepled his hands. "I agree with everything you've said. I'll talk to Chuck."

"We need to change the caveman manifesto." Val rubbed her hands like she did before she typed and thought of what she'd told Brock. "You need to embrace cavemen working as a team to take down a woolly mammoth and—"

"Surviving the Ice Age," she and Darla said in unison.

They exchanged a look. Darla smiled first, but Val felt her mouth shift. She could smile again, something that had felt impossible half an hour ago. She could feel a stirring of purpose—and that deep sense of sisterhood.

Her life was not over.

"Maybe Val might even skate as the woolly mammoth for the next home game." Darla punched her in the arm. "A little 'Caveman on Ice' action."

"You're not serious?" Val choked out.

"So serious." Darla buffed her nails on her own shoulder as she rose off the couch and did a little boogie move. "I'm a media pro with two mega-star parents. Choosing bad men might be in my blood, but so is this. If I weren't happy as a cultural anthropologist, I might hire out. I'd be a great fixer for some entertainer."

"You can be the Eagles' fixer," Ted told her, standing up. "You're hired. Both of you. When we pull this off, you two will have management analyst offers from anyone you want. Sports. Corporate. Maybe even the music industry."

Darla slid her a knowing look. "Part of my plan to turn our cred around, Ted. Like I've told Val, I don't want to live without hot water anymore, nor do I see myself lecturing to a bunch of kids for the rest of my life. We've started a life here—me and Val—and I intend to keep building our foundation."

She took her friend's hand and felt the deep connection they'd been building since boarding school—the pact to protect each other's backs. "Me too."

Her father crossed and kissed them both on the cheeks before sitting next to Val. "It's going to be fun to see what you two get up to next. But for now, do whatever you need to do. I'll talk to Chuck. Darla, send me your preliminary candidates to be in the music video when you have them."

Val watched the two people dearest to her exchange grins. Her father was in his element, delegating orders, and Darla was formulating solutions to the problem at hand. Like usual.

"You would really make a great woolly mammoth on the ice, Val," her father said, nudging her in the side.

Then he winked.

She felt her mouth part. Her father had winked? She couldn't remember the last time she'd seen him do that.

"I'll bet there's a certain Eagles' captain we could get to skate with you." Darla sent her a knowing look. "Unless you want to dress up like a cavegirl. Is that the correct term?"

"I'd rather be a woolly mammoth," she replied, only to press her hands to her mouth. "I didn't mean that. I am *not* skating in 'Caveman on Ice.'"

Darla made a humming sound. "We'll see."

The doorbell chimed.

Darla put her hands to her face in feigned surprise. "I wonder who that could be."

Val's heart started beating hard in her chest. Brock!

"Ted," Darla continued, "you should get a move on and talk to Chuck. I need to call J-Mac. He'll want to fly out here and pamper his baby girl. It's going to be rough with all our father-daughter issues, but I'm doing it for my girl. Val, you should get the door. Ted and I are leaving through the back."

Her father's face turned serious. "Actually, I need to be here a moment longer."

Oh God!

Darla bit her lip before nodding. "Right. Men beating their chests and doing the guy code thing about daughters and the like. Ted, why don't you get the door, then? Val, I'll talk to you later."

The doorbell rang again.

Ted headed to the front while Darla blew her a kiss as she tiptoed out the back.

Val laid her hand over her swirling stomach and rose. She arrived to find Brock standing in the doorway with her father.

"Ted—" Brock began.

"Me first," her father said, holding up his hand. "Brock, I've always respected you. You're one of the few people who dare to look me in the eye. I trusted you with my team. Now, I'm trusting you with my daughter. Because if she let herself skate with you, that says more than anything about how she feels about you. I'll be going now since you two have much to discuss."

She pressed her hand to her throat as she looked from Brock to her father. God, they were both really good men.

With another searching look, her father turned toward her. "Val, honey?"

"Yes, Daddy?"

"It's going to be okay." He sent her a reassuring smile. "You have my word on it. Brock, you have mine too."

He clapped Brock on the back as he left, leaving them both alone as the door closed behind him.

"Jesus, I didn't expect that," she heard Brock rasp out over the wild beating of her heart.

Then Brock was standing in front of her, his heart in his blue eyes, wearing a crisp blue suit and smelling of cloves and pine. "I'm an idiot for walking away like I did, after what we had together. Is there any chance you'll forgive me?"

She tried to smile but her vision started to get blurry. "I was an idiot too. I should have tried harder—"

"*Hey!*" He was wiping the tears running down her face. "Let's agree on one thing. We love each other, and we'll fix this. Together."

"That was three things actually," was all she could manage before he grabbed her waist and hauled her to him.

"My Sexy Librarian," he said gruffly the moment before his lips crushed hers.

Her arms went around his neck as her dopamine levels shot to outer space. She flew into happiness and delight as her mouth tried to keep up with him. He was ravenous for her, his teeth taking her bottom lip gently in a love bite before he thrust his tongue in her mouth and showed her how much he wanted her.

Suddenly he was pausing and growling, *"Mine."*

His mouth found hers again, and she tightened her hold on him. His body radiated heat, and inside the pure joy flowing through her was a flood of desire. He backed her up into the house and slammed the door, swinging her into his arms and starting for the stairs.

"Is this too fast?" His voice was raw, his eyes a little wild. "Because if so, you need to tell me right now."

She laid her head on his strong shoulder and cupped the hard line of his jaw. "No, it's perfect. *I missed you.*"

He stopped. Right there on the stairs. His hand touched

a strand of her hair that whispered down her cheek. "I'm sorry I hurt you."

"I hurt you too," she whispered.

His hand achingly cupped her face. "Unintentionally, and I was too overwhelmed by everything to see a way forward. Well, we aren't letting that stuff define us, are we?"

Tears started to choke her. Part of the yo-yo of that damn human experiment Darla talked about. "Never. I'm not a quitter."

"No, you're a gold medalist." He kissed her swiftly, his blue eyes shining with pride. "Now, I've really got to win the Cup. I need to be your equal when it comes to wins."

She wouldn't tell him how many golds she'd won right now. Later. Later, she would tell him everything. She curled her hand around his neck. "I love your competitive spirit, but I'll still love you even if you don't win the Cup. But I know you're going to win, even if it seems impossible now."

She hadn't believed her mother would love her if she didn't win, and all she wanted was for him to know that her love ran deeper than that.

He swallowed hard beside her ear. "Good to hear. Val, I — You *are* the perfect woman for me. I was an idiot to forget that. I love you. Whoever the hell you are."

The last bit was said with one of his sexy smiles, which she'd gotten used to thinking were hers and hers alone. "You can see my full *curriculum vitae* later. Now, I want you to make love to me."

His sexy smile transformed into a promising grin, and her thighs clenched in response. "With pleasure, Dr. Hargrove. Although I'll always prefer to call you Miss Sexy Librarian."

So he knew...

Thank you, Darla. She tangled her fingers in the black curls at his neck. "I can be on board with that."

"And Val...I've already read your *curriculum vitae* online and a bunch of other articles. You really do love cavemen, don't you?"

"They survived the Ice Age!" She dialed back her geek meter. "I told you earlier."

"Yes, taking down woolly mammoths and all that." He started up the stairs again. "But not dinosaurs."

"Good God, no! That is a common misconception that cartoonists and other ill-informed people continue to perpetuate. We're talking around a sixty-five-million-year difference between them!"

His lips were twitching as he walked into her bedroom. "That many?"

She curled her fingers into his collar and tugged. "Are you laughing at me?"

"Never." He laid her down on the bed and started to peel off his suit jacket.

His muscles bunched with the movement, making her mouth water.

How had she thought she could live without this?

Without him?

She reached up to help him unbutton his shirt because she couldn't hold back from touching him a moment longer. He dug his hand into the back of her hair, loosening her ponytail. Their lips met, his soft and seeking this time, as if he knew the truth at last.

They had all the time in the world.

She sucked on his bottom lip as he tore off his shirt and threw it on the floor. His hands went to her hem, and she leaned back to let him draw her shirt up and over her head, her bra following in quick order. Her hair tumbled down around her as he wickedly slid back and tugged her underwear and pants down, finishing with tossing her socks beside his strewn clothes.

Naked, she lay back as he stood, his heated gaze on her, and unbuttoned his pants. The zipper whispered down. His gorgeous cock shot out, making her want to fidget. His erectile tissue—his *corpus cavernosum* and *corpus spongiosum*—were already impressive.

Then she started laughing. *"Corpus cavernosum!"*

"God bless you." He leaned over her, his expression puzzled. "What's got you laughing at a moment like this? If I weren't a confident guy—"

"Like you don't know that your penis is why words like 'schlong' and 'Mr. Midnight' were invented."

"I'm liking the direction of this conversation more and more." He tickled her ribs as she continued laughing. "'Mr. Midnight,' huh?"

Call it the stress, but a moment later, she was holding her stomach and guffawing. *"Corpus cavernosum.* Don't you get it? It's like the term 'caveman' is hardwired into the penis."

"I have no idea what you're talking about right now, Miss Sexy Librarian."

She cupped his shaft and stroked her hand up its length, making him hiss out a breath. "Your *corpus cavernosum* is part of your erectile tissue. Oh, never mind. I'll tell Darla. She'll get it. Oh, how she'll get it."

She continued to laugh.

He lay down on the bed beside her, resting his hand on his elbow. "I think you're having a meltdown."

"I know!" She pressed her hands to her heated face. "I've cried my eyes out. I thought I was going to throw up. And now I can't stop laughing. I'm a lunatic. From the term 'luna.' Meaning moon. A lunatic. A person with intermittent insanity. Moonstruck. And this is what Darla calls the human experiment! I don't know how anyone is supposed to survive it."

"All right, I think there's only one thing to do here." He stood up and stripped off the rest of his pants, chucking them down and stepping out of them. "You go on and laugh and mumble about my erectile tissue and being moonstruck because of it."

That had her laughing even harder.

"Oh, Val, when you're like this, I can see forever with you so easily."

She sputtered, sitting up. "*Like this?* But I'm nonsensical. I'm babbling in Latin about your man parts, for heaven's sake!"

He was biting his lip to stop from laughing as he covered her with his body. "Don't you know why I love you like this?"

She was already shaking her head as her laughter faded away, the intensity of his blue gaze stealing her breath.

"You make me happy, that's why." He traced her cheek as she fell back against the bed, his gorgeous face staring down at her. "Happier than I've ever been with any woman. Babe, you make me feel like I can fly."

Something caught in her throat as he turned that look on her. The one that she'd cherished from the start. The one she'd feared she'd lost forever.

The one that said she was his everything.

"You make me feel that way too." Darla's words came back to her. "It's pretty great, isn't it?"

"It's everything." He leaned down and slowly kissed her. "You're everything. Now, let's forget the Latin for a bit. Just be with me."

His blue eyes were practically hypnotic when he levered back to gaze down at her. "I want you to breathe me in. All the way. Until there's no place I'm not a part of."

She inhaled deeply and brought his mouth back to hers. Where it belonged.

They took their time, pressing heated kisses to the erogenous zones they'd discussed. She didn't need to catalogue them. She knew the name and shape of his pleasure now like she knew her own. She knew how she could make him moan when she pressed a kiss to the back of his neck and bit down gently. She knew how the mere brush of her fingers along the underside of his buttocks would make him groan. She knew how he'd throw his head back when she stroked the full length of his cock.

Of course, his hands sought out her secret places, some not even known to her before he'd revealed them to her. He'd shown her the full power of her pleasure, the way she'd cry out when he pressed open-mouthed kisses to the sensitive side of her neck, the way her entire body would arch into him as he sucked at her breasts, and the way her body would rise to his mouth and later him as he slid deep inside her and took her where she instinctively knew where to go.

He shattered her breath with his touch, with his mouth, with his very penetration. She surrendered to it all, trusting him with everything she felt, with everything she was. When he tangled his hands with hers, spearing her with a shocked, fiery look as his own pleasure overtook him, she laid her head back and tightened around him, coming with him, like she was always meant to do.

When they rolled to their sides, she pillowed her head onto his shoulder, eyes closed, savoring the awesome choreography of her body in its post-passionate state, the pulsing, the feeling of complete expansion, the riotous heartbeat signaling vitality and the indominable truth that she was alive and she was loved.

Primitive power.

Passionate love.

The human experiment.

When Brock finally stirred, he leaned down and kissed her. From her research, she knew kisses held critical information—they sent messages from one's lips, tongue, and face to the brain, triggering hormones and neurotransmitters along with endorphins.

But in this kiss was something her heart understood. She knew it before he'd lifted his head, his blue eyes warm and bright with love.

"I want you to marry me."

She knew her dopamine levels were accelerated. Doing anything other than smiling was impossible in this moment. Darla had been right to get her brain wrapped around this marvelous possibility. "Is that so?" she bandied back playfully, none of her earlier anxiety present. What a revelation. This must be how people feel when they win the lottery.

"Will you marry me?" he pressed, tucking a sweaty lock of hair behind her ear. "I don't have a ring. My bad. And it doesn't have to be soon. It can be whenever you want. But I want you to know how serious I am about us. That I'm promising you I'm here. I'm fully committed. I'm not *ever* walking out again."

Struggling to rise so she could be on level ground with him, she sensed she was hearing something deeper in his proposal. "I would like to marry you, yes. But why do you feel like you need to assure me so? While also doubling down on something for yourself?"

He looked off. "Because I didn't before, and I don't plan

to do that again." His gaze retuned, searching her face. "Okay?"

She nodded, hugging him tightly, sensing the emotions rolling around inside him. He wrapped his arms around her and buried his face in her shoulder, squeezing her tightly to him. He held her that way for a long time.

There was no need for words. Val could feel their heartbeats harmonize—another magical act of the human heart, one that seemed scripted for partnership.

"So..." He lay back and pulled her onto his chest. "We need a plan. First, I need to buy a ring."

"I think we have other pressing issues right now," she said, tracing the defined muscles of his chest.

He shot her a look. "Our engagement is a priority."

Right. A man claimed what was his with the appropriate adornments, and his voice didn't suggest he'd welcome her view here, so she only smiled. He grunted.

"We should tell your family—and I should tell Darla." Her friend was going to give an earsplitting scream. "And my dad."

"Right. Your dad. I still can't believe he didn't deck me for messing with his daughter."

The mere thought turned her blood cold. "Of course he wouldn't. He's a civilized person."

"Not a caveman, huh?" He gave her a crooked smile, and immediately she knew they would be okay all the way, because they could laugh about it.

"About that..." She tapped her lips. "There's a plan in action to offset the negative press. I believe it's going to be effective. Perhaps legendary, if other similar acts prove a worthy basis for comparison."

"I have no idea what you're talking about," he told her, tracing her shoulder.

"Ever hear of the 'Super Bowl Shuffle'?"

"Yeah, it's a classic." He pressed onto his elbow and stared down at her. *"Why?"*

"Because you might be doing the caveman version with J-Mac." She made a face. "He's—"

"Darla's dad," he finished, squeezing his eyes shut. "God, I just had a vision."

"Of you rapping in a caveman outfit?" she bandied back.

He groaned. "Jesus, you can't be serious."

She patted his chest. "Well, if Darla has her way, I'm going to be dressing up as a woolly mammoth as part of 'Caveman on Ice' at your next home game."

"That's got to be a joke." He sat up and crossed his arms over his naked chest. *"That's"* their idea for turning this around?"

"Cavemen have a lore," she told him. "Besides, I have a plan for St. Lawrence."

"You do?" He brought her hand to his mouth and kissed it. "What is it? Because I've got nothing. Susan promised me Zeke is going to be okay. I'm…trusting that."

She could hear the rawness in his throat and felt her own. They would have to trust it, because another outcome wasn't acceptable.

"I'll endow a new humanities department to St. Lawrence with a small museum of caveman articles I've collected," she told him. "I can't see how they won't see the appeal. Both in terms of the kind of academic attention it will bring the school as much as the seriousness of the person endowing it with me. My husband, the great hockey player, Brock Thomson."

Just saying that had her entire throat clogging up with emotion.

"I like the sound of that, especially the husband thing." He kissed her ring finger and traced it, as if he were imprinting a ring there. "It might work."

She thought so too, but she believed in backups. "If that isn't enough, I'll ask Darla's mom to sing at their high school graduation. And if that's not enough, I'll have my father give their commencement speech."

His face was a mix of pleasure and downright awe. "You *are* thorough. It's playing to win."

"We have that in common. I admit I have not worked out how to convince Reebok to change their mind, but rest assured, I will come up with some ideas for us to discuss."

"Because we work together." He raised her hand to his mouth again and kissed it. "Val, I love you so much."

"And I you." She tangled her hands in his. "Now, are you assured that your future is bright once again?"

"Our future." He leaned over and cupped her face, love shining in his eyes. "I knew it was bright the moment you forgave me and put your arms around me."

Then he was kissing her, and she was throwing her arms around his neck again, like she had when they had come back together like they were meant to. They got all tangled up in the sheets and had a few more of the pleasures of the human experiment.

And after they'd showered later and he'd gone downstairs to find them some food before they went over to his house to tell his family about their engagement, she finally gave in to the one act she'd been pondering for some time.

She picked his towel up off the floor and sniffed it. His scent enveloped her—pine, cloves, and musk. Her man.

Darla was right—as always.

Even though she was on birth control, she could swear she felt herself ovulate.

TWENTY-EIGHT

Why are men willing to look stupid for the woman they love?

Brock frowned at his outfit in the locker room mirror. If this was "sexy" caveman, he couldn't see it. Most of his chest showed—Darla's idea—but it was the brown fake fur loincloth-like drape that had him feeling like the biggest chump alive.

Finn clapped him on the back as he headed to the exit in a matching outfit. "You look like a princess. See you on the ice."

Zeke scowled in the mirror beside Brock, tugging on his junior caveman outfit. Darla had thought it would be cute to have some younger hockey players join their 'Caveman on Ice' pre-game extravaganza. Of course, she'd recruited Zeke in a weak moment. When he'd been grinning like an idiot like Susan and Kinsley after hearing about Brock's engagement to Val.

"I don't want to look like a princess." His nephew pointed to his spiky hair, courtesy of the gel Darla had used earlier, something Brock had declined to consent to. "We look like idiots."

"You need your spear," Darla called, running over from where she'd been talking to J-Mac and Ted Bass in the corner and handing them their plastic props. "Now, you look like primal men who can take on anything. Including the *scary* woolly mammoth." Turning, she called, "Val, where in the hell are you?"

"She's here!" Kinsley called from behind one of the pillars, wearing another new T-shirt that choked him up. FAMILY was emblazoned across the front in the same matching plaid she'd chosen to decorate her new room. She'd taken her tent down the day she'd learned Val was becoming part of their family, Darla a bonus member.

His fiancée emerged shyly, tugging on her gray-fur-covered arms, alongside Susan, who was trying hard not to laugh. Brock fought a smile. Val wore a woolly mammoth headdress with the proverbial trunk and floppy ears along with thick stage makeup. The foam horns swirling on either side of her head were the real showstopper. Her slender legs were clad in gray fake fur tights, as was the rest of her body.

Darla had designed the costume with help from one of J-Mac's famous costume designers, and he had to say, if there was ever a sexy woolly mammoth, it was her.

He gave a wolf whistle, making her flush crimson under the gray stage paint. "Stop that!" she told him sternly, hurrying over quickly on her gray skates, also covered in fake fur. "You're embarrassing me."

He pointed to himself. "*You?* Do you see what I'm wearing?"

Darla tapped his mostly bare chest. "Women aren't going to think you're an embarrassment, Brock, trust me. Zeke, you look like a young guy poised for manhood.

Tonight, you will join the other warrior cavemen and take down the feared woolly mammoth. She will be the sacrifice the gods give you for your service to the earth."

Zeke huffed out a breath and rolled his eyes toward Brock. He could almost hear his nephew thinking, *Man, she's really into this.*

He couldn't disagree. Except Darla's plan had worked from the beginning. They'd turned the caveman circus around to their advantage with the help of J-Mac, who'd produced the shit out of everything so far, tonight included. There was a new manifesto on their lockers, which included the caveman's true legacy, according to the eminent Drs. Hargrove and Jones, better known around the arena as Val and Darla now.

The song J-Mac had collaborated with them on, "Cavemen Like the Ice," was clever with its ice and diamonds metaphor, mirroring their play on the field with living large, something for which Mason was the perfect picture boy. The song and the video had set new records both in downloads and views already.

Of course, Mason didn't know he wouldn't be playing yet. But he'd learn. Tonight. He was finally back after an even longer suspension Chuck had imposed after the leak, which had earned a few other players suspensions as well. They'd apparently only sent Mason the photos as jokes, not realizing he'd break locker room code and splash them over social media, humiliating them as well.

The team had bonded over that disgrace and the wish for redemption. They'd embraced a way out, both with the media and the fans but also for the future of their careers in professional hockey.

With their egos in the ashes, Chuck had helped them

find their inner phoenix. Together they'd become a team. They'd won the last slate of their remaining games.

If they won tonight, they'd win the conference and head to the playoffs.

They still had a way to go, but Brock trusted they would keep winning and take the Cup. Just like he trusted Val's plan was going to work with St. Lawrence, whose coach had called him and softly exclaimed they'd been too hasty. He *was* still valued at St. Lawrence if he wanted to join them. He was letting them stew for a while. It didn't pay to look too eager.

Much like he was doing with Reebok, who'd also come back to his agent with hat in hand. He was still thinking about them too, but he'd been amused by the number of other endorsement offers that had come in since "Cavemen Like the Ice" had gone platinum. He was rolling in profitable opportunities—much like Val and Darla were with offers from other sports teams, record companies, corporations, and even the U.S. military—but they weren't at the top of his priority list right now.

He had a new fiancée to spend time with, and he was deeply dedicated to that task, beyond preparing to win out this season before he retired.

"Are you ready?" he asked her, tugging her left hand to his mouth and kissing the ring he'd placed there the day after he'd proposed.

Of course, she'd told him the emerald ring was too big—even though her eyes had shone when they'd gone shopping, so he knew she loved it. He'd told her that a true caveman, in the best sense, made sure everyone around knew who his woman was. Hadn't he read that in her real report? The one Chuck had finally embraced after realizing he needed to pivot with the media.

She'd caved, of course, with a soft smile he was seeing more and more often. Love looked good on her, Darla said. As he looked at himself, standing practically naked wearing a fake fur loincloth, he had to admit it looked good on him too.

Otherwise, he'd have never agreed to wear this stupid outfit.

Val looked down at herself beside him and then straightened her shoulders, lifting her chin and lengthening her neck—her posture one of pure artistry. "You ask if I'm ready? A woolly mammoth is *always* ready. It's you, caveman, who should think twice about messing with me."

Her hand slapped his butt as she headed to the locker room door.

Darla hooted. Kinsley chortled. Susan guffawed.

She was getting spunkier, his Miss Sexy Librarian, and more than ready for the next phase of her career with Darla, stationed here in his beautiful hometown. Life was more than good. It was awesome.

"Girls are so weird," his nephew said with an aggrieved huff.

"But imagine our lives without them." He gripped Zeke's shoulder. "Come on. We've got a woolly mammoth to take down."

The crowd noise was deafening by the time they reached the ice. J-Mac and his crew were already on the fake iceberg, spinning records, as they said. Mason was skating around in his famous fur coat, setting the stage for the show. Brock couldn't wait to see his face when he realized Chuck wasn't going to play him. Ted had confessed he was trading the kid as soon as he could. It seemed a fitting end to Mason's poisonous influence on the team.

But he wouldn't think about that tonight. Not when he

was skating with his fiancée publicly. Maybe for the only time. He took up his position beside Val and slid his hand around her waist. "You look beautiful. Thanks for doing this."

She ran her hands down her costume, as the announcer began to tell the story of the cavemen's mythical hunt for the woolly mammoth. "You understand why, right?"

He heard Miss Sexy Librarian in her voice. "Tell me."

Her smile lit up every space in his heart. "Love is a great motivator, perhaps the greatest of them all. I'll see you on the ice."

His blood was already racing, a potent drumbeat resounding across the arena. "Don't make it too hard for us."

A wicked laugh escaped her gorgeous lips before she fluidly sailed onto the ice, a sound he intended to enjoy for the rest of their lives.

He watched her lift her arms overhead while skating on a single leg, the movement so exquisite the entire arena went quiet. You could hear a pin drop as she sailed into the next sequence, arms out toward him, beckoning him and the others onto the ice.

He stepped on, the drumbeat loud in his ears.

She was his—his to chase, his to catch.

His to love.

He thought of what had brought her here to him.

It might have begun as an experiment. But it had ended with love.

Val had it right. Love *was* the biggest motivator, he'd finally discovered, and he was going to show her just how motivated he was.

For the rest of his life.

If you liked The Hockey Experiment, make Ava's day and leave a review.

―――――

Want another laugh-out-loud romance to dive into? Get A Very UN-Shakespeare Romance!
Read on for a sneak peek.

A VERY UN-SHAKESPEARE ROMANCE

CHAPTER ONE

Slamming the case file on a bad guy was as good as sex.

Had he really just thought that? Robbie O'Connor filed the paperwork sitting on his messy desk and then picked up his shitty precinct coffee to wash the taste of that sorry realization out of his mouth. Sure, the criminal who was now serving twenty years had hurt his wife and kids like it was his daily right. Robbie lived for getting scumbags like that thrown into the slammer. Work had always been his mission. His source of pride. He loved making a difference in people's lives.

But had he really gotten to a point where he thought putting someone away was as good as a roll in the sheets with a hot-blooded woman?

Okay, he knew he worked a lot. He'd gotten into the habit of taking on extra cases to help out other cops with families since there was no reason for him to go home. He was patted on the back all the time for it. But this notion?

His brothers—all six of them—would likely say he'd become a pathetic excuse for a man. Okay, maybe not Tim. The youngest O'Connor male was the most sensitive one. He'd be more inclined to point out Robbie had become overly cynical since his divorce. Not so far from the truth.

"O'Connor!" his intercom blasted from reception. "The UPS guy needs your pretty signature."

Shoving out of his creaky office chair, he strolled down the hallway, wondering if his sister Kathleen had sent him something from Ireland. She liked to pop the odd stuffed sheep or eerie leprechaun into the post, but those packages usually came in around birthdays or holidays. It was late August, but maybe she'd sent him a *Just Because* present. He was her favorite brother, after all—not that his other brothers would agree, the idiots.

They all adored their one and only sister, and God knew she'd put up with a lot having seven older brothers. But she'd turned out okay. In fact, she was the only O'Connor kid who was happily married with a baby on the way. He was smiling at the thought of his first niece or nephew when he reached the man in the brown uniform beside the reception desk. The guy was belly-laughing with Patty Fitzgerald, both men huddled over the latter's phone.

"Hey, O'Connor!" Patty smacked him on the back. "I was just showing Al here your latest stupid criminal video. I still can't believe that murderer thought he could erase all the evidence by sticking the body in a vat of vanilla ice cream. I about died laughing when the local reporter quoted the suspect as saying the victim loved having his cherry pie à la mode, so he figured he'd appreciate the gesture of burying him in it."

Robbie puffed out his chest, taking pride in spreading his sick version of law enforcement cheer. His family, friends, and fellow co-workers all loved it. "It might be a top ten, given the suspect dropped his cell phone in the vat along with the body. Forensics found the sim card and recovered everything from his threatening texts to his murder shopping list at Home Depot. Idiot thought the ice cream would cure all his troubles."

"A pint of chocolate chip usually cures mine when my old lady gives me fits," the UPS guy said with a snort. "You O'Connor?"

"Didn't you hear me call him that?" Patty walked back behind the reception desk. "What? You got lime sherbet in your ears?"

Robbie shot Patty an amused look before pulling out his ID, tucked beside his badge inside the wrinkled tan sports jacket he really needed to get to the dry cleaners. "Don't mind him, Al. Patty hasn't had his donut quotient for the morning. Thanks."

"No problem," the man answered as Robbie signed for the package.

He immediately noted it wasn't from Ireland as the UPS man took off. Just a simple Next Day Delivery envelope with an illegible return address in Boston. His instincts revved. He hadn't been sent anonymous evidence through the mail in a while, but maybe today was the day. The thought excited him more than it probably should. He needed an interesting new case. Something to hold his focus. The run-of-the-mill breaking and entering was like stale bread.

"That from your sweet little sister?" Patty asked, slurping coffee from his carefully guarded *I'm Too Sexy* cup, an outrageous lie his fellow police officers knee-slapped themselves silly laughing over. Patty had the kind of unmemorable face that had made him great for blend-in-anywhere undercover work. Now, with only a few years to go until retirement, he was proud of his weekly donut intake.

"Doesn't look like it's from sis." Robbie casually rested against the desk and snagged an apple crumb donut from Patty's box. "Maybe I won the lottery. Wait, I just did."

"Hey! Donut stealing is a serious offense. Don't make me cuff you."

"I'm good for it," he called over his shoulder, moving quickly to his office and then dramatically slamming the door. Only one other officer had ever cuffed him—Patty, back when Robbie had been a hotshot rookie. The older officer had taken it upon himself to give him a lesson in police hierarchy after he'd solved one of Patty's cases in a day—a case that had been open for six months. So the big lug had cuffed him to one of his cousin's garbage trucks for revenge.

Robbie had taken the hint to shut up and done his job, letting people come to him if they wanted his help. He'd risen through the ranks faster that way, not that promotion had been his focus. But to this day, he'd never been recreational with handcuffs in the bedroom.

God, here he was again, thinking about sex—or his current dry spell. To be fair, it was of his own choosing. He was turning forty this year, and he was tired. Tired of dating apps that brought strange messages to his inbox, and even more so of the bar hookup scene, including at his brother's Irish pub, O'Connor's.

He didn't want to get married again just for the sake of it, and he wasn't even sure he wanted kids of his own. They were great and all, but they asked so many questions and needed so many things. He'd practically helped raise seven siblings, being the oldest. He was good with living life as a single man. Or so he was telling himself...

He carefully opened the envelope, checking the interior with the eraser end of a pencil from his desk. It only nudged a half sheet of paper. When he withdrew the note inside, he froze.

Robbie,

I need you to get into a taxi right now and go to the Beacon Hill Gym. My babies are there. You have to pretend to be their father and pick them up. Don't try and call me. More information will be waiting for you there. Don't leave this note at your office and don't tell anyone where you're going. Make sure you aren't followed. I haven't been kidnapped, fyi.

Love,

The one who helped you out of Carson Bay after that lion's mane jellyfish stung you.

TARA!

Robbie read his first cousin's cryptic note over again, rubbing the back of his neck as he tried to make sense of it. Jesus, she hadn't even signed it. Just given a detail only he would remember, much more cloak-and-dagger than he was comfortable with. And why the fuck had she thrown in the haven't-been-kidnapped part? His blood pressure was soaring already.

He looked at the UPS envelope, noting she'd sent the letter yesterday. Yesterday...

Why not call or text him? He knew she'd caught her worthless husband, Scotty, cheating with one of her nail salon technicians a few days ago and thrown him out of the house, saying they were done. His brother Danny had spread the news after Tara had stormed into O'Connor's wanting a fully loaded Rueben and a Cosmo.

Why were Tara's two girls at some gym way up in Beacon Hill? Tara didn't belong to a gym as far as he knew, and neither did Scotty. Certainly they didn't hang out in that chichi neighborhood. And what was with the bit about not telling anyone or being followed? Had Scotty hired an investigator for divorce proceedings?

Shit. Divorces sucked. He'd left his cousin a voicemail the moment he'd heard about the O'Connor's incident, saying he was sorry Scotty was such a worthless jerk and asking if she needed anything. Her parents had both passed and she was an only child, so Robbie felt a sort of responsibility toward her. She was almost like another sibling to him and his brothers and sister. But he hadn't worried too much when he hadn't heard back from Tara. He'd figured she had her hands full. Obviously, she did. But with what?

He eyed his gun. He didn't love the idea of picking up kids while he had his service revolver. Technically, he was on duty, however, so he was required to be armed. Shrugging out of his jacket, he refastened his shoulder holster and tugged the garment back on, grabbing his cell phone. He was out the door moments later, walking past Patty with a brief wave. Finding a taxi was always challenging, but he walked up the road until he hit a main intersection and hailed one there.

The ride was over twenty minutes with lunch-hour traffic, giving him time to stew and put extra wrinkles in his pants as he gripped his knees. Tara was a smart, independent woman who handled her own shit like the rest of the O'Connors. Something was wrong. Bad wrong. His gut was flip-flopping like a largemouth bass hooked at Hammond Pond. He was sweating by the time the cab dropped him off in front of the gym, but he was ready for anything. Tara could count on him. She'd always known that. He'd made her that promise when he'd held her after arriving with the police to inform her of the tragic car accident that killed her parents.

The electric double doors of the gym whooshed open as he approached, the blast of the air-conditioning welcome. He approached reception with his best attempt at a smile.

"Hello, I'm Robbie O'Connor." He masked a shaky breath. "I'm here to pick up Reagan and Cassidy."

"Oh, Mr. O'Connor." The woman whose gold nameplate read Brenda gave him a blooming smile. "I'm so glad you made it. Your wife was so worried."

Wife? He compressed a shudder. "Do you need to see my ID?" he asked, already reaching into his back pocket.

Brenda rolled her eyes. "Yes, I do even though your wife showed me your photo. She's never left the kids with us before, so she was a little nervous. Then her boss made it worse when he called her back to work only ten minutes after she'd started her workout. What a jerk. Poor thing was beside herself having to leave them here for longer and asking you to take off work early to pick them up. I felt so bad for her."

He heard this story with more than a little shock. His cousin didn't have a boss; she was the boss, of three nail salons. The lies were clearly necessary in Tara's mind, but why? He made himself nod as he quickly flashed his ID and then signed the kids out, not feeling exactly comfortable with being on record for something he didn't yet understand. He was the guy who put liars away when they took things too far. Impersonating a child's father to remove them from gym daycare was skirting the line, but he knew Tara must have a damn good reason.

"I'll just call and have your kids come out since you don't know where the daycare is," Brenda said helpfully.

Moments later, he heard *"Daddy!"* echo throughout reception.

Robbie's muscles locked hard. The girls were in on it? He swung his head to the right as a young girl ran into him and wrapped her little arms around his leg, gripping it with all her strength.

"Da-da," another childlike voice sounded as a soft lump knocked into his other side, tiny fingers tickling his kneecap.

He hoped the gym attendant hadn't seen his ripple of shock as he automatically put his hands on the girls' heads. What the hell was going on? The smells of workout sweat and pool chlorine kicked up his mounting nausea. Tara had said more information would be at the gym. It had better be. Because now he was super freaked. And he dealt with life-and-death situations daily.

This was family, though, and that made the stakes so much higher.

"Hey, Cassidy and Reagan," he managed to say through a dry mouth as he looked down at the little girls.

Big matching blue eyes in unsmiling china-doll faces filled his vision. He knew Tara's girls, of course. But man, had they grown since he'd seen them at the annual O'Connor July Fourth BBQ over a month ago. Reagan looked inches taller. Was that possible for a six-year-old? And Cassidy's short, curly hair was a darker brown. He tried to smile despite the tension in his jaw. This had to be weird for them too, right?

Cassidy gave him a drool-drenched grin as she clutched the girliest teddy bear in history, decked out in a pink gingham dress with a huge matching bow between her fuzzy white ears. Miss Rosie, if his memory served.

He studied the girls for any signs of further distress as he would on a 911 domestic call. They both had bright bows in their hair, which added to the girly ensembles of flowery sundresses and glittering sandals, Reagan's open-toed and Cassidy's closed. They were dressed just like Tara, who loved her bright colors and bling. The kids didn't have any bruises, thank God. Not even a scratch. He tried to suck in some oxygen in relief, but he caught the worry in their eyes. You could always tell what someone was really feeling by looking there.

This had to be about their father. Robbie hadn't liked Scotty Flanagan from the time they'd shared a playground at St. Stephens Catholic School. He was a weak excuse for a man, but Tara had fallen for him and said he both supported and helped her business aspirations, so Robbie had kept his lips zipped and been pleasant to him at family events.

If Scotty had done something to hurt Tara and her babies, as she called them, they were going to have one hell of a serious talk.

"*Hi,*" Cassidy drew out, hugging his leg harder. He felt something wet touch his knee through his pants and cringed. She was a drool factory, which is why her nickname was Drool Baby while her sister's was Miss Pixie.

"Mr. O'Connor, I'll just grab the diaper bag. Your wife said to make sure you didn't forget it since it's not your fave."

Diaper bag? His balls shriveled, and he immediately looked down at Cassidy. Yeah, she had the puffy outline under her dress that indicated she was still in diapers. His brain shorted. Man, he hadn't changed a diaper since Kathleen was little, and it wasn't something he missed. Then he realized the bag might contain the information his cousin had mentioned was waiting for him, and his palms started to sweat again.

"Thanks, Brenda. I'll just wait here with the girls."

Kneeling to their level as the woman took off, he laid a hand on Reagan's shoulder. Cassidy cuddled into his body with Miss Rosie and laid her head against his chest, smelling of sour orange juice she must have spilled on her dress. "You guys okay?"

Reagan bit her lip but bravely nodded. "Mom said you need to read her letter."

"Is it in the diaper bag?"

"Yes." Reagan curved into him so she could say something into his ear. "Mom said you would take care of us until she came back."

Came back? Where the fuck had Tara gone? His stomach dropped to the floor at that pronouncement, but he hugged them both. They had to be scared, and Tara had to be terrified to have taken off and left her babies. "You know I will. We O'Connors stick together. We'll figure it out." He patted their little backs with assurance. God, they were so tiny compared to his large hands.

Brenda returned with a large bedazzled bag, which said BOSS on the side in white rhinestones. He lurched forward to help her with it as she was straining with effort.

"Your wife is like I used to be," Brenda commented as he gently slid the heavy bag off her shoulder. "Ready for every emergency. I had three boys. My husband joked that hefting around the kids and the diaper bag was like lifting dumbbells."

He tested the heaviness, estimating it weighed about thirty pounds. Did Tara's diaper bag usually weigh this much? Brenda didn't seem to consider it strange.

"It keeps Tara fit too," he said, keeping the conversation

normal as Cassidy hugged his leg again. "I told her she didn't need to join a gym. She looks great just as she is."

"Oh, that's so sweet," Brenda said with a breathy sigh. "I wish my husband thought that. Even so, your wife wanted to join today, but she didn't have time to finish the gym membership paperwork. She said you could bring it with you for her to fill out. I know she wanted to get back here tomorrow to continue her workout."

Robbie doubted she'd be back, but only nodded. "I'm happy to take the papers, Brenda."

"Are you interested in joining too? Your wife said you loved to work out, but not in gyms. That's pretty obvious. What do you bench?"

Her appreciative nod at his impressive build had him shrugging with a little embarrassment. "If there were any gyms I'd consider, it would be this one, but I'm more the outdoor workout type. Well, girls..."

They were staring up at him with their hearts in their eyes. He nearly gulped at the trust there.

"Let's get this show on the road." He made sure to flash Brenda a smile. "Thanks again for your help."

Hefting the diaper bag up higher on his shoulder, he glanced down at Cassidy. How far could a two-year-old walk? Screw it. He swung her into his arms and felt Reagan grab his other hand as they left.

"Mom parked in a garage," Reagan told him the moment the doors whooshed closed behind them. "She helped me memorize the directions."

Tara had left a car? How had she gotten home? But that wasn't a question fit for the kids, so he just said, "All right. Lead the way."

The girls were quiet as Reagan navigated them to a garage three blocks from the gym. He was impatient to reach the letter, but he had to walk like a snail so the young girl could keep up with him. Tara had chosen a parking deck loaded with top-model, freshly washed cars and parked in the corner on the second floor by an exit. When they reached the shiny black Cadillac SUV with dealer's plates—not Tara's—Reagan dug into the diaper bag's front pocket and pulled out a key fob.

"Mom told me to keep the diaper bag safe and I did. When Cassidy needed a change, I got the diaper out and everything."

Her smile exhibited a certain pride, and it made him wonder at the little triumphs that helped build a kid's self-confidence. "You did a bang-up job, Reagan. Did your mom get a new car?"

"No, she got it from someone after all our tires got nails in them." She blew an exasperated breath toward her short bangs, a move she'd clearly copied from her mother. "Mom was so mad, but she said this was the bright side. We got two new cars for our adventure. One for Mom. And one for us."

Battery acid pooled in his stomach. Being in law enforcement, he knew parents used "adventure talk" to dress up bad shit. He popped the trunk and startled at the three suitcases, two girly ones and another in a dark black, along with cardboard boxes loaded with family-size snacks and beverages. He even noticed his favorite beer. Then he saw the giant bag of diapers and winced.

"You're packed for that adventure, it seems." What was the adult-sized case for if Tara wasn't coming?

"Mom went shopping for our trip before we came to the gym." Reagan stood on her tiptoes and pointed to the beer. "She wanted us all to have our favorites."

The beer was a downright bribe. "That was nice of her."

"She brought you some clothes too," Reagan added shyly, ducking her head. "We hope you like them."

"Mine," Cassidy said, pointing to the purple suitcase with the smiling unicorn on the front, decked out with rainbows that made him think of Ireland.

Then he heard an angry meow and looked down at the girls in horror. "Did you bring your cat?"

"Mom said we *had* to take Miss Purrfect with us." Reagan looked at her sister, who nodded, wide-eyed. "She's part of our family, and Mom said we could have her so we wouldn't miss her so much."

How could they not miss their mother? He fought a curse when they both studied their feet. Just how long did Tara plan to be gone—and why? It was time for answers.

"Okay, Reagan. Where's this letter of your mom's?"

She pointed to the diaper bag again. "There's a zipper part on the bottom. Mom said everything you need to know is in there."

He dropped the diaper bag on top of the other suitcases and unzipped the bottom one-handed while balancing Cassidy against his chest. Sure enough, inside the clever compartment was a manila envelope with his name scrawled across it in a hurried cursive.

He pulled out the envelope, hoisted the bag back over his shoulder, and slammed the trunk shut. "Let's get you guys in the car."

"We have our car seats," Reagan informed him as he opened the back passenger door, kicking off another angry meow. "Mom said Miss Purrfect wouldn't be happy being caged in the car, but she couldn't bring her to the gym. Can we let her out now?"

"Sure." Why not add a snarly cat to the party?

She gave him a beaming smile as she leaned down and

opened the cage, her hair bow flopping to the right. The animal's pointed white face snarled at him like he was the reason it had been in feline jail, its green eyes staring at him with as much menace as the serial killer he'd busted ten years ago. Great. He was already on this cat's shit list.

"Look, Robbie! Mom made Miss Purrfect a new collar." Reagan fingered the bedazzled band that had probably been inspired by that Marilyn Monroe song she loved, "Diamonds Are a Girl's Best Friend." Tara had the movie poster of *Gentlemen Prefer Blondes* in her main nail salon, and it seemed like the song had been playing every time he'd swung by to say hello and check up on her.

An image of Tara and his little sister Kathleen doing art projects on the kitchen table in his childhood home rose up in his mind. "Your mother has been gluing sparkles to everything she could get her hands on since she was a kid."

"That's how we make things prettier," Reagan told him matter-of-factly while the cat tugged at the collar with its paw as if it understood their conversation. "I can hold Miss Purrfect on my lap after I help buckle Cassidy into her car seat. Mom says you might not know how to do it."

What did Tara think he was? An idiot? But he was sensitive to Reagan's pride. "She might be right. How about we buckle in after I read your mom's letter?" His fingers were itching for information.

The SUV was designed for comfort, he noticed, as he settled Cassidy in the left captain's seat and then helped Reagan into the right one before fitting himself into the spacious rear middle seat with the diaper bag at his feet. Next, he was going through that. Unsealing the envelope, he pulled out the pages and began to read.

Dear Robbie,

I'm in trouble. I didn't dare call you on your phone because they told me they would find out and hurt my babies.

Let me back up. Scotty has taken off—with that skank nail girl Janice Brewster he screwed at my new location. I know Danny told you that I'd caught them together in the office doing the business on my desk four days ago. I fired Janice and kicked Scotty's sorry ass out of the house, changed the locks, and took him off all the bank accounts, telling him I was getting a divorce. Like my lawyer advised.

Later that day, two of Branigan Kelly's tough guys showed up at my main nail salon. They said they expected things to be business as usual with me even though I'd kicked Scotty out. I didn't know what in the hell they were talking about and told them that they could go fuck themselves.

But the moment I closed for the day, I locked the door and searched every corner of the salon. I found over three hundred thousand dollars, which was like getting hit in the face by a two-by-four. I was sick with worry by the time I finished searching the other two salons. Robbie, I found over three hundred thousand dollars hidden in each nail salon—almost a million dollars total! I gathered it all up in a black suitcase and then put it in my BOSS bag under Cassidy's diapers when I got home—the last place I thought anyone would look. The one I left at the gym for you.

Scotty was laundering money for the Kellys. He's called my phone a million times begging me to let him pick up a few things he left behind at the nail salons. Personal mementos and his precious computer. What bullshit! He showed up when I was out, but my girls told him to buzz off. When he came by the house, I told him I'd call the police if he stuck around. What was he thinking? Doing that in my place of business and risking everything I've worked so hard for? I want to tear him apart.

He had to stop reading. His heart was pounding in his ears. The Kellys? Jesus, he hadn't thought Scotty was that stupid. Everyone knew Branigan Kelly's reputation in South Boston. He was a low-level monster who'd risen to the top by forming alliances with the Russians and the Albanians.

"Daddy really messed up, didn't he?" Reagan said in the quiet of the car.

He looked over to see her holding Miss Purrfect tightly against her chest, her little chin resting in the fur. "What else did your mom tell you?"

"Mom is so mad at Daddy for being a moron and hurting our nail salons by being a bad businessman. She kicked him out of the house when he said he wasn't sorry and wouldn't make it right. Then she told us he left town and might not be coming back and good riddance. We girls are better off."

"Yeah," Cassidy echoed in baby-like support, her tiny fist banging the side of her car seat. "Good riddant."

He tried to give them a smile. As a story, it was a solid one for kids. Believable details. Enough of the truth to make it passable. As a cop, he knew how critical it was for kids to have a story for their minds to hold on to. Otherwise, they might make up a story ten times worse than the truth, which would leave them in a fearful place of confusion and uncertainty. Never a good space for any person, least of all a child.

"I'm sorry this happened, but your mom is correct, and now we're going to fix things." He leaned forward with the letter in his hand and touched both girls' arms, making sure to look them both straight in the eye. He knew how important such a look was. They had to know he could take care of them.

God, this situation was a heavy load for kids to carry. He knew the work it took for kids to keep positive in the face of major family changes and tragedy. He and his family had gone through the wringer when they'd lost their mom to breast cancer. Kathleen had only been five, the youngest of a whole bunch of pissed-off kids who'd done their best to tell her everything would be okay.

But it hadn't been.

Their mother's absence had left a hole in them all. He wondered if Scotty would leave such a hole, asshole that he was.

What the hell was the right thing to say here? "We O'Connors stick together."

"And we're as tough as they come," Reagan added, echoing what she'd heard their family say over and over again. His mother used to say that if you repeated a sentiment often enough, you'd truly feel it, and Robbie believed that. It was the only way he'd gotten over his mother's death.

"You bet we are." He held out his hand for a fist bump, which Reagan gave with a surprising force.

"Me too," Cassidy cried, holding out her little fist as well as her teddy bear's.

His mouth twitched as he included them in the gesture. Tara was tough, and it was clear she was raising strong, independent girls. "I'm going to keep reading, and then we'll...get going."

Not that he knew what his next steps would be yet. He sat back with the letter.

Robbie, the Kellys slashed my tires in front of my townhouse yesterday, and I freaked. Then a man called my cell, said Scotty had taken off with Janice, and that if I knew where he was, I'd better tell them. I said I didn't and that I was divorcing his sorry ass. He said Mr. Kelly expected me to change my mind about continuing Scotty's business arrangement with them or they would hurt my babies. They even told me the name and address of their daycare and said accidents happen and children disappear or fall into the Mystic all the time. At the end, he told me not to go to you or the cops because they had people on the inside and would know.

I lost it. All I could think about was getting my girls to safety. But then what? My businesses have obviously been laundering money for the Kellys, and I have their cash. I think they believe Scotty ran off with it. But if and when they find him, they'll know he doesn't have it. So I'm turning the money in to you as an officer of the law and telling you Scotty is the criminal here. Not me.

But me and the girls are still in trouble. I knew the Kellys would start looking for us the moment I left town. They're already looking for Scotty and Janice. I realized I couldn't get far with two girls their age. Or protect them against Branigan Kelly's guys.

So I'm asking you to take my girls and protect

them with everything you've got. But not with the cops. Like family does. Because I won't bet my girls' lives that Kelly's guys were lying about having people on the force.

Robbie tipped his head to the ceiling as tension gathered at the base of his skull. He couldn't be one hundred percent sure either. The Kellys were legendary for throwing money at people until they caved or, if that didn't work, threatening their families or setting them up for blackmail. They'd already caught one cop working on the Kelly payroll in the last year. But it would be a pain in the ass to handle this without doing it by the book. He didn't want to lose his job by going rogue or become a suspect in this fiasco. Shit.

"Want Miss Rosie?"

He glanced over to see Cassidy holding out her bear. Shaking his head, he let out an uneasy breath when her lower lip wobbled. God, was she going to cry? "Nah, she looks pretty happy with you."

"Mom said to tell you that she trusted you and that she knew it was going to freak you out a little bit to have this adventure with us while she worked things out with the business." Reagan was suddenly pushing Miss Purrfect off her lap and jumping out of her seat, coming to stand in front of him in the short aisle, gripping his forearm. "Me and Cassidy promised Mom we would be really good and make things easy for you."

God, that crushed him. He pulled her to his chest. "You two have always been as sweet as angels. That's not my worry. I'm only worried a little about your mom. Going off on her own adventure like this." Okay, so now he was stretching the truth too. "But don't you guys worry. We're going to get her back here really quick. I'm going to help make that happen. I promise."

"I sure hope so." Reagan tunneled into him. "I already miss her."

"Me too," Cassidy half wailed, eyes full of those tears he feared as she clutched her bear.

This sucked. All of it. "Let me finish your mom's letter."

Reagan pushed away and picked up the cat again. He turned the next page and started reading where he'd left off.

You always say stupid criminals get caught using their own car and their cell phone, so I made other arrangements. I borrowed this car from a client who said I could use it for as long as I need to while I'm getting new tires. He's a dealer and won't miss it. Another client just talked about her vacation in the Outer Banks and how family-friendly it is. I figured it would be the perfect cover for you and the girls if you pretend to be a single dad on a final summer vacation with his girls before school starts. I secured a house through my client's property owners in the Outer Banks. You can pay cash on-site. I told them you were my ex-husband but that I still make reservations for you with the kids because I'm choosier, even though you're a good father.

A good father? He was supposed to continue this charade? He fell back against the seat. Holy shit. As an officer of the law, he couldn't take off with these kids and pretend to be their father. Especially across state lines. That could be called kidnapping if someone like their real father chose to make a stink. Jesus. He gritted his teeth and kept reading.

I know you're going to want to do this like a cop, <u>but you can't.</u> I believe the Kellys when they say they have people on the inside. I can't take the chance with my babies, and neither can you. I'm begging you on your mother's grave to protect them, and I'm telling you that my aunt—your mother—would agree with me.

I'm only asking for two weeks. You've always said the first two weeks after any crime-related incident are the most critical in the way things play out. Plus, you always joke about all your unused vacation time. Something will give. Either Scotty will confess everything to the cops when he realizes he can't outrun the Kellys, which will make it easier for all of us to return to Boston and you to make the case airtight so the inside guys on the police force can't fuck it up... Or the Kellys will find Scotty and deal with him. Hell, Janice might turn Scotty in to save her skin or because she'll hate being on the run.

If and when the Kellys realize I'm gone and so is the cash, I can't imagine how many guys they're going to send out. They might suspect me, but they're more likely to think Scotty is behind it.

I'm disappearing too, although it's going to kill me to be away from my babies, but I know you can do a better job of keeping them safe. Right now, you're the only person I trust. I know you'll know what to do with the cash. And because this vacation is going to put you out, I took out some of my savings and stuffed it into the black suitcase for you to use. Don't get mad. You know we O'Connors pay our way.

Plus, you'll need to pay everything in cash like

you always say is mandatory for people on the run. I did some early shopping since it's a long drive—directions are in the envelope. Also, there's a burner phone in the diaper bag. You know you can't use your regular phone while you're hiding, so I got new ones for both of us. Even though I want to call my babies and check in <u>every single day</u>, I won't. You always say phones are the surest way of getting caught. So when something gives, I'll call you and we'll meet up. If it doesn't—God help us—at the end of two weeks, then we'll meet and make a new plan.

I've written down everything imaginable for you about the girls and put it in this envelope, from their favorite foods to how Cassidy needs to sleep with her feet out of the blanket because they get hot and she starts fussing. I know it's a lot, and I swear I'll make it up to you somehow, but Reagan is a good helper, and Cassidy is as sweet a baby as God has ever made and put here on earth.

Take care of my babies for me, Robbie. I'm trusting you with their lives—and mine.

Your loving cousin,
Tara

His heart was like a jackhammer as he stuffed the letter back into the envelope. He fingered the paper, one zinger repeating in his head. *I'm telling you that my aunt—your mother—would agree with me.* That was like a burr sticking to him.

His chest tightened as he realized what he was going to do—what he had to do. Sitting back, he planted his hands on his knees like he did when he was trying to figure out his next steps on a big case. Closing his eyes, he let the details swirl like dust coughed up from a strong wind off the Bay. He watched them all flash in his mind, fixing his gaze on one and then another, until they all settled to the floor. He could see the pitfalls now, the details that might hurt or injure. He waited for his mind to work out the things he could do now to offset those problems.

The next steps came to him, just as they always did. He was calm on the inside, a signature feeling for him when he was working something out in his mind. Still, when he opened his eyes to find both girls and the cat staring at him, practically holding their breath, pressure returned to his chest.

He could not make a wrong move here.

Pulling his cell phone out of his pocket, he turned it off and took out the sim card. He wasn't going to help the Kellys by letting them track him through his cell phone. Tara had clearly paid attention all these years when he'd talked about cases, way more than he'd ever imagined.

When he looked up, her little girls were staring at every move he made, as still as small china doll statues. The cat looked like a stuffed animal. "Girls, are you hungry? Thirsty? Because I need to make a few calls on this new phone your mom bought me before we take off. But good news. You remember my brothers, Billie and Tim, don't you? Billie's the big giant of the O'Connor clan, the one no one messes with, and Tim's the really nice guy who helps older people at the retirement home."

Poor things both nodded quickly, their eyes as wide as saucers.

"Good news. They're going on the adventure with us."

Because he was going to need some serious backup for this case.

CHAPTER TWO

Her heart was galloping like a herd of wild horses.

Lily Meadows shifted in her seat next to her partner, trying to ignore the feeling that the metal sides of their undercover vehicle were closing in on her. They'd lost their suspect.

How in the hell had Tara O'Connor given them the slip? When her boss found out, Lily's desire for the promotion to the FBI's Child Exploitation and Human Trafficking Task Force would be dead in the water.

She wanted to bang her head on the steering wheel in frustration, but that would be childish. Unprofessional. She might be the polar opposite of the stereotypical alpha, tough-guy FBI agent, but she was a seasoned field agent. She went undercover frequently. Faced down dangerous criminals. Prepared for every eventuality.

How had she blown it?

Lily had judged Tara O'Connor to be a good mother, but she'd just left her two children alone. *At a gym.* Those adorable little girls had been abandoned by the person who was supposed to love and cherish them the most. That kind of shit left scars. She knew from personal experience.

"Are you *wheezing?*" Sheila Morales was known for being one of the most wise-cracking, prank-playing agents in FBI circles, but when she put on her drill sergeant tone, people's spines straightened. "Pull it together, Sunshine. I know this looks bad, but don't make me get out a paper bag. I'd feel obligated to take a photo of you sucking in air on surveillance and pin it up in the break room."

That helped her get her breathing under control. She got enough ragging as it was for having a last name like Meadows and looking like the girl next door, an asset in undercover work. Add in the kernel of positivity she felt toward life despite everything in her past, and she'd been given the nickname Sunshine. Sheila had even given her a *You are my Sunshine* T-shirt for their softball games as well as a key chain, which she used for her apartment in Chelsea, an easy commute to FBI headquarters.

"You even think about telling anyone I wheezed, Sheila, and I'll tell everyone how you forgot to shave your girly parts on your last undercover gig when you were supposed to be a stripper."

"Almost blew my cover because of a bush." Her partner's rough laugh erupted in the hot car. "It was a last-minute assignment, and I still blame the head of the task force for forgetting to include that detail about my outfit in my undercover packet."

Lily couldn't even manage a smile as her gaze cut back to the parking garage they were surveilling. "We're so screwed, Sheila."

Sheila turned in her seat, and Lily focused on her grounding presence. Her black hair was pulled back in a ponytail, showing off dangling gold earrings. She wore minimal makeup and nude lipstick. Her pantsuit was all black with serviceable ankle boots she could run in. They'd been partners since Lily had been transferred to Boston six months ago. Sheila was the more senior agent, having been in the Bureau for ten years in comparison to Lily's five. Her experience in the field came through in moments like this, and Lily nodded to tell her she was ready to listen.

"We are not screwed." Sheila narrowed her brown eyes. "And you stop your rare Negative Nancy tirade. I'm the only person who gets to be Negative Nancy in this partnership. This case still has *golden ticket* written all over it. I'm going to say this slowly in case all the blood in your forebrain has up and left, but the Child Exploitation and Human Trafficking Task Force is going to be doing cartwheels to have you. When we nail Branigan Kelly and close down his operation, Lily, you'll get whatever you want. I'm going to miss you like hell when they put me with some other partner, but I tell myself we'll still work together on the odd case and hang out and talk shop. It's gonna happen. Listen to Mama on this."

God, she must be really freaking out to have Sheila put on her cheerleading outfit. "All right, Mama, dialing Negative Nancy back and putting my sunshine self back on," she tried to joke, flicking her wavy blond hair over her shoulder. "I'm going to miss you too, by the way."

"I know." Sheila lightly punched her in the shoulder. "Now, let's talk about where we are in this case. We know Tara is likely in the wind, which justifies the judge's decision to let us put a tracker on the car she was driving after we saw her bulk shopping at Costco this morning."

"But she didn't take her car, Sheila. Why didn't she—"

"Calm down, Sunshine. I'm telling you... We just watched her cousin, who's an officer in the precinct where we know Kelly has cops on his payroll, pick up the kids and bring them to the car we put the tracker on. That, my friend, is manna from heaven. Why? Because we happen to know there's fifty grand in that black suitcase. The same black suitcase Tara O'Connor was seen taking to and from her three nail salons."

That had been a day. But Lily still didn't believe Tara O'Connor was behind this mess. Otherwise, she wouldn't have removed the cash from the premises...and the Kellys wouldn't have slashed her tires. Sheila wasn't convinced—she'd argued that there'd been some kind of dispute, and Tara had moved the cash as a safeguard. Although fifty thousand seemed kinda light to her. With three nail salons, wouldn't there have been more?

"Your confidential informant told us that money is Branigan Kelly's dirty money," Sheila continued, although she didn't need the reminder. The informant had also told her that it had been laundered through Tara's nail salons. "We have confirmation that the cash is in Tara's new SUV in that garage, and Tara's husband and Janice Brewster disappeared. Enter the new actor today. One of Boston's finest. Lily, we could collar one of Kelly's dirty cops—"

"I don't think he's dirty, Sheila." Lily gripped the wheel. "We've looked at everyone in his precinct, and he didn't even make the third cut. Robbie O'Connor's from a squeaky-clean, toe-the-line proud Irish Catholic family that pays their taxes on time."

Sheila flicked her hand in the direction of the garage where Lieutenant O'Connor and Tara's two young children had entered over ten minutes ago. "And yet his cousin and her husband are suspected of laundering money for the mob."

Lily scanned the parking garage entrance. What was he doing in there with those girls? If the girls hadn't looked completely comfortable with him, she'd be sick with concern. Instead, he'd been holding Cassidy protectively and walking slowly so Reagan wouldn't have to run to keep up. Fact was, he'd look downright tender toward those two girls. Bad guys didn't do that.

"They've certainly been in there for a while," she said, fighting the urge to bite her short, unpainted nails. "You don't think the Kellys followed him, do you? I know we can see all the cars entering and leaving from this angle, but that doesn't mean they didn't go in on foot."

"I know you're worried about the kids," Sheila said, her

eyes fixed like a laser to the garage. "I am too. Let's give it five more minutes before I walk in and look around."

When Tara hadn't reappeared through the main entrance, she and Sheila had gone in, pretending they were considering joining the gym. There'd been no sign of Tara, but Lily had managed to look around the corner into the daycare to confirm her girls were still there and okay. After watching them play duck, duck, goose with the daycare attendant, they'd headed back to the car. They'd barely made it inside before Lieutenant O'Connor had arrived in a cab—not his regular police-issue car—and strode inside with authority, only to exit with the girls minutes later, carrying the same bedazzled BOSS bag Tara had brought into the building. Damn, but she wanted to know if something important was in that bag, because it had looked heavy. More cash? But why split the cash into two pieces of luggage? And why risk it being discovered when Cassidy needed a diaper change? God, she had so many questions...

"He still might turn in the cash and put the kids into child protective services," Lily said with a glance at her partner.

Sheila only made a noncommittal sound in response.

Hating the waiting, Lily started tapping her fingers on her knees, chewing on what she knew of Robbie O'Connor from her file review of potential dirty cops. Thirty-nine. Six-four. Divorced. Residence in the Seaport District in South Boston. On the force for almost twenty years. He'd worked his way up, serving first as a patrol officer, then as leader of the department's tactical unit, and now as lieutenant with whispers that he might even be considered for captain. Impeccable record. Volunteered in the community. Heck, he'd even been a teen mentor for a few years before he'd been handed more responsibility in the department.

Basically, a stand-up guy.

Not a likely accomplice to Scotty Flanagan, whose bigmouthed girlfriend had led to his downfall. Janice Brewster had innocently shot her mouth off to one of Lily's confidential informants in a local casino, telling the CI that her new mink coat had come from the Kellys, whom Scotty was working for.

Brought down by a side piece.

Lily loved the poetic justice of that. Men were always thinking with their dicks. It happened everywhere, especially in law enforcement. "Sheila, I still think Tara kicking her husband out like she did and taking him off the bank accounts means something."

"That could have been because he was screwing the help and got caught. Just because she didn't want her man two-timing on her doesn't mean she wouldn't launder money."

This time she was the one who made the noncommittal sound.

"Tara wheeled that black suitcase out of her three nail salons, and she still hasn't called the cops."

"Maybe she just did by calling in her cousin."

"I know you think he's a Boy Scout..."

Lily wouldn't go that far. He was too rough-looking for that, what with his square jaw that could take a punch and probably had and his masculine, tough-as-nails demeanor. She wasn't going to lie—she liked the look of Robbie O'Connor. Sure, he was handsome enough, and that was part of it, but what affected her more was the sweetness with which he'd held Cassidy and led Reagan by the hand. Call her Sunshine as she was billed, but kids were good at telling you a lot about adults if you paid attention. Just like adults advertised a lot about themselves by how they treated kids.

"We'll know soon enough about Lieutenant O'Connor, don't worry." Sheila cracked open a trio of pistachios, her go-to for their waiting games, before tossing the shells on the floor and popping the kernels in her mouth.

"You know I hate it when you do that," Lily reminded her.

Sheila gave her a lopsided smile. "Yeah, but you'd take a bullet for me."

"Because you're my partner," she shot back, "and only a flesh wound."

"Not that me being your best friend has anything to do with it, of course." She cracked a few more nuts and extended them to Lily. "Come on. You need to eat something."

"You know I can't eat during surveillance." She clenched her knees. "God, what could he be doing?"

"He ain't changing no diaper." Sheila chortled. "That I can guarantee. Did you see that diaper bag? I can't believe an alpha dog like him would be caught dead carrying that. It looked like a bedazzler had thrown up all over it. I swear, I don't get why some women have an addiction to bling." She paused, considering, then said, "I guess maybe it's like men and toupees. But what are they trying to compensate for?"

"Maybe they just want to be more attractive. Some girls like to feel pretty." She thought of those poor kids. Feeling pretty would be little comfort to them if things continued to go south.

Their father was at large, and now that they'd seen the cash, there'd soon be a warrant out for his arrest. Mom was now at large as well, it appeared. A warrant might be in her future. Those two sweet girls couldn't be in a more vulnerable place. She knew. At one time, she'd been just like them.

Come on, you bastard. Don't let me be wrong. Don't be dirty.

"That's our SUV!"

Lily turned on the car, trying not to jump to conclusions. "Lieutenant O'Connor is driving. I think you should—"

"I'm calling Buck right this minute." Buck being their tough-as-nails boss. "It won't sound so bad that Tara snuck out a side entrance on us if we're following a possible dirty cop with mob money. Don't tail too close."

"What am I? An extra in a Hollywood movie?"

Her partner shot her a grin before taking on her *checking in* voice as their boss picked up. When Sheila winced, so did Lily. The FBI office in Boston was a large one with over four hundred agents. It was Lily's biggest office to date, her biggest opportunity too, and she didn't want her career to go down in flames because they'd assumed a mother wouldn't leave her kids in a gym.

From the irate response she could hear through the phone, their boss was chewing out Sheila royally. During her first meeting with Buck, he'd said she only had to remember one thing: don't fuck with Buck. He was going places, and if she didn't help him get there, he'd transfer her butt out so fast her pretty little head would spin. She'd managed to never make him repeat his famous motto since, but she wouldn't be surprised if he'd used it with Sheila today. Lily knew he had cause to be angry. She was upset with herself for the blunder.

Her partner was quiet for a long moment before clicking off the phone and saying, "We're to follow O'Connor and not blink our eyes once. So we won't lose him like we did our last suspect. Like a pathetic rookie who doesn't know his ass from the FBI handbook."

Lily swallowed thickly. "Terrific. If we mess this up, Buck will transfer us out, and we'll be lucky to land in an FBI office in Mobile—"

"Or El Paso." Sheila cranked up the air-conditioning and fanned herself. "You know how much I hate hot weather."

"I'll send you a fan," Lily remarked as she followed Robbie O'Connor onto I-93. "Where is he going, do you think?"

"This certainly isn't the way to his precinct." Sheila rubbed her hands together. "So I'm hopeful we're about to pull in a bigger fish for Buck."

"You're so pessimistic about people." Lily made sure to keep ten cars back, but she kept her eyes peeled.

"I know, and I love that about me. Better to be surprised than devastated. Or dead, for that matter."

Sheila had been shot at, but then again, she'd been in the FBI longer than Lily and had worked in Phoenix, Dallas, and Cleveland before Boston. Lily had only been in Sacramento and Tampa before.

"Okay, you win with the death card." Lily rolled her shoulders. "Do you think he's leaving the state?"

Sheila cracked her knuckles. "If he does, that shoots this whole thing to another level. Can you see your promotion papers in your hands now, Sunshine?"

"Are you going to sing the song? Because with your pipes, it makes me feel all special inside."

"Ah, that makes me want to sing real bad." Sheila stretched her feet out, kicking pistachio shells under her seat. "But I won't start singing the song until we take in Lieutenant O'Connor."

"I'm so hurt." Lily grabbed the volume dial for the stereo and turned it up, pleased Beyoncé was playing on one of their shared Spotify playlists. FBI agents got along best when they were in agreement about a number of things, music in the car being of top importance.

She followed as O'Connor took exit 7 for MA-3 S toward Cape Cod. Sheila cracked more pistachios, crunching as Sia sang about swinging from chandeliers. Lily had a practical side that always cringed from that one. She preferred rope if she was climbing.

They seemed to be on the MA-3 forever when he finally took the exit toward Smith Lane.

"Where is he going?" she mused aloud.

"No clue, but I'm glad you insisted we fill up the tank this morning."

"I always prefer having a full tank when we're conducting surveillance."

Sheila smirked. "Being Miss Prepared and all."

"No, my training officer told a story about running out of gas once when the suspect they were surveilling took off. They couldn't stop for gas, and he went farther than expected. They lost him when they ran out. It stuck with me."

"That sucks, but nice to know our fellow officers have their bad days. Like we did today. It happens."

"That error was probably why he was my training officer, Sheila," Lily reasoned. "Wait! He's turning."

"Slow down. You don't want him to spot you."

"He won't." She took her foot off the gas, slowing her speed rapidly, but then she spotted the sign, her insides pinging. "Oh my God! He's taking them to Maziply Toys."

"What's that? A fancy sex shop?"

She blew a raspberry. "New England's largest toy store, supposedly," she told her. "I heard one of the agents say he'd taken his kids there."

"So he's playing the part of a good cousin, huh?" Sheila threw more shells on the floor. "I don't buy it."

Lily parked well away from Lieutenant O'Connor but kept the engine running in case this was a ruse and he'd only stopped because he'd spotted her. Moments later, he was stepping out of the driver's seat, though, opening the back and plucking out Cassidy, who was still holding her adorable teddy bear. Then Reagan got out and took his hand, and they walked into the toy store like old friends.

"Hmm..." Sheila crossed her ankles. "Bribes for the kids for a long car trip?"

She shook her head. The endless speculation was part of being an FBI officer. She'd turned on some inner question fountain at Quantico, and since then, she'd asked more questions than any normal person alive. In fact, she was pretty sure that if she logged her annual questions number, she could go in the Guinness Book of World Records.

"Why don't you drink your fancy coconut water and turn off the car?" her partner continued. "We can pretend we're working on our phones. Do you remember when it was weird for people to stay in their cars? Now it's so common it makes me wonder what the world is coming to."

"But it makes surveillance easier." She grabbed her coconut water from her little cooler bag in the back. "I've given up trying to convince you how much better this is for hydration than all the Starbucks and Cokes you inhale. Not that I don't like caffeine, but six to ten a day is going to bite back someday, and I happen to like my partner."

"You're not too bad yourself—even if you do like pink water. Why it's pink and not white I still don't understand."

"I've told you it's the oxygenation of the sugars." She took a healthy swig and smacked her lips. "I can even taste the beach it was on. Man, I miss the beach sometimes."

Even at her worst moments as a kid, she could find escape on the beach and then in the Pacific, first learning to swim and later surfing.

"We need a vacation." Sheila patted her belly, her pudge as she called it. "Not that I'm ever swimsuit ready. Doesn't matter if I run ten miles a day like I did when I was at Quantico. I'm always carrying the Morales extras around the bust, hips, and bootie, which I swear are from all the black beans, rice, and tortillas of my childhood."

"Your mother is the best cook I've ever met. If I were an investor, I'd try to get her to quit the bench and open a restaurant."

"I'll tell Judge Morales about your offer when I call her next. Hey! Do you see that black car turning into the parking lot? It screams government issue."

She held up her phone, looking over her shoulder casually, as if she were on FaceTime. "Yeah. I agree. That pops your dirty cop theory."

"Not necessarily. They could be in on it."

When two men left the car with fuck-you strides and shabby suits, Lily straightened in her seat. "Hey, that's O'Connor's partner, Mickey Evans, and—"

"Roland Thomas from Internal Affairs. Dammit! It seems the jig is up. We're going to have to approach and tell them we're onto Scotty Flanagan and his wife for suspected money laundering."

"Not in the toy store," Lily pleaded, putting a hand on Sheila's arm. "There are kids in there, having fun, oblivious to how bad the world can be sometimes."

Sheila nodded crisply. "We can wait."

Fifteen minutes passed, and another car raced to the front of the parking lot. Lily gaped as a forest green Chevrolet Suburban arrived and parked close to O'Connor's car. Two men exited, the bulky one extremely tall with a shaved head, white T-shirt, and ripped jeans. The other was still a sizable height but with a more slender build. He had on a blue T-shirt and brown cargo pants. Lily studied faces for a living, and she caught the O'Connor resemblance in the jaw and brow line.

"Ladies and gentlemen, meet Boston's version of Vin Diesel and his sidekick," Sheila said with a laugh.

"They're his brothers," she said softly. "I'd bet you more pistachios."

Sheila lifted her phone and took a few photos. "You might be right, but I can put their photos in and check for sure."

"Later. Let's keep our eyes peeled."

The men quickly went inside. Sheila lowered her phone, her mouth twisting to one side. "Any ideas? Because I don't think they're here shopping for toys for their kids."

She turned the car on. "It has to be a meet, right? But if we go inside, we'll blow our cover. I say we wait here and see what their next play is."

"And hope they aren't going out the back," Sheila said wryly.

Right. Five minutes later, the tall bald guy exited the store with Cassidy in his arms while the other guy held Reagan's hand. Each girl was carrying a new toy, Cassidy's a furry brown rabbit and Reagan's a new Barbie of some sort. Both men were talking to the kids, and the girls were animated. Happy, even. "If they are Robbie's brothers, then it makes sense that the girls know them."

Sheila threw aside more pistachios and picked up her phone, surreptitiously taking photos. "They sure look chummy with the kiddies. I can't wait to see what happens next."

Lily watched as the brothers took the girls to the Suburban and proceeded to show them the inside of the vehicle. Robbie O'Connor appeared seconds later with the other two police officers. All were carrying gift bags from the toy store. Good cover that. At the car, Lieutenant O'Connor opened the side door, grabbed the diaper bag, and then disappeared around the back of the vehicle to unlock the trunk. The men huddled around it, obstructing their view.

"Dammit!" Sheila leaned closer to the dashboard. "I can't get a bead on what they're doing."

"Neither can I," Lily said. "Take some photos anyway. We'll see if our tech guys can work their magic."

Moments later, Robbie hefted out the black suitcase, handing it over to Roland Thomas, who shook his hand and took off toward his vehicle. Lily caught sight of the diaper bag resting in the back beside the girls' suitcases as Robbie turned to his partner. There was a tense moment when O'Connor laid his hand on Mickey Evans' shoulder.

"Whatever he's communicating is *serious*," she said.

Sheila gave a low whistle. "He's just gone to Internal Affairs and handed over the Kellys' mob money with his partner present. Smart to have a witness he trusts on the force. You're right about one thing. This likely blows my dirty cop theory. If they aren't dirty, O'Connor will be a target now, both from the inside leak on his own force and the Kellys. Because it doesn't look like he's going with them. Interesting..."

She watched as O'Connor and his partner man-hugged. "No, he isn't."

Then he tossed him the key fob and took out the remaining luggage.

"Oh, shit, he's changing vehicles!"

"Good thing you put a second tracker on the cat," Lily said as she watched his partner open the driver's side of the Cadillac and jump in.

"You're the one who said they wouldn't leave the cat if something changed, so that's a win for you. But I risked being clawed by the maniac cat for justice."

"You get major points," Lily said, watching as Robbie carted the luggage to the Suburban.

"You can buy me a drink when we finally get off our shift, Sunshine. My concern is that we have a police officer taking a car with an FBI tracking device on it to God knows where. We don't want the South Boston cops to know we're running this investigation."

Lily winced. "There's no reason to think anyone will find it."

"That's you being all sunshine again," Sheila said with an edge to her voice. "We'd better hope so or this case could go up in our faces."

Lily watched as the bald guy joined O'Connor. They stacked the girls' suitcases in the back of the Suburban, which already had three duffel bags inside. O'Connor dropped the diaper bag inside, and then the brothers crossed back to the Cadillac and lugged over the four boxes from Costco. The bald guy appeared carrying the car seats and the cat in her carrier.

"That pussy just saved our life," Sheila said with a wicked laugh.

Lily didn't appreciate that word, even though she worked around very rough-talking people, men and women included. "I won't have to follow so closely, which is good. Because God knows where they're headed now."

A loud meow tore through the parking lot, and the bald man's disparaging swear word carried, earning him a quick rebuke from O'Connor, who pointed at the kids in the Suburban. Lily rather appreciated his desire to protect the kids from foul language.

The bald guy made clawlike hands in O'Connor's direction before he disappeared from view into the green Suburban. Doors slammed on the passenger side. O'Connor stood alone by the driver's side, watching as his partner followed the officer from Internal Affairs slowly out of the parking lot.

"He looks like he's just lost his best friend," Sheila said with a sigh. "I kinda feel for him. But I'm still withholding judgment until we find out if Roland turns in the money... and where his partner takes Tara's new car."

"They're not dirty," Lily said in a steely tone as she watched Robbie O'Connor's hardened profile in the sunlight. "He's turned the money over immediately and is taking off with some of his brothers to protect those sweet little girls—and his cousin, mind you."

"Don't make him into a knight yet," her own partner wisely pointed out. "We need more—"

"Call our boss and tell him what we saw." She put the car in drive. "Ask him for permission to follow the subject at a distance, even if they cross state lines. Tara O'Connor is going to reunite with her kids, and we want to be there to pick her up as a material witness when she does. She's the key to bringing down the Kellys. I know it."

She wasn't going to back down from the biggest case of her life, and if she could keep watch over those precious little girls, knowing the kind of heat coming for them, then all the better.

Dive right into A VERY UN-SHAKESPEARE ROMANCE!

"...ROMANTIC GOLD – YOU'LL DEFINITELY ENJOY THIS READ!"
~ HOLLY'S LIBRARY LANE

All that glitters is not gold... Sometimes it's just stacks of cash stolen from the mob, piled in a bedazzled diaper bag.

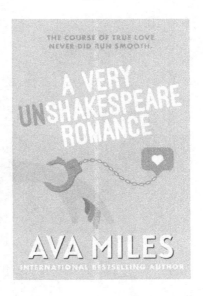

Get A Very UN-Shakespeare Romance novel!

ABOUT THE AUTHOR

Millions of readers have discovered International Bestselling Author Ava Miles and her powerful fiction and non-fiction books about love, happiness, and transformation. Her novels have received praise and accolades from *USA Today*, *Publisher's Weekly*, and *People Magazine* in addition to being chosen as Best Books of the Year and Top Editor's picks. Translated into multiple languages, Ava's strongest praise comes directly from her readers, who call her books and characters unforgettable.

Ava is a former chef, worked as a long-time conflict expert rebuilding warzones to foster peaceful and prosperous communities, and has helped people live their best life as a life coach, energy healer, and self-help expert. She is never happier than when she's formulating skin care and wellness products, gardening, or creating a new work of art. Hanging with her friends and loved ones is pretty great too.

After years of residing in the States, she decided to follow her dream of living in Europe. She recently finished a magical stint in Ireland where she was inspired to write her acclaimed Unexpected Prince Charming series. Now, she's splitting her time between Paris and Provence, learning to speak French, immersing herself in cooking *à la provençal*, and planning more page-turning novels for readers to binge.

Visit Ava on social media:

- facebook.com/AuthorAvaMiles
- x.com/authoravamiles
- instagram.com/avamiles
- bookbub.com/authors/ava-miles
- pinterest.com/authoravamiles

DON'T FORGET...
SIGN UP FOR AVA'S NEWSLETTER.

More great books? Check.
Fun facts? Check.
Recipes? Check.
General frivolity? DOUBLE CHECK.

https://avamiles.com/newsletter/

www.ingramcontent.com/pod-product-compliance
Lightning Source LLC
Jackson TN
JSHW032112120625
86051JS00005B/34